A Fat Virgin Death

Romance and Murder in the British Virgin Islands

J. Tracksler

Llumina Press

Original cover design by bryce creative, kittery point, maine

This is a work of fiction, although certain incidents, names and places, while real, are used fictitiously. The names of some of the characters may have been borrowed from friends, and these, while real, are also used fictitiously, you lucky ducks, you.

© 2007 J. Tracksler

All rights reserved. No part of this publication may be reproduced or transmitted in any form or by any means electronic or mechanical, including photocopy, recording, or any information storage and retrieval system, without permission in writing from both the copyright owner and the publisher.

Requests for permission to make copies of any part of this work should be mailed to Permissions Department, Llumina Press, PO Box 772246, Coral Springs, FL 33077-2246

ISBN: 978-1-59526-836-5

Printed in the United States of America by Llumina Press

Library of Congress Control Number: 2007904498

DEDICATION

This book is dedicated to the real Don Gamble and Arlis Fuglie (and the poems within have really been written by Don), Jamie, Lara and Mikayla Vitiello, The Vermont Symphony Orchestra and the DOMUS Foundation. In addition, thanks to the wonderful people at Radio Vermont WDEV (Kenley Squire and Buster The Wonder Dog), and Mary Jo Loparco for her heroic DOMUS efforts. Great and grateful thanks to Pam Bold for her eagle eye and to my own personal Captain Scumbag for always being there for me.

In addition, I'd like to salute all of the scurvy sailors who have ridden the wind with Captain Jack over all of these years: Cheri and Jim, Susan and Jimmy, Capt. Davie, Art and Wendy, Larry and Val, Paul and Debe, Kathie H., Kathy 2, Sue, Kathy and Jim, Capt. Skip and Cheryl, Capts. Eddie and Karen, Vicki and Connie.

AN ODE TO CAPTAIN JACK

Oh, Jack's a sailor in de Isles, So handsome and so tan…
Makes ladies smile and dat is why dey call him Scumbag Man
He runs Da Southern Cross around and sails da waters blue –
And den he comes to Banjo's Place and eats up calaloo….

He has his man, da Ducky Boy, who keeps it all afloat ….
And Ducky he's da handsomest of all dere in dat boat…
Who cooks de food for Jack as well as all de cakes and pies?
Why Kat, and she's the prettiest of cooks under deese skies…

Oh, Captain Jack, you Scumbag Man..you sail into da sea
Oh, Captain Jack, you Scumbag Man, why don't you play wid me?

Wid Captain Dave and all his girls we have a lot of fun…
Dey catch de fish, dey run de boat, dey sit dere in de sun…
Da GKB, Da Southern Cross, to all de islands go….
Dey love to sail, dey love to dance and drink de High and Lo…

Oh, Captain Jack, you Scumbag man…you sail into da sea…
Oh, Captain Jack, you Scumbag Man, why don't you play wid me?

Wid Bomba Man and his mate Sarge, dey love to do da tangoes
But most of all, dey love to drink dose wicked mango-wangoes!
Dey sail da boat to Billy Bones, and turn around to see
Da wimmin' who go swimmin' over at da Willie-T

Oh, Captain Jack, you Scumbag Man, you sail into da sea…
Oh, Captain Jack, you Scumbag Man, why don't you play wid me?

His Emma-wife, she be da best, she'll never go a'missin'
She loves her Jack an' he loves her –My Word! They're always kissin'
Dey rove da waves, dey fish da sea, dey sail off into space…
But after all is said and done, dey come back to Banjo's Place! Hey!

Oh, Captain Jack, you Scumbag Man, you sail into da sea…
Oh, Captain Jack, I loves you, man, why don't you play wid me?

As heard on many a night at Banjo's Place

THE REVENGE

"...and if you wrong us, shall we not revenge?"
The Merchant of Venice, Wm Shakespeare

Before I commit murder – before I kill him – perhaps I should set it all straight in my mind...how I got to this point, where the taking of another human being's life will bring me nothing but satisfaction and peace.

I divide my life into four parts...well, maybe five...see if you agree.

The first part is called BEFORE. It begins with my birth, or with my first conscious memories and runs through April 11th of my tenth year. During the BEFORE, I lived a life of childish joy. I was the second child and second daughter born to Gordon and Helen Nye. My older sister, who was eight when I was born, was named Deborah, but always called Debbie. I was named Sharon.

We lived in a medium-sized wooden house with a large porch, a garden in both the front and the back of the house, and a wooden garage that sat at the end of a gravel driveway. Our house was on a pleasant, tree-lined street in a prosperous blue-collar neighborhood in Greenwich, Connecticut. My father worked in a bank and my mother stayed home to keep house and care for Debbie and me.

I remember our life as ideal. The sort of life that the Dick and Jane books show...happy pictures...two copper-brown-haired, freckle-faced daughters, both of us pretty, vivacious, well-loved, maybe spoiled a bit, as our father earned a satisfactory living. Our house was always filled with neighbors, friends and relatives. My mother liked nothing better than a kitchen filled with children, and the children in the neighborhood loved my mother. She was sweet and gentle and funny and loving. My father was strong and handsome, always laughing, hoisting me up on his shoulders, letting me dance on the top of his shoes.

Debbie was my ideal. I worshipped her and she adored me. Debbie was bright at school. She was taking a secretarial course and was certain to be a solid success at some important lawyer's office after graduation. Debbie was wonderful...everyone thought so. She was so pretty, popular in a quiet way. She had dozens of girlfriends who giggled together, fixed each other's hair, and dreamed about boyfriends. Debbie had one special fellow. He was named George and he was nice-looking, not really handsome, but tall and pleasant, with an infectious grin. He was nice to me, too, which made me really like him. He always had time to tell me silly jokes and rumple my hair. George excelled at school and, while not an athletic boy, was the drum major in the high school marching band. He wanted to be a doctor and follow in his father's footsteps. I remember especially that both Debbie and George, and indeed, all of Debbie's friends, were always kind to me. Never making me feel as if I were in the way. Both my mother and my father thought that the sun and the moon rose and set over my head and Debbie's head. Even so, they liked George and felt that he was a fitting and proper boyfriend for their marvelous older daughter.

We were all so very happy. Our lives were perfect.

And then, when I was ten years old, the BEFORE stopped and the HORROR began. On the morning of April 11th, I found my sister Debbie dead, hanging from a beam in our attic in our medium-sized wooden house on our pleasant, tree-lined street.

The HORROR lasted for eight years. The first part of the horror was, of course, Debbie's death. Our family was devastated by her death and my mother shriveled into a pale husk in grief and shame. I thought I understood the grief, but didn't understand the shame. Actually, I suppose, I didn't really understand anything. I was pushed into the background; people spoke in whispers and turned their heads when I came into view; and no one ever explained anything to me.

My mother, who had collapsed when she heard my screaming, was unable to walk or eat or perform any useful functions from that time on. The doctor who came felt that she had suffered a complete breakdown. He gave her some pills that kept her sleeping in a drug-induced coma most of the time. She was unable to attend Debbie's funeral. Nor did she ever speak of Debbie again. She barely ever spoke again about anything. My father tried manfully, but, he too, was ravaged and destroyed.

The second part of the horror came a few months later when my mother died - everyone said - of grief and a broken heart. I suppose the third part of the HORROR lasted for four years or so; four years while I tried to be a mother, daughter, housekeeper, cook and friend to the fragile shell that had been my jolly, laughing, loving father. He was never able to work after Debbie's death. He tried, to be sure, and the men at the bank were both supportive and helpful, giving him time and a salary and having him talk to a special kind of doctor who understood grief. But my father was beyond their kindness and generosity. I was fifteen when he was buried in the family plot at St. Mary's cemetery, in between my mother and Debbie. As my sleep had been ever since Debbie's death, so it continued, broken and fitful, filled with galloping demons and unspeakable terrors. Yet, I survived.

Aunt Ophelia, my mother's widowed sister, came to stay with me while I finished high school. Although I had planned to go to college, there was barely enough money left to keep the house. Aunt Ophelia, who lived in upstate New York in a tiny house near Wappinger's Falls, was good to me and tried as best she could to make a home for me. For her sake, and for my own sanity, I pretended that I was coping, and in such pretending, a form of coping emerged. I simply pushed the events of the HORROR to a small, closed place in the back of my head and locked the door.

I graduated when I was sixteen. A kind and benevolent personage, whose name was Countess Ruta-Dagula, had offered a scholarship to a hardship case, and goodness knows, the school felt that I was at the pinnacle of hardship cases. I was awarded enough money to go to Eastbrook College, a small, selective school in rural Connecticut. I accepted, grateful, as I didn't know what else might become of me. I sold the house, which had appreciated enormously, paid off Aunt Ophelia's mortgage and put the excess cash into the bank where my father had once worked.

The HORROR never went away, but in those years at school, it dimmed, helped by the young woman with whom some Providence had picked to be my room-mate, Paula Haskins. I call this period of time my RESPITE.

I had decided that I would attempt to temporarily put the past behind me, to begin anew here, in this verdant place where no one knew my story, my sister's disgrace or my parent's tragedy. I would walk here in fresh steps and try to allow myself to have as normal a life that I could for four years. I squared my shoulders and took the train to school. I was met by a taxi which brought me to the dormitory where I was assigned. The entryway of the building was thronged with girls. Pretty girls, plain girls, chattering girls, shy girls. For a moment, my resolve slipped as I wondered if any of them had been though anything more complicated than hoping to be asked to the prom, or praying for good grades. A cadre of young women with gold badges met each of us and, with sheaves of papers in hand, directed us to our rooms. My own capable young woman, whose badge declared her to be "Karen!" greeted me, checked her list and sent me to Room 222. "You're rooming with, um, ah, someone named Paula Haskins," she told me with a pleasant, but mechanical smile. "Your trunks have already arrived and will either be in your room already, or will be there…God willing…" she made a demented expression meant to convey the difficulty of sorting trunks to the correct rooms,… "or, if they're not in the room, I promise you that they'll be there right after lunch." She checked my name off and told me that lunch would be in the dining room…"Right down that corridor. You'll see all the tables and such." Dismissing me with another pleasant nod, she turned to the next freshman.

An elevator, half-filled with chattering girls, swallowed me and my suitcase. I smiled, nervous, and pressed the button for Floor Number 2, then, smiling and nodding to the rest of the crowd, I hefted my suitcase and walked into Room 222.

I did say that I had reddish brown hair, I think. Although one might suppose that the events in my life might have turned it white, it was not so. I still had reddish hair. It was thick and curly and long, and I usually wore it tied in a pony-tail. My eyes were hazel, my complexion slightly tanned with a phalanx of freckles that marched over my cheeks and the bridge of my nose. I was of average height, slim, not beautiful, but pretty. I tell you this because, as I walked into the room, I saw a girl at the window. She turned, as if waiting for me. She was of average height, slim, with long, thick reddish hair tied in a pony-tail. As we gaped at one another, amazed that we looked so much alike, I saw that her eyes were blue and that she wore round, tortoise-shell eyeglasses.

"And I don't have freckles," she said, "but otherwise…" We stared. It was uncanny. We could have been, well, not twins, but perhaps cousins. I began to chuckle. She started to laugh. I dropped my suitcase and grabbed at her hands. The delight and laughter bubbled out of us, in my own case, becoming unstoppable. She…Paula…her laughter turned to concern as my own laughter turned to hysterical tears.

"What's *wrong*?"

I couldn't seem to speak. Paula led me to a bed and I sat on it, hiccupping and sobbing. The tears I had saved for years poured out of me, soaking the bedspread, blotching my face. Paula gathered me into her arms. "Come on, tell me…tell Paula…"

And I did. The grief I had held inside me, never for a moment exposing it to anyone, came pouring forth to this stranger who looked somewhat like me. I cried into Paula's sweater, gasping, incoherent, my sorrow tumbling out, her young arms holding me, patting me, her voice a soothing murmur to my torrent of memories.

And then, with a last shuddering breath, I was empty. I pulled myself up, knuckled at my streaming eyes and tried a watery smile. Her answering smile warmed me. "Well," she said, patting my hand. "Maybe you could tell me your name now." And we both laughed again, but this time, I was able to stop.

We cemented our friendship that day. We told each other *everything*...and in doing so, forged a bond that would last as long as our lives, and even beyond, as you will see.

Paula's life had been very different from mine. Despite the horrors of my past, I had known – even if it had only been for ten years – the happiness of a normal family life, the love of a mother and father, and the love and companionship of a sister. Paula hadn't even had that much .

She was the only child of Hazel Lorimer Haskins (you remember her, don't you? – so beautiful on screen, so tormented off screen -) brief marriage to Howard Haskins, the oil baron magnate. From her birth, Paula had been a pawn in the daily screaming, scheming machinations of her manic-depressive, movie-star mother and her selfish money-loving father. She had been brought up by a succession of starchy nannies and indifferent nurses, dressed up in too-fancy clothing and paraded briefly, like a pet dog, when her parents felt that it would be advantageous to do so. She never had love of any sort, and when her parents, who had divorced, married others, divorced them and remarried, were killed in a small plane crash, she felt nothing. No grief, no sadness...nothing.

At eighteen, Paula had done some research, trying to find a small college that might afford her privacy and some chance of normal life. And here, in Room 222, we had found one another.

Our time together in our first year was a catharsis for both of us. I was almost able to sleep without my demons, although they still invaded my sleep once in a while, and Paula was able to blossom in our friendship. We were a team. We took strength and delight in one another and we both felt that we could, at last, face the world together. Remarkably, together, we led a happy life at school, made many friends, learned many things, formed some normal and exciting relationships with several young men, and planned to move to New York City at the end of our time at Eastbrook. Wherever Sharon was, Paula was, and wherever Paula went, Sharon went. We served on the Student Government Panel, we sang in the Alleluia Chorus at Christmas time, we served food at the local soup kitchen together, the two of us danced the "Steam Heat" routine in tandem at the Eastbrook Follies, we double-dated every weekend. We were very happy.

We spent the summer of our freshman year in Paris. Paula insisted. I had very little money, she had a tremendous amount. "Why shouldn't I share with you, Sharon," she persuaded me after I had demurred and demurred again. "I can't possibly spend all the loot, no matter how hard I try, and I won't have a good time unless you come with me. It's settled." And she refused to argue any further about it. As I was dying to go to Paris, I agreed, happily conceding to her that I had a very weak character when it came to Paris.

Our sophomore year found us together again, this time in an apartment just off campus. Paula paid the rent; I paid for the food and cooked our meals. It was a bit lopsided, I know, but our personal finances *were* a bit lopsided. She was a multi-millionaire, and I was...well, not. I enjoyed cooking and Paula hated it. Whatever, it worked. She felt good helping me and I felt fine that she was able to do so. We were true friends.

In the beginning, Paula had explained that her parents' estate was worth many millions of dollars. She was the only beneficiary. She received a very large check at the beginning of each month and dealt with her trustees by mail. "As I said before, I could spend ten thousand dollars a day and never even dent the capital." She shrugged, "It's just money."

Our lives continued as pleasantly as before. We had each other, many friends, both young men and young women, and, other than our own personal demons from our early lives, were generally very happy.

The only small snag in our happiness came from Paula's frequent colds. She felt tired and lethargic and I urged her to see the college nurse. The nurse prescribed iron pills to pick up Paula's energy level. Paula took the pills dutifully, and indeed, felt a lot better.

I mentioned that we both went out a lot with young men. We enjoyed dating and both of us even fell in love once or twice. However, when we talked about it – and we talked about everything in our lives –

we realized that neither of us had the capacity to maintain a lasting relationship. Somehow, our experiences, different but devastating, kept us from being able to forge a permanent connection. Would this ever change? We both devoutly hoped so. "I think a few of our friends think we are lesbians," I joked.

"I know. I get those looks every so often." But we weren't physically in love at all, although we loved one another deeply and would have done *anything*, even given our life, for each other. We were just friends. Remarkably good friends. And weren't we lucky to have one another? Yes, we were. I shudder to think of how twisted I might have become had I never met Paula, and she told me many times that she probably would have killed herself had she not met me.

We traveled to Italy in the summer, then to England the following year. Paula's colds became more frequent, and she visited a specialist in New York City this time to see what was wrong. He performed dozens of tests, probed her inside and out, and the verdict was a poor immune system. He urged her to take multi-vitamins, to eat dark green vegetables, to rest. She did, and again, the symptoms subsided. Paula was her own merry self again, but secretly, I was worried about her. I urged her to see another specialist. She promised that she would…soon.

Our years at Eastbrook were coming to an end. We planned to go to New York City, get an apartment and find jobs. "I don't need one, but, shoot, I'll become boring if I don't find some work," Paula said.

"And I *do* need one and I, too, would become boring – and poor – if I don't find some work," I countered.

We entered into all those activities that precede graduation. Studying for finals, the prom, our yearbook photos, aptitude tests, gathering the names and addresses of our friends, checking the New York Times for apartment rentals…it was an exciting time.

As the end of the year got closer, Paula asked me if I would do something for her. "Of course," I answered. "What?"

She looked at me in a very intent way. "You have to *promise* to do it, no matter how screwy you think it is, OK?"

"What the hell do you want me to do? Kill someone?"

"Not quite that bad, but odd, nonetheless. Promise?"

Well, of course I did. I promised and I did what she asked. I had no idea why she asked me to do this, but I did. It was a very peculiar thing to ask, relatively easy and painless, but peculiar. I couldn't figure out why she wanted me to do this and it drove me nuts. I begged her to explain. "*Why*? Just tell me *why*?" She just shook her head.

No matter how I wheedled and cajoled, she refused to tell me. "Maybe I'll tell you someday," was all she would say. "Maybe I'll never have to." I thought a few of our friends would notice what I had done and ask me about it, but, so it seemed, no one even noticed. And in a few weeks, I completely forgot about the whole matter.

And then, three days before graduation, I received the stiff envelope from the bank in Greenwich. The bank where my father had worked. The bank where my money was growing.

And the contents of this envelope moved me from my safe place of RESPITE and onto the dangerous rocks of REVENGE.

CHAPTER ONE

*"Marriage...is a damnably serious business,
particularly around Boston"*
John P. Marquand

Don took off his hat. He held it in his hand and wondered if he had lost his mind. He sneaked a peek at Arlis. She sat, bundled up in a deep red parka that made her curly chestnut-colored hair shine, twisting her wine glass stem in her hand. She looked serene and calm. She was beautiful and he loved her so. Obviously, she had no inkling that he was a quivering mass of Jell-O. She hummed a snatch of *"Let it snow, let it snow, let it snow..."*, and looked out over the two-weeks-before-Thanksgiving-snow-dusted Vermont treetops. He gulped.

"Arlis..." His voice faltered. "Um, uh, Arlis..." She didn't seem to hear his abortive bleat. Don gripped the hat and turned the brim around, seeking courage from the flat black leather. "Arlis..." firmer now... "Uh, will you marry me?"

No comment, no noise, not even a flicker. "Uh, Arlis?" Shit, who would have thought this would be so hard? Who would have thought that these marry-me words would ever come out of his mouth again? He rubbed his chin. A bit bristly. Maybe he should go back into the house and shave before he brought the subject up again.

But, look! Arlis smiled, her attention seemingly captured by a squirrel that crossed the edge of the porch, leaving little paw-prints in the dusting of snow. Arlis' cats, Tinker and Chance, also watched the squirrel, waiting, just waiting for a millisecond of carelessness, when they might pounce.

Don tried again. "Arlis, ah, will you marry me?" He spoke a little louder. Maybe she hadn't quite heard him.

Silence, except for the squirrel. The cats were like statues; only their slitty green and yellow eyes flickered.

Baffled, hoping that he wasn't going to make a gol-durned fool of himself yet once more, Don swallowed hard and dropped to one knee. Arlis' attention was still on the squirrel. "Honey," he said, in what seemed like a very loud voice, "Will you *marry* me?"

Her brown eyes, magnified behind the Art Deco glasses she favored, widened. She whipped her head around, the squirrel forgotten. Stunned, she gasped, "Are you for *real*?"

We will leave Don and Arlis, the squirrel and the cats, for a short time, allowing them to say those sweet and tender things that pass between lovers...especially between lovers who have just realized that their lives are going to be entwined, hopefully, forever.

And then, after the tender kisses and the murmurs, "When do you want to get married?"

"Real soon. How about you?"

"This summer?" She grinned, thinking of herself in billowy white.

"Sure," He grinned, thinking of her naked.

She drained her glass and held it out for him to refill. He took the wine bottle out of the snow-filled bucket and poured. "Hot damn! We're gonna get married!" They clinked glasses. And the squirrel, startled at the noise, ran away. Tinker and Chance shared an annoyed glance and settled back down on the porch to await another opportunity.

"I have a brilliant idea," Arlis jumped up, knocking her glass over. The burgundy stain spread over the snow and she laughed, bent down and scooped the snow and wine back into her glass. She licked at it, making Don's stomach do funny things. "Like an adult sno-cone." She waved the glass in the air. "Nevermind waiting until summer. Let's do it in a few weeks! Let's get married on Virgin Gorda!"

"Hot damn again!" Don reared back and grabbed Arlis. The cats closed their eyes and went to sleep. Too much action going on here on the porch for any squirrels to come by.

And after another short hiatus, Arlis got up and went into the cabin to call Captain Jack.

***

Captain Jack Scambaugh eased himself off of his arthritic knees. Christ, getting old sucked. "I'm getting too ancient for this sort of thing," he groaned. His first mate, Ducky, laughed, showing gleaming, white teeth in his dark face. He smacked Captain Jack's upper arm.

"You're a young pup, Cap. You're just looking for sympathy." With the agile and annoyingly effortless grace of youth, Ducky picked up the heavy folded sail and hoisted it to his shoulder. "Be back in five," he said as he jumped off the boat. "I'm bringing this to the marina for repair." Jack waved at him, flapping his hand, then sighed, rubbing his face, wistfully thinking of himself, forty years ago, and how he could have toted two or more sails without puffing. Nowadays...well...

He looked at the calendar that hung on his bunk wall. Three days and the new group would be here. The passenger list was tacked up next to the calendar. Sixteen new people. Sixteen more passengers, sixteen more lives to entwine with his for two weeks. And then another hefty deposit into his retirement account. Sixteen more trips - less than a year. Sixteen more and he'd be finished. Sixteen more groups to meet, greet, get to know – some more intimately than others. Sixteen more groups to enjoy sailing with...spend the better part of fifteen days with - sixteen more and he could quit. Sell *The Southern Cross* and retire with Emma onto the new boat. Sixteen more trips. He wrote the number on the wall above the calendar, just below the picture of Emma poking her head through a life preserver. Darling, lovely Emma. Sixteen more.

***

"Captain Jack? This is Arlie Fuglie...Arlis, from last year's cruise? Do you remember me?...Yes! Yes! Arlis and Don! Oh, Captain, how *are* you?....And Emma? And Ducky? ... And is Kat still there? Good, us too...We're both *really* good! Yes! Really, really good! Well, we have some great news! Don and I are getting married!"

"Wonderful, Arlis. Congratulations. Don is a fine man and...shoot, if I weren't so attached to Emma...I'd make a play for you myself. I'm so pleased for the two of you."

"Oh, thank you, Captain Jack. If it weren't for meeting on board your boat, well, we'd have never met!" Her infectious giggle poured through the receiver.

"Oh, I'm going to have to move you two from the friends' tabletop over to the romance table top," Jack's laugh boomed back over the telephone wires.

"I called, not only to tell you the good news, but we wanted to ask you a favor," Jack could feel Arlis' sunshine smile through the phenomenon of long distance. He made an encouraging noise. He'd enjoyed the two guests and remembered them well. A romance made in heaven, right from the moment they'd set eyes on each other...the tall, energetic man, whip-thin like a stick of animated licorice and the delightfully rounded laughing woman. Neither Arlis nor Don were youngsters. They each lived with a bit of baggage from their pasts, like most people in their prime. But the magic lightning of The British Virgin Islands struck these two souls immediately. They'd giggled and flirted and were stunned with mutual adoration from the moment they saw each other. It was obvious to Captain Jack; they fell hard right under his eyes, the golden sun of the British Virgin Islands and the dipping and swaying of *The Southern Cross*. He'd gotten a very newsy thank you letter and a birthday card, signed from the two of them. And now, a wedding...not a big surprise to him. His cruises with romantic starry nights on *The Southern Cross* had ended with a lot of weddings. Holding the telephone, he heaved himself over to the cockpit and looked down at the left hand table-top, the one he called the friends' table. There, shut under the clear Lucite top, were dozens and dozens of snapshots, most of them taken right here on *The Southern Cross*. The photo of Don and Arlis was near the rim; a good photo of two tanned and smiling people.

"What can I do for you, honey?" he asked.

"Don and I want to come down to Virgin Gorda and get married on the beach."

"Great! When?"

"Can we do it soon? Maybe in December? And will you give me away?"

"Well, I'd be tickled pink!" Captain Jack's grin split his face. "Let's get all the details and I'll see what I can do to get the ball rolling down here."

Ducky leaped over onto the boat, saw that Jack was on the telephone and foraged in the refrigerator for a cold can of soda. Jack made some loud sounds and then slammed the telephone down.

"Hot damn, Duck, we're gonna have a wedding down here!"

"Who's getting married?"

"Remember last year, that couple...both from New England somewheres...Um, funny name she has, Arlis? Arlis Fuglie? Some fancy Norwegian family name. His name is Don...tall thin guy... baldish?

"Leather cowboy hat?" Ducky laughed. "Bald guy? Always wore a leather cowboy hat down here in the tropics?" He scratched his head. "Oh, sure, I remember *them*! She was cute...glasses and a *zoftig* figure, right?" Captain Jack nodded, grinning, remembering Arlis in her flowered bikini. "And him with the cowboy boots and his skinny white legs?" Ducky chuckled, remembering the sight of Don coming up on deck wearing a white cowboy hat, polished cowboy boots, a blue bathing suit with palm trees on it and nothing else but a grin. The man had guts, that's for sure! "Great!" Ducky shook his head in admiration. "And they're gonna get married down here? Brilliant. When?"

"Not this trip out, but the next one...in December, just before Christmas They'd like to do it on Saturday...let's see" He moved back over to the wall calendar. "That's December 19th. They'll fly down the day before and stay at the Green Flash. Arlis is calling Leslie and Charlie to get things going. And me, I'm gonna give the bride away."

"How about me? Can I be the flower girl?" Ducky's vibrant laugh rang out again. "We'll all have some fun."

Captain Jack smacked his hands down on the table. "We'll incorporate the wedding right into our itinerary...invite the whole boatload along. I'll just jigger the schedule a little and we'll come into harbor the night before. Oh, boy! This will be a pisser and is certain to get the romantic hormones flowing all around."

Ducky popped open another cold root beer. "It will be great publicity for you and your cruises. Who knows? Maybe even *I'll* get romantic."

CHAPTER TWO

*"...while the noiseless chariot of the
Southern Cross rolled over...."*
Pablo Neruda

Passenger List for The Southern Cross :

Your Captain		Jack Scambaugh
Your First Mate		Ducky B. (The Honorable J. Ducksworth Blyton IV)
Your Cook		Kat (Ekatarina Rosseau)
Passengers:	A-1	Annie Sabatino, Greenwich, Connecticut, USA
		Suzie Ruutz-Reese, Greenwich, Connecticut, USA
	B-1	Vinny James Lodi, New Jersey, USA
		Sam Gallofrito, Newark, New Jersey, USA
	A-2	Sarah Lemonowski, Canterbury, Kent, UK
	B-2	Elliott Barringer, Beverly Hills, California, USA
	A-3	Paula Haskins, New York City, New York, USA
	B-3	Duncan MacKinnon, Glasgow, Scotland, UK
	A-4	Martha Temple-Wright, Capetown, South Africa
		Claudia Van Voorhees, Johannesburg, South Africa
	B-4	Lannie Olmstead, London, England, UK
		Michael Beck, Eigan Bally, Ireland, UK
	A-5	Zandra Hoovenmeyer, Amsterdam, Holland
		Corliss Curtis, Bloomsbury, England, UK
	B-5	Hosea Balleau, Athens, Greece
		Elwyn Langdon, Los Angeles, California, USA

Annie eagerly scanned the list. "Hosea! What kind of name is Hosea?" She looked again, "And Zandra Hoovenmeyer. I suppose it's a woman. I mean, it looks like the girls are on the A side and the men on the B side."

"But not for long!" Her cousin Suzie grabbed the list out of Annie's hands. "Hmm? Who looks interesting? I dibs Elliott Barringer or Duncan MacKinnon."

She smoothed a lock of blonde hair back behind her ear. "They've got the private cabins. They must have the most money."

"Trust you to go for the gold."

"Duncan MacKinnon is from Scotland," Suzie theorized as she rubbed her nose. "I smell money there. A Lord or a Laird or whatever they're called…in a big castle. I'd be Lady MacKinnon and go for rides in my carriage." Suzie's eyes softened as she lost herself in imagination.

"He probably wears one of those skirt-things and is old and fat." Annie made a face and rummaged in the packet. She brought out the letter from Captain Scambaugh and read it out loud.

Hi everyone from Captain Jack! All about the BVI trip ….This is a little list that I made up a few years ago. Those of you who have taken a sailing trip probably know it all, but those of you who have never been to the BVI or on a catamaran voyage might appreciate a heads up as to what you can start to collect for the trip. But before you get to the list, the MOST important thing for you is:

Be sure to have your passport in proper order! If you don't have one, start the proceedings to get one NOW!!!! (As it takes a few weeks to get one).

Things to bring to the Virgin Islands:

1. **Be sure your luggage is soft sided so it can be stuffed away easily. There isn't a great deal of room for boxy suitcases, etc. And for those of you sharing a stateroom, well, you are *sharing* a stateroom. Be considerate of your bunkmate! For 95% of the time, we will be very casual (bathing suits, shorts and tee shirts)..bring along two (but NO MORE) dressy outfits…the equivalent of lightweight dresses for the women and slacks and a dress shirt for the men. We will be dining at a very classy restaurant once and are attending one semi-formal beach party.**

2. Camera – Throw aways and underwaters if you do that kind of thing. If you bring an expensive one, be sure to have a good strap, as cameras that fall overboard just don't seem to work as well as they once did. Trust me, I KNOW!!! We do supply throw-a-way cameras, but perhaps you'll want your own.

3. Film – it is VERY expensive down there! Ditto batteries.

4. Binoculars or Video Cameras. If you like. Again, *The Southern Cross* is equipped with binoculars, but many passengers prefer their own.

5. Hat crokies and Eyeglass crokies – EYEGLASSES AND SUNGLASSES Veddy Veddy important!!!! If you don't know what these are, they are little straps and hooks to keep your glasses and hats from going overboard. Captain Jack HATES to have to turn around and go fishing for your Red Sox cap! And, if you wear glasses, maybe bring an extra old pair, just in case you don't listen to me regarding the glasses crokies! And extra eyeglasses if you are blind without them. Just in case you drop them overboard, which HAS happened. Sunglasses are important to many of you. Also, bring reading glasses if you can't read a menu without them.

6. Music. The boat is equipped with a CD player and a cassette player. We have lots of music on board, but perhaps you prefer one or two of your own. Mark your possessions with your name in indelible ink. Perhaps your own walk-man, or IPOD, in case you can't stand Ducky B playing "Hot, Hot Hot!" one more time.

7. Throw away paper back books. Readers can get thru 6 or 7. You can leave your old ones on board or at the "library" at the office at Soper's Hole and trade for some "new" old ones there.

8. Sun stuff. For your skin. The Virgin Island sun is a scorcher. For those of you with fair skin, you may want to go to a tanning place ahead of time to give yourself a wee bit of base before you ventures out to the BVI, and even those with dark skins, like

Ducky B, ought to get a tan ahead of time. Other wise, you will BURN and be miserable. And bring along a tube of "hello Vera", as we call it...some aloe or sunburn soothing lotion to take care of yourself in case you get a little pink.

9. As for make up and hairdressing things, bring the minimum. You are on a boat, for goodness sake! And as for gold and jewelry, bring as little as possible. The BVIs are relatively safe places, but it is foolish – ever – to flaunt your wealth or jewels. We want you to have fun, not regrets.

10. Any and all prescription drugs or medicines you might need. Some of these islands don't have any Brooks Drugs...as a matter of fact NONE of these islands have Brooks Drugs. If you even THINK you might need it, bring it.

11. One beach towel...a cruddy one is good and that way you can leave it when you go home and that will leave you a little more room to bring home some of that great island rum.

12. If you plan to sleep out under the stars with the brave Cockpit Gang, let Captain Jack know so we can sew you up a sleeping bag that will protect you from the occasional, but fierce, night-time rainstorms. Call us and we will try to explain what seems to work. This is not an issue for most people, but for some, it consumes the entire winter as they try to build a better mousetrap to sleep outside in! More about sleeping under the stars later.

13. A waterproof beach bag to carry your wet clothes around after you shower or to tote seashells home.

14. Four quarters per person for the "one dollah shower" on Marina Cay, if you're swift under the spray, or eight quarters if you'd like a leisurely "two dollah shower".

15. Good stuff to keep your hair from turning green and gunky. The water is extremely salty and does a job on one, especially if one uses a bit of Clairol on one's coiffure. A good conditioner is needed here. This applies to anyone that it applies to.

16. Cheap reef shoes. You can usually get a pair at K-Mart or Walmart for about 5 bucks. These are really important, as many of the beaches have coral and little rocks underfoot, and walking on them can be agonizing if you don't have these…they are also good for getting around on the boat as most of them have some kind of non-slip soles.

17. Some bug spray or a bug stick. There are very few bugs down here, but once in a while……The boat has a supply of this kind of stuff, but it is always prudent to bring along your own supply.

18. BUT DO <u>NOT</u> BRING ANY ILLICIT DRUGS. The BVI has an <u>ABSOLUTE ZERO-TOLERANCE POLICY when it comes to drugs, marijuana, cocaine</u> or any such animal. You do NOT want to spend the rest of your life in a BVI jail (VERY unpleasant) so do not even THINK of trying to fool the authorities or mess around with their laws.

I'll be sending you more information in the next week for those who want to try sleeping on the trampolines at night. We call these brave souls The Cockpit Gang, and they are admired by one and all. If this is what you'd enjoy, it is marvelous.

The Southern Cross is air-conditioned. Our galley (kitchen), heads (bathrooms) and staterooms are state-of-the art. However, you will be on a BOAT, not lolling at the Waldorf Astoria Hotel.

And last, if you have some unusual dietary preferences, or are allergic to any foods, please let us know ahead of time. Our sublime cook, Kat, will do her utmost to please your palate. If you need or want any unusual foods or dietary requirements, please let us know ahead of time or bring the items with you. Again, you are going to be on small islands with limited shopping facilities.

On behalf of myself, Ducky B and Kat, we will be awaiting you on the dock at Seven Seas Yacht Basin, Soper's Hole Marina, Tortola, British Virgin Islands.

Captain Jack

"No grass?" Suzie made a face. "Shoot. I was going to bring a few joints in. Maybe they'd help to liven up the party."

"Are you *crazy*?" Annie hissed at her cousin. "Are you nuts? Do you want to spend the rest of your life chained in some prison somewhere? *No* joints! *No* grass!" Horrified, Annie waved the list at her. "What do you think they mean by *zero* tolerance, you nit-wit? Don't even *think* about it!"

"I could put it in a heavy zip lock baggie and put the baggie into a container of coffee beans. I hear that even the sniffy dogs can't smell through coffee beans." Suzie made a puffing gesture.

"If you even *think* about trying any of that stupidity," Annie was so upset that she began to yell, "I'll…well, I'll…um… I'll tell *everyone* about what you did in the Stamford Town *Mall*! I'll take out an ad in the goddamn Greenwich Times…on the front page!"

"You wouldn't tell that!" Suzie's face blanched.

"I would!"

"OK, OK." Suzie made a conciliatory gesture. "But I still think that I could get away with it." Annie shook her head violently and Suzie shrugged. "OK. You win."

***

Arlis had worked and sweated like a demon possessed to get the wedding planned, right down to the favors for the guests (bottles of the local buttery rum, tied in a raffia basket), in the few weeks before the celebration. In a hysterical panic over what she was going to wear, she dragooned her best friend, Carole Singletary, who was, naturally, going to be the Maid of Honor, into driving down to Boston to the bridal sale – "**All Gowns – Couturier Samples worth up to $8,000 - $200 each!!!**" - at Filene's Basement.

On the advice of others who had snared one of the infamous bargain bridal gowns, Arlis wore white tights and a push up bra under her sweatshirt and slacks. The two of them ripped and fought their way through the crowd of brides-to-be, tearing four and five thousand dollar gowns out of the hands of those women who were less demented and less determined to get a bargain. Standing in the middle of three hundred grabbing, screaming, emotional, milling women, Arlis stripped off her slacks and top and stood in a corner in her bra and tights. Carole…God bless her…brought her gown after gown to try on, pushing and shoving against others who were clawing for the selfsame dresses and veils. It was exasperating. The gowns were, for the most part, size 4s and Arlis was, for the most part, especially in the breast and hip areas, larger than that. Nonetheless, she crammed dress after dress over her hair, "They can be altered. All of them. They can be *altered*. Stop worrying!" Carole's soothing enthusiasm triumphed over Arlis' wails that she'd never...*never*...find anything that fit!

Arlis' mother, Alfrieda, who hated to fly, was finally convinced to take a Valium and get her duff onto the plane. "If you want to be at the wedding, Mom, you have to get on a plane. You just cannot swim to there!" Don's three children from his first marriage, two of them happy, one not so happy at the upcoming nuptials, were dragooned into coming. Don spent hours on the telephone, praising Arlis and trying his best to explain just why the wedding had to be held within the next three weeks. Finally, with bribes and thinly veiled promises to disinherit, the kids decided to cooperate. Don was a poorer, but happy man.

The best rooms at The Green Flash were booked, airplane tickets bought. The services of His Honor, J. Ducksworth Blyton III, the Queen's Representative to The British Virgin Islands, and, incidentally, Ducky B's father, were reserved for presiding over the wedding services. The rehearsal supper and post-wedding island luau for all the guests were planned and paid for. The bride and groom's reservations for a Mediterranean cruise on the *MS Noordam* were secured with the last remnants of Don's American Express Card balance. Don didn't care at all. He was, as stated above, a happy, happy man.

Exhausted, all Don and Arlis and their entourage of guests from points all over the United States, had to do was get to The Green Flash Hotel, Big Fish Cay, Virgin Gorda, BVI on time.

CHAPTER THREE

"He is dead and gone, lady. He is dead and gone..."
Shakespeare, Hamlet

Detective-Inspector Carlton Reese stripped off the protective gloves, wadded them up, and stuffed them into a plastic bag. He handed the bag to his assistant, Effalyn Penn. "Dead. Maybe eight...ten hours." His foot gently toed the coconut that lay beside the mushed-in head of the corpse of Two-Tone Hammerly.

"Probably drunk." Effalyn's generally placid face looked down. "I s'pose the coconut fell on his head." She looked up, assessing the probability of the rest of the coconuts falling and prudently moved back a foot or so.

"Mmm. Maybe." Reese followed her gaze. "He was always solidly drunk about midnight. He *might* have fallen asleep under the tree. The coconut *might* have fallen and *might* have hit him on the head. Maybe." The call had come early. He hadn't had a chance to shave. He scratched his chin, then mopped his face and neck with his handkerchief. Eight o'clock in the morning and already, he was sweating like a wart hog. His shirt stuck to his back and his armpits felt damp and uncomfortable. Damn, it was going to be a hot one. He looked back down at Two-Tone. The mottled skin, half dark brown, half light brown, which had cemented the nickname, was fading rapidly to an all-over grey color. Carlton's stomach made a funny noise. To cover the rumbling and preserve the dignity of his office, Carlton made a tsking sound and turned away from the body. As always, when confronted with death, he found himself smiling in a completely inappropriate way and fought down the totally inappropriate delight that engulfed him. It was always the same. He was alive and Two-Tone was dead. Carlton was glad...glad. Not glad that Two-Tone was dead, mind you, but that he – Carlton Reese – was not. He wondered, for the twentieth or so time, if Effalyn felt this strange happiness that the arrow of fate had missed her this time too. He turned around in a complete circle, pretending to look for clues...anything to distract himself from the short-lived, but potent, engulfing thrill that it wasn't *him* lying on the ground with a hole in his head and his brains spilling out onto the sand.

"You think it could'a been murder?" Effalyn didn't seem to mirror his morbid views. Her only expression was doubtful. "Who the heck would want to kill Two-Tone?" Effalyn's early morning ablutions had been more thorough than his. Her uniform was clean and pressed; her hair was wound into an attractive and elaborate pompadour, replete with two artificial sets of curls, one on each side; her make-up perfect. Despite the heat, Effalyn's skin was dry, her white shirt starched and creased and she still wore her protective gloves.

"Dunno." Reese shrugged. "Where the hell is Fullbright? I could use a cup of coffee."

Used to the morning grumpiness of her boss, Effalyn offered, "Want me to get us a cup?" Reese nodded, but before Effalyn could walk to the small string of shops that lined the road, a white SUV drove onto the fringe of the beach. Dr. Sampson Fullbright, Virgin Gorda's Medical Inspector (part-time) and Podiatrist (part-time) heaved his considerable bulk out of the SUV, pushed aside the several dozen curious bystanders who had been gathering ever since the body had been discovered an hour ago, and lumbered to the foot of the palm tree. He set down the satchel that he carried with him at all times.

"Morning, Carlton." Fullbright nodded affably. "Morning, Eff. What we got here?"

"Two-Tone Hammerly." Effalyn offered. "Dead. Hit on the head by this coconut, we think."

"Drunk, Prob'ly." Fullbright and indeed, everyone in the local area knew Two-Tone well. He opened his satchel and took out a towel. "Poor creature doesn't look too good at all." He waved off a group of flies that had settled on the body and in and around Two-Tone's nose, eyes and lips. Effalyn tried not to gag. She wanted to be as professional as possible and felt that vomiting might show her to be weak. Carlton, more used to death's ravages, also felt a little queasy, but would rather have died than show any weakness himself. He was relieved that his grin was under control.

The Doctor swallowed his own bile. No matter how many times he met death, it was always terrible. "Shoot. He looks awful. Hmpf. Not that he ever looked that good on his best day." He spread the towel on the sand next to the dead man's head. Groaning, he knelt, put on protective gloves and gingerly, with his huge, sausage-like fingers, delicately probed what was left of the head of Two-Tone Hammerly. "Smashed him up pretty good." Fullbright grunted. "That the offending coconut?" He made a motion with his head. Effalyn nodded. "Bag it up, honey. Thanks."

Too smart to feel any annoyance at Doc Fullbright's non-feminist remark, Effalyn took a baggie from her crime scene kit and rolled the bloody coconut, plastered with Two-Tone's frizzy hair and other parts that used to belong inside Two-Tone's head into it. Fullbright put out his hand and Effalyn placed the bag in it. The doctor measured the coconut against the gaping wound. "Looks like the offender," he offered. He then took out a thermometer and jabbed it into Two-Tone's chest, piercing the flesh. Effalyn blanched and gasped. "Liver temperature," the Doctor informed her. "Don't worry, it didn't hurt him. Heh, heh." He wiped off the thermometer probe. "Little forensic humor here. Helps us all to cope. Now, give me a hand so I can roll him over," he motioned to Carleton. The two men heaved Two-Tone's body onto its side and Fullbright performed yet another indignity on what was left of Two-Tone. Fullbright lumbered himself to his feet and checked his wristwatch. "Lessee…its 8:17…let's say he's been dead …oh, maybe eight or ten hours…" Carlton allowed himself a small smile.

"How do you know?" Effalyn was fascinated, always avid for information that would help her understand the unfamiliar world of dead bodies.

"Temperature of the body as well as the lividity." Doctor Fullbright pointed to several parts of Two-Tone's skin where the coagulating blood was beginning to settle. "Let's make a guess that he died between midnight and two…and I hope and pray that the poor sonofabitch was stinking drunk unconscious when the damn thing hit him."

"He was always stinking drunk. It *did* hit him, didn't it?"

"Absolutely. Presuming no one helped the coconut along. You know the mantra; Something hits you on the head, a fracture depress. Your head hits an object, a crack is the mess."

"Huh?" Effalyn gaped.

"The little rhyme makes me remember. I know it's silly, but hey!" Doctor Fullbright laughed at her astonishment. "I know I'm not a poet, but…" He spread his big, gloved hands out. "Let's see if I can say it better. If a moving object… say a coconut… hits a fixed object… say Two-Tone's head… hard enough, you get a depressed fracture." He pointed to the bloody depression on Two-Tone's head. "If a moving head hits a fixed object hard enough, you'll get a crack." He grinned at Effalyn's open mouth. "This way, we know that Two-Tone didn't trip over an*other* coconut and hit his head on *this* coconut. Nossir, this coconut fell down and hit Two-Tone, or," he paused thoughtfully, "somebody smacked the coconut down on Two-Tone's head and made it *look* as if it fell on him. Take your pick."

"I'm a little confused with you and your poems," Carlton sighed. "If Two-Tone is *dead*, he got hit on the *head*. Is that what you're trying to say, you fat old poet, you? You done?" Carlton wanted coffee badly. Needed coffee badly.

"Yeah. If you don't like my rhyming, you can buy me a cup of coffee. Let's get him to the morgue at the hospital and I'll do an autopsy this afternoon." Fullbright wrapped up his tools of the trade and snapped his satchel closed. Carlton motioned to Effalyn to get the body moved.

In turn, she motioned to Ganny Johnstone and Armond Hubert, the two patrolmen who were keeping the crowd away. "Get him bagged up and bring him to the hospital." Ganny and Armond approached the body with caution. They were both new on the force and hadn't yet handled a dead body. Effalyn smiled. She was feeling better now, in charge. "Come on, boys, he won't bite you!" She cackled. "Not now, anyhow."

Carton, Effalyn and Dr. Fullbright walked to the coffee shop. "What was Two-Tone's real name?" Carlton asked. "I don't think I ever knew him called anything but Two-Tone."

"Shoot, if your skin looked like his, they'd'a called you Two-Tone, too." Effalyn smoothed her own coffee-with-cream cheeks. "I think his name …it was a funny one, even down here…something like 'Enterprise'? … 'Elemental'? No, no, 'Endeavor'."

"Endeavor? Almost as peculiar as Two-Tone. He had that what-do-you-call-it? Same thing as Michael Jackson…Virgilio? Vitiglio?"

"If he'd been really dark complected, like me," Doctor Fullbright examined his own smooth, deeply colored skin with obvious pleasure, "the pooling of his blood…when it settled after about six to seven hours…would have been difficult to see."

"Ah," Carlton drained his cup and refilled it from the carafe that sat on the table. A huge fan whirred overhead and his sweaty shirt was beginning to dry. "Think it was an accident?"

"I heard once or twice of a coconut killing somebody. Some lady who was at a hotel. She was sitting under the tree and the coconut fell and bonked her on the head. Lots of other people saw it." Fullbright nodded. "And...I think there was a young boy over in Road Town. They...a bunch of kids...were climbing the trees and throwing coconuts around. He was killed by one, but I don't remember if it fell on him or somebody threw it at him." The doctor looked at Carlton. "You remember?"

"Seems like I remember the boy. I'll have to look them up."

"And weren't a couple of chickens killed a year or so ago. Wind storm. They were sheltering under the tree?"

"Don't sit under the coconut tree with anyone else but me," Carlton sang softly. Dr. Fullbright snorted and Effalyn giggled. Effalyn worshipped and respected both the hefty old doctor and her boss. Two terrific men, she thought.

"Lots of poets and troubadours around here." The three of them sat for a few moments, relishing the coffee and the coolness and thinking of how often they, like Two-Tone, had rested under the shade of a coconut palm. Effalyn twisted her cup in her hands. "Again, Boss, You think it was an accident?"

"Who would kill Two-Tone?" Carlton shrugged. And what for? Lazy old drunk, no money at all. Who would be angry enough at him to bop him that hard with a coconut?"

And later, telling Rebecca all about it, he shrugged again. "Who'd kill a harmless old man like Two-Tone?"

"And why?" His wife agreed. "You're always citing me the reasons for murder: greed, hate, revenge, fear...even love, sometimes. Two-Tone didn't have three cents to his name. No one would kill him for money." Rebecca counted on her fingers. "Hate? I never knew anyone who said a bad thing about him. He was a drunk, but harmless. Never heard *him* say a bad word about anyone, either. Revenge? Revenge for what?"

Carlton laughed. "Maybe Two-Tone stole a fish or some breadfruit." Rebecca swatted at him.

"Two Tone was a drunk, but he was always honest. He worked around our house for three years or more." She took a coffeecake out of the refrigerator and put it in front of Carlton. "Never touched one thing. Never! I never worried about him being with Niccola either. I trusted him. My goodness, I never had any feelings that he was anything but himself. A feeble pathetic old drunk. But a thief? No. And, Lordy knows, he could have taken all of our heirloom silver anytime he'd wanted!" She laughed and Carlton watched her with love. "Nah. And as for fear? Fear of what? Two-Tone saw somebody do something bad and was going to blackmail somebody? Doubtful. Two-Tone was usually so drunk he wouldn't notice a bank robbery going on in front of his nose." She shrugged. "It has to be an accident." Carlton nodded, finished his last bite of coffee cake, and then asked what delights Rebecca planned to serve him for lunch.

***

The funeral of Endeavor (Two-Tone) Hammerly was, at the beginning, a sad occasion. Everyone on Virgin Gorda knew the old reprobate and everyone felt badly that his death had been such an unusual one. The Reverend Emanuel Emanuel preached a rollicking sermon full of the delights of Heaven awaiting those who approached the pearly gates with a soul as clear as the soul of the child-like Two-Tone. His sister, Orna, invited the entire church-full of mourners to join her and the Hammerly family in a send-off at the church hall. Carton Reese and Effalyn Penn represented the police force, and they reiterated to all in attendance that the verdict was closed as death due to accidental circumstances. Carlton ate too much and had to take two glasses of Alka-Seltzer before he could sleep. Rebecca, used to her husband's appetite, waited until the following morning to speak to him about it all.

***

To All Guests on the December Cruise of *The Southern Cross:*

So that you can all start soaking up the local flavor of the British Virgin Islands, I have sent you a copy of The BVIsland News, our local newspaper, as well as a provisional itinerary of our cruise schedule:

PROVISIONAL ITINERARY OF DECEMBER CRUISE

Day One - Guests will arrive on Tortola at the Soper's Hole Yacht Basin between 10 and 11:30 AM in the morning. .Some guests will arrive via the 9:30 AM Ferry (The Wild T'ing) from Charlotte Amalie, St. Thomas to the West End and will be met at 10:00AM at the West End Ferry Dock. You will be clearing Customs into the British Virgin Island there and our driver, Cammie, will meet you at the Customs Exit. He will be driving a large white jitney van with a red and white striped awning. The van will have *The Southern Cross* written on the sides. Cammie will drive you and your luggage across Soper's Hole (approximately 7 minute ride) and we will welcome you at the Yacht Basin.

For those guests who will be arriving at the Beef Island Airport on the 10 :45 AM arrival plane from Puerto Rico, you will clear Customs and see Cammie with the jitney as you come out of the exit. The drive from Beef Island to Soper's Hole is approximately 30 minutes. Again, we will welcome you at the Yacht Basin.

You'll be shown to your cabins, have a few moments to get freshened up, and then a tour of *The Southern Cross* will begin, followed by a superb welcome lunch served by our chef, Kat. You can unpack at your leisure after we cast off. Here is our provisional schedule (provisional, as weather and events may change…but, if all goes as expected, this is where you will be and what you will be doing):

Wednesday, December 16th – Welcome, as above, lunch, and then familiarizing ourselves with the boat, rules and regulations of the BVI, rules and regulations of your Captain, safety drill, overview of our schedule for the 15 days you will be on board, and a brief history of The British Virgin Islands. We will set sail at 2 PM and sail to The Bight at Norman Island for the evening. Norman Island is supposedly the place where Robert Lewis Stevenson's Treasure Island is located. You can swim, look for shells, have a cold drink or two and perhaps, if you are lucky, you can find Long John Silver's pieces of eight. Dinner on board.

Thursday, December 17th - Breakfast on board, then over to the Treasure Caves on Norman Island. You can snorkel or ride the Zodiacs and search for treasure and beautiful fish during the morning hours. Lunch on board and then a sail to Jost Van Dyke where we will moor at Great Harbor. In the afternoon, you can explore the shops, swim, pick up shells and relax. Dinner is at the famed Banjo Man's Bar and Restaurant. An island buffet awaits you and then an evening of dancing to the Banjo Reggae Band. Banjo Man, a well-known island character and singer/raconteur, will entertain us with spontaneous songs and comedy.

Friday, December 18th - Picnic breakfast on the beach of Great Harbor. Sail to Big Fish Harbor, Virgin Gorda. Lunch on board. The next two days begins a very special event for our guests. We have all been invited to a wedding! Last year, two wonderful people met one another on this cruise. They are getting married on Saturday, December 19th here in Big Fish Harbor and we will be sharing in their rehearsal dinner tonight and their wedding and wedding banquet tomorrow. The rehearsal dinner will be informal – beach dress, but the wedding will be an occasion for all of us to dress up. So pack a dressy dress, for you ladies, and a pair of lightweight slacks and a dress shirt, for you men. And yes, you are welcome to bring a gift for the bride and groom. On a great second thought, *don't* bring a dress or outfit…BUY one when you get down here. There are many lovely shops for both men and women in Soper's Hole and Big Fish Harbor.

……………..and so on…..

***

"A wedding," Annie squeaked. "A *wedding*!"

"A good omen. If she can do it, so can I. May I be the next one to catch a rich man on the boat." Suzie languidly began to read the newspaper. "Hmmm. Some guy just got killed by a coconut landing on his head." She patted her softly curling blonde hair. "I'll be sure not to stand under any coconut trees."

Annie watched her cousin with narrowed eyes. Yes, If any of them snared a man on the trip, Suzie would be the one. And he'd be a wealthy one, too! Trust Suzie for that kind of unerring instinct! Suzie's best talents lay in the direction of snaring men. She was better at that than anything. Annie chuckled to herself. She should be used to it. After twenty-seven years of watching her cousin's technique…twenty-seven years of trailing Suzie around, picking up the guys that Suzie had dropped, dusting them off and sending them on their way, actually consoling the poor, yearning suckers. Annie snorted, *"You think that I would learn,"* she mused ruefully to herself.

Annie was the smart one, the one who was academically brilliant. Second in her class all the way through school. *Magna cum laude* in college and dead last in glamour and romance. But Suzie, scorning the delights of practical schooling, was *magna cum laude* with the men. Annie patted her own thick, dark hair. Oh, certainly, she loved her cousin, and Suzie, in her own way, loved Annie and Annie's usefulness.

From the beginning, the two cousins were close, close in birth, living a few houses away from one another's family. Annie got the good grades, Suzie got the boys. She had a dozen of them, Annie thought back to their childhood and early adolescence. Suzie would have had *more* than a dozen, if only time had been a little more elastic. Even when they were babies, Suzie had always taken the prize in charm. She was born blonde and fluffy, with huge blue eyes and pink, chubby cheeks. Strangers would stop her mother as she pushed Suzie's carriage. Some lady would lean over and say, "Oooh! My! What a beautiful child!" Annie's mother, harrumphing, would shove Annie's carriage toward the lady, who would smile, a bit uncomfortably, and tell her that her little boy would certainly grow up to be a smart one. Annie quickly got used to being in second place, which, around Suzie, was last place too.

As they grew, Suzie's breasts burgeoned into amazing mounds, perky, pointed, and yet lusciously round at the same time. Annie's breasts were non-existent. Suzie's were truly amazing, the talk and envy of every young girl who changed for gym in the locker room with her and the secret wet dream of every adolescent boy in Greenwich, Connecticut. Even now, after so many men and so many marriages, Suzie's hair was still golden (albeit touched up with a skilled hairdresser's color palette), and rippled down her back, long and straight. Her breasts still caused minor traffic accidents. Annie's beanpole body had adjusted. She did have breasts…small ones. Adequate, but nothing that stopped men in their tracks. Just regular old normal female appendages, nothing more. She also had a small waist, long legs and a pleasant bottom, but no one looked at her twice if Suzie was around. Annie had medium dark-brown hair, straight and thick, usually worn in a bunch at her neck, and medium brown eyes. Not even dark, lustrous ones, just medium. Annie often thought that with her eyes and hair, she might be mistaken for some mongrel puppy dog. Cute, but no worry whatsoever to the silken, purebred Afghan Hound.

Suzie's complexion remained flawless. She never even had a zit in high school. Annie, on the other hand, was plagued with adolescent acne, and, afterwards, freckles dotted her nose and cheekbones. Annie might have been jealous and hated her cousin, but, as Annie was, bone-deep, a decent, humorous woman, she acknowledged the reality that she was plain and Suzie was a dazzler. And she genuinely loved her cousin, admiring Suzie's spunk and daring. Oh, certainly, Suzie was selfish and temperamental, wanting to play with Annie until something better came along, but the two were bound by their cousinship and family ties. And certainly Suzie was sneaky. Sneaky and charming. Charming when anyone else was around, sneaky when it was her and Annie. You know the type. Suzie would get an idea to throw snowballs at cars. Annie might demur, but Suzie would talk her into it. Suzie did what Suzie wanted to do. And then, when the snowball hit a car and the car stopped, Suzie would hand Annie a big snowball and disappear. And there stood Annie, smart in school, but helpless where her cousin was concerned, the obvious-looking perpetrator, in her yellow snowsuit, a huge snowball in her hand, waiting stupidly until the man got out of the car, roaring mad, and looking for Annie's mother. Suzie hung around in the background, blue eyes huge and innocent, wringing her hands and moaning that she had *tried* to stop Annie.

Annie's whole life had been like that. Suzie first, Annie last.

Annie smiled, as she remembered. Suzie often *was* nice to her. Like a person who owned that big, messy mongrel dog and occasionally remembered to pet it. She shook her head and shrugged her shoulders. Who could figure out Suzie? Like when Suzie asked her to be one of the bridesmaids at her first wedding. Her wedding to Callum Converse, whom Annie had a crush on since sixth grade. Had Suzie known that Annie had dreamed about Callum? Kissed her pillow nightly while imagining that the pillow was Callum? Or had she really been ignorant about Annie's adolescent crush? Or would she have cared anyway? Suzie also asked Annie to be a bridesmaid at her second wedding to Craig Curry. And Annie was the first to know about her third wedding, a very small and quiet affair, to Lawrence Guilbert. And then, last year, Annie was the only attendant for Suzie's desperate rush to marry Roland Ruutz-Reese and the one to whom Suzie cried during the nearly instant divorce that followed. The first marriage lasted two years, with Callum leaving Suzie for another woman. Annie often wondered what might have happen had she married Callum instead of Suzie. Maybe he would have left her, too. Suzie's second liaison lasted a year and a half, and the one to Lawrence, only three months as Lawrence preferred his Oriental lawn man's charms to those of Suzie's. The debacle to Roland was three weeks of bliss and then Roland left her in the middle of the night, never to be seen again. So in some ways, Annie mused, Suzie led the pack. And in some other ways, Annie was far ahead of her cousin. It just depended on how you looked at things.

At the end of each marriage, however, Suzie reaped a huge settlement. Annie figured that Suzie earned about a half-million dollars a year while working as an unsuccessful wife. Nonetheless, despite all of Suzie's charms, Annie was glad that she was herself.

Oh, Annie wasn't quite a stranger to love. She was popular, with many friends and even a few boyfriends, stretching to a few abortive couplings...like in bed and all. *"Well,"* Annie told herself with painful honesty, *"actually two times...one, if you don't count Joey Hannigan who was dead drunk when we did it. And Craig? Well, Craig was really just a friend. We'd both been virgins and both of us wanted to not to be a virgin. And thus, a...well...friendly consummation had occurred."* Again, Annie shrugged. *"Friendly, but never thrilling. Where was all the excitement?"* Technically, she was no longer *virgo intacta*, but emotionally, she had never been penetrated. Hopefully, this trip would rectify her longings in a better way than Craig or Joey had.

Several months ago, Suzie had asked Annie if she'd like to go on a cruise. "It's really expensive, but I will pay for you. I don't want to go by myself." Annie wondered why. "The single cabins have already been booked up and there are only double cabins left. I don't want to share with a stranger." Aha. "It is supposed to be a cruise to meet your true love." Suzie showed her the advertisement. Annie saw a long, white catamaran with a huge white sail, turquoise waters, and an impossibly blue sky. "ROMANTIC HOLIDAY! SAIL *THE SOUTHERN CROSS*", the brochure clamored. "Somebody...I can't remember who...told me that lots of rich men go on these cruises, so I signed us both up. You'll love it" Suzie told Annie. "And you might even find someone for yourself." Suzie was often magnanimous, and sincerely wanted Annie to be happy, as long as Annie's happiness didn't interfere with her own desires.

"How can I say no?" Annie agreed. Maybe she would find someone. Maybe. But most likely, she'd watch Suzie walk off with the prize. Annie sighed again. Maybe Suzie might find real happiness this time. Maybe. It seemed upside down, but, in truth, Annie was sorry for her cousin. In what really mattered, Suzie was pitiful. Rich, beautiful, adored, but pitiful. She wanted every dream that came her way, and she got every dream fulfilled. But, somehow, the dreams turned to crap. Every time.

CHAPTER FOUR

"And they sailed away, for a year and a day..."
Edward Lear, Nonsense Songs

The plane took them briefly to San Juan, Puerto Rico. "I wonder if any of our fellow passengers are on this plane?" Annie scanned the faces of the other travelers as they debarked into the falsely chilled air of the airport. She was excited to be in Puerto Rico, marveling at the unusual fauna and flora, the heat that shimmered outside the building and the chattering of the gaily-dressed locals. Suzie urged her to try to be more soigné, not gawk like a first-time tourist.

"But, I *am* a first-time tourist!" Annie pointed out. Embarrassed by Annie's exuberance, Suzie merely stalked ahead to the gate where they were to get on the small plane that would take them the ninety or so miles to Beef Island, Tortola, British Virgin Islands. Annie followed, carrying the soft-sided duffle bag stuffed with three new bathing suits (two of them bikinis), a pair of cheap reef shoes, and a collection of easily folded sports clothing. As Captain Scambaugh had suggested, Annie had left lots of room and planned to buy herself an outfit or two in the islands.

A woman stood at the head of the line. She was older...maybe in her fifties, with a coil of thick, coppery hair skewered to her head with a comb, dressed in obviously expensive beige linen shorts and a white gauzy long-sleeved top. Suzie glanced at the woman's shoes and mentally calculated their cost. Large money. The woman turned to them, "Excuse me for asking, but are you going to Tortola?" She was attractive, Annie noted, thin, almost too thin, with a tanned face, greenish-brown eyes, and a pair of round, gold, eyeglasses. There were lines of tension on her face and her hands gripped a small leather bag too tightly.

"Oh, yes," Annie gushed, always ready to talk to strangers. "And you?"

"I'm going on a catamaran cruise...on *The Southern Cross*...with Captain Jack."

Annie squealed, "Oh, we are too! How nice to meet you! I'm Annie Sabatino and this is my cousin, Suzie Ruutz-Reese. We're from Connecticut." Annie's eager and friendly grin lit up her face. The woman's eyes widened at the mention of Connecticut. Annie wondered why.

"I'm Paula Haskins. From New York City." Paula didn't mention Connecticut, but extended her well-manicured hand. Suzie shook it, approving of Paula's obvious breeding and fashion sense. Annie waved, a small cheerful wave and moved closer, wanting to talk to their first co-passenger.

A loudspeaker interrupted, in Spanish and then English, announcing the imminent departure of Flight Six-Four, San Juan to Beef Island, Tortola. "This is us!" Annie danced with excitement and even Suzie found herself grinning. "Let's go!"

"Tortola, dead ahead," the captain's voice crackled over the speaker. Everyone in the plane, even the sophisticated Suzie, leaned to peer out of a window. "We land in five minutes." The water, so far below, was an incredible shade of blue and those passengers on the right side could glimpse a necklace of green islands, humping out of the ocean, like a giant handful of emeralds that some huge, mythical creature might have scattered.

The plane banked suddenly and passengers heard the pilot's voice: "We are now flying over Tortola, the largest of the British Virgin Islands." Annie's mouth dropped at the spectacular topography; sparkling beaches, and breathtaking rock formations lining the shores. The interior of the island was undulating green, with peaks and valleys and incredible rock formations. Tiny colorful houses – pink and yellow and pale green – dotted the thread-like roads that meandered up and down the mountains. The plane leveled out and then banked again sharply heading for what looked like a tiny strip of runway cutting through a jungle. As the plane zoomed down, small buildings came into view, then more roads, and then cars and people. Annie gripped Suzie's hand and let out a yell of pleasure. The plane slowed and bumped – hard - onto the asphalt, brakes screeched and Annie saw three goats running across the runway, racing the slowing plane.

The plane rolled to a stop. The goats slowed their gallop, pleased at themselves for beating the plane to the end of the landing strip. Several chickens, prudently hiding while the plane came down, bravely stepped out onto the runway, pecking at some bugs that crawled in the cracked asphalt. "Look at the chickens! Just like being at JFK!" Annie marveled, shouting over the noise of the propeller. Their fellow passenger, Paula, smiled, thinking that Annie would be a good companion for the rest of the trip.

The pilot shut off the engines. The air conditioning hissed and ceased. A soft, moist, quiet descended on the passengers and immediately, Annie could sense the heat curling up. They gathered their belongings as a rickety metal staircase was pushed to the door of the plane. The stewardess…Annie wondered if they were still called stewardesses…opened the cockpit door and with the hiss of air, the heat punched into the cabin. The passengers gingerly climbed down the creaking steps, holding fast to the handrail. The air was gaspingly hot, humid and almost liquid. A hot, stinging breeze accentuated the humidity and all of the passengers were dripping with sweat as they walked to the Quonset-hut building that served as Beef Island's airport. Suzie's march was slowed slightly by a goat that was attracted her to scarf. The goat bit at the end of the scarf and Suzie let out a desperate scream.

Just before the passengers reached the doors, another plane swooped in from the sky, roaring its engines and sending dust and sand into everyone's ears and eyes and crevices. "De plane from England," Annie overheard a fat black man call out. The goat turned, tired of Suzie's scarf, and began another race with the next new toy on the runway.

If possible, the temperature in the corrugated shack they called the Beef Island airport was even hotter than the air outside. Clothes stuck to bodies, sweat dripped and body crevices began to send out tendrils of strange odors. The passengers passed from the corridor and through two heavy swinging doors into the Customs Area. Ahhh! Air conditioning! Blessed, blessed Twentieth Century comfort! Annie stopped for a moment and dropped her bag, lifted her arms out and let the chilled air surround her. She felt a bit self-conscious…perhaps travelers didn't wave their armpits about. She turned, slightly abashed, only to realize that *everyone*, even Suzie the pseudo- sophisticate, was doing the same thing.

The procedure through Customs was quick and efficient, but even so, Annie was sweating as she was spewed out of Customs and into a large hall. Suzie grunted and groaned behind her, cursing in a loud voice about the heat.Their progress into the hall was halted by a large, fat lady, carrying a tray of plastic glasses filled with some highly- colored pink liquid. "You!" She called out with a jovial smile. "Have youselfs some island punch! Free island punch!" Everyone grabbed a glass, drained the sweet, cold drink, then, grabbed another glass and drank it off. Ahhh! "You like?" the lady asked. "Dere's more when you get inside" She waddled off to greet the next plane filled with visitors and the passengers walked, slightly refreshed, into the main lobby. Perhaps Beef Island didn't have all of the amenities of JFK, Suzie thought, but no one had ever offered her free drinks in New York.

Another coffee-colored woman pointed them to a circular area in the middle of the lobby. "Your baggage will be there in a moment. When you find it all, there are cabs at the front of the building." Annie, Suzie and their new friend, Paula, stood, uncertain of what to do. They were surrounded by a teeming mass of humanity. A jolly, laughing, friendly mixed bag of people...all races, colors, sizes and shapes, some, like the three of them, dressed almost too well in creased traveling clothing, others, probably locals, comfortable in bright cotton clothing, some with straw hats perched on their heads, and all sporting cheerful smiles. Annie poked Suzie, motioning as a fork lift truck deposited a mound of luggage onto the floor.

"There's our stuff." At the same time, Paula saw a tall, thin man holding a cardboard sign that read "***Southern Cross*** **– Captain Jack Scambaugh**". Annie grabbed her soft sided duffle and dragged it over to the man.

"You fo' *The Southern Cross*?" the man asked. He was older than he had looked at first glance, nearly bald, lanky with a small, wispy moustache, tanned, with a lopsided, creased smile. Annie nodded. He stuck out his horny hand. "Ah'm Cammie. Ah'm yo' driver." Annie shook hands and fanned her face. Cammie laughed and motioned to another woman standing along the side of the crowd, holding yet another tray of pink-filled glasses. She shuffled over and Cammie handed Annie more punch. "It's good an' cold. Make you feel happy."

"*Dang*," Annie told herself. "*That's why I'm here, isn't it? To feel happy*." She tossed off the glass and the woman laughed again and offered her another. A pleasant glow started to unwind from the vicinity of Annie's stomach.

"You the only one?" Cammie asked, his eyes scanning the crowd. "I t'ink there supposed to be eight of you on dis trip...t'ree from the United States and five from England."

As if in answer to his question, Paula and Suzie dropped their luggage at Cammie's feet. He introduced himself, and the woman brought more drinks, kissing Cammie soundly on his cheek. "Hey, Branda!" He squeezed the woman around her ample waist. Paula and Suzie each grabbed a glass, but Annie, feeling a little woozy, waved off a fourth...or was it fifth? Cammie's eyes, like those of most men's eyes, settled on Suzie and he whistled "Yellow Bird" softly. "Welcome to de islands." Annie, Paula and Suzie introduced themselves and he checked off their names on a sheet that he carried. "The odders, dey be here in a jiffy." He made a motion and a porter, pushing a large carrier, came to our side. "Hey, Heff, put dis stuff in da jitney," Cammie told him, or at least that what was it sounded like to Annie. Branda, the woman with the drinks and Cammie talked in some fast-paced, incomprehensible language. Annie reached into her fanny pack and held out a dollar tip for the drink lady. Branda laughed again and waved the money away, telling Annie to save it, that she was gonna need it down here.

Cammie held his sign aloft and in a few moments, four more people joined his group. Each gave his name to Cammie: a spare tallish woman, dressed in severely tailored slacks and a suit jacket announced herself as Sarah Lemonowski; an even taller, somewhat bulky mature man with a tanned, humorous face introduced himself as Duncan MacKinnon; Lannie Olmstead was pudgy, with soft, hot hands; and last, an overly-made-up woman, calling herself Corliss Curtis was outfitted in colorful stretch Capri pants and a wildly printed top. Her hair was frizzy and red and her manner breezy and loud. Annie watched Suzie's reaction to them all. She could see Suzie's mind dismiss the Lemonowski and Curtis women as lost causes and the effeminate Lannie as no one she would bother to cultivate. Suzie approved of Paula Haskins and her distinguished, obviously wealthy ways, and she was dismayed that her cherished, imaginary vision of the Scottish Lord was not quite what she had thought he might be...Suzie's blue eyes narrowed a bit and her face almost shouted her disappointment... Duncan MacKinnon was much older than she had anticipated. Handsome, though. Tall, with piercing blue eyes and bushy white eyebrows. Cammie introduced the four newcomers to Annie, Suzie and Paula, never making a mistake on anyone's name or where they had come from. Annie was impressed.

Branda passed around more of the pink creations and Heff lifted away the rest of the baggage. "Only one more to come," Cammie assured us, "and den, we' be on our way." His eyes scanned the crowd. "A Mister Michael Beck, we be waitin' fo'. From Ireland, I t'ink."

Branda said something to him, which none of them could understand, and the two islanders began to laugh.

"Is it a special language that you speak?" The woman who had given her name as Sarah asked. "Is it an island language?" Cammie and Branda laughed even harder.

"It's really English," Cammie explained. "Only we talk it so fast dat no one else kin unnerstand it." He smiled kindly. "We call it *patois* or *Papiamento* and I guess it mixes de English wid a liddle bit of African, some Spanish, a bit of French and…well, whatevah!" He ducked his head. "A'h'll try to slow de speech down so you kin hear me plain." And with that, he waved at a man of medium height, slightly balding, but with a pleasant, open face, dressed well, perhaps, for a rainy day on the cold moors of Ireland, but amazingly overdressed for the tropics. "You for *De Southern Cross*? You Mr. Beck?"

The jitney left the airport, scattering chickens and one small donkey and turned onto the road that rimmed the coast. Annie sat in the back seat, squished by the luggage and the over-warm thigh of Michael Beck. She hung her head out of the side, trying to catch as much of the breeze as possible. Cammie called out, "Everybody know each udder? Good. We'll get to be good frens in a jiffy." He downshifted and the jitney began to climb a hill that wound through a sparsely settled cluster of houses. "Dis side of de island is de hot side," he explained. "We be goin' t'roo Roadtown, dat's de big town here, and den, we'll be on de bettah side, de West End. De wind blows bettah on de West End. You'll see."

"I certainly hope it will be cooler," the woman known as Sarah huffed, pulling ineffectually at the neck of her blouse. Cammie nodded at her.

"So, let me tell you 'bout where we is and were we be goin'," He tooted his horn at a group of children playing in the surf. The children turned and waved, giggling. Several of them were black, some several shades of tan, and a few were blonde and obviously Caucasian. "Now, as I tol' you, my name is Cammie Fernald. I'm a Belonger here." He grinned at the questioning looks. "A Belonger," he explained, "is a person who is born in de British Virgin Islands. If you're not born here, you can nevah be a Belonger. It's not just some nickname, it is a legal term and has many privileges dat go along wid it." He looked at the group with a prideful face. "Up until a few years ago, only Belongers could own land here. Dey… dat is, da Legislature, changed da law a liddle, but, unless you are a Belonger, it still is very difficult, and you gotta be a rich person, to own land on de islands. A stranger, after obtaining a permit, has to live in de islands and make money...maybe have a business or work...for t'ree years before dey can begin to try to buy land or a house. Den dey be called a sort-of-Belonger. Not really one, but sort of. And de business, it gotta be profitable. Make money for de government. Gotta make...I t'ink, about a quarter of a million dollahs. Dat way, de government gets mo' money from dem, but it isn't easy to be livin' here and owning land. You gotta give to de government a lot."

"In Scotland, we certainly are all familiar with giving the government a lot," Duncan MacKinnon commented with dry humor. Annie tried to see around his bulk. He was handsome...well...maybe distinguished would be a better word. Too old, though. *I like the way his voice sounds*, she thought. *Kind of burr-y.*

"De gov'ment, dey take it all!" Cammie agreed with fervor.

"Do you own land here, Cammie?" MacKinnon asked in his clipped Scottish accent. Cammie nodded, pleased with the question.

"Yass. I own many acres here and on Jost Van Dyke. My family is a very old one. We wuz slaves 'way back when de copper mines were runnin'. Den, after de uprising, we got land." Again, he tooted his horn at a passing driver and the jitney crested the top of the hill. The passengers gasped aloud at the view. The jitney slowed for a moment, so that everyone could see the vista below. The road was perhaps a mile up the side of a mountain, a ribbon on the edge of a sheer cliff that fell to the rocks and the sea below. Huge turquoise waves crested and broke with silvery blue spume on the jagged rocks at the bottom. The passengers could see conical lumps of green that jutted out of the ocean, small islands, larger islands, some just piles of rocks, others with tiny houses and roads criss-crossing, visible even from many miles away.

"Are...are we going down this road?" Paula asked in a timorous voice, her eyes wide and apprehensive behind her sunglasses. She held on to the side of the jitney and the knuckles of her hands were white.

Cammie smiled with kind patience. "Doan you worry none, Mizz Paula. I drive dis road six times a day. I neffer have any trouble. You jess relax and I'll tell you more about de islands." Paula's hand relaxed slightly, but her eyes remained wide and fearful. The jitney started its journey down the corkscrew road. "See dat cluster of buildings down dere?" Cammie pointed. "Road Town, our capital and largest city in de

BVI. Lots of interestin' shops, lots of good food. Captain Jack and *De Sothern Cross* will be moored here for a few days so dat you can shop and explore and eat de best barbecued ribs on de planet. Yessum. And I'll be drivin' you." He nodded. "I been working for Captain Jack now for, oh, more dan fifteen years. Never lost anybody yet, and..." He turned around in his seat, making Paula grab once again at the side of the jitney..."We had a lotta romances happen on dese trips ovah da years, too."

Annie looked at her fellow passengers, wondering who might be her Lochinvar. Lannie Olmstead looked a little too effeminate; Duncan MacKinnon, certainly Lochinvar-like, but an older Lochinvar...handsome and distinguished, but – alas - too old; and her seatmate, Michael Beck, although passable and about the right age - too sweaty. "*Ah, well*", she thought, "*perhaps the next batch will be a bit more to my liking.*"

Paula forced herself to relax. Cammie, for all of his casual ways, seemed to know the roads and perhaps, with Cammie's driving skills and God's grace, the jitney would stay on the road and not plunge them five hundred feet down into the sea and the rocks below. She made herself look away from the cliff's edge and look at the trees and colorful bushes. "Those flowers are incredible," she called out as they passed a large tree covered with thousands of bright orange colored blossoms. "What are they called?"

"They be flamboyants," Cammie informed her. "They be everywhere." He pointed to a pink hedge that covered a gate. "That be bougainvilla." Paula nodded, relaxing a little more. Cammie was an interesting guide. A man who obviously knew his islands, garrulous, clever, and...as Cammie again blew the horn and waved to a man walking along the road...knew everyone.

Cammie continued his tour. "Only Belongers can fish and get shellfish. If you want to fish and you're not a Belonger, you gotta get a permit and go wid a Belonger."

"Can we fish on *The Southern Cross*?" Again, the man from Scotland asked a question.

"You a fisherman, Mister Duncan?"

"Aye. I do a fair bit of fishing. Fly fishing. Usually salmon. You must have permission from the owner of the stream and a fishing license back in Scotland."

"Mmmmm, hmmm. A bit different here." Cammie nodded with vigor. "Ducky B, de first mate, he be a Belonger, even though Captain

Scumb…I mean, Captain Jack isn't. Dat way, all de passengers can fish." He thought for a moment. "I t'ink, though, dat if your group wantsta do sport fishin'…you know, barracuda, bonita, wahoo, tarpon, swordfish…dem kina fish…den Captain Jack will set up a special trip for you to go 'way offshore wid Captain Dave and his All-Girl Crew for a day of big fishin'…"

"All girl crew? What in Hades is an all-girl crew?"

Cammie laughed, a booming sound. "Effrybody asks dat! Yup, Captain Dave, he got only ladies who work his fishin' boat. And dey good fisherladies, mark my word! He got Susan an' Lenny an' Tracey and dat new one…Miss Lynn. Da best!"

The traffic had increased as they came to the bottom of the mountain. The jitney wound its way through ever more crowded neighborhoods and entered into the outskirts of Road Town. The passengers oooh'd and aaah'd as they spotted stores, and a tented bazaar area. "You'll all be spendin' a few days here. Lots of bargains, lots of nice things to bring home," Cammie assured them. "You all are nevah gonna be bored here."

CHAPTER FIVE

"I met murder on the way...he had a mask..."
from The Mask of Anarchy, by Percy Bysshe Shelley

"Carlton?...Fullbright here. I'm at the bungalow of Antony and Ellen Marsden, Fifty One Overlook Drive...up off the turnoff of the Coppermine Road. Yeah.....Well, Mr. Marsden has just, um, expired..."

"And you want me? What's up?"

"I think you should amble up here. Rather interesting, I think."

"I'll be there in fifteen minutes. Do you want Effalyn and the crime scene kit?"

"A wise man would bring it all along. And ask that the boys come around here with an ambulance or a hearse about a half-hour after you get here so that they can take the body back to the morgue."

Sampson Fullbright hung up the telephone. He harrumphed and went back into the bedroom where the body of Antony Marsden lay. Death had not been kind to Mr. Marsden, the doctor mused, viewing the dull gray-blue skin, the contorted limbs and the claw-like hands that clutched the still-damp and sweaty sheets. Mrs. Marsden sat in a chair, clasping a handkerchief and dabbing at her eyes. He wasn't positive that she was actually crying, though. "Now, Mrs. Marsden, why don't you wait in the kitchen? Matter of fact, I'd appreciate it if you'd make me a cup of coffee. And it wouldn't hurt for you to drink one too. I'm going to do a few, uh, things here and then I'll join you."

Ellen Marsden, a small woman in her early sixties, gave a sniff. "What are you going to do?"

"Oh, some medical tests," the doctor answered blandly. "It will only take a moment."

"And then can I call the funeral director? The heat...I mean...I think..."

"Well," the doctor spread his hands out, "The police will be here in a few moments to do their report. We have to wait..."

"The *police*? Why the police? You can see what happened!" Mrs Marsden gasped. "Antony...oh, Antony..." She reached toward her husband's remains. The doctor gently took her hands and turned her toward the door.

"You go into the kitchen, Mrs. Marsden. I'll be right with you."

The doctor closed the bedroom door and turned back to Antony Marsden's body. He touched it and moved a limb or two, then shrugged and joined Mrs. Marsden in the kitchen to have a cup of coffee and talk about anything – anything at all but the body in the bedroom.

***

Cammie sounded three long blasts on the horn of the jitney as it turned into a large gateway that proclaimed itself to be Soper's Hole. The road wound around pink, pale blue and salmon-colored buildings, drenched with bright flowers. On the opposite side of the buildings, the passengers glimpsed tall sailboat masts, and the waters of a large harbor. "Dis be Soper's Hole," Cammie told them. "Dis be where de Seven Seas Yachts are and where Captain Jack keeps his boat when its not cruisin'." He turned his lean body, rested his elbow over the seat back and continued in his sociable manner, "Nice people own de marina here. Roland and Judy. Young couple from South Africa. Dey bought da marina mebbe five years ago, just when da sailing bug bit everyboddy and everyboddy wanted to come sailing here. Smart people, Roland and Judy." He turned back to the wheel twisting it just before the jitney hit a large bush. Annie was proud that she hadn't screamed in panic.

The jitney rolled to a stop. Paula Haskins, following Annie's thoughts, thanked whatever Heavenly Power that had kept them from crashing into the ocean or running into a boulder. With a stifled groan, she eased herself down onto the path by the side of the roadway. In front of the jitney was a large arched gate with a sign that said "Seven Seas Yachts."

"Yo! Cammie!" A tall deeply-mahogany-colored young man, his head crowned with tumbled black curls, pulling a large blue cart, greeted them. "Welcome to the Virgin Islands!"

"Hey, Mr. Duck. Here is yo' group!" Cammie's long legs climbed down. He turned to the passengers. "This be Ducky B. He's yo' first mate. No," he instructed Duncan MacKinnon, who had picked up his duffle bag. "Ducky will get the luggage. All you need to do is follow me and we'll get this trip started. You all be our *guests*, heah!"

Annie watched Suzie watch Ducky B. The young man was gorgeously muscular and handsome, and gave them a dazzling white grin. He wore a pair of disreputable white shorts low on his hips, no shirt and his feet were shod in flip-flops. Annie could hear Suzie's chops lick.

The vision grinned and lifted the luggage, as if it were filled with air, into his blue cart. "Come on, all of you. Let's get ourselves into vacation mode!" His accent was upper-class British – the kind you'd hear on television – his dark eyes danced and Suzie bit her lip, her big blue eyes rolling in appreciation.

Ducky led them around the building and onto a wharf-side dock area. The passengers stopped to gasp. There, in various slips, were at least two hundred sailboats, monohulls, catamarans, and a few trimarans, all riding majestically in their slips. The air was cooled by a soft breeze, the scent of flowers filled the air. The passengers each gave a sigh of pleasure. At last, their vacation had properly begun. Ducky led the little parade down past several stores, an office with a sign that announced "Seven Seas Yachts", a public toilet and shower building, several more stores and a restaurant to a huge boat that was tied to the dock, all by itself in splendor. Ducky stopped, turned and announced, "This will be your home for the next few weeks. Ladies and gentlemen, behold *The Southern Cross*!"

As the passengers gaped in awe, a heavy-set man with a luxuriant head of white hair, a luxuriant moustache and an even more luxuriant beard leaped gracefully over the rail of *The Southern Cross*. 'Welcome!" he cried in a deep voice. "Welcome to *The Southern Cross*! I'm your captain, Captain Jack Scambaugh. And you all, for the duration of this voyage, are my scurvy crew!"

As if on cue, Ducky began to laugh. "And he's often called, both in front of and behind his large back, Captain Scumbag!"

Captain Jack laughed too, a rollicking sound, and each of the passengers had nearly the same vision of Captain Jack at the helm of a boat, facing into the wind, sailing into blue waters. He was the perfect caricature of a sailor man, with a movie-star version of wavy white hair and a full white beard. His hazel eyes were outlined with sun-kissed wrinkles etched from a lifetime of watching the sea and the sky.. His shoulders spoke of strength, and his well-balanced body tapered into surprisingly slender, shapely legs for such a big man. His grin was eager and real and he came toward them with a rolling gait. Each passenger immediately felt as if they could rely, hug or cry on those massive shoulders. Each of them, in that instant, trusted Captain Jack implicitly. Each of them sighed happily, knowing that this was going to be a memorable vacation. And how right each of them was.

"Welcome to a couple of weeks of sailing, swimming, snorkeling, lazing around, limbo dancing, great food and drink, remarkable rum, fun and a bit of romance." He turned to Ducky. "Did I miss anything?"

Ducky kicked off his flip-flops and planted one huge foot on the rail of the boat. "Oh, there'll be a few surprises." He tossed the luggage onto the cockpit. Bare-chested, Ducky's physique and his laughing, gleaming eyes promised something special. He turned, gave his hand to Suzie, and pulled her onto the boat. Suzie, seemingly stunned, turned to Annie and grinned.

"Oh, I'm gonna like this trip!" Her exuberance was interrupted by a young girl who came out of the closed cabin and stood next to Suzie on the deck. She was tiny, curved, with long, streaming dark hair and brilliant blue eyes and wore the smallest white bikini that Annie had ever seen. The attention that Suzie was used to getting was immediately transferred away from her and to the young girl. Suzie's eyes bulged. And then narrowed. The eyes of every male passenger also bulged. Even Annie's eyes bulged.

Ducky laughed again, sensing Suzie's discomfort. "And this, my fellow crew, is your cook for the journey." He waved at the group standing on the dock. "Group, this is Kat. Kat, this is the group...or a bit of the group. The rest are coming with Cammie's next delivery and they should be here in about twenty minutes."

Kat, with a lithe movement, jumped from the boat onto the dock and began to introduce herself to each of the passengers. "Hi, I'm Kat and I will cook for you." She had a charming, unusual accent and seemed familiar with each of their names and where they were from. "Michael...from Ireland? Pleased to meet you...Lannie? Ah, yes. You live in London. One of my favorite places on earth...Paula. How cool and elegant you look. And yes, you are from New York City? Also a wonderful place...Annie? How nice to meet you...and Suzie...you two are cousins, no? And you will have to tell me where Conn-ect-i-cut is...that, I do not really know...And Sarah...from England. Canterbury and Kent is wonderful. I was visiting friends there two months ago...and last, but not the least, Duncan...and from Scotland! So easy to remember that! Such a...Scottish name!" She giggled, a silvery sound, and Annie watched Suzie's face scowl. Kat stepped back and smiled. "You must be sure to tell me what you really like or what you dislike to eat and drink. I will do everything in my power to please each of you...gastronomically, that is!" The group laughed, at once charmed by her. Even Suzie smiled, despite herself. "We will come on board now and while we wait for the others, perhaps you would like some light refreshments and Captain Jack," she giggled, "whom I *never* call Captain Scumbag...I call him Captain Sweetie...will talk to you all."

The passengers stepped onto the huge and impressive catamaran's shiny teak decks. Fascinated by the place that they would call home for more than two weeks, one by one, they began to prowl its gleaming decks and interior. Annie was the last to get on, helped by Ducky's strong and willing hand. "I'm looking forward to the trip," he said with pleasure, giving her hand a squeeze. "We'll have a great time."

Annie watched Kat's white clad bottom disappear into the cabin. "She's just beautiful," Annie exclaimed with evident sincerity. "My goodness, all the men will be falling at her feet."

Ducky laughed again, softly this time. "Then, I will tell you a secret that is really not a secret." He leaned closer to Annie. "These men, they will be very disappointed." Annie's eyes flew to his face.

"Huh?"

He winked. "You will be the first to notice." His eye brows wiggled up and down. "Watch and see." And with that, he hefted three of the heaviest duffle bags and disappeared into the interior of the boat.

***

Carlton and Effalyn knocked at the door of the bungalow. Dr. Fullbright answered the door and motioned them inside. His bushy eyebrows signaled to them to be vigilant. Carlton's own eyebrows signaled back that, naturally, they would be.

Mrs. Marsden appeared from the kitchen, clutching a tea towel. "I still don't understand why the police are here."

"Mrs. Marsden? I'm Detective Inspector Reese." He smiled reassuringly at her and flipped his identity card out. She glanced at it nervously. "This is Detective Penn." Effalyn also showed her identification, but Mrs. Marsden ignored it. In Carlton's experience, everyone got nervous when visited by the police. And Mrs. Marsden had more than enough reason to be nervous. After all, her husband had just died under peculiar circumstances, to say the least..

"We are very sorry for your trouble, Mrs. Marsden," Effalyn said in her quiet voice. "Can I be of any assistance to you?"

"No. No. I don't want...I just don't understand...why...the police...he just..." The tea towel dropped out of her nerveless hands and onto the floor. Effalyn stooped and picked it up, folded it neatly and handed it back to Mrs. Marsden.

The doctor patted her on her shoulder. "Is there a neighbor...a friend, perhaps, who might come and keep you company for a while?" Mrs Marsden looked frightened and then nodded her head.

"I can call Neil and Damson...they live nearby...."

"Good. Please call them and see if they can help."

"All right..." Mrs. Marsden went to the telephone. Doctor Fullbright motioned with his head and Carlton and Effalyn followed him into the bedroom.

"She OK?" Carlton jerked his head backwards.

"Mmmm...who knows? She seems upset, naturally," the doctor made a face. "But, I think we may have a little situation here..." He pointed to the body on the bed. "Take a look at the poor sonofabitch."

"Goodness!" Effalyn gasped. "The pittiful man!"

Carton whistled softly. "Son of a bitch died in agony, I should think." Effalyn squared her shoulders, took a deep breath and regained her usual composure. She handed Carlton a pair of gloves and put a pair on her own hands. They stood for a moment, looking at the corpse, each of them thinking about how wonderful life was. Carlton suffered his usual reaction to a dead body; a deep and sincere gladness that death had passed him by yet once again. He coughed to cover the embarrassing grin that rippled swiftly across his own face. He couldn't help it. He was alive and Mr. Marsden wasn't. Unaware of her superior's brief spate of non-professional glee, Effalyn reached into her bag and took out a tape recorder. She looked at Carlton and he nodded, solemn again. She began to speak into the recorder.

"We have here a Mister ...?"

"Antony Marsden. A-N-T-O-N-Y...M-A-R-S-D-E-N...age, perhaps late sixties to early seventies. White. Scrawny. Malnourished. Looks as if he'd been ill...maybe as if he had eating problems." She held the microphone up towards Dr. Fullbright. He motioned her to keep talking while he took another slow and careful look at the corpse.

"Found at about eight o'clock on the morning by his wife...?" Again, she looked at Doctor Fullbright for further information.

"Ellen Marsden...white. Age, maybe sixty."

"Mister Marsden appears to have suffered a distressed death. His body is contorted, with limbs in unnatural positions, as if, perhaps, poisoned." She leaned over, very close to Mr. Marsden's mouth and sniffed. She nodded. "Smell of cyanide or something similar. Maybe a plant alkaline? *Ricin*?" Her eyes questioned Doctor Fullbright and he nodded, shrugged and then leaned over and spoke into the microphone.

"Body is blue-gray...slated... with dull skin. Little elasticity. Lips are bluish and mouth in a rictus. Hands in a clawlike position, clutching at his chest as if trying to get air. Sheets are stained."

Effalyn asked, "Did he vomit?"

"Quite a bit." Doctor Fullbright pointed to a number of small yellowish stains spattered on the sheet near the head of the victim.

"Suspicious." Effalyn said with a firm nod.

"Definitely...but there may be some mitigating history here."

"Oh?" Carlton spoke, finally getting his inappropriate smile under control.

"The Marsdens have been my patients for...oh, maybe six years. They moved here from Australia, I think...or maybe New Zealand. Quiet, respectable people. He was a wealthy businessman...I think paper products or some boring, but necessary thing. She married him just before they moved here and after he retired. I think both of them were married before and are both widows." He harrumphed. "I mean she was a widow and he was a widower." The doctor glared at Carlton, daring him to make a sarcastic remark. Carlton, looking like a dark cherub, forced himself to gaze up at the ceiling. The doctor continued, "Nothing remarkable about either of them until..." He looked up at the ceiling too, seeking inspiration. "Mebbe two-three years ago."

"And?"

"Marsden started down the path to senile dementia. Maybe Alzheimer's. He began to forget things. Started to roam. Classic symptoms. Mrs. Marsden came in a lot to talk to me about it. She told me that he often went for a walk and then she'd go looking for him and he usually went down toward the beach." He gently opened one of Marsden's eyelids and peered at the bluish-white eye. "Hmm," he spoke into Effalyn's machine, "Eyeball really sunken in." He rubbed his gloved hands together. "This will be a very interesting autopsy." His voice was gleeful. "Can't *wait!*"

Effalyn's mouth pursed and she rolled her eyes. "Just like one a' them body snatchers, you are." She sniffed. "Can't wait to get to the juicy parts!"

Carlton snorted down a chuckle. "So?"

"So, when I finally got her to bring in her husband, he was covered with welts and skin burns." Carlton and Effalyn stopped and straightened up, watching the doctor closely. "She told me that he went and sat under a manchioneel tree. She said that was where she'd found him. It had been raining that afternoon and the manchioneel oils had dripped off the trees onto him. I had no reason to doubt her. The man was dazed and confused. She told me that was the way he had been in the past months. I never did see him before that when he was supposedly in dementia. Only what she told me. I'll have to check my records, but I don't think he ever came in except that one time with those welts and manchioneel oil poisoning. Only her to tell me about him. Seems that I suggested that he come in, but I don't think he did. She said he was really losing his ability to think and remember. She said he was getting worse and worse. I gave her some Benadryl for the skin reaction and also gave her a tube of soothing cream to make him comfortable."

"Mmmm?"

"I told her to bring him in and we'd do some testing to see what could be done to alleviate the dementia." He shook his head, looking like an old water buffalo. "Not much we can do for dementia, but there are a few new experimental drugs that seem to slow the symptoms down...but she never brought him in."

"Hmmm."

"This happened two or three more times in the past year or so. She said that he'd take off and go under the trees and then she'd bring him home with manchioneel skin poisoning."

"Manchioneel poisoning?" Carlton rubbed his chin. "Could be fatal...rare that it kills anyone...could have contributed to his delusions and mental state. Jeez, we don't see much of this anymore. Most people here know to stay away from the manchioneel trees. Hmpf ...but there's no welts or burns on him now." He twitched the sheet aside and examined the twisted limbs. "And what's with the contortions?"

"She told me that he got away again and she found him in the garden, eating plants."

"Plants?"

"Mmmmm. She said that there was datura there. You know, angel trumpets, or whatever you call them. And oleander bushes. She thought he might have eaten poison."

"By mistake, you think?"

"Mebbe. Or mebbe she helped him and chose a few delicacies for him to nibble on. He was pretty far gone. He'd probably have done whatever she suggested."

Effalyn, her mind sharp and suspicious, asked, "Do you think she might have wanted to get rid of him? The Alzheimer's...he might have lasted for years with it and maybe she didn't want to have his life drag on."

"Donno." Doctor Fullbright's heavy shoulders shrugged. "That's why I called you. I don't really know that he has...ahem...had Alzheimer's at all. Only way to tell is with an autopsy and doing some further tests on his brain, and even then...sometimes you can't really tell."

Carlton groaned. "This is gonna be a screwy one. I can tell by the ache in my big toe." He shook his foot in the air. "And maybe he didn't walk under the manchioneel trees...she might have led him there and told him to lie down and take a nap."

Effalyn asked, "*Cui bono*? Is there money? Does she have a boyfriend? Or was she tired of taking care of him?"

"Oh, you suspicious woman, you. Maybe she's telling the truth." Carlton thought for a moment. "Maybe it was just as she told you."

"Mebbe." Doctor Fullbright pulled the sheet up to Antony Marsden's neck. He snapped off his gloves. "Hot diggity. Let's cut him up!"

Effalyn touched the cheek of the corpse that had once been a viral man. She peered closely into his one open eye. "Antony? Where are you now? What can you tell us, Antony?"

"He's somewhere beyond our knowledge" Doctor Fullbright addressed Mr. Marsden's body. "What's it like there, Antony?"

They waited for a moment, but Mr. Marsden, wherever his soul might have been, wasn't giving away any secrets. Effalyn gently closed his one open eye.

CHAPTER SIX

*...A harbor, even if it is a little harbor, is a good thing,
since adventures come into it as well as go out*
***Country Byways* by Sarah Orne Jewett**

"Mikayla!" Her mother called. "Madeline is here!" Mikayla, a bright and precocious child, even though she was only two-and-a-bit-more, knew that anything to do with her baby-sitter, Madeline, meant fun and pleasure. She toddled into the kitchen and grabbed her mother's knees.

"Maddie. Where Maddie?"

"Boo!" Madeline jumped out from behind a chair, scaring Mikayla in a most delicious manner. "Here I am." Mikayla left the shelter of her mother's knees and leaped into Madeline's arms. "Wanna go to the beach?" Mikayla's blue eyes, slanted slightly, opened wide and she nodded, eager.

"Beach!" she yelled, cementing her approval. "*Beach!*" The telephone rang.

Like one of those transformer toys that switch from one thing to another, Mikayla's mother switched from being a doting parent to being Lara Vitiello, artist and owner of the newly opened Big Fish Cay Art Studio. "Big Fish Cay Art Studio. Lara speaking. How may I help you?"

"Lara? This is Joyce O'Sullivan...Hi. I'm bringing in two of my paintings this morning. Is ten o'clock good for you?...Great. Oh, and Lara, I have two new people who want to join the school. Yes! I met them at the Library. Two men who just relocated down here from California...yes, they are....I'll have them stop in to see you this afternoon. Who? Oh, yes, Howard and Bo. Yes, Bo. OK, see you at ten, Lara. Byee."

In her transformer mode, switching yet again, Lara now dropped all pretense of being a dignified business professional, and transformed herself back into a mom. She grabbed her daughter by both hands. "Hooray! Mikayla's going to the beach!" She swung Mikayla's sturdy little body in a circle and then pressed a huge kiss on her daughter's forehead. "Let's get you into a bathing suit and you can go."

"With moom!" Mikayla said firmly.

"OK, punkin'." Lara understood her daughter's prattle. "With moom." Lara plucked a pink scrap of nylon off the counter, stripped off Mikayla's overalls, and dressed her in a ruffled bathing suit with a crescent moon on the front of it. Sitting in the crescent moon was a caricature of a cow.

"Cow and moom", Mikayla grinned.

Mikayla, strapped into her big-wheeled push chair, babbled cheerfully as Madeline pushed her along the path that went from the Vitiello's house to the section of beach that was fenced in especially for children. They passed Neel's Five and Dime Variety Store, the hairdresser's shop and the spice store, crossed the narrow street and turned at The Alice W. Rabbit's Hemp Emporium. The street widened into a paved path that led along the harbor. Madeline waved at her neighbor, Trisha Flynn, as Trisha, the owner of Flynn's Fashions, and mother of four young girls who were all best friends with Madeline, trundled out two trendily dressed manikins and arranged them at either side of her shop door. "Hey, guys," Trisha stooped to tousle Mikayla's dark curls, "Whassup?"

"Beeeeach!" Mikayla crowed. Trisha nodded, wishing she could leave the shop for an hour and sink herself into the water. Ah, it just wasn't to be. Trisha sighed and turned to go back into her shop. "Oh!" She stopped, as she remembered, "Maddie, tell your mom that I have that scarf she wanted." Madeline nodded. "The white one with the poppies on it." Madeline nodded again. Maddie was reliable and dependable. Trisha knew that the message would be passed. "Bye, now."

"Bye, Mrs. Flynn." Madeline stopped to shake some sand out of her sandal and then, spurred on by Mikayla's cries, continued to the beach. The pushchair went up and down the curb, and then passed by Lara's Big Fish Cay Art Studio, then, stopped in front of the furniture and gift shop owned by Madeline's parents, Mike and Jami Uretsky. The store was whimsically named "All Washed Up - Beach Furniture and Gifts".

Jami looked out of the large window and saw her daughter pushing Mikayla. "Hi, honey. Going to the beach?"

Mikayla agreed. "Beeeach!" and waved her hands.

"Yup. I'm going to keep her there until noon and then bring her home. Oh, and Mrs. Flynn said for me to tell you that your scarf is in. The one with poppies." Madeline, intelligent, reliable and amusing, was much in demand as a baby-sitter. Everyone in and around Big Fish Cay wanted Maddie to care for their children. Madeline could pick and choose her clients, and today, as usual, had picked Mikayla, an easy child whose parents paid top dollar for her services. "Lara gave me some money to get buns and stuff."

"Ok, sweetie," Jami smiled at her daughter. "See you a little after noon."

Madeline stopped for a moment and took a scrunchie out of her short's pocket, gathered up her long, abundant light brown curly hair and tied it back on her neck. "Hot, Mikayla. Hot", she crooned. The two continued along their way, noting that Captain Dave's boat was steaming into the harbor. "Boat," Maddie informed Mikayla. Dependably, Mikayla parroted her word. They rolled next door to Aunt Fanny's Tea Shop Bakery and pushed open the screen door. Aunt Fanny, a tall, pleasant woman who adored children, came around the bakery counter, cooing to Mikayla.

As if on cue, Mikayla said, "Bun," delighting Aunt Fanny, whose six grandchildren had moved to St. Thomas last year. She missed fussing over them.

Armed with a bag filled with sugar buns and two cold bottles of milk, Madeline passed Captain Fatty's Freedom Bar, crossed over to the top of the sand and opened the gate onto the children's beach. She tugged Mikayla out of the push chair, put down a thick blanket and the two of them sat down to enjoy their snack.

"Boat," Mikayla had remembered the word. She pointed to a large sailboat tugging at its mooring out in the harbor.

"Good girl. That's a boat. Yes. And the name of that boat is…can you remember this?…the *Jumbie Jamboree*."

Mikayla squinted up her forehead, and lisped, "*Jumbie Jam!*"

"Good enough," Madeline wiped Mikayla's mouth. "Now let's go and paddle in the water."

On the other side of the harbor, especially at the Green Flash Hotel, early preparations for the wedding of Arlis Fuglie and Don Gamble were beginning. The wedding guests would be filling up most of the rooms and the barbecue area in front of the hotel would be hosting not only the rehearsal dinner barbecue, but, on the following day, the wedding luau. Leslie and Charlie Janes, the proprietors of the hotel, sat at a table to formulate their strategy for the upcoming events.

The Janes, like many of the residents of Big Fish Cay, had moved from elsewhere to the British Virgin Islands in the past ten years, following the turn in fortune the beautiful islands had reaped. The upturn in sailing and rental of cruising boats, coupled with the constantly beautiful weather and easy sailing of the British Virgin Islands, had lured more and more visitors to their little paradise. And along with the visitors, new residents, eager for a new and lucrative career, seeking a different way of life, followed.

In Maryland, where the Janes lived for twenty years and raised their family, Charlie had toiled, very successfully...maybe too successfully... as a Mortgage Broker and Leslie's career was in nursing. Their children were grown and married, their house was paid for, and the stress of keeping up with inflation, bigger sales goals, and the relentless American obsession with *more* was wearing them down. At Charlie's last checkup, his blood pressure was soaring. Leslie's stress levels were becoming serious. How could they rectify these situations aggravating their health and their lives?

They'd talked everything over and decided to sell the house, chuck their ever-increasing race for *more...more things...more possessions...more, more, more of everything*, and move somewhere else. Somewhere peaceful, restful, warm... A chance article in a magazine suggested the Caribbean as the new spot for people like themselves. They visited St. Thomas and found it too busy; Paradise Island in the Bahamas and found it just like Las Vegas; and then, on a whim, took the ferry over to the islands of the BVI.

The ferry itself, a remarkable steel apparition called *Da Wild T'ing*, piqued their sense of humor. How could a place with a ferry boat named something as funny as that be anything but wonderful? A friendly cab driver told them about the opportunities at Big Fish Cay. "It's a growin' place. Beautiful harbor, soft, white sands...Lots a' room to spread out. The sailing business is comin' down here. More and more people are discoverin' how easy and pleasant it is to sail around the islands. Property is still cheap..." Charlie, ever interested in the housing market, had perked up his ears... "You guys gotta meet David and Barbara Wessel. They're a couple...he's from England and she's from the States. They came down and started buyin' up property and findin' people who wanna leave their own personal rat race and settle into a more relaxin' life."

And thus, Leslie and Charlie, like many like-minded people, came to Big Fish Cay. The first thing they learned is that "cay" is *not* pronounced as it looks....Oh, no. One says "key" and one is understood to be in the know. The second thing they learned is that Big Fish Cay had once been a haven for drug smugglers and was still referred to as "Hash Harbor". The third thing they leaned is that the British Virgin Island government had taken a firm stand against drugs five years ago and that anyone caught with any kinds of illicit drugs or drug paraphernalia would be jailed in extreme discomfort immediately. The fourth thing they learned was they could easily afford to buy a beautiful bungalow, perched on a cliff overlooking the entire chain of islands for a pittance of what their ranch house in Maryland could be sold.

David Wessel, a tall, thin, distinguished man who affected all of the accoutrements of an English dandy...foulard printed ascot, Malacca cane, clipped speech, elegant tweeds, even in the heat...had come to Virgin Gorda a few years ago, seen the potential, and moved in quickly to buy up property, option what he couldn't purchase, become an almost- Belonger, and seat himself on various governmental boards and committees so as to be in position to develop the harbor and make himself huge profits at the same time.

Barbara Wessel, a petite blonde dynamo, had been a Development Director in her earlier life. She was so tiny, so pretty and so feminine, that she was able to close deals, bamboozle investors, and make even the most hard-hearted man succumb to her wishes, even before he realized that under her fluffy, adorable personage lay a mind of steel. Wessel and Wessel, Ltd. ruled the Big Fish Cay area, and ruled it well. They acclimated themselves to island life and together with their beloved wired-haired terrier, Teddy, lived a busy, but enviable life.

The Janes were steered, willingly and excitedly, into hotel management, and Wessel and Wessel partnered with them to construct the Green Flash Hotel, named after the extraordinary sunsets that could be seen from all of their balconies. Charlie, who had been in the food and beverage business before he had gone into mortgages, fell back like a duck into a pond to a life that he'd always enjoyed. An affable, cheerful host, he epitomized island hospitality and soon had the hotel running in the black. Leslie loved running the front of the house. The Janes both glowed with happiness and good health. Charlie's blood pressure dropped and Leslie lost that anxious look that had marred her pretty face. The success of the hotel brought others to the booming little harbor.

The Neels, Sue and Curt, from Florida, also tired of the American rat race, invested in a pharmacy and soda fountain, using Curt's expertise in the drug industry to insure their success.

Lynn and Irene Sorenson, he a football coach from Nebraska and she a housewife, opened a Bicycle and Mo-Ped rental shop, guessing...correctly...that sailors who came to the harbor might want to explore the interior. The Mo-Ped Shop raked in money and the following year, Lynn added a sports equipment and sports shoe section at the rear of the rental store, calling the addition The Husker Sports Shop in honor of his beloved Nebraska football team. Lynn, a huge blonde bear of a man, straight from the corn field to the defensive line of the University of Nebraska football team, was called "Coach" by all who knew him. Although he had suffered early in life from jibes at his feminine first name, as soon as his muscles grew, the jibes ceased. "I just made them understand not to make fun of my name," he explained with his easy grin, flexing his huge ham-hands. "They sure got the idea right away!"

The Coach had also endeared himself to the children of the island, teaching them the rudiments of American-style football, together with Mike Uretsky, Madeline's father, on Saturday mornings in the empty lot next to the nursery school. Dozens of little boys conversed knowledgeably about a "third-and-goal-to-go" or a "touch-back" and many parents had to be dragged to the Coach's shop to purchase a genuine football jersey with Tom Brady or Donovan McNabb's name on the back. Coach was no dope. "I have a ball teaching them and then they come and buy cleats and sneakers from me. We all win."

Ginny and Walker Vought, sailors who had completed their dream of sailing around the world, took over a decaying rum distillery, turning it back to producing the island's buttery rum (Walker's part) and a gift shop (Ginny's part) that sold island crafts. Two Pakistani sisters, Mahji and Hadji, opened a spice shop; and an older veterinarian and his partner, both formerly from South Africa, opened a pet care center. A retired musician who was the leader of his own swing band, Ray Leach, gave trombone lessons in a room above the spice shop, while his wife, Shirley, took a job at the Big Fish Cay Library. Everyone who left their harried lives was delighted to now live in the bright, sun-kissed, easy time, no-rush little harbor.

Madeline's parents, Mike and Jami Uretsky, came to get their children away from inner-city violence, crowded cities and the American rat-race. Mike left the financial world to make eclectic furniture from driftwood and Jami started yet another gift shop, this one featuring Mike's furniture and handmade toys. Their children, Madeline, who was seven when they moved to the island, and Mitchell, who was five, traded a long bus ride, hostile classmates with violent tendencies and indifferent teachers for a land of sunshine, a more relaxed, but yet more rigorous British- based educational system, and a sunny boat ride each morning to pick up other island children. The boat, riding over the sparking waves, brought fifty children each school day to Spanish Town, the largest town on Virgin Gorda. Mitchell and Maddie could no longer imagine that anyone might want to live their childhood anywhere else but here.

Mikayla Vitiello was born here in the hospital behind Spanish Town. Her parents, Lara and Jamie, had also been trapped in the rush for financial success in New York City. Jamie, a tall, dark haired, blue-eyed man, half Chinese, half Italian, was becoming ill and tense with the stress of new-and-ever-spiraling-higher sales goals every three months. Lara had fallen in love with Jamie's easygoing nature and ability to befriend anyone who met him. But, after a few years in the New York atmosphere, even Jamie's cheerful demeanor was becoming strained. Rents in New York were rising astronomically. Lara's job in the financial sector left her stressed and unable to relax enough to conceive the child for whom they wished. The death of an aunt resulted in a decent-sized legacy to Lara. "Let's leave here," she begged Jamie. "Let's go…oh, anywhere where it isn't New York!"

Lara's secret dream had always been to paint, and thus, through the offices of Wessel and Wessel, the Big Fish Cay Art School was born. And a few years later, so was Mikayla. Lara found dozens of islanders who wanted art instruction. She expanded the school to include an art gallery, where her pupils sold their work, and where Jamie found his own creative fulfillment as a sign designer, making unique, three-dimensional signage for the burgeoning new businesses in the group of islands. Jamie and Lara became new almost-Belongers and belonged so well that Jamie was elected Mayor of Big Fish Cay.

Bob and Muriel Cherico, from Rome, didn't want to start up any sort of business. Retired from a busy life as a businessman, Bob only wanted to paint. Muriel wanted only to watch Bob be happy. And thus, Bob joined the artist colony, painting wild, colorful landscapes, each unique because Kyle, his old, black Labrador retriever was painted into each picture. Sometimes, the dog could be seen plainly, and sometimes, the viewer needed a discerning and knowing eye to be able to pick out Kyle's dark figure. For those in the know, each of Bob's pictures fetched a goodly sum. Muriel, a comfortable homebody who had retired from a lifetime of teaching, spent her days on the beach, knitting, gossiping, watching the children play, and occasionally helping Mrs. Leuzarder, who ran the Infant Nursery, to hand out the morning snack.

Joyce O'Sullivan, a short bespectacled woman from Ireland, who had moved to Boston, Massachusetts, raised a family and kept the family going with her earnings as a nurse, also retired from a life of hospital stress. Joyce, happily rid of all of her obligations as a wife and mother, came to paint the remarkable plant life of the island. She was a left-handed painter, a rarity in the art world, and also played the flute in the island's fledgling orchestra. She sold her botanical prints in Lara's store, but her artistic passion was the book about native plants she was writing and illustrating which had been commissioned by the Brooklyn Botanical Gardens.

Likewise, Pat Biase, from the United States, came to relax and paint. His specialty was painting houses...not painting the walls and ceilings, but creating a painting *of* the house...with the inhabitants plunked into the picture. When you ordered a custom-made painting by Biase, you got your house's best side, with flora and fauna, featured, with you, the purchaser, your spouse, kiddies, if you wished them, and dog or cat posed in front. Like Bob Cherico's, Pat's paintings were scooped up as soon as the acrylic was dry and his list of commissioned pictures zoomed into at least ten more years of success. Between paintings, Pat enjoyed playing the piano with the island orchestra and exercising with a bit of tennis, swimming and golf. He had recently rented the upper half of his duplex to another couple from Europe, Tony and Joyce Ginise. Tony was also immersed in the relaxation of painting and Joyce was happy to join Muriel and a few other women who sat in the sunshine and did good deeds for the less fortunate on the island. Tony's paintings were enthusiastic blobs of color with less success in sales, but he was a cheerful, gregarious man who only wanted to be among a group of others. He was as happy having morning coffee and cream buns at Aunt Fanny's as he was completing a successful sale. Tony played, with great joshing from the rest of the musicians, the triangle in the island orchestra.

Not all of the business-owners were from "away". Many of the Belongers, sensing an opportunity, moved into the older block of stores along the harbor and lining the adjoining streets. Aunt Fanny Loparco brought her considerable baking skills into a small shop that sold cakes, buns and cookies and served high tea. Her long-time friend and neighbor, Marie Rudisell, maker of island-famous fruitcakes, leased Aunt Fanny's kitchens in the late afternoon to bake and ship her magnificent fruitcakes worldwide. She was well known locally, and her bright orange boxes with her portrait on them proclaimed her as The Fruitcake Lady.

Captain Fatty, a Belonger, with a varied cast of ancestors, opened a bar on the right hand side of the harbor and his son, Fat Matt, opened yet another bar…this one with a sports motif…on the other arm of the harbor. One bar served island food, and the other served American-style burgers and fries. There seemed to be plenty of business to keep both successful.

Eva Mae Moulton opened a jewelry shop and called it Eva's Jewels of the Sea. Her original creations were snapped up by the wealthy sailors who came…more and more and more…to Big Fish Cay. And just last year, two couples from New England, Paul and Robin Blanchette and Trisha and Brian Flynn gasped when they heard the price of land now, but bought nonetheless. Robin and Paul, long time followers of the rock bands of the 1960's, opened a hemp product shop, and Trisha and Brian called upon their previous talents to open a fashionable women's clothing shop (Trisha) which sold custom rugs and carpets in the back (Brian). Brian and Paul, both avid, enthusiastic musicians, played in Fat Matt's establishment three nights a week in a band. The band, featuring Brian on drums and Paul with a guitar, was called The Island Boys. Upon a bit of arm twisting from Joyce O'Sullivan, Paul and Brian had been forced to join the orchestra's grouping, and, would be attempting to provide the music for Don Gamble and Arlis Fuglie's upcoming wedding.

Even the very waters of the Big Fish Cay harbor filled up with commercial life. Captain Eddie and his wife, Captain Karen, both certified charter boat captains, moored their sailboat, the *Jumbie Jamboree*, off the commercial dock. Retired from the US Army, Captain Eddie was known as Bomba Man and his wife as The Sarge, as her job in the Army had been that of an MP. Bomba and the Sarge advertised in sailing magazines around the world, and, like Captain Jack Scambaugh, their boat was filled to capacity on every charter.

Captain Davie Holt ran a commercial fishing boat that fished for profit and also ran day-trip fishing ventures for those tourists who wanted to bring home a trophy fish. His boat, the *GKB*, had a unique feature that drew curious tourists to it like an ant to a picnic…Captain Dave only hired pretty and well-developed women as his crew. His boat was always referred as "Captain Dave and His All-Girl Crew" and was a smashing success.

The Wessels, drowning in their success, hired a successful businesswoman, Gail Gallagher, from her high-powered job in Washington DC. Gail was to run the office and give David and Barbara a chance to wind down and spend more time with each other and Teddy. Gail was all that they could wish for and her first year was tremendously successful, but she left the Wessel establishment to open a hairdressing emporium, finding more joy in styling hair-dos and manicures than in the world of business. Sighing in resignation, the Wessels were putting ads in the Wall Street Journal and the London Times, hoping to find someone else to take over their burdens. Philosophical, Teddy whined a bit at being once again ignored and then sat back on his haunches hoping in his doggie way, that a new office manager would be found quickly.

At the back of the harbor were the municipal buildings, the fire and police stations, the Big Fish Cay Post Office, presided over by Postmistress Holly Dulac, the offices of government, the Wessels real estate conglomerate, three banks, a sail loft and a small supermarket. On the other side of the harbor were other, older stores and offices: a dentist, a clock-repair shop, Doctor Fullbright's Foot Parlor, The Virgin Gorda Dance Studio, two Laundromats and a meat market, run by Lou Seraso, a retired butcher from Spain. Together with his wife, Muriel, who operated the cash register, they supplied choice cuts of sirloin or goat meat to the island residents.

And in the aforementioned police station, Detective Inspector Carlton Reese stopped to eat a cold pork sandwich that his wife, Rebecca, had made for him this morning and, at the same time, re-read the autopsy report on the late Antony Marsden. It confirmed Doctor Fullbright's hypothesis of some sort of internal poisoning, but, the exact nature could not be ascertained until the toxicology reports came back from the laboratory in Road Town.

"And that will take a couple of days." Carlton waved half of his sandwich aloft at Effalyn.

"Well, that means no burial just yet. Mrs. Marsden isn't gonna be happy about that."

"Tough tittie," Carlton coughed on a piece of gristle. "She's just got to be patient."

"Accident? Just an old man who was so senile that he caused his own death?" Effalyn mused, "Or a clever murder?"

Carlton dusted pieces of bread off his shirtfront and stood up. "I'm going over there to talk with her and interview a few neighbors and friends. Wanna come?"

"Do the buzzards fly over the dead mongoose?" Effalyn joked with vulgar humor, grabbed her purse, checked that her notebook and pen were stashed within, "I'll get the car and meet you out front."

Carlton watched Effalyn's neat backside leave the office. He smiled with appreciation. Effalyn was terrific. He didn't know what he had ever done without her. She had been an inspired choice for the police force. Attractive and neat with a sharp sense of what was right, Effalyn was admired and respected by everyone. Hired right out of high school as secretary in the police station, she had shown intelligence and loyalty. The rise of the women's liberation movement had given her impetus to improve herself, and, at the first available opening in the police force, Effalyn had applied and been hired as a patrolwoman. She took advantage, as Carlton also had, of the generous Virgin Island University's free tuition for Belongers and went to college at night to get her degree, specializing in Criminal Justice. Carlton's own university degree was bolstered by a Master's Program in Criminology and moved him from Detective to Detective Sergeant and then to Chief Inspector. Even now, Effalyn was managing, despite being the sole caretaker and provider for her elderly mother, to return to school to study law. Carlton just knew that she would someday be one of the first woman judges in the Virgin Islands or perhaps the very first lady Prosecutor.

Carlton dialed Rebecca. "Virgin Gorda Dance Studio," Rebecca's New York accent, even after all the years of island living, was strong. "Oh, hi, honeybun."

"Hi, sweetie. What's for dinner tonight?"

"Carlton, do you ever stop thinking of food?"

"Only when I'm wrapped in your lovin' arms." She giggled.

"I'm gonna grill some skirt steak and make fajitas. Ok?"

"Oh, goody-goody," the hard-boiled policeman rubbed his hands together as if he were seven years old. "I'm off to see Mrs. Marsden, our grieving widow."

"You know, Carlton, I heard a snippet of gossip today at Gail's. There were two women there who were neighbors of the Marsdens. Live a street or two away near their bungalow. They were making insinuations about her being very chummy with some man who lived a few streets away. This fellow has a sick wife and they were joking about her being knocked-off."

"Do you know the women's names?"

"No, but Gail will know them. She said they came in every two weeks for a shampoo and cut."

"Ah, the bush hair-do telegraph. I ought to make Gail a deputy."

"She knows everything, I swear."

"What do you have on your agenda this afternoon?" Carlton heard the beep of the horn from Effalyn.

"Tap dancing class for juniors. Island dancing rehearsal for the wedding group entertainers."

"Good. Good." Carlton's mind, relieved at knowing that fajitas were on the dinner menu, was already planning his interview of Mrs. Marsden. "I'll see you about six. Love you."

"Love you, too."

***

Jack Scambaugh watched the rest of the passengers climb down from Cammie's jitney. Another group of chickens for his coop, ready for fifteen days of sailing instructions and hell-bent on finding romance. He chuckled and stood up to greet them. Ever since Emma had the brainstorm to change his advertising to emphasize romance, they had more business than they could handle. And he loved it. He drove the boat and Emma ran the business side. Ah, and here came Emma now, ready to join them in the welcome to the boat speech. Good, he always did a better job when his Mrs. Peel was there.

Two dark-complectioned young men heaved up their own duffle bags and came towards the boat, laughing and talking. Probably the two from New Jersey; Vinny James and, um, Sam...um, Sam...funny name...what was it? Ah, Gallofrito! Emma, who could speak fluent Italian, told him that it translated as "fried chicken". Sammy Fried

Chicken. OK, he'd remember *that* one. The young men were followed by two women, ages in their early thirties, Scambaugh estimated. The girls from South Africa? If so, their names were Martha Temple-Wright and Claudia Van Voorhees. Both were tall, with blonde hair, tied back because of the heat. Both dressed in attractive shorts and tops. An older woman, tall with wild red hair, came next. Corliss Curtis from England or Zandra Hoovenmeyer from Holland? And then a shorter woman, bouncy and grinning. And then two men, one in his thirties, one perhaps sixty three or so. The older one had a sour look on his handsome, but discontented face. The younger man was obviously not an Englishman nor an American as he wore baggy, ill-fitting shorts, sandals and white socks. The older man was more likely one of the remaining Americans, either Elwyn Langdon or Elliott Barringer.

The man with the socks stopped suddenly, dropped his bag and spread his arms out as if to embrace the harbor scene. Captain Jack grinned, understanding how the beauty of the islands and the boats at anchor might affect a city-bred traveler, and got to his feet to greet them. The man following the socks bumped up against him.

"Sonofabitch! Watch what you're doing, you fool." The second man ejaculated angrily, confirming Captain Jack's first opinion of him as a passenger hell-bent on being a misery to all. And an American. Such a blight on the usually happy and easy-to-get-along-with typical guy from the USA. Jack sighed. Such passengers were *so* tiresome and always disrupted the harmony of a cruise. *Ah well, all this shall pass*, Jack thought. Only fifteen more times.

"Oh, so sorry!" The socks turned and offered eager apologies. "I was looking and so was stopping without thinking." He offered his handshake to the American.

The American stepped around him, ignoring the proffered hand. "Try to be more watchful. This is a small ship and I hate being crowded."

Looking a bit bewildered, the socks bent to pick up his bag. Before he could lift it up again, the man whose name meant Fried Chicken scooped the bag up. "Hey, man, no problem at all," the easy drawl chuckled out. "This is supposed to be a fun time here." Fried Chicken offered his own hand to Socks. "I'm Sammy...Sammy Gallofrito. From Jersey."

"Jersey! The island of Jersey? Oh, so happy to meet you, sir." Socks almost cried with happiness. "I am Hosea Balleau. I am from Greece."

"The island of Jersey? What's that?" Sammy's handsome face showed his puzzlement.

The short woman laughed. "Jersey is an island off the coast of England. I think you are from America, no? Maybe from the state that is called *New* Jersey?"

"Ah!" Hosea looked at her with gratitude. "I am so foolish. Two Jerseys. One in the Channel Islands, one in the United States, but that one is called *New* Jersey." He slapped his forehead. "I am to learn much!"

The older American sneered and stalked into the coldness of the air-conditioned cabin.

The last passenger, a tall black man, watched the little scene in front of him with interest, then, shook his head and came over to the boat. "I'm Elwyn Langdon." His smile lit up his handsome face. "I'm so pleased to be here."

As Ducky put the bags away, Captain Jack gathered his entire group together in the voluminous cockpit. The American came out and stood, looking bored, in a corner. Jack spoke: "Welcome to all of you. It might seem a bit confusing today, but we'll all get to know one another quite well in a day or two. First, I am your captain and your host. Captain Jack Scambaugh," he slapped his chest. "Better known as Captain Jack, and even, some of the time behind my back, Captain Scumbag." The group laughed. Even the American smiled. A few of them had already heard of Captain Jack's affectionate, albeit irreverent, nickname.

"This is my wife, Emma." An attractive woman with light brown curly hair, dressed in khaki shorts and a blue tee shirt which proclaimed her as a member of crew of *The Southern Cross*, grinned at all of them and flapped her hand in greeting. "Emma...some of you have already had some phone calls and correspondence with Emma...Emma runs the office and takes care of all of the problems, leaving me free to sail the boat, drink a little rum and have fun." Again, the group laughed, enjoying their first few moments of their Captain's hospitality and cheerful personality.

"And this handsome specimen of manhood over there," Captain Jack's arm swept to the back of the group where the tall dark man who had carried the luggage down into the boat stood. "This is my First Mate, Ducky B." The young man bowed, displaying white, even teeth in a perfect face. Annie could feel, even from across the cockpit, Suzie's hiss of indrawn breath.

"And here," the lithesome young woman in the white bikini popped out of the galley. She held a large tray filled with chilled glasses. "With a welcome-on-board cocktail, is Kat, our cook." Kat, perhaps feeling that her official introduction deserved more formality than the white bikini, had adorned her slender, yet curvy body with a transparent blue scarf, which she wore tied around her hips like an island *pareau.* This time, Annie sensed the hiss of indrawn breaths from every male in the group. Her eyes flew to Ducky's face, wondering just what he had meant from his previous comment to her, and he grinned at her and winked a slow, knowing wink.

"We are here to make you happy. We are your hosts and your servants." Captain Jack continued. "We will do anything to make your trip memorable and to give you the best vacation you have ever known." He put out his hand and Emma came to his side.

"Now, Emma will give you her little spiel." He sat down and Emma spoke to the group.

"I'm Emma Scambaugh and *no one* calls me anything but Emma." She gave them all a mock glare and they laughed dutifully. "I will not be with you on most of the trip, although I will join you now and then on some special social occasions, especially, this time, the wedding that we will all be attending." The group murmured and she continued. "We advertise this as a romantic trip, and it often is. Although we cannot guarantee that you'll find love and romance," She stopped for a moment and her glance took in each face in the group. "I *will* promise you sunny days and tender, velvet nights. If you can't find romance within these setting...well!" Her audience sighed happily.

She pointed to the two tables in the cockpit. "See these tables?" Everyone who was seated began to look. "This one is the friends table. Here, your pictures will be added to those of the people who came and sailed with us." She moved towards the other table. "This table is called to romance table. These pictures were taken *after* the cruise and sent to us by the couples who found romance with one another. See how many there are?" She pointed to the dozens of photos, some of smiling couples, some of weddings, some of families and children. "We all hope that a few of you here with us for this cruise will, one day, send us a picture of yourself, linked with another of your fellow cruisers."

She laughed as some of the passengers sneaked a look at one another and a few of them blushed. "That's sort of the way Jack and I met and one night, when he was full of rum and playing on his guitar. He was very sexy and very romantic, and perhaps, if you can manage to twist his arm on this trip and get him to have a few drinks..." She dropped a kiss on her husband's head... "Maybe he'll tell you all about it." She moved back to Jack's side and took his huge hand in hers.

"Now, I know some of you might think this is high-school-ish, but, if you're like me and can't remember your mother's name, we've figured out a way to get to know one another fast. Please bear with us and wear these name tags for the first day or so." She passed a basket around. "There are eighteen of you and it is hard to remember eighteen names all at once." Her smile was so genuine and cheerful that anyone who might have demurred kept quiet. "We'll go around. Please give your name, where you are from, and tell us one or two things about yourself." She looked at Ducky. "Duck, you go first and then Kat and then we'll start here."

"I'm Ducky B. That's not my real name. My real name is a mouthful; The Honorable J. Ducksworth Blyton the Fourth. I'm descended from a long line of Ducks." The group laughed, mellowed by the glasses of island punch. "I am a Belonger, born and educated here until I went to University in London. I am reading Political Science there and am on a sabbatical until the end of next summer when I will return to read Law at Oxford. I have sailed since I was a toddler and am lucky to have this opportunity to crew with Captain Jack." Ducky threw is head back laughed and the strong muscles of his throat and chest rippled. "I will also be teaching you...those of you who need teaching, that is...to snorkel, wind surf and even, if you dare, to do some para-kiting." Kat had slipped below to refill the pitchers of punch. As she placed the pitchers on the tables, Ducky turned the floor over to her. "Kat?"

"Hello to all of you. My name is Ekaterina Rosseau and I am from Croatia. That is, like Ducky's name, too long to say, so please to call me Kat." She laughed, like a peal of silvery bells. "I have been here since two years, cooking and crewing for Captain Jack. Like Ducky, I, too, am a sailor from my baby days. I am a Cordon Bleu cooking school graduate and like to think that I can cook you any special dish that you might desire." Annie's treacherous mind jumped to the thought that many of the men on board would certainly desire Kat as their special dish. She pushed her thoughts down and took a ladylike sip of her drink, again envying Kat her gorgeous figure, lustrous dark hair and beautiful face. *She's everything I'm not and more*, Annie sighed to herself. *And, she can cook*!

"Every morning, we will meet here on the deck in the cockpit. Breakfast will be served at 7:30 AM, but I am an early wake-up person and the coffee and juices will be ready at 6:30 for those of you who are like me. At the time of breakfast, we will talk about our plans for the day and I will tell you what my menus will be for lunch, if it is on board, and for dinner. If you do not like what I am to be serving, please let me know and I will prepare something that you do like. I am always happy to listen to your requests and I promise you, that I can prepare any dish at all. You must let me know of your wishes and I will comply with them." She stepped backwards and then stopped. "Oh, yes. And there are always cold drinks in the ice chests on the deck, and in the refrigerator. There are snacks and nibble foods in the galley at all times and you are all welcome to come and eat anything at all." Her dazzling smile lit up her lovely face. "Even if you eat the steak that I planned to serve for dinner, that's OK, too." She grinned. "I will think some very private thoughts about you, but..." her hands made an expansive gesture, "You are our guests." She bit her lips and rolled her eyes, as if trying to remember her speech. "Ah! And, if you like to cook or bake, I will welcome you into the galley with me. You can prepare a whole meal, if you wish, or help me peel potatoes. Or, if you are like most of our guests, just eat or drink! So, welcome to all of you!" She waved a small wave and turned back to the closed glass door that led to the galley area. "And now, I am going to bring all of you my delicious lunch."

Emma spoke again. "And, speaking of food and drink, and I am sure that you are all ravenous after your flights and the trip here, we are equipped with almost every kind of wine, beer or liquor. If you desire some sort of special drink and we don't have it on board, please ask and it will be delivered." She laughed again. "We often have fun learning about new drinks. Last year, one of our passengers told us about a drink called a Mango-Wango[1]. We will have some of them ready this afternoon for you to try." Ducky rubbed his washboard stomach and rolled his dark eyes in appreciation. "Yes, Mr. Duck is especially fond of the Mango-Wango. And, as a matter of fact, you'll hear a song about them and a few of us passengers when we get to Banjo's place on Jost Van Dyke."

"All right, now to you." She motioned to Hosea Balleau, whose guileless face blushed like a child. "You start. Tell us who you are, where you're from and a little bit about yourself."

---

[1] See the recipes at the end of the book.

Hosea, a chunky middle-aged man, stood up nervously. "I am Hosea – that is spelled H-O-S-E-A, pronounced Hoe-see-ah. Hosea Balleau. I am from Israel originally, and now I am in Greece where I work for a multi-national company that manufactures computer parts. My mother is Israeli and my father is French. I speak seven- no - eight languages; Greek, French, Hebrew, Pharsi, German, Italian, Egyptian and English." He ran a sweating finger around his tee shirt collar. "I do not know sailing. I have never been on a boat. I would like to learn." He sat down, grateful that his turn was over. Annie's heart went out to him. He wasn't handsome, as a matter of fact, he was sort of homely. Obviously, he didn't have a great deal to offer in social graces or witty dialogue, but she felt drawn to his honest earnestness. *"He'll make someone ...not me nor certainly not Suzie...a good, faithful husband,"* she thought.

"And next." Emma pointed.

"I'm Vinny James." Vinny spoke sitting down. He was a good-looking young man in his late twenties, perhaps early thirties. "I came here with my good buddy, Sam. We live in *New* Jersey in the US of A." His grin was infectious and Hosea grinned with him. "I always wanted to learn how to sail and I'm here to do just that."

"And do you work, or...?" Emma asked.

"Oh, yeah. I forgot!" Vinny blushed becomingly. "My family is in waste management ...sanitation and disposal. I'm the manager of the operations."

"And you?"

"I'm Sammy Gallofrito. From *New* Jersey, as Vinny told you, not the island of Jersey." He spread out his hands and chuckled to Hosea. "I'm so dumb, I didn't even know there *was* an island called Jersey!" Hosea beamed at him. "So, anyway, Vinny and me...We've been friends since we were kids. I'm an attorney." He shrugged and made a gesture with his hands. "With a name like Gallofrito, you gotta know I'm Italian, no?" The group laughed out loud. "I have a speedboat, and I love to take girls out into the ocean, but I don't know about sailing. We're here to have a good time and learn about the boat and all." He turned toward Kat. "I can cook, and I cook really good, but I don't wanna cook on my vacation!" Again, the group laughed. Kat bowed towards him and made a shooing motion with her hands.

Annie gazed hard at the two friends. Both looked alike. Dark curly hair, dark eyes, great shoulders. Annie adored great shoulders. They were most likely about her age – passable, definitely passable. Nice sense of humor for both of them. She wondered what life as the wife of a garbage magnate in New Jersey would be like…maybe like an episode of *The Sopranos*?

"My name is Paula Haskins. I live in New York City." The woman who had come on the plane with Annie stood up, pulling herself to her feet with the aid of the table edge. As she had come on the boat with the first bunch of travelers, she had already been to her cabin. Annie noted that she was now wearing a straw hat and a long, loose, finely meshed long-sleeved shirt. Annie thought that she looked ill and tense. Paula spoke, "I have never been on a vacation to these islands. I have never sailed on a boat, and, as a matter of fact, I can't swim." She appealed to Ducky. "I'm hoping that you can find a few minutes, when we get to a shallow beach, to help me to learn to stay afloat."

"I'd be honored," Ducky bowed to her. "You'll find, Paula, that the water here in the BVI has a high saline content. Very salty for those of you who eschew technical talk," he grinned and Annie was again bowled over by his dark good looks and breathtaking personality. "It is very easy for a person to float in this kind of water; the salt makes you very buoyant. It will be easy and fun to teach you how to do a decent dog-paddle, or, maybe even get you to swim well enough to be an Olympic contender."

Paula smiled and sat back down. Annie thought, *She didn't really say much about herself, did she?*

"I am Sarah Lemonowski. I am from Great Britain." She was tall and thin and her age perhaps forty-five. Her salt and pepper hair was cut short, almost cropped to her head, she wore large, square rimmed eyeglasses covering slightly bulging eyes and she didn't smile when she spoke. "I am a financial consultant. I can sail competently and would be happy to help out where I can, if I am not in the way."

Captain Jack answered her indirect question. "We'd love to have your help. This boat was built to my specifications and can be easily sailed in any kind of weather by Ducky and me. Hell, I can do it myself if need be…but this is a vacation for all of you. We'll teach you the rudiments of sailing, docking and navigation, if you want to learn. We'll let you steer, sail the boat, and even dock it if we feel you have the ability. We want you to haul the sails…" He laughed, a big, booming guffaw, "although nowadays, these boats are so automated that we do it by the push of a button…It's all up to you. You can loll around on a cushion and sip Mango Wangos and eat Kat's great food all day and all night and never lift a finger. That's fine with us too." He bowed his head towards Elwyn.

Elwyn stood up. "Elwyn Langdon. Los Angeles, California. Home of movie stars and palm trees," the group chuckled with him. "I am certainly not a movie star. I'm a pilot. I fly commercially and also do private jets. I'm a widower, have two wonderful daughters, two decent son-in-laws...sons-in-law? Never can remember which is correct." Again, he made the group laugh. "Best of all, I have four grandchildren and I promise each of you that before this trip is over, I will have forced you to look at their pictures."

The other man from California, the rude one, Elliott Barringer rolled his eyes, showing his boredom with this little bit of getting-to-know-one-another. Annie took an immediate dislike to him. Langdon didn't seem to notice and continued, "I can sail a little bit. Took some lessons and, as a pilot, know something about navigation. I've never seen such a beautiful boat as this and I simply can't wait to get going." He sat down to a few whistles and cheers of agreement.

"I'm Elliott Barringer." His voice was cultured, languid and slightly bored. "I also live in California, not in LA," his lip curled, "but Beverly Hills. Beverly Hills is where the movie stars *really* live."

Who gives a rat's ass? Annie asked herself. He was very handsome, tall, tanned and fit, looking as if he swam or played tennis every day. His clothes were tailored and expensive-looking and he wore, contrary to Captain Jack's advice, a heavy gold chain around his neck and a matching gold bracelet on his arm. A wrist watch, glittering with diamonds around its face, adorned his other wrist. *Oh, my! Suzie will latch right onto him, even if he's a bit too old for her*, Annie mused. *Too bad. The man was poison*, she knew it in her bones. She looked up and saw Ducky watching her. He winked again.

"I have a lucrative law practice in Beverly Hills," Elliott continued. "And yes, I represent many movie stars and wealthy businessmen."

Who asked you, dickhead? Annie found herself disliking him more and more.

Elliott glanced at the wristwatch. "I am taking this trip, not for romance, heh, heh," his glance raked the faces around him, "but because I needed a break from the stress of my work. I have a very important trial coming up...I'm sorry that I cannot share with you the name of the movie star that I represent, but...you will see, in the fall, probably on television," he smoothed his hair, which was dark-blond with attractive grayish wings above each ear, back from his forehead, "It is vitally important that I get some relaxation before I begin my work again."

"I am Martha...." One of the tall, blonde South African women began to speak. Elliott Barringer cut in, glaring balefully at her interruption.

"Excuse me, but I hadn't quite finished." Martha blushed and stammered. Elliott began to talk again.

"I am an expert and experienced sailor. I have sailed and captained boats much larger than this. If I felt like it, I could sail this one myself, but, as I am paying a fortune for this experience, I will leave the driving to you," he bowed with a wintery smile towards Captain Jack.

Captain Jack nodded back to him without smiling. "And now, Martha..." the words *before you were so rudely interrupted* hung, nearly visible in the air..."please go on with your introduction," Captain Jack smiled gently at her.

Martha glared at Elliott and gathered herself together. "As I was saying, I am Martha Temple-Wright. I am from Capetown, South Africa. Claudia," she gestured to the woman who sat next to her, "is my sister. I am a widow with one grown son. He is an engineer and also lives in Capetown. He is married, but, as of yet," she turned and smiled at Elwyn, "I have no grandchildren or pictures to show." The group chuckled with her, happy that the slight tension was over. "I can show you a picture of my cat, but, maybe I will wait until we have drunk a few of those mango drinks." Again, a chuckle rippled. "I have sailed a little, but only as a passenger. I would adore sitting on that chair and pretending that I can steer this beautiful boat." Again, a smattering of laughter. "I am a doctor in Capetown and my specialty is microsurgery."

"We are so proud of my sister," Claudia rose. "She is an inspiration to our family. She will never brag to you, but she has helped many children who were born with difficult birth defects to lead a normal life after she has fixed them." A few passengers applauded and Martha ducked her head and pushed at her sister's arm. "And she does it for no charge at all to the child or the family." A murmur of appreciation swept through the passengers.

Claudia continued: "So. I am the younger sister of the doctor. My name is Claudia Van Voorhees and I have never been married. The men of South Africa are stupid, no?" A long guffaw came from Elwyn's throat and he nodded, agreeing. "My family has a ranch and I keep house for my father and mother and help them to run the ranch. I have been a passenger, too, on boats, but know nothing about sailing one. I am happy to learn anything and also happy to help with the meals or anything else. I am happy...happy to be here and happy to meet you all." Blushing prettily, she sat down.

"They look very much alike", Annie thought. *"Pretty women, such thick, blonde hair and such blue eyes...funny, obviously intelligent and pleasant. The men of South Africa must be idiots, all right! I think we will get along well."*

Kat interrupted the introductions by bringing out long platters of smoked salmon, rare roast beef, sliced turkey and ham. She deftly dealt out plates, white and blue with a shell motif, silverware and napkins to each guest. Ducky followed her with platters of lettuce, fresh juicy tomato slices, onions, capers and small pots of mustard, horseradish and mayonnaise sauces. Kat passed baskets of fresh, hot breads, rye rolls, and squares of steaming cornbread. As if by magic, crystal glasses appeared and Ducky set pitchers of wine, iced lemon water and beer on the tables. Kat returned with a huge frosty jug of a creamy liquid. "Mango-Wangos!" She held the pitcher up. "Who wants to try?" A chorus of appreciation greeted her and Ducky assisted, pouring large glasses of the foaming, icy drink. Kat crowned each glass with a spear of sliced mango and a dusting of nutmeg and the passengers subsided into bliss.

Each of the two tables held ten guests with room to spare. "We will pause one moment while we set up our lunch," Kat explained. "Then, the rest of us will speak."

She put out round plates filled with olives, pickles, sliced cheeses and salamis. "Now, who needs anything else to drink?"

"Bring me a scotch, single malt, if you have anything like that on board," Elliott snapped his fingers.

Kat nodded with a smile that didn't quite reach her eyes. Annie swiveled her head back to Kat. *She seems like a very pleasant woman, this Kat.* Annie thought. *But I don't think she likes having fingers snapped at her.* "Anyone else?"

Murmurs of *this is great...who could want anything more?...I've got everything I could ever want here...*floated in the air. Kat nodded again and went back into the galley. The guests happily tucked in.

"Who is left to talk?" Emma turned to Duncan MacKinnon. "Perhaps you can start again?"

Duncan rose, putting a thick sandwich of roast beef and mustard down on his plate. "Aye, this is magnificent food. Thank you, Kat." He gestured to her as she returned with a large glass containing a hefty amount of amber fluid. "The whisky looks good and I'll have a wee dram later." *What a nice man*, Kat watched him. *He just knows the right words to simmer the situation down. I hope he finds love on this trip. Someone to keep him happy out there in Scotland.*

Duncan scratched his chin. "I am Duncan MacKinnon, from the island of Skye in Scotland. I'm sixty-four years old. I know my listing says Glasgow, but that is where our company shipping offices are. My farm, for I am a sheep farmer, is on the island away up north and over the sea to Skye, as the auld song says," his voice was melodic. "As I live on the sea, I've been a sailor since I was a wee boy. But in small boats, never anything like this lovely thing." He gestured to Captain Jack. "This, this is magnificent. I am honored and pleased that I had the brilliance to choose this vacation." Captain Jack raised his water glass to Duncan. "I am a widower. My dear wife, Mairi, died four years ago, leaving me with three strong sons and one beautiful daughter. All are wed and happy. Some live in our village, some in London, some in Hong Kong. I, too, will force you all to see the pictures of my wee grandchildren, and maybe, if you are very lucky, a few snapshots of my sheep." He sat down to raucous laughter. The group was relaxing.

My turn, oooh, I hope I don't say anything too stupid, Annie worried. "Hi, I'm Annie Sabatino. I'm here with my cousin, Suzie and we both live in Greenwich, Connecticut. For those of you who are not familiar with the geography of the United States, Connecticut is in the northeast part, and Greenwich is situated on the waters of Long Island Sound." She looked around nervously. *Am I talking too much?*

She watched as Paula's eyes widened and then narrowed. *What does she know about Greenwich?* Annie wondered. *That's the second time she has made a peculiar expression when I mentioned the town.* "I have never been married. I work as the Director of Human Resources for the Greenwich Hospital. I like my work. I, too..." She turned to Vinny and Sam, "am Italian and come from a big, noisy family with branches in waste management."

"Just like all Italian families," Sammy said and there was laughter. "We rule the world because we rule the garbage!"

"Garbage and food. That's us!" Vinny waved his fist in the air. "We rule the garbage and food!"

Annie nodded fervently. "We're smart, we Italians. First we make you eat our food and then we have you pay to have us clean up the leftovers." Again, the passengers laughed, relaxing more and more. Annie continued: "I'd be so happy to help you, Kat, in any way I can. I love to cook and am even very qualified to wash dishes." More laughter. "Already, even before we have left the dock, this is so super!" She sat down to a smattering of applause.

Suzie stood up slowly and tossed a lock of hair back from her forehead. "And I am Suzie Ruutz-Reese, Annie's cousin. From Greenwich, and you all know where that is now." She gave Annie a wink. "I *have* been married, but that was long in the past." She dimpled, letting every man feel that anyone who had been married to her, even for a moment, was one lucky guy. "I don't have a real job, but I do a lot of charity work." Annie's mouth fell open. "I do lots of good things," Suzie said firmly. "Lots." She managed to twirl around in the small space in front of her chair. "I am sooo looking forward to the sun and fun and dancing under the stars." She smiled enchantingly at each of the men, lingering her glance for a moment into each of their eyes and then gracefully sat down.

"I'm Lannie Olmstead. I am from London. I was born in a small village near the coast of Cornwall. I work for a fashion magazine called *Lady*," Several of the women gasped and nodded. "Yes, you may have read it perhaps," Lannie continued, pleased that his publication was familiar. "I have never been married," his pink and white complexion blushed. "I have never been sailing at all. I have never been to this part of the world. I am very excited to be here and hope that we will all have a very nice vacation." He sat back and then popped up again. "Oh, I would be thrilled to help out in any way I can." Annie noticed that Elliott Barringer rolled his eyes and looked towards the heavens. *Rude bastard*!

"Zandra Hoovenmeyer. So happy to meet all of you and I will try so hard to remember all the names!" She blinked her blue eyes in an exaggerated way. Her bouncy curls quivered. "I am Dutch and from Holland where beautiful tulips grow. As a matter of fact, I help them to grow even more beautiful. I am a horticulturalist and work for the Holland Tulip Company. We grow lovely flowers and ship the flowers and the bulbs all over the world. As Holland is crisscrossed with waterways, I have sailed, but never on a ship like this!" Her enthusiastic voice squeaked with pleasure. "I have not married, yet. And who knows?" She winked at Duncan who raised his eyebrows and grinned. "Maybe next year you will come to *my* wedding" She sat down, giggling and blushing prettily, to chuckles.

"I am Michael Beck. I live in Ireland where the weather is chilly and rainy. Not like this lovely sun and this heat. I think I have to buy some new clothes!" He laughed, pulling at the thick sweater he wore. "This is too…too…heavy for here." Captain Jack gave his wife a glance and she rose and went through the galley door.

"I am a funeral director in Eigan Bay, the third generation to run Beck's Funeral Parlors. I enjoy my work." His pink-cheeked, fresh face beamed at them. Annie thought she'd never seen anyone who looked, on the surface, less like a funeral director. "Although I went on a long voyage, when I graduated from University, on a tramp steamer to India, I have never sailed. I enjoyed the tramp steamer, the good days and even the bad days. I was never seasick and I know I will enjoy this trip, too." The sweat gleamed on his bald head as he sat down.

Emma came back into the deck, her arms filled with blue tee shirts. "Here, Michael," she offered one to him after checking that it said X-L on the tag. "These are our first-day gifts to all of you. The official *The Southern Cross* crew tee shirt, just like mine." She tossed the pile onto the ice chest. "When you're done, come and take one each. We hope you'll like them."

Michael clutched his tee shirt happily. "I will go and change as soon as you," he bowed to the woman who sat next to him, "speak. I think you are the last of us."

"I'll be quick, then. I hate to see a handsome man suffer," she giggled. "OK, I am last, but never the least. I am Corliss Curtis and I am from the UK. This is such an adventure to me! Imagine me, Little Corliss, here on a zillion dollar yacht!" Her frizzy red hair stood on end and she clasped her hands ecstatically in front of her. "I work for The Bank of Scotland. I'm single and available and looking for my Mister Right," she looked around the tables slowly at each face. "Isn't that why we are all really here?

CHAPTER SEVEN

"...the way of a serpent upon a rock..."
The Bible, Ecclesiastes

Carlton dispatched Effalyn to sit in the kitchen with Mrs Marsden, ostensibly to have a restorative cup of tea, but, in truth to pump her, woman-to-woman, about the events leading to her husband's death. Carlton, while Mrs. Marsden was occupied, would be searching their bedroom and the desk drawers for any clues that would give them more than a glimpse into the Marsden's life...their checkbook, their correspondence, the medicines in the bathroom cabinet, the pills in the bedside drawers.

Mrs. Marsden was, at first, reluctant to talk. Effalyn, professing sympathy, urged her to have a small glass of brandy, "So you can relax a little. It's a great restorative for a woman's troubles, my Auntie Jean has always told me." Effalyn bustled around the kitchen and found some small glasses. "Here. One little sip will be good for you, and, you know what? I'm going to join you." Effalyn poured the amber liquid. "I get so tired of having to listen to my boss tell me what to do every minute," she confided. "I don't know what kind of bee he gets in his bonnet over a sad death like your husband's. Silly old man sees a boogie man behind everything." She reached out and patted Mrs. Marsden's arm. "We should be comforting a woman like yourself, not rooting around in your nighties."

Mrs. Marsden nodded morosely. "I just want to get Antony buried respectably. He'd be mortified if he had been in his right mind and saw all this folderol." She drained the glass and poured herself some more.

"How did you meet?" Effalyn leaned forward, arms on the table. *Safe subjects and go slow*, she told herself.

"We met in Melbourne. I was a widow and he and his wife retired and bought the house next to mine. We were good friends for a long time. She, his wife, was very ill...very demanding...complained all the time and made Antony's life difficult."

"He had to cater to her?" Effalyn's voice was warm with sympathy. "Tough to be caring for someone like that. I remember when my auntie had to care for my uncle. He was such a difficult man. Wanted her to stay by his side all the time. She never could even go to the bathroom without him whining about where she was." Effalyn sipped at her brandy.

"No one understands how hard it is," Mrs. Marsden complained. "I had no life of my own." Effalyn tsk-tsked in womanly understanding.

"How did Mr. Marsden's first wife die? Heart attack?" Effalyn's question was delicate.

"A stroke, I believe," Mrs. Marsden sniffed.

"And you were a widow at the time. You must have been a comfort to him in his grief." Effalyn touched Mrs. Marsden's hand. "Thank goodness he had you!"

"Oh, yes. He needed me. He came to me and said that he had always admired me..." she blinked. "Not that he and I did anything...nothing...before, you know..."

"Oh, of course. I can tell that you are not that kind of woman." *Oh, Effalyn*, she scolded herself, *so many lies you are telling today*!

Mrs. Marsden sniffed. "It's hard."

"Mmmm," Effalyn said soothingly. "And how will you possibly manage now? I mean, this is a beautiful bungalow. In such a nice area. How can you afford, I mean...I don't want to pry into your personal business, but how can you afford to live like you did when Antony was alive? I know how it can be... my poor mother, when my father passed, had to come and live with me. She lost his pension and his savings just melted away with the funeral costs," Effalyn sniffed a bit herself. "And then, oh, my, she was so lonely!"

"Antony was so thoughtful. He took out a large insurance policy when we moved to the islands. He always said that he wanted me cared for, even after he was gone." She touched her eyes with her fingers and sniffed again. "He always told me that he loved me more than he loved his first wife." She touched her eyes, but Effalyn noted that they were dry. "And, he willed me the house, too. There's no mortgage, so I can afford to live just the way I want to...I mean, the way I am used to." She glanced up at Effalyn, but Effalyn was looking down at the tabletop.

"Thank the Lord that he was so considerate of you. He must have loved you very much."

Mrs. Marsden finished the last drops in her glass. "He was a gentleman, even to the end. Just a few days before he...sniff...died, he told me that he would always take care of me."

Remarkable. Man has dementia, and yet he's capable of telling her that he'll keep her in style when he's gone! Effalyn kept her suspicious thoughts to herself. *The Boss is gonna love all of this! Proves nothing, however.* "Such a thoughtful man. I sure hope you can find someone else one of these days...after your grieving has settled. Someone that you can share your life with. It's tough for a woman alone."

"I've been a lucky woman," Mrs. Marsden confided. Behind her, there was rat-tat-tat on the kitchen door. Before Mrs. Marsden could get up, the door swung open and a bald-headed man came in.

"Hi, Ellie. It's me...Oh," he stopped as he saw Effalyn. "I'm sorry, um, ha, Ellen. Didn't realize that you had company." Effalyn smiled at him and noted that he was somewhat discomfited. She looked at him and saw that he was perhaps ten years older than Mrs. Marsden, a man with a barrel-body and short arms and legs that looked disproportionate. Mrs. Marsden's mouth opened and then shut. She seemed disturbed and uneasy. The silence stretched with Mrs. Marsden and the man...was it the neighbor, Effalyn wondered? The one who was so, um, helpful?

"Good day," Effalyn spoke into the vacuum. "I'm Effalyn Penn and I'm here to comfort Mrs. Marsden." She held her hand out to the man. He shook it briefly. His handshake was damp. "I'm with the local police."

"I'm, um, Neil Zuster. I live near, um, not too near, but, um, on the next street away with my wife, um, Damson. We're from South Africa. Um..."

Aha! thought Effalyn. *Not too near, huh*?

"Oh, Neil. I am so glad that you decided to stop in." Mrs. Marsden got up, twisting her dress in her nerveless hands. "We were just..." She appealed to Effalyn. "Neil has been a god-send to me. Making sure that I don't get too sad."

"I can see that he is invaluable," Effalyn agreed.

***

Arlis' phone bill nearly rivaled the National Debt. She spoke almost daily with Leslie Janes, her mother, Carole Singletary and ten or twenty of her friends, all of whom offered (except for Leslie) unneeded and unwanted advice. The guest list was growing by leaps and bounds, and what was initiated as a simple wedding on the beach, was growing to hysterical splendor.

"Are there enough rooms for everyone?" Arlis moaned to Leslie. "I get nightmares thinking that my mother will have to sleep out on the beach under a coconut tree!"

"We've got everyone who called taken care of." Leslie soothed. "The few that can't be put up here are going to the Pelican Guest Houses. They help us out and we help them, when there's a big event and not enough rooms. Have no fear, your mother has a nice single room, with a queen-sized bed, all to herself..." here Leslie giggled, "Or, should she meet someone nice from Don's side of the family...who knows?"

"Ooooh! Shudder at the thought," Arlis giggled back. "And the food?"

"OK, here's the menu, and I'm going to e-mail it all to you as soon as we're off the phone so you can check it out and make any changes. Rehearsal is a barbecue on the beach. Grilled chicken, fish and ribs, salad, rice...." She read the menu and then switched to the Luau that would take place after the wedding. "Grilled Caribbean lobsters, two large steamship beef roasts, roasted pork fillets...."

"And the music?" Arlis' panic came through the wires. "This is so hard, doing all this by telephone! I wish we were sitting at your bar like last year!"

"You will be, you will be!" Despite hosting hundreds of people in the intervening year, Leslie remembered Arlis and Don well. Arlis had been so puppy-dog cute, bouncy and happy and obviously delighted with everything that came her way. Don had been a memorable individual, with his long, skinny legs and passion for leather vests and hats that were more suited to a ranch in Texas than the beaches of the Virgin Islands. Don's eyes had never left Arlis' face and Arlis had confided to Leslie that he had slipped a poem to her under her cabin door every morning. The fact that they were going to be married came as no surprise to anyone who had watched their obvious romance growing under the palm trees.

"Ooooh, God! I hope everything goes well!" Arlis sounded just this side of hysteria.

"Keep your hair on." Leslie laughed. "We do this all the time, you know. I have an island band for the rehearsal dinner. They'll do reggae music and island-type rock and roll. Dancing on the beach. Open bar an hour before dinner with hors d'oeuvres, open bar during dinner and open bar after dinner. Everyone will be so snockered that they will remember this as the best time they've ever had, bar none, if you'll excuse the pun!"

"I'll drink to that!" Arlis was feeling better. "And the music for the wedding itself?"

"The island chamber orchestra will be set up on the deck, overlooking the beach. They'll do some nice stuff before the wedding, like Pachabel's Canon and that sort of thing, do the Wedding March as you parade down from the deck onto the beach with Captain Jack and then do the Triumphal March from Aida as a recessional. The orchestra will play during the luau, and the island band will take over for dancing afterwards. Again, open bar and open bar and open bar."

"Sounds great, barring, ha ha, any unforeseen problems."

"It will go like silk," Leslie promised. "We have a little entertainment when the band takes a break. I forgot to mention it to you. Rebecca Reese, who operates the local dance studio, has a group of local dancers who are going to put on a little show for you. Do some limbo and some other do-dahs calculated to make the dead get up and boogie." Leslie was gratified at Arlis' gasp of pure pleasure.

"Cool!"

"Everything OK with your gown?" Leslie now was anxious.

"It's just beautiful. Has a long train and I've been practicing with a bedsheet so as to not fall flat on my face."

"You're gonna be gorgeous. Are you ordering flowers?"

"Some jasmine for my hair and local informal bouquets for the tables. I called the Spanish Town Floral Shop. Are they reliable?"

"They're fine. I just made a note here to check with them on Tuesday and remind them of the time we'll need the flowers here." Leslie made yet another note on the voluminous pad of paper marked "Don and Arlis – Wedding" "What else? What have you been doing to relax yourself?"

"*Relax*! What relax? We just did the American Legion USO show here last week. Don was the Commander there for many years and loves to put on a show to raise money for the troops."

"I didn't know he was a show business kind of man. With his hats and that vest, I thought he was a cowboy from out west."

"He was. He came from Colorado."

A giggle exploded from Leslie. "Is he wearing the cowboy hat at the wedding?"

"He'd love to. I insisted on a beautiful grey silk tuxedo, but who knows? I think he's going to surprise me and wear a special hat. I saw a bill...an astronomical bill...from that western goods place that he always uses." Her giggle was infectious. "His brother-in-law, Tom, is going to stand up with him and he's gonna look pretty spiffy too."

"So does Don sing or dance in the USO shows?" Somehow, Leslie just couldn't picture lanky, laconic Don dancing around on stage.

"No, he does back-stage stuff. Just like I've done with the Lyric Theater. Neither of us is *that* extroverted. We're both back stage people. We do tickets, props, make-up, costumes...everything but strut around or emote on stage."

Leslie stretched. "Gotta go...oh, one more thing...who's special that will be here? We have this blackboard to greet people. Put their names down so they feel special...I'd like to be sure that we have the names of your greatest friends..."

"Goodness, you'll need a huge blackboard! I have friends from my hometown of Winona, Minnesota. Ever hear of it? ... I thought not. All with Norwegian-German names, all with dark hair and brown-green eyes. Buddies from my college years at Valparaiso University, friends left over from my wild days in New York, Boston and San Francisco. Even two old pals from my memorable life in Paris are coming. and, of course, Carole and Esther, my best friends. Oh, and my co-workers from the Vermont Department of Education."

"Geez. Is there room for anyone on Don's side?"

"Oh, he's got a mob coming, too. His kids, Jim, Amy and Todd, a few family members from Nebraska, some of the poets from Don's poetry group, some good old boys from the American Legion, a couple of old Air Force buddies, some co-workers, people who worked on shows with him.... his sister...oh, we'll send you a loooong list."

"My hand is cramped. I really have to go. Sixteen people have just shown up for dinner. Yow!"

"Bye, Leslie. Thank you for everything," Arlis was fervent.

"Bye, Arlis. Don't worry about *anything*! Love ya!"

And they finally hung up.

***

Madeline and her brother Mitchell shared baby sitting duties on Tuesday. Mitchell's pockets were empty as he had spent the cash his father paid him for helping in the store on a computer game and Christmas was fast approaching. His sister, feeling a surge of brotherly love, offered to share Lara's generous pay if Mitchell would share the pushing of Mikayla's carriage. As always, they stopped at Aunt Fanny's to collect a bag of oatmeal cookies and three cans of grapefruit soda.

"Boooat!" Mikayla screeched, as they plopped onto the sand. "Big."

"Big *white* boat," Mitchell wanted to increase Mikayla's vocabulary.

"Big wide boooat," Mikayla obliged. Then, getting to her feet, she lurched toward the water's edge. "Sfim."

"She's really learning a lotta words," Mitchell leaned back on the blanket. "Now, I'm gonna learn a new word…nap." He crossed his arms over his eyes, shielding them from the hot sun. "A great word – nap."

Madeline scooped up a handful of sand, and in a sisterly fashion, trickled it over Mitchell's chest. He flicked the sand away and wiggled into a more comfortable position. Madeline scooped up more sand.

"Ess is for snake," they heard Mikayla say. "Ess. Ess." Madeline looked up to see why she said that particular letter.

"Oh, my *God*!" Madeline jumped to her feet.

"Fifty cents to me for swearing!" Mitchell mumbled.

Madeline kicked him and ran down the beach. "Get Help, Mitch!" she screamed. "It's a *snake*!

Mitchell, usually a slow and purposeful mover, leaped up. He saw his sister grab Mikayla and drag her up, yelling all the while. Standing, he could see the ribbon of color that writhed along the water's edge. "Damn!" Mitchell swore too. He was a good student in natural science and recognized the colorful bands that marked the serpent. "It's a goddamn *coral* snake!" He looked wildly around for some kind of weapon and found some driftwood pieces under a bougainvillea. He grabbed two and ran to his sister.

"Stay *here*, Mikayla. Don't *move*!" Maddie's voice was sharp. Mikayla, a bit frightened now, sat down and stuck her thumb in her mouth.

Mitchell waved the sticks and walked carefully, watching the snake. Madeline joined him and took one of the sticks from him. "It's a *coral* snake!" she whispered in a voice that almost screamed.

"It didn't *bite* her, did it?"

"No, but it *might* have!" Madeline danced on her bare feet. "Thank goodness, she's fine."

"What should we do? Can we kill it with these without being bitten ourselves?"

"I sure hope so. Come on." The two children slipped on their sandals.

The snake, feeling the sound of their footsteps through the sand, stopped moving. The tiny head rose. Glittery, flat eyes watched them.

"OK." They moved closer to the snake, branches upraised. "When I say now, we'll both smash at it. Be careful, don't let it get near your feet." Mitchell's hair was standing on end and Maddie's eyes were fervent with effort. "OK?"

"OK."

"One, two, three...*Now!*" The sticks slammed down, hitting the snake hard. Mikayla's shriek rang out, bringing Mrs. Leuzarder out of the school house. She gasped as she saw Mitchell and Maddie, hysterical, hitting and hitting and hitting the snake. "There! There! *There!*"

Mitchell stopped. "I think we killed him good," he said laconically. "He's certainly dead."

"Damn snake!" Madeline raised the stick again, just to be sure.

"Oooh, hoo," her brother crowed. "You swore, you swore!"

"I'll hit you if you don't shut up!" She waved the stick, with its gory bits of smashed coral snake stuck onto the end, at him. "Of course I swore! The damn snake could have bit Mikayla!" Mitchell pretended to be cowed.

Maddie hit the snake one more time, just to be sure. She grinned with triumphant glee, whirling her stick in the air like a club. "OK. We got him."

Mrs. Leuzarder ran down the beach on her arthritic legs as best she could, stopping to check that Mikayla was unhurt. "Ess is for snake," Mikayla told her gleefully.

"Thank goodness for Sesame Street," Mitchell told Mrs. Leuzarder.

***

Carlton and Effalyn's patrol car bypassed the road and drove over the sand to the huddled group. "What happened?" Carlton jumped out of the car. "We got a report of a poisonous snake. Anyone get bitten?"

"Nope." Mitchell told him with careless nonchalance. "We killed it."

"You *did*? Killed it? Brave kid." Carlton patted Mitchell on his head. Mitchell smirked.

"Not just *him*," Maddie rolled her eyes, glaring at her brother and wanting some praise from the police. "Me, too."

"You're a brave girl. You two did very well. You are both heroes." Carlton patted Madeline's shoulder. "I think we should get a little write-up in the local paper about watching for snakes and maybe commending the two of you for your fast action and courage."

"I haven't heard any sightings of coral snakes around here for years," Effalyn looked around nervously.

"I checked, Ma'am," Mitchell assured her. "I looked under all the bushes and there was only that one."

"Good," Effalyn nodded. "Let's hope he's an orphan."

Effalyn walked home with Mitchell and Maddie, helping to steer Mikayla's chair. "I'll explain to Lara what happened and then you can tell her yourselves." She stroked Maddie's head. "You two were very brave, very quick-thinking. "Your mother and dad will be proud of you."

***

"A freaking *coral* snake! I haven't seen a coral snake outside of a dictionary down here in thirty years. What the hell was it doing there on the beach?" Carlton's appetite was sharpened by the day's events and Rebecca's *rouladen* and potato pancakes disappeared as fast as she shoveled them onto his plate.

"I didn't even know there were coral snakes around here." Rebecca touched Niccola's shoulder. 'Be careful, honey. If you're near any rocks or bushes, keep an eye out for any snakes."

Their daughter, nine years old and unafraid of anything, nodded her head and promised to be on the lookout for whatever might come her way.

"It's an assault from Mother Nature!" Carlton exploded. "First a coconut kills Two-Tone, then some plants kill poor old Mr. Marsden, and now we have a coral snake! What's going on here?"

Rebecca looked at Niccola. Niccola looked at Rebecca. Both of them shrugged and helped themselves to another potato pancake.

***

The telephone rang just as Effalyn and Carlton sat down to hash over the Marsden case. "Hey, Carlton. This is Lynn…the Coach, you know?"

"Hi, Lynn. What's up?"

"Remember those leather jackets that disappeared a few weeks ago?"

"Of course I remember," Carlton made a disgusted noise. "I'm sure it was one of those rotten boys from over Spanish Town, but I can't get anywhere with any of them. Clammed up tight, they all are and stiff with pride at stymieing me. I'd like to kick their collective delinquent asses."

"Bring back the rack any ole day, right, Chief?" Lynn chuckled.

"Don't let the Island News hear me say this, but, hell yeah." Carlton laughed, albeit with frustration. "What can I do for you?"

"I want you to come over to the store." There was a note of deep satisfaction in the Coach's voice. "I have a nice surprise for you."

On the ride over, Effalyn went over Doctor Fullbright's autopsy findings. "Doc said he's never seen so many toxic plant seeds in one corpse in his entire life." Effalyn shook her head. "He also told me that he was going to write this whole thing up and have it published in the medical journals because no one would believe that one poor man could ingest so many poisons."

"What did he find?" Carlton turned the patrol car into the Big Fish Harbor area.

"Ricin…that's from the castor bean plant. Common name down here is the coffee-tree bean. Causes nausea, vomiting, convulsions, coma and death." She looked out the window at the beautiful foliage and plants that were massed on the roadside.

"Nice…great way to go."

"The beans are deadly. They have a very hard shell, though," she read. "A person could probably swallow a couple, and if they didn't chew them up, might not even get sick."

"But lucky old Mr. Marsden chewed them?"

"You guessed it. Doc found at least ten of the beans, all masticated. Enough to kill six grown men."

"Hmmm."

"Doc says that there was a famous true murder case in London in 1979 that most likely used ricin." She checked her notes. "This

Bulgarian man, Georgi Markov, who was a spy or a dissident, was walking down the street. He felt a sting on his leg. Another man was passing by and he had an umbrella...later, they figured that the umbrella had a point on the end with a pellet of ricin in it and some kind of tiny explosive device. The umbrella man probably stuck Markov in the leg with the point of his umbrella, released the ricin dart, and continued strolling down the street, probably twirling his umbrella." She stopped for a moment and shook her head. "God! What will they think of next?"

"What happened to Markov?"

"The little pinprick on his leg became infected and he died four days later. The thing about ricin is...well, it is metabolized quickly and disappears from the body in a day or two. The pathologists found the tiny metal capsule, but no trace at all of the poison. Lucky for us that we found the beans in Mr. Marsden right away."

"Not so lucky for poor old Mr. Marsden, though."

"Mr. Marsden seems to be the most unlucky human being that I have ever heard of. Seventy thousand plants on the islands, seven poisonous ones...and Bingo! He eats three of the poisoned ones!"

"Amazing. Amazing." Effalyn muttered darkly. "Well, can you believe he only ate three, not all seven? How did she miss the other four?"

"Now, now...we don't know that he didn't just happen upon them, do we? Poor bastard, how did he miss the rest of them? What do you think? Accident or murder?"

Carlton parked the car in front of Island Mo-Ped Rentals and Husker Sporting Goods. "Donno," Effalyn shrugged. Let me read the rest of Doc's report." She flipped some of the pages over.

She looked up and continued; "Well, poor Mr. Marsden didn't have an iceberg's chance in hell. I don't think he ate six or seven poisoned things, but he sure ate a lot of them! Even if he survived the castor beans, he had also ingested some rhododendron roots..." she thought for a moment, ..."Did he dig up a root and eat it? He was old and shaky and disoriented. How did he get rhododendron roots? This whole thing smells to high heaven." She made a tsking sound and continued reading; "Rhododendron produces vomiting, seizures, diarrhea, and paralysis...all kinds of horrid things." She laughed, a harsh sound. "And the old man also had some *other* kinds of toxic seeds in his digestive tract. No way he could have survived *one* of these poisons, much less three!"

"Either he was the unluckiest camper in the woods or someone….our nice lady, Ellen?.. .*really* wanted him to die in the worst way possible."

"And Doc says that there might just be a few more things floating around in Mr. Marsden's stomach cavity, or what used to be his stomach cavity, but he needs the lab in Miami to finish testing the rest of the stomach contents, the liver and…oh, a few other organs."

"Was he really senile, I wonder?"

"The lab is doing the Alzheimer's test on his brain. That will take about two weeks or so, but, even if they get some results, they're not always accurate. Doc says Alzheimer's is very difficult to diagnose positively."

"Sheesh!" They got out of the car and went into the store.

Irene Sorensen's cheerful Midwestern smile and flat vowels from Nebraska greeted them. "Hello! Wait until you see what Lynn found!" She pointed towards the back of the store.

CHAPTER EIGHT

The Pharmacist
A calm, respectable lady went into the pharmacy, walked right up to the pharmacist, looked straight into his eyes, and said, "I would like to buy some cyanide."
The pharmacist asked, "Why in the world do you need cyanide?"
The lady replied, "I need it to poison my husband."
The pharmacist's eyes got big, and he exclaimed, "Lord, have mercy! I can't give you cyanide to kill your husband! That's against the law! I would lose my license! They'll throw both of us in jail! All kinds of bad things will happen! Absolutely not! You CANNOT have any cyanide!"
The lady reached into her purse and pulled out a picture of her husband in bed with the pharmacist's wife. The pharmacist looked at the picture and replied, "Well, now. That's different.
You didn't tell me you had a *prescription!*"

"While Kat cleans up, Ducky will give you all a tour of the boat. The heads…the toilets for those of you who are new to boating…are electric and easy to flush, but we have a rule for toilets on a boat. 'Do not put anything into them, other than toilet paper, that hasn't been eaten and digested by you.' We'll all save ourselves some trouble if we follow that little rule." He laughed.

Ducky agreed with a rueful face. "You can't imagine what trouble it is if they get clogged up. Nosir! And as I am the one who gets to mess around down there, I will personally kill anyone who forgets!"

Captain Jack continued, "We don't have too many other rules out here. The big rule is to be careful; this is a boat. Everyone has to look out for themselves. Don't do stupid things, don't annoy your fellow passengers or me, Ducky or Kat. Especially me." He laughed, but no one was fooled.

"We don't mind if you drink, hell, we don't mind if you get a bit shot in the ass, but please, don't get so drunk that you're a danger to yourself or others. When push comes to shove, I *am* the Captain. In any emergency or dangerous situation, you will all listen to me and obey me immediately." He laughed gently. "I don't expect that these sorts of things will ever happen, but, I *do* want you to know that I can wrestle an alligator if needed."

His head moved from side to side. "Be sensible and there will never be a problem. You are all adults and I expect you to act like adults." He sat back. "Ah, and one more very important reminder; Illegal drugs in the BVI are *illegal*. Remember that our laws and prisons are not like those in the United States or Great Britain or anywhere else. I guarantee that you won't like the prison hereabouts, and you won't have any rights or one-call-to-my-lawyer as you do elsewhere. These prisons *stink*. And they never let you out, especially if it is drug related." His voice was stern and he obviously meant what he said. Everyone was frozen into their seat, although Suzie squirmed around. Jack looked at each of them, meeting each passenger's eye. "Any questions?"

No one had any questions at all.

***

"Come on back here," The Coach beckoned to Carlton and Effalyn. "Just wait and see what I found today!" His pale blue eyes behind his squared off glasses gleamed with delight. He brought them into the stockroom. Piled neatly on shelves were rows and rows of boxed sport shoes. Lynn pointed to four white boxes that he had taken down. "One of my football players came in this morning and needed a pair of sneakers. He has a big foot, size 13 American. I brought out a couple of styles that I thought he'd like."

"Mmmm?" Carlton asked.

"Ha!" Lynn threw back his head and laughed. "Here, let me put on these gloves so that I don't mess up your evidence…" He took a pair of yellow kitchen gloves and pulled them over his big hands. "OK, now I won't spoil anything." He opened one of the boxes.

Inside, lying in the tissue paper, was an old pair of sneakers.

Lynn opened the second box. "And here…" Effalyn backed up, holding her nose.

"Eeeeyuu! Who was wearing *those*?"

'Who do ya think?" Lynn laughed, a big, booming sound. "The little bastards who stole those leather jackets from me three weeks ago, doncha think?" Carlton's mouth dropped open as he realized what the Coach was showing him. He reared back and began to laugh.

"No shit!"

"Yea, shit! The little stupid pricks… 'scuse me, Eff…must have decided that they'd not only scarf the jackets, but that they'd treat themselves to new shoes, too!" He opened the third and fourth boxes. Each held a disreputable pair of used sneakers.

"Oh, my, my." Carlton's face held an expression of glee. "And so stupid that they left their old ones behind." He did a tiny dance of glee. "And I'll bet I know just whose crappy sneakers these are. Sid Lefferts, Davis Petrosky, Hecky Ruthers and...what was the other kid's name...?"

"Lemuel." Effalyn's smile was like the sunshine. "Lemuel Gandolph. The four scourges of Spanish Town." She rummaged in her handbag and took out two pairs of protective gloves. She handed one to Carlton, put down her purse and pulled on her own pair. She lifted out one sneaker. "Smelly. Just like its owner." She held the sneaker away from her and made a face. "There will be gorgeous fingerprints on the box...and inside the sneaker...People don't realize that toes have fingerprints too..." She looked perplexed. "Or should I say toeprints?" She peered inside the sneaker. "But wait! What's *this*?" She held the sneaker open and pointed. "My, my. Hecky Ruthers. Nice of him to write his name on his old sneakers." She handed the sneaker to Carlton and picked up its mate. "And on both of them. What a thoughtful lad!"

"No!" The Coach was ecstatic. "His freaking *name*?"

"His freaking name." Effalyn put the pair back in the box and then carefully, one by one, examined the rest of the sneakers. "and, I will presume, his freakin' fingerprints!"

"I love it!" Carlton guffawed. "I just love it!"

"Sid's name is on both of his. The other two probably didn't know how to spell their names."

"May we borrow these for a while?" Carlton bowed to the Coach.

"With my most gracious permission. Who the heck would want them back?"

"Got a nice, new plastic bag?"

"One here with my logo on it." Lynn handed the bag to Effalyn. She placed the boxes carefully in it.

'Let's take a little ride over to Spanish Town," Carlton graciously ushered Effalyn out of the store, stopping only to plant a big, smacking kiss on Irene's cheek. "I want to speak with Chief Halliburton. He's gonna love it all as much as I do. We soon will have four young men who will be spending a lot of time in prison waiting for the years to pass."

Effalyn giggled. "And the years will pass without them getting any new sneakers!"

***

The passengers settled their belongings in their cabins. The cabins were located in each of the two hulls with the men's on the left and the women's on the right. There were four private single cabins, which could also be used as cabins for a married couple or for children, and six double cabins for the passengers. The singles held a queen sized bunk and the doubles, two single bunks. Each cabin was outfitted with a private head, shower and sink, and each had ample storage. The cabins were not particularly spacious, but each held its occupant or occupants in comfort. In addition, each cabin sported an easily reachable window hatch that opened onto the deck. The cabins were gleaming with pale yellow wood cabinets and each bed sported a dark blue coverlet with the name *The Southern Cross* embroidered at the top. The cabins were also equipped with air conditioning unit controls, electric lights, fans and electrical outlets. "Wooo! These are spiffy!" exclaimed Corliss.

In addition to the passengers' cabins, there were two narrow crew cubbies at the rear of the boat. One was for Captain Jack's use, and the other shared by Ducky and Kat.

"Lucky you," Vinny enthused to Ducky. Ducky merely grinned and raised his eyebrows up and down.

From the spacious cockpit, which was shaded with a blue and white striped bimini awning, the passengers could open a sliding glass door and step down into the main saloon and galley. The galley was state-of-the-art, with gleaming stainless steel ovens, an ice machine and dishwashers. The cabinets were of shiny rosewood and the countertops were polished granite. The rest of the room was equipped with two large oval tables surrounded by comfortable banquette seating with storage underneath.

"We put the extra beer and water under the lazarettes…what's a lazarette? It's these," Ducky pointed to the banquette benches. 'Everything on a boat has a nautical name. The toilets are the head, the kitchen is the galley, a rope is a line and a line can be a sheet…" The passengers looked confused…and Ducky laughed again. "You'll learn, believe me. We'll make able bodied seamen of you scurvy landlubbers in a day or two."

In an alcove off the main saloon, was a desk, with charts, the boat's communication devices, a CD player and the electrical switches. "This is the Navigation Station, more commonly called the Nav Station. We'd prefer that no one move these things around unless the Captain asks you to." Ducky waved at the desk area. "You'll become familiar with all of this, but get yourself acclimated to the rest of the boat first and then you can decipher the mysteries of the Nav Station." Ducky's voice was easy and pleasant, but it was obvious that he had just warned them to not touch anything in or around the Nav Station.

He showed them the lockers up at the bow..."The front of the boat is called the bow..." He took them up front where the anchors lay with their chains coiled. "Those big nets are called trampolines, and you guys will most likely stretch out there a lot." He waved his arm. "Often, Captain Jack and a few hardy souls like to sleep out here on the trampolines at night and gaze up at the stars."

Annie bounced and balanced herself on the wide netting straps of the trampoline, then dropped down and lay on the netting, her arms crossed under her head. "Sleep like this?"

"Yup, but with a special sort of sleeping bag."

"Sounds wonderful. I think I'll try it." Annie squinted up at the sky. "I'll bet the stars are spectacular."

"Amazing. The constellations are very different from the ones you are used to in North America, although you'll see a few familiar ones like the Big Dipper."

"Great!"

"There are no lights at all at night out on the water. It is velvety dark and the stars seem to loom huge. You'll see The Southern Cross, a necklace of stars, lots of shooting stars and even a satellite or two circling the earth."

"Really?" Annie squeaked. "Oh, heaven!" She realized her unintentional pun and began to giggle. Ducky thought she was a thoroughly nice woman.

"Only problem is the sudden squalls that pop up once in a while. That's why Captain Jack has devised these special sleeping bags." Ducky winked at her and helped her to her feet. "OK, now, let's all go to the stern of the boat...that's the back end..." He showed them the lazarettes in the cockpit which housed the snorkeling equipment and the custom-made stainless steel Weber barbecue grill, the storage at the stern and on the swim deck, and allowed them to peek under the hatches at the tiny, immaculate rooms which cradled the steel and brass engines.

"The two silvery blow-up boats are called Zodiacs and they hang up, on these hooks called davits. The davits keep them neatly hung up out of the water when we are not using them. Naturally, the Zodiacs have pet names. This one is Betelgeuse and this one is Sirius. Named for two stars. We try to bring the boat up to a dock when we are visiting a harbor, but sometimes, the docks can't accommodate anything as big as *The Southern Cross*. Then, we have to moor the boat out and use the Zodiacs to ferry ourselves back and forth from the shore."

He turned and continued his lecture. "*The Southern Cross* is a custom made catamaran. Eighty-five feet long. Made in South Africa..." Ducky bowed to Martha and Claudia,... "At the Seven Seas' yacht basin there. Captain Jack and Emma sailed it over here three years ago. The cost?" He grinned. "A lot of dough, as you Americans say. A lot."

"It's magnificent," Elwyn touched the smooth wood of the rails with reverence.

"This is Captain Jack's third boat. His first was a 30 foot Cat. He could take three couples and he and Emma did everything. The second boat was a 45-footer. Held four or five couples. Five if they were friendly." His laugh rang out. "And three years ago, he upgraded to this little love boat."

"What a life!" Hosea breathed with envy.

"Yeah, but it's a lotta work. The Captain, Kat and I are on duty for fifteen days. No breaks, no days off, just work." Ducky sat down and took a plastic bottle of water out of the ice chest and gestured to his group to help themselves. "It's a lot of fun, sure, but we get tired toward the end." He took a deep swig. "And a lot depends on the group. Some groups are fun and easy from the minute they come on board to the minute they get off. Some are a bit more stressful. Depends." He drained the bottle. "I can see you guys are going to be one of the good ones. Piece of cake."

"I hope so," Hosea nodded, his eyes earnest. "I hope so."

***

"Ok, just hold that line," Captain Jack handed the line to Duncan. "Keep it taut...good...good." The powerful twin engines throbbed. A few of the passengers were sprawled on the trampolines at the bow, some were watching the cast-off with great interest, and one or two were inside the saloon reading. Ducky held the stern line and Captain Jack slid into the captain's chair at the right side of the open cockpit.

Emma kissed him and waved good-bye to the passengers. "See you all in two days on Virgin Gorda!" She jumped lightly off the boat.

"Ready, Mr. Duck?"

"Aye, Cappie!" Ducky cast off the stern line and swung himself into the cockpit with strength and grace that Hosea envied. On the dock, Emma stooped and neatly coiled the line. She straightened up and waved as the huge boat, sails down, turned into the center of the harbor and then, a few moments later, pointed out to the mouth of the harbor toward the Sir Francis Drake Channel.

"That island is Frenchman's Cay, and that one is Little Thatch. The big green thing over there is another country entirely. It's St. John, part of the United States Virgin Islands. We'll be passing Pelican Island in a while and then you'll see our destination, Norman Island." Captain Jack kept a running commentary. "As soon as we're out in the Channel, we'll get the mains'l and the jib up."

"Treasure Island, here we come!" Kat came out from the galley with drinks and snacks to keep body and soul together on the one hour journey to their night's mooring.

***

"You nose around with the neighbors," Carlton instructed Effalyn. "You know what to do, right?" She nodded firmly. "I'll talk with those...what's their names? Zusters."

Damson Zuster watched him as he walked toward her door. She saw a medium-sized man, perhaps in his late thirties, dressed in a blue short-sleeved shirt and dark pants. His crinkly hair wreathed a small bald spot. He wore dark sunglasses, so she couldn't see his eyes. He terrified her and she clutched her sweater to her neck.

"Mrs. Zuster? I'm Detective Inspector Reese." He held up his identification folder.

She nodded, reluctant, and slowly opened the door. Carlton stepped into the air-conditioned coolness. She was afraid. He could smell her fear. She looked strained and sickly. He smiled pleasantly. "I'm here to try to get a little bit of background about poor Mr. Marsden."

"Come in," she stepped back. "What can *I* tell you?"

"Mrs. Marsden tells me that you and your husband were their best friends. I thought you could clarify a few points for me." He lowered his voice and looked around. "She's so upset, you understand. I hate to ask her too many questions and intrude on her grief."

She nodded with grudging agreement and motioned him into the living area. The house was a substantial one and the rooms were scrupulously clean…almost museum clean, he noted. Not a magazine nor a book nor any flowers anywhere. The chairs looked uncomfortable and brand new, the floor spotless. Mrs. Zuster, what the heck was her name? Something really odd…like a fruit or something…ah, Damson, Damson the plum, he grinned to himself. Unlike a nice, juicy plum, this Damson was a dried up stick. Lackluster hair, screwed into a knot, a plain, ugly green-colored dress, ankle socks and utilitarian shoes….didn't look like a fun girl.

"Thank you for assisting us," His eyes asked if he could sit down. She nodded and sat down herself, perched on the edge of a stiff chair. Carlton chose a matching chair. He took out his note book. "Sure is hot out there," he began. "This is lovely," he gazed around the room with every expression of envy. "My wife would be green with envy. She'd love a home as beautiful as this." *Was I putting it on too much? Nah. She was obviously house proud and even seemed to thaw a bit with all the compliments.* "Cool and everything so nice. How long have you and Mr. Zuster lived here?"

"Four years." She felt safe enough with his question.

"Where did you live before you came to the BVI?"

"Johannesburg. South Africa." She relaxed slightly.

"Do you miss it…have relatives there?"

"I didn't like it there. We are originally from Holland and I wish we had moved back."

"Holland! What a beautiful place that must be! I wanted to go there last year on vacation." He leaned forward. "I'm a big garden man and I just think that tulips are the most beautiful flower." She smiled, a faint smile, but it was a beginning.

"Yes, they are beautiful."

"I wish we could grow them here," he sighed, "but…"

"It is too hot. The heat…too much." She joined in his sigh. "I miss them."

"Gotta go where the hubby's work is. Too bad."

"No. He does not work. We moved here because I am ill and needed a hot climate, but not a dry heat like Johannesburg."

"You're not well?" His voice was concerned. "Is it better here? Your health, I mean?" He leaned in closer towards her.

"It is better. My respirations...I need a lot of moisture to breathe."

"Well, you poor little thing." He made a face of worry and she actually smiled at him.

"Thank you. You are kind."

"Ah, now, Mrs. Zuster. I need you to help me. Please tell me about your neighbors. Tell me about Mr. Marsden and his wandering."

"Well, I do not know too much. They were more Neil's friends than mine." She made a sour face and Carlton wondered what she was *really* thinking. "He is...Neil...he was an accountant and he has helped Mrs. Marsden to do her bookkeeping and take care of her house expenses and so forth when Mr. Marsden could no longer function."

"Oh, how nice and neighborly. Did he spend much time over there? I mean, would he know more about Mr. Marsden's sickness?"

"Yes. I didn't visit much. But Neil, he was always stopping there." Carlton watched her carefully. Was there resentment in her tone?

"With you so ill, was it all right that he spend so much time away from you?"

"I didn't mind." She shrugged, listless.

"He was a good neighbor, but I think...as a married man...that he should be with you." He wondered if he had gone too far.

She turned her face toward him and he thought he saw tears glistening. "He...he...he was always helping others."

"My wife would kill me if I spent a lot of time at ...well, I really shouldn't even talk to you like this...but she'd kill me," He shrugged sheepishly, "if I was over at a neighbor lady's house a lot." His shoulders shrugged. "But my wife is the jealous type." He laughed quietly. "She's from New York in America and not very understanding when it comes to helping a pretty neighbor." Damson's head jerked up and then she lowered her glance. Carlton thought he had suggested enough. He changed tactics. "Enough of that stuff. I didn't mean to put you and my jealous wife in the same basket." His laugh was nervous. "Let's go back to important things. I want to know more about Mr. Marsden's wanderings. Did you ever see him wander off? Maybe toward the beach area or out into the gardens?"

"I never saw him."

"Oh? Gee, I understood that he was always walking away from home. That he went down to the beach."

"I never saw." Her face was stern and her chin was up in the air.

"Ah, then...I'll have to speak with your husband. Where is he, by the way?"

"He is at the Marsden's. He is helping to pack the clothing." Carlton let his face show what he thought of that. Damson's mouth twisted.

"Well, I'll just sit with you for a few minutes. Maybe he'll be back soon."

She sat, unblinking and not offering a word. Carlton tried again. "I really like this house. Did you choose it?"

"No, Neil chose it. He liked it too."

"My wife would really like to live up here where the breeze is always blowing. Are the houses up here, um, uh, expensive?" *Geez, Rebecca would likely kill him if she knew how he was bandying her name around.*

"I think they are. This house, which belongs to me, cost me three hundred thousand dollars when we first came." He wondered why, after her reticence, that she had offered such detailed and intimate information.

"My! I'll have to tell my wife to save her pennies, won't I?" He tried a little laugh.

She gazed at him and then got up. "I am tired now and want to lie down. Can you come to see Neil another time?"

"Certainly, Mrs. Zuster. Thank you for your time and kind consideration." He stood up. "I'll call ahead of time, perhaps tomorrow, to be sure that your husband is at home and not somewhere else."

She nodded, a sour, unhappy nod from a sour, unhappy woman, and let him out.

***

"How did it go?" They drove back toward the police station.

"Interesting." Effalyn flipped out her notebook. "I went over to Gail's beauty parlor first. She told me that two of her customers...Marsha Stelman and Cynthia Kochanek...one lives next door, next to the Marsdens and one lives a few blocks away, but knew them casually from their church... had been blabbing in the shop about Marsden's death. The two ladies think there was definitely hanky panky going on between Mrs. M and Mr. Zuster. They both felt sorry for Damson. Said she was a...how did Mrs. Stelman put it? 'She was a lackluster woman, but, nonetheless, he shouldn't have been cheating on her'." Effalyn sighed, her breath gusting out. "I wonder if anyone sees me as lackluster?" Carlton laughed and assured her that however anyone viewed her, it was never with a word such as lackluster.

Effalyn scrunched her mouth up and continued, "Gail also said that she had heard other rumors, but she can't remember who…she's gonna try to bring it up casually as she's doing hair and see if she can get more skinny for us."

"Carlton chuckled. "Tela-phone, tela-graph and tell-a-hairdresser!"

"Well, ladies do tend to gossip when they're getting beautified. My mother gets all sorts of interesting tidbits when she goes to get done." Effalyn flipped a few pages on her pad. "So, based on Gail's stories, I checked with the people to the right. There's Marsha…that's Mrs. Stelman…and Lenny…His last name is Sisitzky. Different last names…I'm not sure why…anyway…They've lived there for seven years. Tried to be friendly, but…'Mr. Marsden was daft as a brush'…their words exactly. They, the Stelman-Sisitzkys, have a great way with words. They also said, and I quote from him, 'Damson is such a pretty name. I wonder what her mother was thinking when she named her Damson.' And then she said, Marsha, that is, that *she*, Mrs. Marsden, the aforesaid Damson, was stand-offish. Said that Neil Zuster was always there at the Marsden house." Effalyn peered at her scribbles. "They, the Stelman-Sisitzkys, kind of looked at each other and their eyebrows were raised. I asked if there was any visible hanky-panky, but they said no. Nothing that they really saw. Mrs. Stelman offered that now that the old man was gone, well, who knows what might happen. Mr. Sisitzky…Lenny…winked and made a comment that poor Mrs. Zuster had better keep her own eyes peeled for danger."

"I asked him what he meant and he said, 'Well, we can't be sure that she killed him, but if Zuster's wife comes a cropper, well, then we'll really know that the two of them were in it together.' Then, Mrs. Stelman giggled and poked Lenny's stomach and then the two of them hugged one another. Hmpf. Lots of smoke, but I can't really see a fire. Just a lot of innuendo."

"Hmmm. So the neighbors thought that there was something funny going on?"

"Not really funny, but potentially funny." Effalyn was fair. "They don't remember seeing Mr. M wandering, but they do remember Mrs. M taking him for walks once in a while. She held his arm and sort of guided him." Effalyn dropped her attempt at fairness and said, sotto voice, "She sort of guided him right into the rhododendron bush and then sort of pulled out the rhododendron root and sort of mashed it up and sort of made him eat it!"

"Whooo, Effalyn, you cat, you!"

She shrugged. "It's suspicious, you gotta give me that much." Carlton nodded.

"Any arguments or disagreements? Could they hear anything?"

"Nope. They...Marsha and Lenny... have air conditioning and couldn't hear much of what went on outside."

"And what else?"

"On the other side..." she flipped a page over..."live Lou and Cindy, um, Kochanek. They're from Latvia. Lived here for a few years. He's a diplomat or some such thing...he was rather cagey about what he did and she also worked for the Latvian government. They're retired and their son lives on St. Thomas. They wanted to be close to their grandchildren, but not too close." Carlton nodded. "They don't know the Marsdens well at all, really. Lou Kochanek said that the old man was crazy in the past three years or so and never spoke to them except to shake his fist at them and mutter. Cindy said that Mrs. Marsden seemed to go out of her way not to speak with them." She peered at her notes. "Oh, I see I got it wrong. *They* went to church with the Zusters, not the Marsdens. Ah." She made a mark on her pad. "OK, so, they *did* know the Zusters, as they go to the same church on Sundays, but very casually. They said that Neil Zuster did visit the house now and then, sometimes in the evening, but that was all. They didn't want to speculate. Not much help from there." She sat back and looked out of the window, a tiny smile on her face.

"Ah, my dear Effalyn, what *else* did you learn? And why do you have those canary feathers at the side of your mouth?"

"Boss, you are a real detective." Her face broke into a full grin. "A girl can't hide anything from you." Carlton rolled his eyes and pulled into his parking space. He turned in his seat, keeping the air conditioning running.

"And so?"

"So, I spoke to the lady across the street. Ann Leuzarder. An older woman, a retired teacher. She runs the nursery school down at the harbor now. Sharp old lady, very attractive even now. She must have been a stunner when she was young."

"Our own Miss Marple?"

"Not far from it. Always out in her garden. Always notices what's what. She says that the house belongs to Mr. Marsden and was in his name only. She understands that has been a bone of contention from the very beginning. The wife was a whiny, grasping person. I quote from Ann Leuzarder, 'She's a snake. I wouldn't be surprised if she poisoned her husband to get the money and to get free from his illness'. I asked Ann if she really thought that Mrs. Marsden might have poisoned her husband and she thought for a moment and said, 'Sure. She controlled everything ever since he got that manchioneel poisoning and his whole demeanor changed. The husband was a loud, virile man before that happened and after that happened, he was a frail puppet. She fed him, she pushed him here and there; she killed him'. That was Ann's statement and her fervent belief."

"But no proof."

"None whatsoever. But Ann Leuzarder has bet me a large gin and tonic that our investigations sooner or later will show that she murdered him."

"And you love gin and tonic, don't you?"

"I do. I do."

***

That evening, Effalyn and her mother sat outside, under their flamboyant tree, enjoying their after-dinner coffee. Mrs Penn looked forward to hearing about Effalyn's day. She was immensely proud of her daughter's work and loved to be her confidante with police business. "Hmpf," she sniffed. "I certainly hope that she doesn't get away with it."

"So far, we only have innuendo and gossip, Mama." Effalyn cut herself a piece of her mother's famous rum and coconut cake.[2] "Want a piece?" Mrs. Penn shook her head.

"No, thank you, dear. My stomach is acting up. I'd only be going to the toilet all night if I eat that rich cake." She sipped at her coffee. "I can make it, but I can't eat it anymore. Oh, my, Effalyn, your father sure did love that cake!" She sat back and thought of times gone by. She sighed, "You know, I remember when I was first married, hearing

---

[2] See recipes at the end for Mrs. Penn's Famous Island Rum and Coconut Cake

about a woman who killed her husband and no one could prove anything."

"How did she do it?" Effalyn licked the white icing.

"She fed him to death."

"She *what*?"

Mrs. Penn chuckled. "She fed him. She was a wonderful cook...Mama told me about her. Said she was a big, fat lady herself...I don't remember the names of these people, mind you...And he was fat, too. This was back in the days before everyone was worrying about cholesterol or what they ate and all that nonsense."

"Go *on*, Mama!"

"Well, supposedly she just kept feeding him...all rich foods, gravies, desserts, potatoes, whipped cream...and he ate and ate and ate. One day, he died. Just like that. Burped and groaned and rolled over dead as a goat." Mrs. Penn made a satisfactory sound. "He died happy, but, nonetheless, he died. She fed him to death."

"Oh, Mama, that's silly," Effalyn scooped up the last bite of coconut and rum cake. "You can't kill someone like that!"

"Well, she did." Mrs. Penn rubbed her hands together. "Maybe I *will* have a piece of that cake after all."

***

Carlton belched softly. Undaunted by stomach stresses, he held his plate out for another slice of mango pie. "Have you finished your homework?" he asked Niccola.

"Yup. All done, Daddy. Mrs. Shields is going away to Italy for her Christmas Holidays and she's not giving us much to do this week." Niccola's face was happy.

"Can I walk down to watch the movie tonight?"

"Who are you going with?"

"The Flynn girls are coming by in ten minutes, if it's OK with you."

"What's playing tonight?"

"*Father Goose* starring Carey Grant."

"Sounds good." Carlton's eyes questioned Rebecca's.

She nodded. "I love Carey Grant. How about we stroll down too?"

It was only in the past year or two that homes on Virgin Gorda had been hooked up to cable television. Prior to that technological advance, there was little in the way of mass communication on the island. Leslie and Charlie Janes at the Green Flash Hotel, sensing a chance to improve business, had hooked up a large television set eight feet up in the trees of their empty side lot. They placed chairs and some old wooden church pews facing the television, and, on Tuesday nights, instituted an evening of the seven o'clock news followed by a free movie. The residents of Big Fish Cay, every Tuesday night, strolled down to the harbor, watched the goings-on of the world around them, and then enjoyed a family-themed movie. Mothers, fathers, grandmothers, little children – everyone bought drinks and snacks from the hotel and settled into their favorite pews for a night out. Young couples sat in the back seats, little children up in front, families in between. An excellent business move on the Janes' part and an excellent social time for the island residents. Even after cable TV came their way, Tuesday nights were generally spent out under the trees.

The four Flynn daughters and Niccola walked ahead of Carlton and Rebecca. "We've lost her to early adolescence," Rebecca mourned. 'She'd rather be with her friends than us."

"Naturally," Carlton picked up his wife's hand and swung it. "And, if the truth be known, I'd rather be with you than with a gaggle of preteen girls."

As they walked slowly in the heavy, sweet night air, Carlton mused on the happiness of his life. Rebecca…the finest wife he could dream of, was his. He thought back on their first meeting. He'd been a fledgling patrolman, nervous and anxious to do well, dressed in his uniform and heavy shoes, hoping that nothing *too* exciting might happen…nothing that he couldn't handle, and also hoping that something a *little* bit exciting might happen…something just thrilling enough to make him shine in his new job.

There'd been a screech of brakes and a loud crash. He ran ahead to see what had happened. There, on the roundabout, were two cars mashed up against one another. One car was a rental and it had clearly caused the accident. From a quick look, it seemed as if the rental car had been going the wrong way around the roundabout. Carlton's eye widened and he fished his ticket book out of his pocket. Damn foreigners didn't know zip about driving around roundabouts. The other car was a dark sedan.

The rental car was smashed in the front where it had hit the dark sedan's grille. Steam was shooting out of the radiator on the dark car.

The occupants of the dark sedan – two men – had gotten out of the car. They seemed unhurt. In the rental car, a young woman sat, stunned and bleeding from an obvious head wound. Her hair, abundant and red, was in wild disarray and Carlton hurried to see if she was badly injured. He called out, "Everyone, stay quiet and still. I will call for a doctor and some back-up and we'll get this taken care of quickly!"

The young woman, who was clearly unable to function, stayed slumped over the wheel of her car. The two men from the car whispered to one another in low, urgent tones. Carlton quickly reported the accident into his radio-microphone, and asked for assistance. He stuck the ticket book back into his hip pocket. Time enough for that later. Already, in the distance, he could hear the sirens of the patrol cars and the ambulance coming.

"Are you OK?" He touched the young woman's shoulder. She turned her face toward him and, as if Cupid's arrow had hit him in his heart region, Carlton fell in love. He gasped and clutched at his stomach. She was bloody and bruised, trying hard to stay conscious and she was the most beautiful creature he had ever seen.

"It's all my fault!" the creature wailed. "I can't drive these goddam cars!" She swept her glorious hair off her face. "Why don't you drive on the *right* side of the road?"

"Oh, I am so sorry!" Carlton touched her head with a tender hand. "Here, take my handkerchief." He reached in his pocket as the sirens got closer. "Help is coming right away."

The vision wiped her face and lifted her head. "Oh, boy, did I cream their car or what?" She looked at the dark sedan. "How come...? Wha...wait a minute! Hey! You guys! What are they running for?" She pointed a white, freckled arm and Carlton turned to see that the dark sedan's trunk was open and that the two men were running away, each carrying a satchel.

"Don't go away!" he pleaded with her. She smiled, a wide grin with the blood running down her face.

"Go get 'em, Tiger!" she urged. In some reckless daze, he bent and kissed her cheek and then turned to chase after the men who were running away.

The two of them were hampered by the satchels which bumped and banged against their knees as they tried to run. Carlton, buoyed by the combination of adrenalin and love, easily overtook them, and pushed one to the ground. The other, seeing a police car stop near his path of egress, gave up his flight and sat down with the satchel on his lap, his face resigned and lugubrious. Two policemen jumped out of the car. One ran to the sitting man and the other ran to help Carlton. But Carlton had the situation easily in hand. Heady with triumph, he stood over his victim with his newly issued police shoe on the victim's back. He opened the satchel…"Jesus!! Look at all the *money*!"

"Can you take care of these two? I think they just robbed a bank or something!" Carleton didn't realize how true his statement was. He really didn't care. He turned his prisoners over to his fellow police and ran back to the redheaded vision in the rental car. She was still in the car, her head unnaturally bent against the backrest cushion, watching the entire show of cops and robbers evolve in front of her.

"You got them?" Her voice was nasal, foreign to him. Huffing somewhat from his exertions, he nodded. "Good." The vision then groaned.

Ohmygod, she's hurt! Carlton blanched and his heart dropped. *I can't lose her now!* "Let's get you out of the car." Trying not to panic, Carlton opened the door of her rental car and put his hand under her elbow. He noticed that her arm was so white, pale and freckled, and that his hand was so brown, hard and callused. She groaned again and lifted herself slowly out of the car with his help. He noticed that she was as tall as he was, maybe even a few inches taller, slender with long legs and that she was white and pink and freckled. His heart yearned. "Are you injured?" His voice was nervous, soft and concerned.

"You handsome idiot, you hero, of course I'm injured!" She began to laugh. "Are you going to arrest me? Are you going to give me a ticket?" and then she collapsed into his arms.

He went with her, feeling in his island-bred-superstitious bones that he must never let her go, sitting in the back of the ambulance, holding her hand all the way. At the hospital, he accompanied her into the Emergency Room. Asked for her identification, he opened her handbag with her permission and took out a New York license that identified her as Rebecca Goldberg, age 23, of 2098 East 73rd Street, New York, New York 10016. Rebecca Goldberg. A Jewish sort of name…Goldberg. He wondered what his father would think of a Jewish daughter-in-law.

A nurse pushed him aside and cleaned Rebecca's face. "How is she? Will she be OK?" He pulled at the nurse's arm.

"She's just fainted a bit. She seems fine." The nurse, a large, black woman, patted him with kind sympathy. "I'll be back in a jiffy. You watch her."

Rebecca's voice whispered, "Are you watching me?"

"Forever. I'll watch you forever," Carlton's hand clasped hers. "For always."

***

"A penny for those thoughts," Rebecca pulled at his hand. "We're here, you dolt!"

"I was thinking of when we met," His grin was sheepish. "And how you bamboozled me so that I never did give you a ticket."

"A girl's gotta do what a girl's gotta do!" She winked at him. "Marry the cop so that you get away with reckless driving." She smiled and the night stars shone for him. "Let's sit in the back seats and neck."

CHAPTER NINE

"A ship, an isle, a sickle moon – with few but how splendid stars..."
To a Poet A Thousand Years Hence, by Gustave Flaubert

As *The Southern Cross* sailed over the Sir Francis Drake Channel, the passengers, already beginning to settle into their new home, started the age-old dance of man and woman. The large group split into smaller ones, with some sitting two by two on the trampoline and some gathering in the cockpit.

Kat was busy in the galley. Lannie was with her, helping to put away the lunch dishes and start the preparations for dinner. "We will have steaks tonight, Lannie." Kat confided. "Steaks and potatoes in their jackets with fresh green beans and almonds. And for dessert!" She rolled her eyes heavenward, "I'm doing hot chocolate lava cakes with custard cream!" Lannie expressed a groan of happiness. "What would you eat for dinner on a typical night in London?"

"I like to do my own cooking. I might prepare a steak and kidney pudding from Marks and Spencer's freezers or go out for a fish and chips supper. Sometimes I have to work very late, especially when we are getting the magazine out. The people I work with are quite dedicated, but after work, we all enjoy socializing. We usually go to a pub and wind down and then, maybe out for supper."

"What was the reason this cruise appealed to you?"

"I thought about Christmas..." His cherubic face was wistful..."It's really a family holiday and I have no family. I thought it would be fun to be away and not have to spend the day...Christmas day...all alone."

"A handsome man like you? Alone?" Kat's face was surprised.

"You are too nice, Kat. I have a lot of friends, but...no one special..." He sorted the silverware, head down, avoiding her sympathetic glance.

"Sometimes, I, too, am lonely in a crowd," She spoke softly. "Sometimes it is less lonely all alone." He looked up, but her head was turned away as she chopped onions for that night's sauce.

Suzie and Elliott were sitting together on soft cushions up at the bow. They both sipped large glasses of iced wine and spoke in low voices, their handsome heads close. Annie, from her perch on top of the cockpit, hoped that Suzie would take care. From what she'd seen of Elliott, he wasn't going to be the man of Suzie's dreams, no matter how gorgeous his looks or how much money he had. She turned suddenly and saw Duncan watching her.

"A wee bawbee, as we'd say in bonny Scotland, frae yer thoughts." His accent was broad and exaggerated.

"Could you tell what I was thinking?" She bit at her lip.

"I think you were being like a fierce tiger, protecting your cousin," His eyes were kind. He shinnied up to sit next to her, a bulky man who moved with unusual grace. "You're younger than Suzie, yes?"

"A year younger."

"But you want to protect her…"

"She's…she's beautiful…but, sometimes she makes poor decisions…" Annie sighed. "I just want to her to find some good man and be happy."

"Ah, lass. You can't protect her from herself." He moved closer and leaned against the huge mast, his shoulder touching hers. She felt heat from where they touched and he looked somewhat surprised. Did he feel her heat, too?

"Why do you speak like an Englishman some of the time and then like a Scottish laird some of the time?"

He laughed, an easy, open guffaw. "Och, lassie, I can pretend to be a toff if I so desire…I scrub up weel, as they say. I went to public schools, which are the same as your private American schools, and I can be as stiff as a guardsman at Buckingham Palace. But deep in my soul, I'm a Scottish farmer." He moved his hand toward her cheek, but stopped just short of touching her. Instead, he simply said, "Now, how about a wee drink with this auld man to celebrate our vacation's start?"

"You're not so old."

"Old enough to be your father, lass."

"Young enough to get me an iced tea?" He laughed again, his blue eyes crinkling and the skin around them breaking into lines. He slid down to the deck. He really was very sweet. And very handsome in an older way. She speculated….If he were ten years younger, maybe…

"I'll be right back. Don't even think of moving."

She nodded, closing her eyes to the sunshine, being sure to not even think of moving.

In another corner of the trampoline, Zandra and Hosea shared their life histories, and Claudia and Martha, Sam and Vinny sat with Captain

Jack, trying to learn the intricacies of steering a multi-million dollar boat. At the table under the cockpit awning, Michael, Corliss, Paula, Elwyn and Sarah studied a large chart of the Virgin Islands and tried to track their upcoming journey.

"Norman Island straight ahead!" Ducky yelled. "Treasure Ho!"

***

Carlton drove home for lunch, leaving Effalyn to collate her reports. Rebecca's car was already at the house. "What's for lunch?" Carlton's stomach rumbled with anticipation.

"Bagels and cream cheese with smoked salmon," Rebecca kissed him hello. "You can cut and toast the bagels." She set a bag and a knife in front of him. He poured himself a cold beer and started slicing.

"A good Jewish island lunch," his eyebrows danced with anticipation. "You're turning me into a good *mensch*."

"You are a *mensch*, even my mother agrees now," Rebecca laughed. "It only took her an hour to realize what a catch I made that day I went the wrong way around the round-about and rammed into the robber's car." She cocked her head, remembering. "Well, it took her an hour to get over the shock of your being black! I thought she was going to pass out, the first time she saw you! She was smart, though, my mom. She realized, right off the bat, that you might not be Jewish!" They laughed, comfortable about their love, comfortable about the path that their lives had taken that day when Rebecca broke the law and got away with it...*and* got away with the policeman.

"Lordy, but you were beautiful then, and you are even more beautiful now, my sweet passion flower, you." He dropped the knife and kissed her.

She put down the fork and kissed him back. The kiss deepened and she turned off the toaster. "The bagels can wait," she began to unbutton his uniform. "I can't."

A while later, as they devoured their bagels, their appetites whetted by the noontime delay, Rebecca told him about the dance program for the wedding. "I have two groups; one is for kids and one for adults. There are fifteen children, including Niccola, Maddie and the Flynn girls, and ten adults. The kids are going to do a sort of island dance with a limbo finale and we grown ups are going to do some stylized ballroom dancing with an island twist and then join the kids with another limbo. Hopefully, we'll get some of the guests to join in. Should be fun."

"You're wonderful," he reached across the table and wound a lock of her hair with his finger. "The bride and groom will love it." He upended his beer glass and swallowed the last gulp. "Gotta go. I'm off to question Neil Zuster."

"Think he had anything to do with Mr. Marsden's death?" Rebecca dusted off her hands and began to clear the table.

"Could be, but not a shred of proof that it just wasn't a tragic accident." He stood up. "What's for supper, by the way?"

Rebecca shooed him out the door. "Do you ever think of anything but food?"

"Got a few more minutes? I'll show you what else I think of!" He made a grab at her and she backed away giggling.

"Pah! It would take you a lot longer than a few minutes!"

He was still chuckling as he drove away. Who would have thought that their marriage would have been so perfect? An island man, his paternal half descended from slaves that were brought here to work the sugar plantations and his maternal half descended from Portuguese sailors who came to the islands generations ago, happily married to a New York Jewish girl whose ancestors emigrated from the horrors of the Holocaust. They'd brooked disapproval and disproved the dire warnings from both sides of the families. Him, dark-complected, dark-eyed, frizzy-haired…what was left of it anyway…of medium height, chunky build and wide, flat feet married to a tall, willowy goddess with milky skin, no matter how long she sat in the hot island sun. Her fiery red hair, soft and silky, her graceful limbs, her freckles and her long, elegant high-arched feet were diametrically opposed to everything physical about himself. He was clumsy; she danced like a butterfly. His voice was a frog's croak; she sang like celestial bells. He was a tenacious cop, with fierce intelligence and determination; she was a freer spirit, who charmed everyone who met her. Who would'a thunk that it would be the most perfect of unions? And the fruit of this union…Niccola…the best of both of them. Red, curly hair, Rebecca's freckles with smooth tan skin, bright as a gold coin, as natural and friendly as the sun. A joy. He was still grinning as he turned the car into Neil Zuster's driveway.

Before he could reach the house, the door opened up. An older man, somewhat squat and balding, stepped outside. "Are you the police?"

Carlton nodded, flipping out his identification folder. "Good afternoon. Is it Mr. Zuster? I'm Detective Inspector Reese. We met very briefly at the Marsden's house..." Carlton thought the man looked like a troll. His body was dumpy and his arms too short. Not exactly the man he'd think of killing for, but, as Carlton had deduced, many times over, there as no telling....never.

"Come in Inspector. My wife told me that you were coming." Zuster motioned him in and led him into the kitchen. "Can I get you a beer or a cold drink?" Zuster seemed affable and relaxed.

"No thank you. On duty, you know, just like in the movies," Carlton spread his hands out in supplication. "But you go right ahead if you'd like..." Zuster grunted and opened his freezer door, took out a handful of ice cubes and put them into a large tumbler. Carlton noticed that the kitchen counter held an assortment of liquor bottles. Zuster picked up the familiar squat bottle that held Virgin Gorda's famous Walker's rum and poured out a hefty amount. He gestured to the chairs and the two men sat down.

***

'We're heading into one of the safest harbors in the BVI. It's called The Bight at Norman Island and it is famous for many reasons," Captain Jack spoke to the group in the cockpit and imagined that Ducky, up in the bow, showing the group that clustered around him how to pick up a mooring, was telling the same story. "This is the island that Robert Louis Stevenson wrote about in his famous book, *Treasure Island*. Supposedly, the book was written about the many pirates that cruised these islands, stole gold and jewels and hid their treasure in the many caves that are all around us." The passengers looked around them. They had sailed into a large sheltering bay and the two arms of the bay wrapped them in rocky arms. Even from the catamaran, they could see tantalizing nooks and crannies in the rocks. "Yup," Captain Jack's voice boomed into their imagination, "the treasures could be anywhere around here." He spread his arms wide and then, as the boat approached the round, white mooring, slowed down as Ducky signaled him with his arms...a little to the left...slow down...there! Ducky bent down, a study in fluid grace, boat hook in hand, and snared the loop of the rope that floated from the mooring ball. Ducky stood up, making a prizefighter's triumphant hand gesture.

"First time, every time!" Ducky and Captain Jack's voices rang out in tandem.

"It's very bad luck to miss the mooring on the first attempt," Ducky explained. "Only a dyslexic land-lubber would do such a thing!" His laugh rang out and Suzie wondered if what he said was true or was it only part of the boat's stories.

Captain Jack pointed to a low white building in the center of the sandy beach ahead of them. "That's Billy Bone's restaurant on the beach. We can ferry you in on the Zodiacs if you want to explore the beach, go up some of the trails and see if you find any gold, or just relax at the bar there." His strong arm pointed to a large, back sailboat, rigged with a pirate flag, that sat in the water to their right hand side. "And that's the infamous William Thornton, a real pirate ship named for the man who was the architect that designed the United States Capital building...Better known down here as 'The Willie T' ". Captain Jack began to chuckle as Elwyn asked the inevitable question.

"Why is so infamous?"

"Many reasons. One of them is because cruisers go there to get rip-roaring drunk and dive off the rail, but the primary reason is that a lot of women go there, get plastered, and take their tops off and dance around."

"You're joking!" Paula was incredulous.

"Not at all. The Willie T is known all over the world for wet-tee-shirt contests and it can be the site of many broken romances and the start of many divorces." Captain Jack's face was bland. "My wife never has set foot on it."

"Is it dangerous? Or just fun?" Suzie's eyes were shining.

"It can be fun and it can be dangerous." Captain Jack shrugged. "Depends on what you're looking for. Don't get me wrong. The Willie T *can* be a lot of fun...it has good drinks, great hamburgers and often has a good band. But...and this is a big but...it can get out of hand over there." He turned off the engines and got up to stretch. "Anyone want to go ashore? Anyone for the Willie T? We have two Zodiacs and...oh, I forgot to ask...can any of you drive an outboard motor?" Several hands went up. "Great. It's three-thirty...We'll begin cocktails and munchies about five....who wants to go to the beach and Billy Bones?" Almost everyone raised hands.

"I'll take a boatload over," Ducky offered. "I can take eight of you at a time and I'll come right back for the rest of you unless you wanna go over too, Cappie?" He turned to Captain Jack.

"Oh, I'll go over for a lemonade and a sweet talk with Valerie." Captain Jack heaved himself over to one of the lazarettes. "Put on your reef shoes and here's some plastic bags if any of you want to gather shells." He grinned and looked around. "Anyone want to go to the Willie T and take off your clothes? No?" His grin was infectious. "Smart people here."

***

An hour later, Paula, Annie, Duncan and Lannie had tired of the sun and sand. Captain Jack was ready to go back, too. "Who wants to drive?" Captain Jack pointed to the Zodiac with his broad, bare foot. Duncan raised his hand and, after a few moments of instruction, managed to start the Zodiac and steer them, without too much difficulty, back to *The Southern Cross*. "OK, cut the engine now and let it glide gently against the swim platform," Jack instructed. "This is the toughest part...docking." He stood, sturdy, his broad, strong body facing the wind and held the line, ready to tie up. Kat came out of the galley and bent to help. As she bent down, Annie could see the tops of her breasts and she wondered, with a small, surprising stab of jealousy, if Duncan was looking at them. Kat looked up suddenly at Annie and grinned, winking. Annie blushed and wondered what it was exactly that Ducky meant about Kat.

Kat whipped the line around a cleat and assisted Annie and Paula up the steps from the water to the cockpit. Annie jumped off, lithe as a mountain goat, but Paula had to be assisted off the ladder. She seemed winded and a little tired. Captain Jack's eyes were worried for a moment. Some passengers, and she looked like one of them, took a few days to acclimatize themselves to the potent punch of the Caribbean heat.

Lannie, grunting, managed to get off without any help. His face showed his pride. "Nice, Lannie." Jack complimented him. Lannie beamed, forever now in thrall of his Captain. Turning, Jack instructed Duncan in the tying-up procedures that would secure a large Zodiac. He nodded. "You did well, my boy. Very well." Jack patted Duncan on his shoulder. "We'll make a scurvy sailor out of you in no time."

Pleased with his accomplishment, Duncan accepted Kat's invitation to a cold beer and they all went into the cold air of the galley. "What can we do to help you, Kat?" Annie offered.

"You are wonderful. Thank you for thinking to help me. Annie, you can scrub the potatoes and then oil them up," Kat pointed to a huge basket of spuds. "And you, you handsome man" she pointed to Lannie, "can wash and start the salad." She pulled a huge bag of greens from the refrigerator and tossed them towards Lannie's blushing countenance.

"And me?" Paula sipped at her beer. She seemed less tense, cooler and more relaxed now.

"You can...oh, let's see...Ah, you can set out some salsa and chips...here are four little bowls and four big baskets..." She smiled at her galley crew. "And my many thanks all for the help. Let me tell you, many of our passengers never even think to ask." She made a graceful motion with her hands. "Not that they have to...but it is nice to have a few extra hands here, and, best of all, I like the company."

Duncan and Jack delved into the intricacies of the ship's communications systems as the rest of them washed and peeled. "Annie?" Paula's voice was soft. "Greenwich, Connecticut?" Annie, her hands greased, looked up. "I had a friend...my best and most wonderful friend...and she was born and raised in Greenwich."

"Really? Gee, my family has been there for ages and we know everybody. What's her name?"

"Well, she's gone now. Died years ago," Paula's voice caught. "Her name was Sharon...Sharon Nye." Paula's voice faltered. "Have... have you ever...heard the name?"

"Oh, I'm so sorry...."Annie scratched her nose, getting a spot of Crisco on it, "I don't think I know any Nye family.. Was she, um, your age?"

"Yes. Somewhat older than you, my sweet. We met at college and were friends since we set eyes on one another. She was a wonderful person and I miss her every day." Paula looked out of the windows at the sea and the sky. "She would have loved this....all this..."

"Um, what happened? I mean, how did she, um, die?"

"She became very ill with a rare neurological disease. There was no cure and she slowly slipped away. Even now, so many years later, I mourn her." Paula's face was tense and her eyes were bleak with memories.

"Oh, Paula. How sad." Annie wiped her hands on a towel and hugged Paula. "I'm sure she is somewhere at peace and is watching you..." Annie's eyes twinkled... "She's making sure that you don't go over to the Willie T and flash your boobies around." Everyone, including Paula, laughed, although Paula's laugh held an odd note. Paula hugged Annie back.

"Thanks, you made me feel ever so much better." Her thin face relaxed. "Actually, she might have urged me to go over there and do a bit of...whatever."

Duncan, listening, came over to the counter. "When my wife died, I felt as if my world fell apart. I had a hard time functioning or wanting to be happy or to enjoy myself." He put his hand on Paula's arm. "I felt guilt that I was still here and she was gone." Paula's hand covered his. "It took me a while to realize that the best thing I could do for her memory was to live my life to the fullest." He swallowed the last of his beer, tipping his head back, and Annie watched his Adam's apple bob and felt a warmth at his kindness and consideration. Paula's face nodded in rueful understanding.

"I know. I can feel Sharon sometimes, especially in a place like this...where the beauty of nature overwhelms...she's out there...watching me and enjoying all the things that I am doing."

"Is that why you came on this cruise?" Lannie prowled around her like a curious dog..

"I came on this cruise...to...finish my mourning. To...honor the memory of the dead and to complete...well," Paula's words stumbled. "To finish my mourning, I guess, is the best way to say it."

"Look to the stern," Captain Jack's voice interrupted. "There's one of the finest views you'll ever see." He pointed to the mouth of the Bight's harbor. In the narrow opening, clouds had gathered in the sky and the shapes of the distant islands looked dark green and lumpy.

"Why it *does* look like a bunch of women lying in the water!" Annie exclaimed. "See, that one? Look...her head, her breasts...her tummy...and even her toes are sticking up!"

Jack laughed, rich and rollicking. "Imagine those sailors so long ago. Supposedly, they were the crew that was with Christopher Columbus on his second voyage to the New World. Imagine Old Chris and his men. They'd traveled for months on the ocean...storms...boredom...fighting for their lives...and then...this lush and green land. Can't you just see them approaching here...and seeing those huge shapes, lolling in the water. A big fat virgin over there," he pointed to another island, "Look at her voluptuous belly and her thighs..."

Duncan chuckled. "Land ho and I'm gonna jump right out and grab a breast!" He popped another beer open. "No women for months and months. No wonder these islands beckoned to them!"

"And that's why they're called The Virgin Islands, although another tale of why they're called The Virgin Islands has to do with Saint Ursula." Captain Jack snitched a taco chip and dipped it into the salsa. "She, supposedly, led a group of eleven thousand virgins…" He rolled his eyes.

"Ahh, eleven thousand of them…Great God! A brilliant thought!" Duncan smacked his lips.

"Well, they may have been virgins, but silly virgins, I think. Rather than submit to marauding Huns in Fourth century, they all killed themselves."

"Silly buggers." Duncan jokingly mused and was hit in the shoulder by Annie's fist.

"Male chauvinist pig," she mocked him and then, she stopped and bit her lip, looking at her hand with a peculiar expression. Duncan rubbed his shoulder and bit his lip. He avoided Annie's gaze.

"Ah, it's only a story," Jack soothed. "Would it have been better to submit and live, or sacrifice yourself instead of a fate worse than death?"

"I'd kill myself…" Paula's voice was small. "Except…" Her face was white and she held onto the knife in her hand with a tight grip.

"Ah, lass. It's a story. Only a story," Duncan soothed her. She smiled bleakly at him and relaxed her death grip on the knife.

"Well, that's the story and now you understand, sort of, why we call these The Virgin Islands." Jack ate his taco chip. "And day after tomorrow, we're going to the one that looks the cutest…Virgin Gorda, or The Fat Virgin. She's got the most protruding belly of them all."

Annie sucked in a deep breath and rubbed her stomach. "Oh, I don't know. If I keep on eating all of Kat's wonderful food, I will have the most protruding belly of them all." The tension was broken as they all laughed together, binding themselves in friendship and creating memories.

***

"I got the name of Marsden's former wife back in South Africa and her date of death. Mrs. Marsden wasn't happy about telling me, but she did. I'm going to check and see if there was anything peculiar about her death." Effalyn made some notes on her pad. "I took a walk with her out in the garden and asked her if she knew which plants were toxic. She made a big fuss and told me that she knew nothing at all about poisonous plants. As I know nothing about poisonous plants, I went over to the library and checked out these three books," she pointed to a pile on her crowded desk. "That nice librarian, Shirley Leach, researched them for me." Effalyn smirked. "She also researched just who *else* had taken out these books in the past few years…" She waited.

"OK, OK, *who*?" Carlton bit.

"Ha *Ha*! Who do you think?"

"No! Really? Mrs Marsden?"

"Yup. She took out these three twice." She checked her notes. "And not only that, our little widow also checked out a book about poisoned mushrooms and one called, um…*Deadly Doses, a Guide to Poisons*. I followed the library habits of the Widow Marsden and took that one out too."

Carlton rubbed his hands together. "Maybe we are getting somewhere here."

"And…" Effalyn let the word hang.

"There's *more*?" Carlton's mouth gaped open. Effalyn was a wonder.

"Guess who else took out these books?" Effalyn waved a small blue pamphlet in the air.

"Mister Zuster?"

"Bingo!"

"We need some expert help here. I know diddly squat about plants and that kind of thing." Carlton's eyes were gleaming and he stood up, unable to contain his excitement.

"Slow down, Boss." Effalyn soothed him. "Even if they did research poisons, it *still* is circumstantial. She could say that she was just trying to see what she could do to protect him from these kinds of plants," Effalyn thought for a moment. "At least that's what I'd say to you if you were suspecting me."

"If you killed anyone, no one would ever know. You, my dear, would be a murderer to be reckoned with."

"Bet your bippy." Effalyn chuckled. "Anyway, I'm way ahead of you. I got Ganny and Armond going over to the college to speak with a Professor, um, Stambaugh…Carol Stambaugh. Almost like Captain

Jack's name, but a little different. Stambaugh, Scambaugh." Effalyn giggled. "Anyway, she's the head of the biology department and supposedly an expert on plants of the islands. She can tell us a lot about poisonous plants and then, maybe, she can come and check out the Marsden's yard to see what's out there.

Carlton nodded approvingly. Effalyn was gold. "Did we get the reports back from toxicology yet?"

"Not yet. Some tests will take a few days, some up to two weeks."

"They did it, Eff, didn't they? I feel it in my big toe."

"They did it. All we've got to do is prove how."

***

At precisely seven thirty-two, the sun went down over the Bight at Norman Island. It was a beautiful sight, the clouds refracted the rays into a panorama of colors...red, gold...orange and purple. "If you're lucky and keep your eyes on the horizon," Captain Jack told them, "you might...just *might*...see the green flash."

"And what, pray tell, is the green flash?" Elliott's voice drawled.

"*What is it about him*," Annie thought, "*that makes my flesh crawl every time he speaks?*" She noted that Suzie's face was rapt.

"The green flash is a rare phenomenon that happens when the sun sets and the light is exactly right. There is a flash...an actual flash...that occurs, or rather is seen to occur, just as the last of the sun goes down. It is a green sparkle, like a beautiful emerald. I've seen it only twice, but once seen, it will never be forgotten." The passengers, in a state of stuffed happiness, were sipping after dinner drinks.

"I've only seen it once." Ducky chimed in. "I was with my girlfriend, Lisette, and the saying goes that the next person you kiss after you've seen the green flash will be your true love forever." He grinned.

"And did you kiss her?" Hosea and everyone else wanted to know.

Ducky made a silly face, his eyebrows wiggling. He shrugged and laughed. "Well, she's still my girlfriend, ya' know." He rose and stretched. "OK, before I fall asleep here, who is brave enough to want to sleep out tonight? Who wants to be part of the cockpit gang?"

Suzie shook her head, her fair hair falling like a cloud, "Not me. How silly to sleep out here when we have such lovely mattresses and air conditioning!" Several voices echoed her feelings.

Elliott made no bones about what he thought about sleeping outside. "Damn stupid thing to do, really!"

Elliot's negativism cemented Annie's enthusiasm. "I'm game," Annie raised her hand. "I'll try it anyway."

"As a Scotsman who has oft' slept out on the heather, I'm in." Duncan joined her. "Who else is man enough...oops!" He avoided Annie's fist..."*Person* enough to join us?"

"I'll try it," Hosea turned to Zandra. ""Will you join me, Zandra?" She giggled and nodded why not.

"Any other *real* sailors?" Ducky goaded. "Man or woman?" The rest shook their heads, murmuring that one would be crazy to sleep on the netting all night. "No one else? OK, you four wise people, come on with me and I'll show you what you have to do."

He opened up a hatch up forward and removed four wrapped parcels. "Each is a sleeping bag...sort of...see, you fasten the corners to the netting like this..." He rolled out a blue tarpaulin, each edge of the roughly five by eight rectangle had a bungee cord attached. Ducky hooked the bungee cords securely around a square of the trampoline netting so that the tarp lay flat and secured. "Go get your pillow and bring it up here," he instructed and each of them scurried to their cabins to comply while he hooked up the other three tarps.

When they returned, he had brought out four sets of sheets and lightweight blankets each folded and sewn into an envelope. "OK, you each put these sheets into your tarp, like so." He opened the side of the tarp, which had been closed shut with a heavy Velcro tape. "See? You have your own little sleeping bag. Now, we gotta blow up your air mattresses." He brought out four limp and slippery rubber forms, fitted one of them with a small pump, and began to blow it up. "Here," he handed Hosea one of the mattresses and the pump, "You get the rest of these blown up."

Nodding happily, Hosea bent to his task. Zandra watched him with a fond, proprietary smile. "Now, we slip the blown up mattress into this pocket underneath," Ducky put action to match his words. "And now, you have a comfy bed."

"Ohh," cooed Annie, "How sweet!"

"Most of the time, yes," Ducky grinned at her. "But...but!"

"But what?"

"But if it rains, well, now we have to show you what to do. This is the most important part and the part that separates, excuse me Miss

Feminine PC," he tipped his head to Annie and she laughed. "The men from the mice."

"First, you slide the blanket and sheet envelope into the sleeping bag." He neatly showed them how to do this. "Then you fold the top down, just like folding down your bed before you go to sleep. Then, tuck your pillow here, on top of this flap." He held his hand out to Zandra. "Come on, Miss Zandra. You will be my guinea pig." He opened the sheet and blanket and showed her how to slide in. "I'm gonna get you into bed." He wiggled his eyebrows and Zandra giggled. "You in OK?"

"Snug as the bug," she giggled some more. "I like this!" She folded her arms over her head and looked up. "Oh, my gootness me! Look at the stars!"

"I'm gonna give you a tiny lesson in star gazing in a few minutes," Ducky promised. "Just let's all get finished here, because I only show you this the first night. After that, you are on your own and if you don't do it right, you will be very, very wet. I promise you. Very wet!"

"Everyone done theirs?" He checked each one. On one side of the trampoline was Annie's and Duncan's sleeping bags, on the other side, those of Zandra and Hosea. "Everything looks OK to me. Fine." He bounced over to where Zandra lay. "The thing is, every so often, especially at night, it rains. It rains very hard...not for a long time, maybe five or ten minutes, but when it rains, it *rains*! You'll feel like you are under a huge waterfall!"

"We won't get wet, my man?" Duncan looked doubtfully at the contraption on the trampoline. "This wee floppy thing will keep us dry?"

"If you do it right, it's a hoot and you'll be so proud of yourselves. Usually, you can just lie here, under the sheet with the blanket folded back. If it gets cool, you can then pull the blanket over you." He rolled and pummeled Zandra and she slid in and out of the blanket with ease. "So long as it doesn't rain, you're all fine. But...a big but here...OK, if you feel even a drop of rain, yell out to everyone else. Then, quick as a bunny, pull the sheet and blanket over yourself and then, take a second to do it right...fasten the Velcro all the way up, making sure that there is no space that isn't shut securely. Yup, just like that," he approved as Zandra closed up her envelope, securing all but her head in stiff plastic.

"And the last thing," he showed Zandra how to fasten the flap over her head and the pillow and secure it in front of her neck with the Velcro strips. "You can keep a tiny spot open so that you can breathe...ha ha...It's really not as difficult to do as it is to explain it. As soon as you are lying down, you'll catch on when you need to do it." Each of the four went into their cocoon and pulled and fastened until Ducky was satisfied that they understood how keep dry if the need should arise.

"And this will be fun, ha, ha?" Hosea's eyes blinked.

"Not only is it fun, but it is wild!" Ducky laughed. "The water is storming down on you, but you are warm and dry. If you do it right, you won't get a drop of rain on you."

"And if you don't do it right?" Duncan asked.

"You'll be flooded back to East Jabip! You'll be drenched to the skin! You'll be cold and soaked and one sorry bastard!" He slapped Duncan's pillow. "You guys are gonna be just fine. I can tell. OK, now everybody into your bag and I'll tell you about the stars down here..." He lay back with them, his head on Annie's legs, and showed them the Corona, a necklace of stars that looked like the most expensive bauble in any jewelry store, Orion and the Southern Cross. Enchanted, they all were ready to snuggle down. Laughing, Ducky jumped up. "Just get your pajamas on whenever you're ready. And if you think the stars look good now, wait until we put out the lights. The stars seem so close, you'll think you can reach up and pick them like grapes."

The rest of the passengers came to see the cockpit gang's layout. Some scoffed, some were sorry that they hadn't participated. Some, like Elliott, were verbal in their disdain. "Stupid to do this," again was how he put it. Annie vowed, no matter how wet she got, that she'd never give him the satisfaction of going below to sleep.

Captain Jack had brought out his guitar, Ducky picked up a mandolin and they began to sing old songs...the ones that everyone knew that words to. *"We come on the sloop John B, My grandfather and me..."* and then, *"Yellow is the color of my true love's hair, in the morning"*... All around their boat, other boats floated, little pools of light in the darkness of the Bight. Annie looked around at her fellow passengers and sighed with happiness. She noted that Suzie and Elliot had gone inside, then re-appeared and wandered up to the bow of the boat. She could see the tips of their cigarettes glowing closely together. *"She's a big girl now,"* Annie thought. *"I guess she knows what she is doing."*

"If we get caught, they'll throw us into jail," Suzie shivered.

"Do you want a joint or don't you?" Elliott offered. He lit his cigarette and drew in the acrid smoke.

Suzie reached for his hand and the cigarette. She giggled. "I wanted to bring in some stuff, but my stupid cousin wouldn't let me. How did you get these past the Customs check points?"

"I didn't, you silly girl." Elliott's face held an expression of intense satisfaction. "I bought the stuff after we landed.

"Bought it? From who?"

"Oh, I can spot someone who wants to sell in a moment. There were several men at the airport who were looking for a rich man like me."

"Clever."

"Yes. I pride myself on things like that. There's always some local yokel who wants to make a buck and doesn't care how. These natives are so lazy and stupid and don't have any fear of police reprisal. You just have to know how to spot them."

She gulped the smoke and then, slowly blew it at Elliott's face. He grinned wolfishly and grabbed her hand. "That's what you get for bringing along a nanny." He bent and kissed her softly, then harder.

"I needed a roommate. I couldn't get a single cabin."

"She's up here for the night. Now you have a single cabin." He kissed her again and his hands moved to her breasts, softly first and then with cruel pinches. She rubbed herself against him.

"You have a single and I have a single. Aren't we lucky?" Her peal of laughter floated back and Annie hoped that Suzie wasn't making yet another horrible mistake.

***

It had been a long day for the passengers and one by one, or, in a few cases, two by two, they went to bed. Only Captain Jack, Ducky and Elwyn Langdon were awake, sipping a fine old brandy.

"How did you get into this game, Jack?"

"I was always a seafaring man...even as a kid. I was born in New Jersey – just like Sammy and Vinny - where my parents had a summer home on Monmouth Beach – on a little spot between the ocean and the bay. I could swim and sail before I could walk. I worked on boats when I was a young boy and always yearned to sail. My parents wanted me to be a doctor or some such respectable thing, but I was only interested in boats." He sipped at his brandy and strummed his guitar softly. "*Tell me what were their names? Tell me what were their names? Did you have a friend on the good Ruben James?...*" Ducky accompanied him, but this time played on a beat-up harmonica. The mournful music floated into the star-filled night and made Elwyn's eyes glisten.

"As soon as I was able, I started to crew on sailboats. This area was just beginning to thrive, and I loved the heat, the people and the water down here. It's easy sailing, and I'm basically a lazy guy. I was crewing on a biggish yacht and there was this passenger from England. Emma Anderson. She was the most gorgeous thing I'd ever seen and I vowed, right then and there, to keep her right by my side." He chuckled reminiscently. "And I did. Emma. I was her Steed and she was my Mrs Peel. Just like The Avengers on that old television show." Jack chuckled to himself as he thought of the games he and Emma had played with one another. Silly, lovers' games, generally involving him in some situation with a black homburg and a furled umbrella and Emma wearing nothing but a black cat suit and a lascivious grin. "We were married three weeks later, much to the horror of her family and mine. I hocked everything I had and bought my first boat and Emma waited on tables and helped me to start a charter company. We almost starved, but, one way or another, we managed. The sailing business down here grew and we grew with it. We have two children, Adam and Dorothy. Both married, one set in England and one set in California. They're all good kids and we enjoy seeing them when we see them...three or four times a year. They're happy and Emma and I are happy."

"Sounds like a great life."

"It's about to get even better for me. I've got a plan for retirement in a year or so." He grinned in the darkness, his teeth gleaming. "Ducky here will be going back to school and Kat will be leaving me in March. I'll be selling the boat...I already have a buyer who is salivating to get his hands on it... Unknown to Emma, I have bought another boat, just right for two old farts like us to retire on. It's being refurbished in South Africa and will be here next summer. The boat will be called *Music*."

Ducky began to sing in a soft, smooth voice.... "*She is all that I have left, and Music is her name...think about it....*"

"*When you see The Southern Cross for the first time....*" Their voices, mellowed by the brandy, floated over the water.

"When I named my first boat *The Southern Cross*, it was kinda original, but now, every fifth sailboat is named the blamed *Southern Cross*. No originality at all!" Captain Jack's tone was mildly aggrieved.

"Hence, *Music*." Elwyn nodded, understanding perfectly. "Just right." He clinked his glass. "I'll drink to that." He drained his brandy and stood up, yawning prodigiously. "Bed for me."

"Sleep well, Elwyn. Glad that you're on board." Elwyn slid open the glass door and was swallowed up by the air conditioning.

"Another little sip?" Jack beckoned Ducky with the bottle.

"Just a splash and then beddy-bye for me, too."

"Your thoughts?" Jack made a motion towards the cabins.

"A few romances are perking. Hosea and the delectable Miss Zandra," Jack nodded unseen in the darkness. "The New Jersey boys and the two luscious blonde cousins from South Africa, um, Martha and Claudia…Clow-dee-ya…love that name." Ducky rolled the syllables. "Our vamp, Suzie has her talons out for that shithead, Elliott."

A soft, "Hmpf" came from Captain Jack's corner. "Can't stomach the jerk."

"They'll deserve each other," Ducky judiciously commented. "Maybe that Corliss, the nutty one and Michael Beck. They seemed to hit it off. The rest, I donno."

"Duncan our Scot and the sweet one, Annie?"

"Interesting, those two. Not really matched – he's quite a bit older - but there *is* some electricity. I don't think they know it yet themselves." Ducky's voice was slurred.

"Go to bed, son." Jack ordered. "Get a few hours of kip and then relieve me at three or so." He waved his glass. I'll just keep the jumbies off the boat."

"I thought I smelled pot tonight," Ducky yawned. "I think Elliott scored some stuff somewhere."

Captain Jack stiffened like a dog on point. "Sonofabitch! I'll drown him if I find he's using on this boat!"

"I can't be absolutely sure, Cap." Ducky held up his hand. "I tried to get close to them and he threw his cigarette into the water. Fucker sneered at me."

Jack rubbed his beard. "We'll get him. If he's using, I'll make sure he rots in jail."

"I'll keep vigilant," Ducky smothered another prodigious yawn. "Night, Cappie." He shambled into his tiny cabin, careful not to wake Kat.

"Night, Duck."

CHAPTER TEN

*"And hand in hand, on the edge of the sand,
they danced by the light of the moon...."
Edward Lear, The Owl and the Pussy Cat...*

If Suzie had known Elliott – really had known Elliott, instead of their last night's biblical knowledge, she would have run away screaming. But Suzie was Suzie, and all she wanted was a few kisses, the potential of a future with someone with money, a joint of marijuana, and a satisfactory screw.

She hadn't been privy to Elliott's past, his excesses and the horrors he had wrought as a youngster, his lies, the hurts and the disasters he had carelessly left behind. She didn't know that he had been caught cheating at college and only the huge sum of money that his father paid as a bribe kept him from being thrown out. She didn't know that his father had actually approved and muttered, "chip off the old block" as he shoveled out the cash which had always smoothed the way. She only saw his exterior skin, his handsome face, his sardonic wit that diminished others and the smooth mask that dazzled. She saw the wealth, ostentatiously displayed in a gentlemanly-like manner, the cleverness, slick and manipulative, that mocked others, and the success, gained at the distress of those he had stepped on. In other words, Elliott was made for someone as selfish as herself. The only mitigating circumstance was that Suzie's selfishness wasn't evil. Just selfish. Elliott's, on the other hand, was always meant to hurt. And often to harm.

Had she known about his own four marriages, would she have balked? Had she known how spectacularly unsuccessful a husband he had been, even to terrorizing his ex-wives now so that they were frightened to ask for alimony? Had she known that upon learning that his second wife was pregnant, that he kicked her down a flight of stairs, with a few extra belts to her abdomen, to be sure that the baby was aborted? How she, the second wife, was still in a mental hospital, unable to cope with her life?

Did she see the gloss and veneer of success in Elliott's part of the law firm, not understanding that his lucrative practice represented only crooked corporations? Did she realize that he had failed the bar exam three times and the only way he was finally able to pass it was with an enormous bribe from his father? No, to her credit, she knew nothing of these matters.

And if she had known, would she have cared? Not really, when he touched her in all the right places, rolled her a joint, made her laugh by whispering viciously biting remarks about the inadequacies of their fellow passengers, mocked Captain Jack's kindly manner, and sneered at Kat, who had already rejected his advances.

***

The cockpit gang, after spending their first night on the trampolines, a night blissfully free of any precipitation, awoke and sat up, disheveled and warm, as Ducky brought them glasses of iced orange juice and cups of hot coffee as they stretched and congratulated themselves on their cleverness at sleeping out. "I feel funny," Annie exclaimed.

"Funny how?" Zandra's hair was a birdsnest. Hosea blinked at the sun shining on her head and thought she was the loveliest thing he had ever seen. He couldn't believe that the two of them had slept, secure and innocent in their respective cocoons, a few feet apart.

"Funny that we are sleeping out here, all together, and that up to yesterday, we didn't even know one another!" She shivered in a delicious way. "Ya! Almost indecent!"

"Almost gorgeously indecent!" Duncan swallowed the rest of his orange juice. He peered through his glasses at Annie. She was sitting up, half-in and half-out of her sleeping bag, her hair tumbled and messy, her face still rosy from sleep. Beautiful to see in the morning sun. He felt a sharp hurt to his heart that he was so old.

"I didn't think I'd sleep well out here," Annie murmured. "But, I don't even remember closing my eyes and I was gone! Good thing there was no rain." She pulled herself up and began to fold her bedding carefully. Duncan got up too. As he tucked his pillow away, he was buffeted by a wave and bumped into Annie, trying to keep his balance. The two of them, clasping hands, felt a hot stab as their fingers met. For a moment, they swayed on the trampoline web, hand-in-hand, stunned by the touch of one another.

"Excuse me, Annie," Zandra's voice cut into their reverie. "I am going to put my bedding away and get a bathing suit on."

"Uh, me, too." Annie stepped back and dropped her hand. Her face was pink and her breath came unevenly. "Me, too." Her eyes met Duncan's. His mouth was open slightly and his blue eyes were bemused.

"Uh," he said. "Uh."

Annie went down to the cabin to brush her teeth, complete her morning ablutions and change into a black one-piece bathing suit for snorkeling. As she folded her pajamas, Suzie came in. "Oh, hi, cousin dear." Susie's voice was acid.

"Good morning, Suzie," Annie thought she'd be casual and nonconfrontational. "Enjoying the trip?"

Suzie looked into the mirror and carefully checked a small blemish. She opened her make-up box and applied a medicated lotion and then covered the tiny spot with a dot of foundation cream. Satisfied that she would pass inspection, she brushed out her hair into a fan of gold. Annie thought that Suzie's actions seemed artificial and affected. *Better not to even rock her boat*, she thought. Pretending indifference to her cousin, Annie used the head and then slipped a pink tee shirt on over her bathing suit. Suzie eyed her from the reflection in the mirror. "What's with you and the Duncan geezer?" Her voice was insolent. Suzie at her very worst.

"He's a very nice man, Suze," Annie kept her temper. "Nice sense of humor and good company." She smiled at her cousin, refusing to be drawn. "I like him a lot."

Suzie mad a sour face. "Elliott reckons he's a fag."

"Elliott is no child himself. I think he might be even older than Duncan." Annie's voice was quiet but firm. "And besides, Elliott's a pompous crab."

"How *dare* you?" Suzie's face contorted.

"Oh, Suzie. Let's not argue. If you think Elliott's words are gold, well, then…fine. I simply have my own opinions about him and the other passengers."

"Elliott is worth fifty of *any* of them. What a boatload of losers!" Suzie's face was flushed with anger and annoyance that Annie didn't seem bothered by her criticism.

"Oh, I'm pleased to hear his high opinion of me," Annie grinned and took her reef shoes out of the cupboard.

Suzie turned and hissed, "I'll thank you to remember just who paid to have you take this trip…" Annie frowned. Suzie's venom and fury seemed to be growing out of proportion. "You wouldn't even be here if it wasn't for me and my money!"

Annie sucked in her breath and turned to counter her cousin's unfair and hurtful remark. She noticed that Suzie's face had reddened and flushed. What was wrong with Suzie? Annie bit her lip and decided to ignore Suzie's nasty jibes. "Are you OK, Suze?" Annie asked, her tone concerned and conciliatory. Suzie opened her mouth and wheezed and choked. Her face suddenly flushed and her eyes were glittery. "Hey! What's *wrong*?" Annie touched Suzie's arm. Her skin was hot and flushed.

"I'm fine, damn it. Just leave me alone." Suzie's voice rose to a shriek. She seemed almost out of control. *What the hell...?* Annie's mouth opened, but before she could say anything, Suzie began to laugh and laugh until she was gasping for air. She dropped to a bunk and pounded the coverlet, nearly hysterical with some uncontrollable glee. Annie's eye narrowed. *What the hell was going on?*

Then, Suzie began to cough. Her eyes streamed tears, as Annie watched with trepidation. Just as swiftly, her mood changed and Suzie started to laugh again, "Don't you get it, you innocent idiot?" Annie shook her head, wordless at this display. "It's the stuff...the *stuff,* you know?"

"What stuff?" Annie was whispering in horror.

"The native stuff, you goose!" Suzie's giggles made the hair on Annie's head rise. "*Da ganga*. The coke. The maryjane. All that beautiful stuff." Suzie wiped her streaming eyes. "Oh, my God, how can you be so *stu*pid? *Cocaine!*"

"Co*caine*?" Annie's lips mouthed the word silently. "You...you...*cocaine*?"

"Ohhhh, you dumb cousin. A little dab'll do ya!" Suzie began to laugh again and then, sucked in a deep breath and whispered, putting her finger to her lips, "Don't tell anyone. Shhhh!"

"Are you crazy, Suzie? Are you off your head? You heard what Captain Jack said. You know about the jails and the law!" Annie was aghast.

"Oh, screw Captain Jack!" She stood up, seemingly recovered from her bought of hysteria. "Oh, simmer down, Annie. Everything is cool. I'm fine. And no one will find out anything. Elliott is too smart to be caught."

"Elliott! Is that where...? Did he give you cocaine? Oh, *Suzie!*"

"Oh, stuff it! I'm fine and no one is any wiser and if you tell anyone...well...you won't, will you?" Suzie suddenly changed her tone and wheedled. "I didn't mean anything about me paying for you. I was just...." She shook her head violently back and forth and her blonde hair flew out, looking like gold in a shaft of morning sunlight. "I don't know why I said anything at all to you. If you tell on me and Elliott, if anyone says anything, I'll just swear I was kidding and you'll look like a fool." She smiled, the same smile she had smiled when Annie got caught with the snowballs.

Visibly upset, Annie went to the door. "You're family and I won't say anything, but – think about this – it isn't me who'll look like a fool if you and that shithead are caught." She sighed in despondency. "Take care, Suzie. Don't make a mistake that you can't reverse. You're playing with danger and dynamite and you don't have a clue as to how stupid you are being. This kind of danger is 'way over your head and if you get caught, you're not going to be able to smile and charm your way out of this." As she shut the door behind her, she heard a crash. Presumably, Suzie had thrown something.

***

"This morning, we have Caribbean Hash and Eggs Benedict with a Passion Fruit Hollandaise," Kat offered loudly, grinning to herself as she watched the romances unfold. After all, wasn't this what the cruise was all about? "Or plain old Eggs Benedict with plain old Hollandaise." It was easy to tell what Kat thought of plain old. "I also made fresh croissants this morning and we have gorgeous fruit." She pointed proudly to the table.

"Today, after breakfast, we are going snorkeling at the Caves here on Norman Island. Great fish to see and perhaps you will find those gold doubloons that you couldn't find yesterday." Captain Jack waved his coffee cup in the air. "Then, we'll go across The Sir Francis Drake Channel again and go to Jost Van Dyke. We'll moor there for the rest of the day and the night. You'll enjoy the shops there and perhaps buy a dress for the wedding, or, if you can't find anything in Jost Van Dyke, there are many shops in Big Fish Cay the next day."

Ducky chimed in, "And tonight, we are all going to the Banjo Man's Bar on Jost Van Dyke. Banjo is a very famous personage here in the islands. He sings songs that he makes up on the spot, about you, about me, about anyone. He's very clever and perceptive, quickly making rhymes and jokes, and you ought to enjoy yourselves a lot. The band is very good, the music and songs are fantastic and their food, while not as great as Kat's, is terrific."

"Naturally," added Captain Jack, "the entire evening's cost, the dinner and all of your drinks, are included in your cruise cost, so don't be shy, order whatever you want and enjoy it."

"There is a great buffet, or you can order off the menu," added Kat, "and their specialty is conch chowder. I recommend it."

"What's conch chowder?' asked Hosea.

"Conch – it is spelled c-o-n-c-h, but pronounced 'konk', is a large shellfish," Jack appealed to Kat who immediately went back into the galley and brought out a large picture book showing shells of the islands. "The meat is tough unless it is beaten with a mallet for a long time. Then, it is velvet and tasty. The chowder is made with the bits and pieces of the conch that isn't used in the fillets. It is spicy and good, the chowder, that is. They also make conch fritters, a specialty of all the restaurants down here. Those are fried bits of batter with onions, conch pieces and spices. Again, delicious and spicy hot. Yum."

"Who wants to dance with me tonight?" Ducky made some suggestive moves.

"Me, me, me." Claudia got up and made some moves of her own. "Oh, this is so great!"

"Why is this place called Big Fish?" Lannie asked.

"Big Fish Cay." Here, Captain Jack laughed, a booming sound. "Used to be nicknamed Hash Harbor back in the old days when islanders bootlegged drugs." Sixteen pair of eyes swiveled to his. Annie watched Suzie and then Elliott. Suzie looked nervous; Elliott merely bored.

"That was a while back. Then, the government of the British Virgin Islands, with the cooperation of almost all of the residents, except, of course, the few that were making a living from delivering drugs, made their minds up that they would be a *tourist* destination, catering to visitors and sail charters instead of a drug capitol catering to criminals and thugs." Annie's eyes slid to Elliott's face. There was no expression at all on his handsome features.

"It was a wise decision, both financially and crime-wise. These islands are now very peaceful and there is very little crime here. No islander would steal…well, I won't say there aren't still a few reprobates sneaking around, but they are widely condemned by everyone…because our very livelihood depends on people coming here in safety to have a memorable vacation in the sun. If there were to be stealing or pirates or boat vandalism, the entire structure of the islands would collapse. Thus," he spread his big hands out, "there is very little crime and Hash Harbor is no more."

"Oh, well," Zandra laughed. "I'll have to get my fun some other way." Everyone laughed. Everyone except Suzie and Elliott, Annie noticed. The two of them looked at one another and then looked away.

"I'm glad that the drugs are completely off limits," Ducky said, his handsome face sober and solemn. "Before, kids died and there were terrible fights and problems. If you want a drink or two, well, enjoy yourself. If you want to break the law…well…go somewhere else." He shook his head. "My father represents these islands and he is one hundred per cent committed to keeping drugs out of here."

"My uncle died of a drug overdose in New Jersey," Sammy's face was bleak. "We have a big problem in the United States. Kids think it's cool to get toked up and then they do stupid things to get more drugs. They get hooked and then they rob and steal and the women turn to prostitution." His face was wooden.

"Enough of this gloom!" Jack got up and moved towards the captain's seat. "Just keep away from anything illegal and you'll never have any problems." He sighed and then brightened up. "OK, those who want to snorkel, go to the lazarette at the stern and find flippers that fit your feet and get yourself a mask that fits you. If you have never snorkeled, Ducky and Kat will help you." He turned to Paula. "Paula, it's difficult to snorkel here without being a good swimmer. Maybe you had better wait until we get to Jost Van Dyke where there is a nice, sloping beach and Mr. Duck can give you a swimming lesson." He winked at her. "We all have gotten to like you and we don't want you to drown just yet." He turned as Elliott whispered into Suzie's ear and muffled laugh came from Suzie.

"Did I miss the joke?"

Elliott's face was smooth but Suzie had the grace to blush. "It was a personal comment," she explained. "It had nothing to do with Paula's swimming."

"I would like to think it didn't," Captain Jack's own face was smooth.

***

On Big Fish Cay, Pat Biase and Joyce O'Sullivan huffed and puffed, pushing the grand piano that normally resided inside Rebecca

Reese's dancing studio out onto the concrete apron that fronted the sand in front of the Green Flash Hotel. When the piano was in place, Pat wiped his forehead. "Damn hot work, pushing this thing around." He sat down and rippled his hands over the keys. "I think we pushed a little too hard." He laughed. "We pushed the entire tuning out!"

"It will be fine." Joyce spoke in her Boston accented voice. She played an arpeggio on her custom-made left-handed flute, then put it back into its case. "Everything sounds fine to me."

"Humpf!" Pat made a face. "That's because you have no ear for the finer nuances of music!" Joyce smacked him on his shoulder and went to pull eight folding chairs around the piano.

"One for me – flute. One for Paul – guitar. Two for Janet and Bo. Two for the violins and one cello and one bass." Joyce slapped a pile of music on each chair.

"How about Brian?"

"He's bringing his drums over tonight. He has his own chair." Joyce plunked a stack of music on the piano. "Wanna go over a few songs?"

Pat fiddled a bit more with the pedal of the piano, played a snatch of melody, and pronounced the piano as good as it was going to be. "Let's do *Sheep May Safely Graze*." He began the slow, sonorous melody and Joyce again took her flute out of its case and joined in. Barbara and David Wessel walked by with Teddy trotting at their heels. "Good day, Pat. Good day Ms. O'Sullivan," David bowed in his elegant way.

"Beautiful music," Barbara complimented them. Teddy barked and Barbara remarked, in the way pet-owners sometimes do, that he was confirming her opinion. "Should be a fun time, Pat, what with the dancing and the wedding and all. Has anyone bought any artwork yet?"

"Not yet. We are going to put out easels and a big banner and hopefully, by this time tomorrow, the art show and sale will bring in a few bucks." Joyce put her flute up and the notes of *Summer Wind* floated in the air. Pat joined in and several more passers-by stopped to listen.

"Whatcha' doing?" an old woman asked.

"There's going to be a wedding here in two days." Pat slipped from *Summer Wind* back to *Sheep May Safely Graze* and Joyce turned the page of her music to keep up with him. David and Barbara stepped back slightly to let the passer-by goggle. Teddy ignored the entire musicale and sniffed at a shrub on the sand.

"Nice." The old woman beat time with her hands. "Who's getting married?"

"Some people from America." Pat's hands climbed from one side of the keyboard to the other. "You can come and watch. I think the wedding is at four o'clock in the afternoon."

"Do I have to get dressed up?" The woman eyed David's splendiferous attire and swished her housedress. "I love a good wedding."

Pat's nimble fingers moved into *Pachobel's Canon*. "No. You can wear anything you want. You'll have to stand out beyond the wall, but I don't think anyone will mind a good audience." Pat shrugged as he played. He supposed half the island would be on hand to gape anyway. This old lady wouldn't even be noticed. He finished the *Canon* with a soft note and turned all the way around on the round stool. He crashed down on the keys, playing the first bars of *The Wedding March* and then got up, stretching his fingers. The old lady clapped her hands.

"We'll do very well," Joyce put her flute back into its case. "Now, let's start on the art show."

"Music, art, shoot, I can do anything!" Pat grinned. He covered the piano with a quilted rug and he and Joyce went to the other side of the harbor where an area had been roped off for the art show. Barbara, Teddy and David walked back to the office. The elderly lady wandered along with Pat and Joyce, sensing that tagging along might be beneficial. Might even be a drink of beer for her if she was in the right place.

Tony Ginise, Lara and Bob Cherico lifted wooden easels off a dolly and set them along the waterfront wall. "We're going to string a banner up here," Lara pointed to an open area between two trees. "Jamie is finishing it up now."

"Sure hope we sell some pictures," Bob stood, hands on his bony hips, and smacked his lips. "Maybe we ought to put a sign up saying something like 'These original pieces of art would make a great wedding gift' or something like that."

"Great idea," Lara agreed. "What would be nicer for the bride than a picture of the harbor where her wedding took place?"

"Maybe a picture of where her honeymoon took place." Tony snickered.

Mikayla's push chair appeared, with Mikayla sitting and Madeline steering. "Hi!" Maddie screeched. "Hi, Mommy! Saw doggie! Saw Teddy!" Mikayla was fond of doggies, especially Teddy who always licked her face politely and could be counted on to retrieve Mikayla's rolled ball.

"Hi, honey." Joyce patted the little girl on her head. Lara waved.

"Hullo, Mrs. O'Sullivan. Hello, everyone," Madeline greeted the elders.

"We're gon' beeeach," Mikayla offered. And Lara smiled.

"If it gets any hotter, we're gon' beeach, too." Pat lifted his arms in the air to cool himself.

"What are you doing?" Madeline asked, curious.

"Art show. There are going to be more than a hundred guests for the wedding. They're all coming tomorrow and we hope they'll buy lots of stuff, paintings, clothes, gifts..." Lara's arm swept the entire harbor.

"Should be fun," Madeline was torn between hoping that she was asked to baby sit and hoping that she was free so that she could enjoy the celebration.

"Are you part of the dancing entertainment?" Pat asked her.

"Yup, we're going to dance around to *Hot, Hot, Hot* and then do the limbo. I think the idea is to get all the wedding guests up and dancing." She laughed as Pat pretended he was shuffling under a limbo bar. She liked Pat, Joyce and Tony, even if, to her young eyes, they were all as old as the rocks that lined the harbor.

Mikayla thought that all these conversations had gone on much too long.

"Beeeach!" She ordered, giving an unmistakable hint that she wanted to move on.

"OK, beeach," Maddie shrugged and pushed the chair onto the sand of the children's beach. Mikayla's legs pumped happily. Weren't grownups boring, the way they just wanted to stand around and talk?

***

On the other side of the harbor, Leslie and Charlie's staff began to set up the tables and chairs for the rehearsal dinner. Inside The Green Flash, chambermaids made up beds, checked the min-bars, cleaned bathrooms and the kitchen staff began preparations for two – well, more like three - full days of cooking and entertaining.

Rebecca and seven of her young pupils paraded along the waterfront, carrying poles and two wooden stanchions. Rebecca spoke with Leslie, "Where do you want the dancers to do their stuff?"

Leslie shrugged. "I think we'll have the regular dancing right there," she pointed to a concrete area, "And you guys can do the limbo out on the sand. That way, if anyone falls over...and I am *sure* that there will be a few who fall over..." The two women snorted with laughter... "They'll land themselves on the sand."

Meghan and Allison Flynn, the 14-year old blonde haired Flynn twins, overheard and began to giggle. Leslie rolled her eyes. "What are you two laughing at?" She jokingly scolded them. "You're too young to know about people falling in the sand!"

Emily-Ann, the twins' younger sister, scoffed. "Even I'm not too young to know about drunks!"

The youngest Flynn daughter, Cailyn, who was nine, turned to her best friend, Niccola Reese. "How disgusting!" she sniffed. "I hate it when people fall!" Niccola agreed and then the two youngsters wondered why everyone else laughed at them.

"What are you all wearing to dance?" Leslie decided that there had been enough talk about drunkards in front of the girls.

"Bright island dresses," Allison pirouetted around. "Mine is pink and Meghan's is blue. And Mitchell and his buddies Howard and Jared are wearing white shirts, shorts and a tie-dyed sash."

Rebecca made an admiring noise and handed the poles to the twins. "Can you two please put these right over there, behind that big coconut tree. No one should bother them there." The girls ran to obey.

"Are there only kids dancing?" Leslie did a sort of hula.

"No, no." Rebecca smacked Leslie on her rear end. "I'm jazzing it up and my island ladies' dancing class....just wait until you see them, they're great...are going to do a number or two." She shimmied suggestively and the younger children snickered and poked at one another. "Do you want to join us?"

"I just may." Leslie giggled. "By the time you get to the entertainment, I may take all my clothes off and ...who knows?" The girls gaped at her and then collapsed into a heap of laughter, torn between giggles and embarrassment at the talk of these older women.

"Shhush! They'll go home and tell their mother that you and I are stark, raving crazy!"

"And we're not? By the time this wedding and all that goes with it are finished, I may just go quietly bonkers!"

"You must be swamped. Lot of work?"

"Yeah, but I like Arlis and her beanpole boyfriend, Don the cowboy-man, with his hats and his boots. The two of them were nice and sweet and funny. I'm glad they're bringing the wedding down here. We're making a lot of money these next few days, so I don't mind the work."

"It will be a lot of fun. Just fun and sun and no problems!" Rebecca laughed and gathered her girls up. She put a cassette tape of *Shake, Sonora* into her tape player, set the player in the sand, and the group began to dance. "Let's do a little bit of practice, children." Leslie stood back, together with several interested passers by, and watched the girls cavort on the sand.

"Sun and fun and no problems, huh?" Leslie shook her head. "We'll see…"

***

The Southern Cross sailed back around the Windward Passage heading for Great Harbor on Jost Van Dyke. The passengers, tired after swimming and snorkeling, albeit in vain for the treasure of Long John Silver, ate a lunch of cold Caribbean lobster, salt rolls steaming out of the oven, and Kat's special International Falls Hot Cheese Ball Salad[3]. Most of them were draped in various snoozing positions, exhilarating in the salty spray and the sun on their backs. "This is the life for me," Lannie sighed with happiness. "I must work on winning the football pools so that I can afford to do this for the rest of my days."

"Jost Van Dyke ahead. Land Ho!" Ducky announced. "Great Harbor coming up!" A large, high mountain of green lay dead ahead of them.

Duncan rolled over and got to his feet. With his height, he was able to see a white, crescent beach intersecting the mountain. "Why is it called Jost Van Dyke?" He carefully echoed Ducky's pronunciation of *Yost Van Dike*.

Ducky nodded with approval. "You said it the right way. A lot of people don't know how to pronounce the name and call it *Just Van Dick*."

"As a canny Scot, I never say anything that is more difficult to pronounce than *haggis* until I hear someone else say the word."

"There are only about 300 people who live here full time. Great Harbor, ahead of us, is the largest settlement." He pointed ahead. "The mountain rises up from the harbor more than a thousand feet. There are two other good harbors; Little Harbor and White Bay, but Great Harbor is the official point of entry into the BVI and this is where most of the

---

[3] See recipes at the back of the book for this delicious and unusual salad.

inhabitants live. See that white building there? That's the Custom House and the police station." Duncan picked up the binoculars and peered out at the beach.

"Here," he handed the binoculars to Annie. She took them gingerly, not touching Duncan's fingers. Duncan smiled. "Can you see?"

"Yup," she swept the harbor. "What is that pink building over there?"

"That's Banjo's. That's where we'll be tonight. We'll moor over by Banjo's, but we have to go through these reefs carefully." He gestured forward. "See the channel markers? It's tricky here for a bit and then the harbor opens up." He checked a chart and then called out to Captain Jack that he was going to furl the jib, put down the mains'l and start the engines.

Captain Jack went forward to warn the passengers on the trampolines that they were rolling up the jib. "Watch your heads!" he cautioned.

"OK?"

"OK here!" Jack called back to Ducky.

"Jib coming in!" Ducky pushed a button and the stay at the bow began to furl itself, the winch humming, as the jib rolled itself up neatly. Ducky grinned to Duncan. "A lot easier these days with all these newfangled electronics. Even a landlubber can do it."

"Lowering the main!" Captain Jack checked out his lines as Ducky pushed another button and the huge, heavy main sail rumbled down, folding itself like an accordion in the lazy jacks that held the canvas. Ducky slid to the top of the cockpit and carefully coiled the lines.

The engines rumbled into life. That done, Ducky leaped into the captain's chair and steered the boat through the channel markers and into the harbor. "Here's a bit of local lore," Ducky told Duncan, Annie, Claudia and Sarah. "The island was named after a Dutch pirate and was the birthplace of Doctor John Lettsome. Doctor Lettsome was born here in 1744, went to England and founded the London Medical Society and the Royal Humane Society." Duncan nodded as if he knew about the Royal Humane Society. "He was supposedly a great humorist, too. On his tombstone, supposedly, is this –

'I, John Lettsome, blisters, bleeds and sweats 'em.
If, after that, they please to die – I, John Lettsome.'

"I think our innocent minds are being spoofed," Annie laughed.

Ducky spread his hands out in supplication. "Would I lie to you?"

"Tell us more about Banjo's." Claudia begged.

"Ah, Banjo's. Banjo Larkin was born here, right up above the Customs House in a tiny bungalow." He pointed and Annie swung the binoculars up. "His family was in the restaurant business...small time...and Banjo was always singing, playing the banjo...hence the nickname...making up silly rhymes and cavorting around instead of being a good cook. When Banjo got to be about twenty, he talked his father into letting him be the entertainer at the restaurant and Banjo just skyrocketed into island fame. He put together an island band and his specialty is making up island-music songs, right on the spot, making fun of the customers, his family...politics, the Queen...*every*body! He's been all over the world, dressed in ragged shorts and a tie-dyed top, barefooted, singing topical and silly songs. He's a rich man, with dozens of recordings, concerts and a lot of fame."

"But all Banjo really wants to do," Captain Jack broke in, "Is sing and drink some rum and cavort around. You'll be hearing him tonight, and if you're lucky, he'll make up a song right on the spot about you."

"He's done a great one about Captain Jack and *The Southern Cross*, and another about our other friends, Bomba and the Sarge." Ducky began to laugh. "It's to the tune of *All Day, All Night, Mary Ann*."

"*All day, all night, Bomba Man...In the Virgin Islands and so tan...*" Jack sang. "*Bomba Man, Oh, Bomba Man, what did Emma see? Nuttin' but perfection, on Marina Cay. Captain Scumbag likes it there because it is so nice...*"

And then Ducky and Captain Jack sang together, "*It's got cheeseburgers in Paradise!*"

Duncan and Annie stared, openmouthed. "Yup, Ole Captain Scumbag here is famous," Ducky feinted to the left to avoid Jack's swat. "You'll all see and hear it tonight."

"Yo, everyone!" Jack shouted. "We'll be mooring over there, to the right." The rest of the passengers got up, stretched, and came into the cockpit. "This is Great Harbor." He gave them the lecture that Ducky had already given to Duncan, Annie, Claudia and Sarah.

"There are some wonderful shops over by the Customs House...three dress and clothing stores and two gift shops...a bakery back there and then, over by Banjo's, there's a group of Banjo gift shops...clothing, island gifts, Banjo's CDs, an ice cream shop and a few bars and other restaurants. *The Southern Cross* will be anchored here all night, making it easy for you all to get on and off. You're welcome to wander anywhere you want, but watch out for wild goats if you go up in the hills." Elliott blinked and then decided that Captain Jack was joking.

"Have a fine afternoon exploring," Kat spoke to them. "Don't eat too much as you are scheduled to gather at Banjo's at seven o'clock..." She bowed to them. "Me, too. I have the night off tonight. I will let Banjo and his family cook for me." She dimpled. "And they cook very well, so save your appetite. They offer a grilled island buffet with ribs and chicken and fish and all kinds of great food. Or, if you don't want the buffet, you can order anything you want from the menu. All the food and all the drinks are included in the price of your vacation, so I urge you to enjoy yourselves and sample lots of island drinks and punches." She mimicked sipping a long, tall glass of something delicious. "And then, after the food is cleared away, we will be treated to Mr. Banjo himself, The Banjo Man, together with his famous band, playing and singing for our pleasure. We hope you'll kick off your shoes and get up and dance and have a ball."

She leaped onto the top of the lazarette and did a little jig. *"Oh, Captain Jack, you scumbag man, you sail into the sea..."*

Ducky touched Paula's arm gently. "How about some swim lessons, Paula? The water here is clear and slopes very gently."

Paula's face tightened. "N...no. Not yet, Ducky." She bit her lip. "I'm...I'm afraid. It's too soon. I'm...I don't feel ready." Her eyes darted from left to right.

Ducky gave her his best smile. "No problem at all, Paula." He moved between her and the rest of the group and lowered his voice. "I'm here whenever you are ready. I promise you that I won't pressure you or try to make you do anything that you don't want to do." He patted her arm and she flinched back. Behind his smile, Ducky was slightly concerned. Her fear was almost palpable.

"Its not that I don't want to learn," Paula whispered. "I just...I can't..."

Ducky bent and kissed Paula gently on her cheek. "I won't mention it again until you are ready. You come to me and ask and we'll do whatever is best for you." He chuckled. "Hey, there are a lot of things that I don't really want to do. I hate to try new foods. I hate liver. I hate anything slimy like okra. I hate snakes and have no desire to walk in any jungle. I'm not too fond of heights. We all have our physically vulnerable points." Paula's smile was tremulous but genuine. What a marvelous young man he was!

"Thank you, Mr. Duck. You are a credit to your mother and father." She hugged him back with a light touch. "But I am dying to go ashore and do a bit of shopping! *That*, I am *always* anxious to do!"

***

Carlton slammed the telephone down and made a face. "What's the matter, boss?" Effalyn sympathized.

"Goddamn snakes! This is the fifth call about goddamn snakes!"

"Well, there *was* one snake, after all. Maybe there is another snake or two around," Effalyn's tone was reasonable.

"That was a coral snake! Bah!" Carlton shook his fist at the telephone. "These calls are all of sightings of boa constrictors, giant snakes eight feet long! Bah!"

"Are you going to check it out?"

"Of course. If I didn't, we'll have an anaconda scare in our midst." He laughed, his good mood restored. "Let's go and bring your snake catching kit with you, just in case."

"Snake catching kit? What's that?"

"I don't know! An umbrella, maybe." Whistling, he bowed her out of the office stopping to snatch an umbrella from the round metal container next to the front door.

"I saw it under them trees, I swear it was ten feet long and as big around as a large pig!"

"What color was the snake, Mrs. Lawrence?" Carlton was politeness itself.

"Brown, with green stripes. It was *huge*!" Mrs Lawrence hugged her sweater tight around her.

Effalyn, armed with the umbrella, poked gingerly into the bushes. Carlton warned Mrs. Lawrence to stand back. Rolling his eyes at Effalyn's hesitant search, he took the umbrella from Effalyn, waved it in the air like a rapier and ducked under the mangrove tree. A large, sinuous broken branch lay across a tree trunk. It was dappled with long green leaves from the frangipani tree behind it. "Is this it?" He held up the branch.

Mrs Lawrence screamed, covered her head with her arms and crouched down. "It's the *snake*! It's the *snake*! Kill it! Kill it!" Carlton sighed and beckoned Effalyn to handle the matter from then on. Disheartened at his ongoing onslaught of nature, he trudged to the car and sat in the passenger seat with the air conditioning on until Effalyn came back from ministering to Mrs. Lawrence and her imagination.

"I'm going to slit my throat." Carlton said sadly. "Freaking snake!"

"Come on, boss. She really thought it was a snake." Effalyn began to laugh. "You can't blame her for being honestly mistaken, can you?"

"Freaking snake!" No one was going to make Carlton feel any better.

CHAPTER ELEVEN

"...So, so, break off this last lamenting kiss..."
John Donne, Songs and Sonnets

It was so easy to write poetry about Arlis. Especially after...well...*after*. Don got up, quietly, being sure not to disturb her curled-up slumber. He lit a cigarette, thinking that maybe, after the wedding, he'd quit. Maybe. He put a robe over his shoulders, wide awake now, and padded into his office. His computer beckoned – winking green lights at him and his imagination spilled into his fingertips and his word processing program.

"How, why you came into my life is yet just a mystery
But there you were and the rest is mere history –
Norwegian, Minnesotan, a dark-haired beauty,
You'd have been a treasure in any pirate's booty:
Quiet, soft-spoken, with a smile that just glowed,
A soft laugh, and a heart that overflowed
With love for all critters, whatever their size
And a marvelous sense for joy and surprise.

Has it been just a year? Seems more and much less;
Forever? Since yesterday? How long has it been?
Tomorrow, forever, will I see you again?
Well, goodnight for now, and may God bless.

If all could love just the way that you do
Christian, Muslim, Buddhist, Hindu and Jew
The world would be a more peaceful place
And we could stop running this frightful rat race.

A lifetime with you, no more and no less –
Well, goodnight for now, and may God bless,
And hold you tonight in His warm caress."

Don sat back, all passion spent. He printed out the poem to leave on Arlis' pillow and went back to bed. She was warm and soft and nestled into his arms. Well, perhaps, he grinned into the darkness, not *all* passion spent.

***

A night at Banjo's. An easy evening with not much to do but sit back and enjoy Banjo's outrageous songs. Thus like Captain Jack Scambaugh, many of the charter captains usually planned together to bring their boats into Jost Van Dyke's Great Harbor to treat their passengers to an evening of terrific food, conviviality, Banjo's music and tall, cool island drinks. As well, *their* passengers might just enjoy meeting someone *else's* passengers, enhancing the vacation experience for all concerned. And, certainly, it was fun for Jack, Ducky and Kat to spend a convivial hour with Karen and Leigh, Captain Dave and the rest of the charter captains and crews. And thus, joining Captain Jack Scambaugh's catamaran group was the *Jumbie Jamboree* with its four passengers, Captain Dave's fishing boat, the *GKB,* with its all-girl crew, Leigh and Karen Brethauer's 45-foot motor launch, *Looney Tunes*, with its six passengers, and *The Spanish Doubloon*, a 50 foot monohull out of San Juan, run by Esteban Cabrillo and his brother, Feliz with the four Puerto Rican couples who had chartered it for a week, each couple hoping to perk up their sagging marriage.

The night fell and the passengers from *The Southern Cross* took seats at a huge round table that was reserved for them. The four men from the *Jumbie Jamboree* sat next to them at a table with their Captains, Eddie and Karen, better known as Bomba and The Sarge. Captain Dave and his four fisherwomen, Lenore, Susan, Tracey and Lynn sat with the passengers from Puerto Rico and Leigh and Karen Brethauer. Huge trays of drinks appeared as if by magic and in the time it took to drink two rounds, all of the passengers from all of the boats had made friends with one another. Torches were lit and the smells from the roasting meats filled the air. Despite her infatuation with Elliott, Suzie noted that the four men from the *Jumbie Jamboree* were all tall and very good looking. One of the men, dark and heavy-set, sporting a bushy moustache winked at her and she smiled back. She wondered if there was anything there that she might be missing, but Elliott touched her thigh underneath the table and she jerked her attention back to him.

As the meals were consumed, and the food preparation and serving area was cleared, the band came onto the sand in front of the dance floor and began to tune up their instruments. Lannie, who was a devotee of reggae music in England, watched the drums being dragged into place. "They make those drums from old oil cans," he told Zandra. "Then they pound out the tops to different levels. That makes the drum sound out the notes when they hit the top in different spots." Zandra craned her neck to see. "They can play reggae music or the most delicate classical sounds on those drums...Oh! That must be Banjo himself!" Lannie joined the rest of the audience in getting to his feet and applauding.

Banjo seemed larger than life. He was tall and coal black, with a short beard and a large gold earring. He looked like a benevolent pirate dressed in a colorful shirt opened all the way down in front. His chest was draped with dozens of gold chains and medallions and he sported a bright purple cummerbund tied around his waist. His pants were ragged and cut off below his knees and he was barefooted, with large, splayed feet.

"Hey, evryboddy!" He called.

"Hey, Banjo!" The crowd chorused back.

"You reddy fo' some music?"

The crowd cheered and clapped. They were ready. The drums began and Banjo grabbed a guitar and began to sing. The song was raucous and bawdy and mentioned many of the people who were in the audience. The crowd loved it, stamping and clapping and swaying and Banjo fed off their enthusiasm and when he was done, stood for a few moments basking in their applause. The crowd roared and he began again, this time singing an island song, *"She Shake her 'Ting"*, moving his huge body in lascivious postures to the music and lyrics.

Banjo spied Captain Jack at the back of his table. "Hey! Captain Scumbag! How you do?" He roared. "Come up here, man and we do your song!" Grinning and pleased with the attention, Jack strolled up, shook Banjo's hand and clapped in time as Banjo told the crowd that he was going to do the Captain Scumbag Song. "And get up here too, you Bomba Man!" He called to Captain Ed. "And you, too, Lady Sarge and you, Captain Dave! All-a-you in dis song, come on up here!" Captains Dave, Karen and Ed, grinning, ambled up to stand next to Captain Jack. The beat of the drums was hypnotic as Banjo, the band, and many of the regulars started to sing. *"Oh, Captain Jack, you Scumbag Man...you sail into da sea....."*

"Get up and dance!" Banjo ordered, and many in the audience did. "Hey, you, Kat, you beautiful t'ing! Hey, you Duck-Man! Dance!" Sammy and Claudia, Vinny and Martha, Zandra and Hosea and Michael and Corliss took to the floor, bumping and grinding together with dozens of others, stamping and shouting the lyrics. Annie watched as Captain Dave's girls got onto the floor and Kat joined them, gyrating and moving to the raucous music. *"Dey rove da waves, dey fish da sea, dey sail off into space...But after all is said and done, dey come back to Banjo's Place! Hey!"*

"Come on, let's join the action," Duncan held his hand out to Annie. She grinned and shrugged and took his hand as they moved into the crowd on the dance floor, shoving Kat with her hip as they both grinned and sang the easy lyrics. *"Oh, Captain Jack, You Scumbag man, Why don't' you play wid me?"* Was it the heat or the night or the man? Annie didn't know or care. She was having a fabulous time. She threw her head back, tossed her hair and moved her body in rhythm with Duncan's arms and hips. For such a big man, he danced well, with balance and rhythm and she gloried in the music. Each touch burned and made her warmer. Their hips bumped, their backsides touched, their arm entwined. It was wonderful.

"Such bourgeoisie," Elliott sneered from the dark corner of the table. "Let's get out of this crush."

"Can't we dance just once?" Suzie wheedled.

"Don't be such a whiny little bitch. If you want to dance, go right ahead." Elliott's sneer was visible, even in the darkness. "Just don't expect me to be here when you come back."

"I like to dance, Elliott. I...you're probably a good dancer, too. You have such...you're so athletic..."

"Stuff it, babe. You wanna dance with a bunch of losers or come with me? I've got a nice surprise for you. Something new that I got." He patted his pocket and smiled. Suzie noticed that when you did what Elliott wanted, he was all smiles and sweetness. If you wanted to do what he didn't want...well!

She smiled back at him, a slightly lopsided smile. "I'm with you, Elliott. You're my man." She hoped for a reply that showed that he cared for her.

She got, "Let's get away from this stupid bunch of yahoos." He steered Suzie out of the restaurant, ignoring the droop of her mouth. She went with him, wanting his approval and the stuff he had procured. But couldn't she have had it both ways? Dance a little and then go under the trees? Or go under the trees and come back, exhilarated, and then dance? Suzie was used to getting her own way. She generally led the parade. Sighing with reluctance, she followed him. It looked like a lot of fun out there on the dance floor and she did so love to dance. But Elliott's face told her plainly what he thought of a bunch of strangers dancing to what he referred to as jungle music and she wanted to please him.

"Where are we going?" She asked him, trying to keep the disappointment out of her voice as they moved into the inky darkness along the shore.

"Somewhere private, baby. Somewhere where no one is going to see us or what we do." He stopped for a moment and took her into his arms. "Somewhere dark and alone."

She giggled, capitulating to him, and molded herself to him. To hell with the dancing. "Whatever you want, Elliot."

"You got it, honey. Whatever I want."

***

The passengers drifted back in small groups or two by two, some sober and a few who had more than they should have had to drink. Up on the trampoline netting, as if by tacit consent, Zandra and Hosea moved their bedding closer and lay on top together, arms entwined, watching the stars glow.

Annie wanted to move closer to Duncan, but was too shy. Duncan wanted to move closer to Annie, but was frightened by his fierce feelings for a woman he had known for just a few days. Even worse, he was worried that the gap in their ages made his feelings almost indecent. She was the same age as his daughter, for God's sake! Thus, they got ready for bed and lay apart, both yearning, both rather silly, if the truth be told.

Silly or not, Duncan began to talk, telling Annie about his early life, how he met and wooed Mairi, his family, his farm, the sheep and the lambs and her death. He told her about the braes and the lochs of Scotland and the beauty of his homeland. He spoke into the darkness about his children and grandchildren and his love for them. And, how this love, although boundless and joyful, was not quite enough.

Annie listened and her heart turned over, hearing the echoing loneliness to her own soul as Duncan whispered in the darkness. Duncan's voice stopped and he waited. Into the void, Annie tentatively began. She told him of her happy childhood, of her huge and wonderful family, her cousins, her parents, "Even Suzie was part of my good childhood memories – *most* of the time," she confided with a rueful chuckle. In the inky softness, she heard and felt him move closer to her. And, despite trying to not eavesdrop, she could hear the soft sounds from the couple on the other side of the trampoline.

Annie gulped. The darkness was a wonderful cover for embarrassment and shyness. She began to talk about her job, her hopes and the few men who had wandered quickly in, and even more quickly out, of her life. "I have so many men friends. I date a lot and always have a partner for dances and movies and dinners." She poked her bare foot out from under the covered and wiggled her toes. "But the one that I hoped for hasn't yet shown up." She sighed softly, appalled at her own audaciousness. *Wonder if he thinks I'm a man-eating hussy?*

"Hmmm," Duncan mused up at the stars, "I wonder…"

"Wonder what?" *Where was she getting this ability to spill out her thoughts?*

"Wonder if you just need to look to your left." She sat up with a gasp.

"What do you *mean?*" Her heart hammered and she was sure that it could be heard all over Great Bay.

"I mean, little hen," he rolled over onto his side and propped his head up with his hand. "That maybe we …. I mean, I…Ah, Annie. I am too *old* for you!" His voice was anguished. "From the moment I saw you…I was attracted. But you are so young, lassie. You're my daughter Kirstie's age!" He groaned from the depths of his soul.

In the blackness, Annie grinned. If *he* felt uncomfortable, why then it was easy for *her* to feel confident. Was *that* what has been missing all these years? That and a big ox of a Scotsman? Sure he was older, but…did she care? Not really. "Duncan, I felt…well…" and she felt herself blush and was grateful for the enveloping dark. "I, um, I, thought you were so distinguished and kind and nice…"

"Kind and nice? I don't want to be kind and *nice*! Sounds like my grandfather! Kind and nice!" He made a groaning sound and rolled over to lay right up against her. Only the thin blanket was between their pajama-clad bodies. "My bonnie wee Annie, to hell with kind and nice!" He enfolded her and kissed her and kind and nice disappeared, replaced immediately by hot and intense.

I guess I'm not too old after all, was Duncan's last thought before he slept. Annie's last thought was indescribable.

***

It was very late, very late, when Suzie and Elliott stumbled onto the boat. She began to giggle and he put his hand over her mouth to stifle the sounds. "Shut up, you silly bitch!" He shook her until her head bobbed back and forth and her giggles turned to moans. "Don't make another sound!" He pushed her into the cockpit and down into the cabin area. Ducky raised his head and listened. *This is not good*. He and Jack would talk over the potential problem in the morning light. Sighing at the imbecility of some passengers, he rolled over and went back to sleep.

It was even later when Kat crept onto the boat. She was smiling and wrapped herself in a light blanket to catch one hour's sleep before she had to be up to make breakfast.

***

Annie was awakened by the bleating of goats. She sat up, suddenly and stared at the sheet-rumpled lump that was obviously Duncan. Still asleep, he made some inarticulate noise and burrowed into the blankets. Annie's eyes were wide. A noise from her left made her turn her head slowly to see Zandra poke her own tousled head out from the single bump comprised of herself and Hosea. She grinned at Annie and gave her the thumbs-up sign. Annie blushed furiously and ducked her head. Quietly, so not as to wake Duncan, Annie slid out of the nest of blankets and went down to her cabin to gather her thoughts and brush her teeth. The cabin was empty. She shrugged. Suzie was probably with Elliott, but, as a fierce blush covered Annie from head to toe, who was *she* to criticize? Grinning widely and humming a song, Annie tossed aside her pajamas and put on a blue and white bikini. She slid a navy blue sun-dress over her head. What a beautiful day!

***

In the galley, Kat was also singing as she prepared omelet's to order. "Nice night?" Ducky queried, giving her a quizzical look.

"The best," she answered, her smile inscrutable. "And you?"

"Good, but not as good as you." Ducky laughed, a booming sound and went to bring coffee to Captain Jack.

***

"*What?*" Carlton listened to the hysterical babble at the other end of his cell phone. "I don't believe it!" He listened for a moment more and then slammed down the phone. He was hot and sweating and his shirt was already stained with a smear of jelly-donut. "Sheesh, Eff. You are not gonna believe this!"

"What won't I believe?" Effalyn was crisp and professional. Carlton, again, marveled at her early-morning prettiness and wondered why at least one of the stupid men on the island hadn't scooped up this prize.

"Come on. Get the car and I'll knock your socks off," He glanced down at Effalyn's neat panty-hose covered legs. "That is, if you were wearing socks. Let's go, girl!"

As the car swept out of the parking lot, Effalyn asked, "OK, where are we going, Boss-man?"

"To Salt Cay Bay." His excitement abated for a moment. "Mother Nature has kicked me where it hurts again. Another death."

"Death?"

"Uh, huh, this time by manta ray or sting ray." His face had lost its grin.

"*What*? I didn't think they were lethal."

"Not usually, but I think…Doc said this guy was allergic, apparently."

"Who is it?"

"Some Chinese guy. Cousin of Jackie Sing's."

"What happened?"

"I don't know much more. Geez, I can't take all these deaths, Eff. We go along for years not having anything more than a broken leg on a drunk or a kid who gets sunburn." In his rising agitation, Carlton began to chew his lip. "And now, in the space of a week or so, we have Two-Tone, Mr. Marsden, and the goddamn snake!"

"Well, Two-Tone and the snake, they were accidents."

"Maybe. Maybe. I'm beginning to see a Jumbie behind every palm tree!" Carlton swerved the car into a short, dusty road that led to a rocky bay. Doctor Fullbright's car and two trucks were parked by the edge of the sand.

"Mornin, Eff. What do you think of this situation, Carlton?" Doctor Fullbright's pants were wet at the bottom. He had obviously waded into the surf to examine the body and his face held a doleful expression.

"Hey, Doc." Carlton waved a limp hand. "Shit, I'm tired of all this flora and fauna screwing up my crime statistics. What happened?"

"Jackie Sing's cousins, three of them, came over to visit from China. One of them," he peered at a piece of paper, "name of Sing Fong...I think they use their names backwards...died from a sting ray spike going into his forehead. Seems Mr. Sing or Mr. Fong or however it goes was allergic to the sting ray poison." Doc Fullbright's heavy arm pointed to the water's edge where several men stood, clustered near a long, wet blanket-covered shape. "Poor bastard."

They walked slowly toward the group. One of the men standing at the water's edge detached himself and walked to meet them. It was Jackie Sing, owner of the Sing-Song Chinese restaurant in Spanish Town. "Ho, Inspector Reese. See what tragedy has befallen my family." Jackie's eyes were wet with tears. "My cousin, Fong. He is dead."

"We are so sorry for your family." As always, Effalyn said the right thing. "Can you tell us how this horrible thing happened?"

"They are all – Fong and his cousins Henry and Eddie – good swimmers and experienced divers. They all, in China, often swim and dive for shellfish. Fong...he is the one who died..." Jackie bowed his head, "He was once bitten by a blowfish some years ago. He had a bad reaction and the doctor there told him that if was ever bitten again, it would be a serious thing."

"But a blowfish and a sting ray?" Effalyn asked. "They are two different things. Why did...?"

Doctor Fullbright spread his hands out. "Might be a similar toxin." He shrugged. "I know you can get mighty sick from a blowfish or a sea urchin or sting ray, but I wasn't aware that one could die from the poison." He scratched his chin. "But if the toxin was similar, perhaps the original bite left him...what was his name? Ah, yes, Fong." He bent forward with a little bow that reminded Carlton of a Charlie Chan movie. "Might have left Fong with a susceptibility to a more massive allergy problem." He bowed towards Jackie again and Jackie bowed back. "Let's take a look at him." He stepped towards the body and then turned back. "Are you all right with this, Jackie? Why don't you and your cousins wait here and I'll, um, take care of..." He harrumphed delicately. Jackie nodded slowly and called to his cousins in a chirrupy language. The two men looked again at the bundle and slowly came back up the beach.

As they passed, Carlton and Doctor Fullbright nodded to them and they nodded back. Effalyn's eyes were sympathetic and the men gave her a half-bow. The two men joined Jackie, who began to speak in their native language, no doubt explaining what the doctor had said.

Carlton lifted the blanket back and covered his mouth to hide his involuntary grin. Here was a dead Chinese man named Mr. Fong Sing. And here was a very alive Black man, himself – Mr. Carlton Reese. Naturally, he was sorry and shaken that Mr. Sing was dead, but also, naturally, he was delighted that he, Carlton Reese, was not. Doctor Fullbright made a puffing sound and knelt in the sand. Effalyn bent over and took out her microphone. By that time, Carlton's delight in his own mortality was under control. "What have we got?" he asked.

"Adult male, perhaps thirty-five years of age, Asian, well-nourished," Doctor Fullbright spoke into the microphone. "From visual examination, he is certainly dead. Get me some gloves out of my bag, Carlton." The doctor pulled on a pair of gloves. As Effalyn and Carlton did the same, Doctor Fullbright performed his ritual acts. "Tough for me to say with certainty, as he's been in the water and died there, but, based on what the other men have told Jackie, he died at about seven AM. I'd have to wait until the autopsy is finished, but, from the verbal anecdotes of the two other swimmers, he died of some anaphylactic reaction and did not drown." He peered into the mouth of the corpse and moved its hands and arms. "The cousins told Jackie that they were swimming underwater, over there by those rocks, and Fong here saw several sting rays or manta rays...they're not sure which...One of them watched as Fong got very close, probably trying to peer closely at one of them or perhaps take a picture. Fong had an underwater camera strapped to his wrist.. The ray swam towards Fong, presumably, and his stinger pierced Fong's forehead. Fong convulsed and was thrashing about for maybe thirty seconds and then went limp. The cousin closest grabbed him and brought him immediately to the surface and up on a rock, but, when he ripped off the mask, Fong was already dead. They tried to resuscitate him, but it was too late. The puncture hole was obvious – already red and swollen." He asked Carlton to help him turn Fong's body over and he dictated more of his observations into the microphone as the mortuary hearse pulled up to the edge of the sand. Two sweating mortuary attendants pushed a wheeled gurney over the sand.

"Uuufff! Help me up, Carlton." Doctor Fullbright struggled to his feet, dusting the sand from his knees. "I'm getting too blamed old to play on the beach." He motioned to the mortuary men to take the body away, "I'll do the autopsy tomorrow. I don't think there was any foul play. I think this was just another one of those peculiar accidents we seem to be having." He looked at Carlton for his opinion.

"Too many of these accidents for me," Carlton made a sour face. "But, I think you are right. This isn't murder." Effalyn nodded in agreement and the three of them followed the gurney to the edge of the sand.

***

"I've brought you a good, illustrated book about toxic poison and plants," Professor Carol Stambaugh peered at Effalyn and Carlton through round, wire-rimmed glasses. She was tall, with pepper and salt hair cut in a Dutch bob. She wore an attractive print dress and sensible dark shoes. She looked like somebody's mother, a teacher, a librarian, but she was the foremost expert in plant poisons in the Southern Hemisphere. "These are the two that have been positively identified." She showed them a picture of a beautiful vine with large white flowers. "This is the castor bean plant, pretty as they come. It looks so innocent and is so deadly, if one chews the seeds."

"And that's what Mr. Marsden did, huh?"

"So it seems. He had eleven seeds, each fully masticated, in his stomach. From what we can tell, the beans had been digested eight hours before. Poor man, he must have been in wrenching agony with cramps, diarrhea and a burning in his mouth." She made a face. "He must have been truly incapacitated to not convey his distress to his wife or some passer-bye. I wonder that he wasn't screaming in agony. I can't believe that no one would have heard his cries." Professor Stambaugh's eyes, behind their glasses, magnified her puzzlement.

"We will check again, won't we, Eff?" Carlton watched Effalyn make her notes. "But, I don't think anyone said that they heard anything, Professor."

"Could he have had a gag in his mouth?" Effalyn asked, writing furiously.

"Call me Carol. Yes. Could have," Carol Stambaugh made an unhappy moue. "If he was old and in poor physical shape, especially if he was confused, he might not have been able to make any effort to extricate himself from something blocking his screams. The beans could have been mashed with a mortar and pestle, no way that anyone could tell if they were mashed or chewed..." Effalyn shuddered as she thought about Mr. Marsden's last few hours. "And it would be relatively easy to force them down the throat of such an ill person. He wouldn't be able to physically protest or stop a determined, sadistic murderer." Carlton swallowed the bile that had risen in his own throat. *Jesus! Could anyone do this to their own husband?*

"And the rhododendron? Was it just regular rhodies, like I have in my garden?"

"Yup," Professor Stambaugh nodded. "It is amazing how toxic some plants can be. Almost every part of a rhododendron is poisonous, but, only the root will kill you outright. The rest of the plant will make you very sick, but it isn't a plant that anyone would try to eat unless the person was nuts. The leaves are leathery and tough...it would take a superhuman with teeth like a dog or a wolf to masticate one of the leaves or stems, although the flowers are pretty and maybe some child would suck nectar out of the blossoms."

"Really? Gee whiz," Effalyn was aghast. "I wonder if I ever ate any of those plants when I was a kid? Who could know they were poison?"

"They'd make you very sick." Carol shook her head. "But it would be doubtful that you would die. You might be very ill but you'd have to ingest the roots before you'd really be in trouble."

"And who would eat a plant root? Wouldn't it be difficult to get to?"

Carol nodded. "You'd have to dig it up, cut the root off...and they are tough and fibrous roots, very difficult to cut by mistake...then mash up the root and eat it. It would be like eating a tree. No one in their right mind would do it."

"So, Mr. Marsden would have to be crazy or sick, or...?"

"Or." Professor Stambaugh nodded. "Or."

"And then we come to the mystery seeds..." Carlton turned the pages of the book. "What is your educated guess?"

"I think it might be Jimson Weed. That's the name it is called in the United States. The official name is *Datura stramonium,* called The Angel's Trumpet or the Devil's Trumpet here in the islands...take your pick..." She showed them a picture of a delicate blossom, shaped like a trumpet. Some of the flowers were pale purple and some were pure white. "It is part of the nightshade family, a particularly nasty group of poisons, and contains a horrible selection of poisons like atropine and scopolamine." She pointed to a list of symptoms. "One of the problems with *Datura* is that the symptoms don't appear for an hour or so, leading the eater to think that the plant was just fine to munch on." She went on to tell them that many young adults eat the plant, daring one another to see who can come closest to death. "A dangerous, deadly contest that kills more than a thousand people every year." She took off her glasses and polished them on the hem of her dress. "There is a saying in the medical profession about jimson weed victims: 'Hot as a hare, blind as a bat, dry as a bone, red as a beet and mad as a hatter'." Her head swayed from side to side. "These people, before they expire, hallucinate like crazy, argue with imaginary aliens, scratch bugs that aren't there off their bodies, do wild dances or maybe stand, catatonically still, for hours before they die." She put her glasses back on with a careful motion. "They, too, die an unimaginable death."

"Shit." Effalyn used a word that she hardly ever used.

"Right." Carol agreed.

* * *

By late morning, the airplanes that carried most of the wedding guests had disgorged their passengers. The wedding guests were hot and eager to get to their hotels, cool off in the air-conditioning and then jump into bathing suits, the ocean and perhaps a few island drinks. The stores on Big Fish Cay filled with shoppers, the bars and restaurants held crowds of visitors and the art show and beaches had more than their share of excited throngs.

"No, Ma'am. Although the name of the shop mentions hemp, we do not...most emphatically do not...sell marijuana." Robin thought that if she had to explain this one more time, she might go bonkers. "There is a very strict law in the British Virgin Islands about the illegal use of drugs. You might just take a look here," she pointed to a luridly colored photo of a dripping cell block room, with a hole in the floor for a toilet, furnished to all merchants by the Chamber of Commerce, of the inside of one of the Road Town jail cells. "This is where you'll spend the rest of your life if you even *think* of lighting up a joint." Robin smiled with sweet patience. "We sell *hemp* products here, products made from a very different kind of plant. There are woven belts, sandals, ropes, placemats, jackets of a linen-like hemp material...all kinds of wonderful products made from the hemp plant." She showed a braided basket to a heavy-set woman who was bulging out of a bathing suit three sizes too small.

"And is Madam going to the wedding? Oh, your cousin's niece! Now nice." Robin steered the woman toward a display of tableware. "If you haven't yet selected a wedding gift, we have many wonderful things for you to look at. *And* we wrap for free..." She left the woman to move herself to a spot that was right in the path of the air-conditioning and fluffed her short blonde hair.

"I told you early on that naming the store The Alice W. Rabbit's Hemp Emporium would give out the wrong impression." Robin's husband, Paul, hissed. He turned, "No, sir, this is a *hemp* shop, selling *hemp* products..."

The hefty lady finally departed, toting several hundred dollars worth of woven tablemats, four belts, a skirt and six purses. Robin watched her go with mixed feelings and turned to the next customer. "No, we do not! This is a *hemp* products store selling...." It was going to be a very long, albeit very profitable day.

On board *The Southern Cross*, Hosea greeted the breakfast group, "*Goedemorgen! Hoe gaat het?*" Blank faces looked at him while Zandra's smile stretched huge. "*Magik mezelf aan...um, um...*" He looked at Zandra for assistance.

"She nodded with encouragement. "*Goed! Magik mezelf aan u voorstellen.*"

"*Ja*," Hosea beamed at them all. "*Mijn naam is Hosea*!" He bowed. "I'm learning Dutch!"

"I wonder from which little Dutch girl," Elliott said, but his smile didn't reach his eyes.

"Wonderbar!" Lannie leapt up, ignoring Elliott. He slapped Hosea on his shoulder. "Man, you are going to be the...the...the most *linguistic* person that I know."

"Good show," Duncan saluted Hosea with his tomato juice glass. Everyone joined in, everyone talking at once, *I should learn more in the way of languages...Boy, isn't it clever?...He sure is smart....How can he remember all those words?* Elliott took his plate of toast and went inside the cabin. Suzie glared around the table and huffed after him.

"We have a name for people who can dish out the mickey, but can't take it," Duncan tried to hide his smile.

"The mickey?" Sammy looked baffled.

"You call it giving someone a verbal insult, we call it 'taking the mickey'".

"What do you call such a person?" Claudia leaned in.

"A dickhead," Duncan's tone was neutral. Everyone laughed. Covering his mouth, Duncan said, "I shouldn't have said that. I'm as bad as he is."

"No!" Zandra was adamant. "You are just joking. He means to hurt." She put her hand on top of Hosea's. "Hosea has worked hard to learn. I am very proud."

"And so say all of us!" Duncan again hoisted his glass.

Sitting on the swim platform, a little ways away from the group, Captain Jack mused on how well a pain in the ass passenger fused all of the other passengers, well, except for Suzie, who should get herself away from Elliott, into a much more cohesive group. Elliott was poison, pure poison. A nasty piece of business and he'd be happy if Elliott suddenly got an urgent telephone call from one of those rich and famous clients that he could never talk about calling him home. He sighed. He needed a little Emma time.

As if on target, the splash of oars made him turn around. And here she was, his own wonderful Mrs. Peel, rowing a tiny dink out. He stood up, his bearded face aglow with delight and tied the dink up; then nearly pulled his wife bodily into his arms. "Geez, I have missed you!"

"I love you, too." She kissed him with enormous enthusiasm. "What's wrong? You look a bit upset."

"Tell you later." He patted her behind with tender appreciation as the entire group at the breakfast tables waved and called to Emma.

***

Continuation of Itinerary of *The Southern Cross* ....

Saturday, December 19th - *The Southern Cross* stays moored in Big Fish Harbor. Breakfast on board or, if you want to explore alternate places to eat, there are wonderful restaurants on the island. Lunch is a packed picnic lunch for you to enjoy on the beach. And in the early afternoon – the wedding! Put on your dress-up dancing duds and get ready to have a wonderful time. Don't forget! A good guest gives a nice present...hint from your Captain Jack...

Sunday, December 20th –You sleep late and recuperate from the wedding. While you loll in bed and have a cup of restorative coffee, we will sail you in the early morning to The Baths, one of the most remarkable natural formation of huge granite boulders, with magical pools of water and sun light. Snorkeling here is excellent and the adventurous walking trail through the boulders is fun. After a picnic lunch on the beach, we will travel a short distance to Spanish Town and the Virgin Gorda Yacht Basin. Once again, we will be tied up at the dock, making for easy egress. The afternoon activities include a horseback ride up to the Copper Mine or speed boat rides with water skiing. If you want less action, you can relax and shop in the many stores and boutiques that line the harbor. Night will find us all traveling to the Olde Yard Inn, known for its excellent cuisine and gardens.

Monday, December 21 – Breakfast in the tiny, exquisite garden in the middle of Spanish Town. The restaurant is noted for its rum and banana pancakes. Then, a leisurely morning in Spanish Town . The Southern Cross will depart at noon with lunch on board as we cruise to the North Sound of Virgin Gorda. The boat will travel into oceanic waters and you will hang onto your hat as we skim the waves at more than 18 knots. The truly brave can ride on the trampoline, holding on tightly, for the ride of their lives. We'll turn the boat before we reach Portugal (ha) and head into the North Sound for several days. You can now look forward to para-kiting, a snorkeling expedition off of Necker Island (guest island of the stars and the really, really rich). sailing your own small boat, more horseback riding, SCUBA diving, and The Bitter End Yacht Club.

Tuesday, December 22 - We will leave The Bitter End Yacht Club on the GKB, Captain Dave's legendary sport fishing boat. Captain Dave's crew – the only all-girl crew in the British Virgin Islands – will serve you breakfast on the way to the secret fishing grounds where no-one doesn't catch big fish. Dave promises you sailfish, barracuda, blue or white marlins, dolphin or tuna...many of the fish are more than 300 pounds of fight! Captain Dave can arrange for photos and/or preserving your trophy fishes, and he will ship your fresh catch to your home

should you so desire. Lunch on board and, upon arrival back at The Bitter End Yacht Club, those still able to keep awake will enjoy a magnificent dinner at The Carving Board at The Bitter End.
 ….more later…..

CHAPTER TWELVE

"Three things I shall never lend – my horse, my wife and my name..."
R. S. Surtees, Hillington Hall...

Don and Arlis sat in First Class...his first time in the luxury of the front of the plane. Arlis had once gone, long before he had met her, to Paris on a First Class ticket. She'd raved about it so much that he had once again upped the credit limits on his new AMEX card. What the hell...how often does a man get married? Well, he retracted his thought...How often does a man get married to such a prize as Arlis?

Arlis sat next to the window, dividing her time between reading an engrossing new mystery, *The Ice Floe*, and staring out of the window at the world spread beneath them and then poking Don in the ribs and exclaiming, "Oh, my goodness! Look at that ship below! Is it a big ocean liner?"

He began to doodle on the pad that he always carried, just in case a poetic thought floated to him. He drew a caricature of Arlis' cat, Tinker, then a few floating clouds. He drew a picture of a man with a bow-tie around his neck. The man had a smile on his face...did that mean that under it all, he was happy at being married? Certainly. Under it all and over it all.

He began to write:
This is for Arlis, who loves a good story:
Mystery or murder, if it isn't too gory,
As long as no animals are injured or maimed,
And in the end, the culprit is named.

She'll take a good book with her to bed –
Each night, a chapter or two will be read –
A cat might come up and snuggle beside –
Or nuzzle a page as she tries to decide
Who wins the contest, the cat or the book?
Then over her face comes a whimsical look.
She purrs to the cat, and he purrs right back,

They're on the same page, on the same track –
I look at them both, and all is all right,
And thus so it goes, most every night.

"Why do you have such a goofy look on your face?" Arlis nudged him. "Look! We are coming up to a big, green hump in the ocean! Do you think it is Tortola already?"

***

The two Zodiacs ferried the passengers to Big Fish Cay. Immediately, the one with Captain Jack and Emma was greeted with shouts and hails! "Captain *Jack*! Captain *Jack*! Emma! Emma, darling! Here I am! Me! Arlis!" As Jack tried to step onto the dock, he was nearly torpedoed off by Arlis' exuberant hug. She threw herself in his arms. He laughed uproariously and whirled her around with her soft, white arms strangling his neck. "Oh, my goodness! I'm so excited to see you! Don! *Don*!" she shouted to the tall, cowboy-hatted man who was watching the show with a mixture of fierce pride and a bit of embarrassment.

"Hey, Don, my man!" Jack extricated his hand from Arlis' fervent grip and pumped Don's up and down. "Congratulations to you both!" He turned to announce to the rest of the passengers, "This is the bride and groom! Arlis, our beautiful, beautiful, bride, gorgeous outside and gorgeous inside. And this is Don, the luckiest man in the world." Most of the passengers crowded around to be introduced and to congratulate the ecstatic couple.

Arlis and Don eventually dragged Captain Jack and Emma to The Green Flash Hotel to be schooled in the mysterious ritual for the morrow. The rest of the passengers stood by the Zodiacs, gazing around. They were charmed by the shops and art show, the beautiful sandy beach and the friendly atmosphere of the harbor.

"I could stay here for the rest of my life," Sarah sighed. "This is the loveliest spot I have ever seen."

"Let's just stay!" Sammy echoed. "Let's just get off the boat and find a place to live." He gazed in awe. "I could be a bartender. I could wait on tables or be a fisherman. No worries, no cares. What a place!"

The passengers split into groups; Elliott and Suzie started out towards the bar at The Green Flash but noticed the sign for the Hemp Emporium and turned that way; Claudia and Martha sauntered off with

Sammy and Vinny; Annie, Elwyn, Zandra, Hosea, Paula, Lannie and Duncan wandered toward the art show. Michael Beck and Corliss walked over to where the fishermen were taking out their catch and Sarah sauntered towards the back street.

Pat sold six pictures to the tourists and passengers, two of them showing some of the glorious harbor scenes he had painted to be given as wedding presents for Arlis and Don. Joyce O'Sullivan, explaining her left-handed painting technique, sold five botanical studies, one of which was going to be given to the bride and groom. Bob Cherico sold four oil paintings, each with his dog, Kyle prominently displayed, Tony Ginise sold two watercolors of boats in the harbor, and Lara sold four of her brilliantly colored island impressionist works. Six of the other artists also sold pictures. The Big Fish Cay Art Association called the day a triumph.

At Fashions By Flynn, Trisha Flynn sold five thousand some-odd dollars worth of clothing, shoes and handbags, including a yellow spaghetti-strapped outfit and a pale pink striped strapless, more formal dress, to Annie; a pink and white island sarong to Zandra; a tropic print sheath with a matching long-sleeved jacket and hat to Paula; and six pair of shoes to Corliss... "I just can't ever buy enough shoes!" she gushed, waving the large plastic bag filled with shoeboxes.

In addition, Walker Vought nearly denuded his shelves of his island rum and Ginny's gift shop made more than three thousand dollars in the morning hours. Jamie Vitiello had orders for eleven commercial signs and one for a single-family house that stated that 'The Signorello Family Lives Here' emblazoned with bas-relief bunches of grapes, to be made and shipped worldwide; Aunt Fanny had to shut her doors to bake more for the afternoon tea hour; Leslie Janes had to send her bar manager to Spanish Town to beg a few more cases of rum from one of their warehouses; every single mo-ped and bicycle was rented from The Coach (and most reserved for the next day); and Gail Gallagher had to lock her hairdressing shop's doors to keep out the women who begged her to "do" them. "The brazen bitches were waving sheaves of twenty dollar bills at me through the glass display windows." Gail laughed, tossing her own just-coiffed hair. "They think that I might just succumb to a big bribe."

"And as well you might," Leslie laughed at her. "I've known you to grab at the green now and then."

"Yeah, but today, I'm too pooped to be driven by mere moolah." Gail poked at the crown of her head. "I want to save up my energy to dance the night away."

The shoppers continued to mob the stores. The All Washed Up Beach Furniture and Gift Shop had only two rickety tables left of their stock. "You have to go to the beach," Jami Uretsky begged Mike and Mitchell. "Drag anything you can find here...sticks...beach debris...logs...and we'll knock some chairs together." She tugged with frustration at her blonde pony-tail. "I cannot *believe* that people are spending so much money!"

"We can retire after today!" Her husband whirled her around in the air while Mitchell watched with his mouth open.

Neel's Five and Dime did an enormous soda fountain business and sold every single roll of wrapping paper, every wedding card, even the tacky ones, and Sue Neel finally had to resort to crossing out "Happy Birthday" on a group of suitable cards and inking in "Best Wedding Wishes" in its place. Another huge seller at Neel's was film, as passengers, guests and wandering tourists snapped photos of the harbor, the shops, the flowers, the fishermen and their catch and each other.

The Spice Shop ladies sold out their gift packets of island vanilla and nutmeg and Eva Mae's Jewels of the Sea showed only empty shelves. Corliss had been there early and bought an even dozen of Eva Mae's specialty island shell necklaces. "I've got most of my Christmas gifts bought!" she exulted, showing Kat all of her treasures.

The store that outdid every other store, however, was The Alice W. Rabbit's Hemp Emporium. Despite a short, but emphatic discussion with Elliott and Suzie, the other customers quickly realized what the merchandise was really about. Robin and Paul had to shut the shop at 3 PM with a promise to re-stock and open early on the morning of the wedding. It was an amazing day for the economy of the harbor. "We ought to stage a wedding here every week-end," Paul told Robin. "We'd be rich in no time."

***

As the harbor filled and ebbed with customers and onlookers, the official toxicology report was delivered to Doctor Fullbright, who, incidentally, had seven patients drop into his office in the morning to have corns and calluses removed prior to the next night's anticipated dancing. He immediately phoned Carlton.

"That lady plant professor sure does know her stuff," he began. "She was absolutely correct. The official name is, um...lessee...*Da-tur-a, um...*"

"*Datura stramonium?*"

"Yeah, that's it, smartass. *Datura stramonium.* Stickweed, Jimson Weed, Angel's Trumpets. He was stuffed with them. There were sixteen berries all chewed up. That's in *addition* to all the other shit he had stuffed into him. The man's stomach could have killed everybody in town!"

"I'm going to see if Carol Stambaugh can come to the Marsden's yard and then to the Zuster's yard. I want her to check and see if these plants are located in either yard."

"I thought you said there were poisonous plants in the Marsden's yard."

"I did, but I want the Professor to double check. This just can't be an accident! There's too much going on."

"You got my vote, but can you convince a jury of hard-headed islanders?"

"That's what we'll aim to do. Maybe we can get enough evidence to make one of them confess."

"Sheesh. Lots of luck on that one." Doc Fullbright made a disgusted noise. "You going to the wedding?'

"Yup. Rebecca's dance crew is doing some shindig and I want to be there…Effalyn too, she can be in plain clothes - and the boys from the station in uniform…to keep crowd control and see what's what." Carlton, too, made a rude noise. "Way things are going here, a whale will jump out of the ocean and eat the bride!"

In the bar at The Green Flash, Arlis and Don and dozens of family and friends gossiped and hugged and kissed and talked. In a corner, Kat sat at a table with her good friend, Belinda, from Ireland. Belinda also worked as a chef on one of the Puerto Rican yachts. At another table close by, Ducky sat with his father and mother, and his French girlfriend, Lisette, a tall-pale-haired beauty who was studying to be a doctor at McGill University in Canada.

Charlie Janes, together with his crew, were busy setting up the chairs, tables and the arbor for the rehearsal and rehearsal dinner, which was to begin at six PM. The band gathered, put up their chairs and arranged their instruments. They'd play for the rehearsal and had been hired to play island music during the rehearsal dinner and for two hours afterwards.

Elliott and Suzie, stymied by their erroneous expectations of The Hemp Emporium, had walked behind the larger shops and restaurants that ringed the harbor. Several streets behind, in a less commercial area, they finally found what they were so earnestly seeking. "Suzie, meet Mr. Thigpin Odette," Elliott introduced her to a whiskery, disreputable figure of a man. Mr. Odette. "Mr. Odette, this is Suzie. Isn't she beautiful?" He pinched Suzie's upper arm.

Thigpin nodded in a mechanical way. He wasn't interested today in pretty ladies. Today, all he had time for was his business dealings. Suzie said "Ouch," sharply and tried to wiggle away. "You're hurting me. Stop it!"

Elliott's eyes gleamed. "Let's get this business done and then we can talk about our love life." Thigpin snorted his appreciation. Ha! Here was a man who knew how to treat his bitch *and* had money!

***

Carol Stambaugh brought two of her colleagues, her camera and her large illustrated book with her. "I took the liberty of asking Randy and Mary Corke...it's 'Corke' with an 'e' at the end...to join us. Randy is a botanist with the University of Massachusetts. Mary is his assistant, and, also his wife. They've helped me a lot with research in the past and just happened to be in Road Town on vacation. I called them and asked if they might come along and lend me some expertise."

Carlton and Effalyn shook hands with the Corkes. "Nice to meet you, Randy and Mary Corke with an 'e'," Effalyn laughed. "I'm Effalyn with two effs and no 'vee'...I get my name spelled wrong a lot, so I understand." On the way to the Marsden house, Effalyn filled them in on the situation.

"Not a very nice way to murder your beloved husband," Mary mused.

"Don't jump to conclusions," Randy chided her. "Just because you'd murder me that way in a nanosecond, doesn't mean that every woman would murder her husband that way." He made a funny face. "You have to watch these women who know all about plant poisons."

Effalyn and Mary eyed one another and then burst into guffaws as they all arrived at the Marsden home and knocked on the door. There was no answer. Shrugging, Carlton motioned to his entourage and they walked around to the gardens at the back of the house.

"Lots of rhododendron. Not surprising. They're everywhere." Carol poked at the gnarled roots. "I can't see where anyone has dug anything up, but with the fertility of the island plants, any trace would be long gone." She pointed to a beautiful vine that climbed over a fence at the rear of the yard. "And this is our castor bean vine." She picked one of the flowers and smelled it.

Mary smelled it also and then crumbled a leaf in her fingers and touched the tip of her tongue to the leaf. She spit it out, making a moue. "Lovely, isn't it? Like a beautiful vampire that will bite you to death. *Ricinus communis.*" She twirled the flower around and then put it and a few of the leaves and berries into a glassine envelope.

Randy took a stem in his hand. "This little plant, in the hands of a terrorist organization, might be able to poison the entire water supply of a city." He took a camera out of his satchel and began to snap photos of the castor bean vine and then one or two of the rhododendron.

Carol shook her head. "This is one of the deadliest poisons in the world. And so pretty." She laughed. "Makes you wonder, doesn't it?"

"Do you see any of the other one, the *Datura*?" Effalyn stood three feet away from Carol and Mary with her arms folded around her. "I'm not going to touch anything out here, no sir!"

"I don't see it." Carol shook her head. "Randy? See any?"

Randy was wandering among the bushes at the back of the house. He came back, his hands dangling and empty. "Nope. Don't see any at all. Let's try the neighbor's yards. Maybe she only had to go next door."

No one was home on either side of the Marsden's house. Shrugging again, Carlton moved his merry band of accomplices into the adjoining yards and they searched for poisonous plants. There were rhododendrons a-plenty, but no other castor bean plants and no *Datura*.

At the Zuster's house, Effalyn rang the bell. After several moments, Mrs. Zuster answered the door. "Again? You people are here *again*?" She seemed flustered and angry.

"We just want to look at the plant life in your yard, Mrs. Zuster," Carlton spoke politely. "Are you feeling all right?"

"Why do you ask?" Her eyes were darting and sharp.

"You just look tired and we're worried about you," Carlton tried to be soothing.

She shrugged again. "I have been feeling poorly."

"Is Mr. Zuster at home? Perhaps we don't have to bother you at all."

She shook her head slowly. "No, he is in Road Town with her."

"Her?" Effalyn pretended ignorance and Carol, Randy and Mary tried to fade into the background.

"Her. That Mrs. Marsden." There was a wary look in Mrs. Zuster's eyes. "He had to go to her attorney's office."

"Oh?" Effalyn allowed a sympathetic grimace. "Maybe Detective Inspector Reese and Professor Stambaugh and her guests can look in the yard and I can make you a cup of tea." Mrs. Zuster watched Effalyn for a moment and then nodded grudgingly. Effalyn put her hand on Mrs. Zuster's thin arm and guided her back into the house. Carol, the Corkes and Carlton moved around the yard, seeking the white or pale purple trumpet flowers.

"I'm worried about you, Mrs. Zuster." Effalyn busied herself with the kettle as Mrs. Zuster sat heavily onto a kitchen chair. "You seem very exhausted. Have you seen a doctor to ask about a tonic of some sort?"

"No." Mrs. Zuster's voice was a whisper. "You know...I did tell you that I am often ill." Effalyn nodded and poured out the tea.

"Here. Do you take sugar? Let me help you?" She set the teacup on the table and poured herself a cup, too. She sipped the hot liquid. "Yes, you did tell me, but I think you look even more tired than when we saw you last." She put her hand over Mrs. Zuster's arm. Her skin felt hot and dry. "I think...I know again I am speaking out of turn, but I like you, Mrs. Zuster. I think that your husband should be here more, caring for you." She busied herself pushing her spoon around on the tabletop, feeling her way carefully.

"Yes," it was a soft sound. "I am feeling that way too sometimes." Mrs. Zuster's lackluster eyes sought hers. "I think he spends too much time over there." She sipped at her own cup. "Ach! And then I feel badly as she is alone and has no one." She rubbed her chin.

"But when he is over there, *you're* alone!" Effalyn's sniff of indignation was sympathetic. "I'd be...well, I'd be angry."

"Sometimes I am angry." Mrs. Zuster's eyes were averted. "Sometimes I wish we had never met the Marsdens and not gotten involved in their business."

"Are you lonely?"

"Sometimes." Mrs. Zuster coughed and clutched at her stomach.

"Are you OK?"

"I'm fine. I'm just so tired all the time," she sighed. "I just have a touch of stomach flu or indigestion." Effalyn's head flew up.

"How long have you had…uh…the flu?"

"A few days only. It is nothing. Just a bit of upset and diarrhea. It will pass."

If you don't pass first! Effalyn thought. *She's a poor specimen, but I don't think she had anything to do with any of this. Maybe she'll be the next victim. Maybe he's practicing on her already!* "I want you to promise to take care of yourself. Please call your doctor and tell him about your stomach flu. You don't want to be more tired than you are now." She spoke in a gentle, but admonishing tone. "Do you want me to call your doctor for you?"

"No. No, don't be silly." Mrs. Zuster finished her tea. "I will lie down now and sleep for an hour. Neil should be back by then." There was a knock at the back door. Effalyn made a sign to Mrs. Zuster that she would get up and answer it. Mrs. Zuster nodded in defeated acquiescence.

"Effalyn? All through here? We're done." Carlton asked a question with his eyes and Effalyn's eyes answered that she'd tell him when they were in the car.

"Good bye, Mrs. Zuster," Effalyn put her hand gently on the woman's bony shoulder. Underneath the ugly housedress, Mrs. Zuster's bones were fragile. "Remember, just call me…here's my personal card…if you want any assistance or even just to talk."

"We found two of the plants. Both white trumpets. They're tucked away in the back, by the stand of palm trees." Carlton was exultant. "What did you scope out?"

"She's getting tired of him being over there and she's been sick to her stomach and is always exhausted. I'm a bit worried about her. She's weary and thinks she has a stomach flu and diarrhea." Carol looked interested and asked if perhaps Mrs. Marsden was being slowly poisoned.

"A minute bit of ricin…not enough to kill you…will make you ill and anemic. It attacks the red blood cells. You said she was tired. I think it would be a good idea if she got a blood test."

"We had a murder a few years back," Mary informed them. "A man killed his wife and his mother-in-law with low doses of ricin."

"Well, his mother-in-law," Randy rolled his eyes. "We can all understand murdering a mother-in-law. I presume they let him go then." Mary poked him and they all laughed. "But, seriously, I'm worried about her symptoms. He just may be trying out doses on her."

"I think it's a distinct possibility. I tried to get her to go to the doctor's, but she didn't want me to be involved."

"Should we try to force her? Might she really be in danger?" Carlton was worried.

"Perhaps we can speak with Neil Zuster and point out to him that we are mightily interested in his wife's well-being."

"Good idea. We'll see him on Monday morning."

"It's rather interesting, don't you think," Carol's eyes were huge and bright behind her glasses, "She may be ingesting ricin, which isn't at her house but at the Marsden house, and Mr. Marsden ingested, or was forced to ingest, *Datura*, which is found at the Zuster house but not at the Marsden house."

"Very interesting indeed," Carlton agreed. They dropped Professor Stambaugh and her guests at their car with fervent thanks.

"I'll do some more research and Mary and Randy will check for anything further when they go home next week, if you still need more information. We'll let you know what we find." They all waved goodbye.

At the police station, a message had been left from a Colonel Haug of Johannesburg, South Africa. Ganny Johnstone wrote it down: "The late Mrs. Marsden's death was of natural causes. She had been ill for some time with a heart condition and under doctor's care. Her doctor had been mildly surprised that she had died earlier than his prognosis, but…often these things are not measurable and the death was ruled not suspicious, although he did hear that the doctor was elderly and had a few complaints of stupidity and negligence informally against him. Colonel Haug thought you would understand and would be available to talk, if you wished to get back in touch." Carlton sighed. Maybe he'd call, but it would be for nothing. An old doctor, a failing patient. Who could say now? So much for that.

CHAPTER THIRTEEN

"With this ring, I thee wed" –
The Book of Common Prayer...

Arlis, decked out in a turquoise sundress, splattered with red, yellow and green parrots, her naturally glowing complexion even more enhanced by the facial Carole had forced her to endure, greeted her family, Don's family, their guests, their friends from last year's vacation in Big Fish Cay, and the sixteen new passengers from *The Southern Cross*. "God! Isn't this fun?" she crowed, accepting gaily-wrapped gift after gaily-wrapped gift. "Thank you so much! You shouldn't have..." She giggled, "What is it I'm supposed to say? 'Your presence is present enough?' Hogwash, I love gifts!" Don stood behind her, his lean face, shadowed by the pale grey Stetson on his head. If possible, his grin was even broader than his fiancée's.

The Honorable J. Ducksworth Blyton, dressed informally for a change in blue Bermuda shorts and a white shirt, escorted his wife, Alliana to the table that Leslie had marked with a big RESERVED FOR THE DUCKS sign. Ducky and Lisette joined them, Ducky, also for a change, was wearing something more formal than his usual ripped shorts and bare feet. Lisette fussed over the collar of his blue and white patterned shirt, touching Ducky as often as she could. She wore a slender sheath of green linen and her pale blonde hair was tied up in a knot with tiny tendrils that escaped framing her face. Alliana wore a yellow skirt, a white blouse, and a yellow cardigan in a lightweight cotton.

"I bought the skirt and sweater this morning at one of the shops in the harbor," she told Lisette. "Such lovely clothing there, yes?" Lisette agreed. The Honorable Duck Senior rolled his eyes and ordered a Red Stripe beer. His son followed his father's wise example.

The sand and concrete apron at the rear of The Green Flash began to fill up. Behind the fence that separated the hotel from the public beach, hundreds of locals and guests from other yachts began to assemble, everyone curious to watch the rehearsal ceremony and gape at the party afterwards. The old lady who had listened to Pat and Joyce play the day before was there, right in the front, pressed up against the fence. She'd brought a folding chair and a bottle of some liquid with her and was prepared to stay put until the crowd surged forward and maybe she might snag some refreshments in the melee.

Brian heaved his drums into place and Paul sat next to him, strumming on his guitar. Pat seated himself at the piano. Ray Leach dusted off his trombone and polished the slide until it gleamed. Joyce stood, flute in hand and the rest of the Big Fish Cay Orchestra tuned up instruments. With a pencil stuck into her hair, Leslie stood in the middle of it all, directing. "OK," she yelled, I want Arlis and Don, His Honor, the Best Man, the Matron of Honor and any other attendants to come here. She motioned them all to the front of the arbor. "I've conducted a lot of rehearsals in my time and find...*No!*" She hollered at Arlis' mother. "We don't need you up here yet. Go back and stand over there for a few moments. I'll tell you when to come up and where to stand." Leslie's glare stopped Mrs. Fuglie in her tracks. "Thank you," Leslie nodded regally as Mrs. Fuglie retreated. Leslie was always gracious when she got her own way.

"The easiest way for you to know where you want to wind up, is for you to start at the end of the ceremony." She pulled Arlis and Don gently together, just in front of the arbor. "Your Honor," she turned and winked at Mr. Duckworth, "You will be here, right in front of them." His Honor, Mr. Duckworth let himself be maneuvered into place. "That's how you three will be at the very end of the ceremony..."

"When I say: 'You may kiss the bride?'"

Leslie was pleased. "Exactly." Don grabbed Arlis and kissed her soundly. The crowd laughed and applauded and the lady on the other side of the fence dabbed at her eyes, remembering her own wedding so many years ago.

"You have that part down pat," Leslie giggled.

"Want me to rehearse that again?" Don was hopeful.

"No, not until you are legally married," Leslie parried. "OK, Carole...you stand here and pretend you are holding Arlis' bouquet." She handed Carole a palm leaf. "Captain Jack, after you hand off Arlis, you'll be standing here through the ceremony." Jack nodded, amicable as ever, and moved to his chosen spot. "And you, what's your name?"

"Tom Douglas," the tall man with the chipmunk-cheeked face grinned. "I'm Don's brother-in-law."

"OK, Tom Douglas, brother-in-law. Your position is here at Don's side and make sure he doesn't attack this woman until tomorrow afternoon!" The crowd laughed, especially the lady on the other side of the fence sitting on a folding chair.

"Any other bridal attendants? No? How about immediate family?... Yes, Mrs. Fuglie...Alfrieda...At last, that means you!" Leslie arranged Arlis' mother, her sister and brother-in-law Larry and their two daughters on one side, with Arlis' great friend Esther just behind them. On the other side, she placed Don's three children, Jim, Amy and Todd, together with Don's sister, Joleen. Leslie stood back, her hands on her hips and critically checked out everyone's position. "OK, now, good friends and other relatives of Arlis' on this side...you will all be seated there. And ditto for the groom's friends over there." She turned and yelled. "Charlie! Get the boys to bring out the chairs so that everyone knows just where they are to be." In a few moments, Charlie and six of his helpers brought out stacked chairs and placed them in a semi-circle following Leslie's orders. "Now, all of you who will be sitting, sit!" And they did quickly and quietly. Leslie was in charge.

Leslie then led them backwards through the ceremony, ending up with Arlis and Captain Jack at the door of the door of the hotel, Carole and Tom in front of them. Leslie made a very satisfied face "Very good. Now we'll do it the right way with music." She raised her hand at the orchestra. Nodding, they crashed into the opening bars of *The Wedding March*....tum, tum, te tum-tum-tum tum, dad a dad a, dada!

Sipping a cold beer, Captain Jack ran a finger around his collar. "Shoot, I'm getting really nervous! I'd better do it right tomorrow! If I screw up, Leslie will kill me!"

"Kill you?" His Honor harrumphed. "All you have to do is trot her down the aisle. Me, I have to do all that talking!" He snared a cocktail from a passing waiter. "I'd better go home early and practice!"

At the other end of the fence, Carlton watched the festivities. The dancers, including Niccola, performed their island dance to huge applause and were only allowed to leave the floor when they promised that they would all be back after the wedding ceremony itself. Mitchell and his friends, using the darkness as cover, each snitched a lurid-colored cocktail from a forgotten tray and drank the sweetish contents down in long gulps, darling one another not to be a sissy. The band played for three hours and then, exhausted, wished everyone a goodnight. "We'll see you all tomorrow," Brian promised. "Go home, get a good night's sleep and be here, ready for eating and dancing and the wedding tomorrow!" The lady on the other side of the fence managed not only to join the wedding-rehearsal party and eat a heaping plate of food, but also stashed two bottles of white wine into her carryall to bring home.

CHAPTER FOURTEEN

"I'll woo her as the lion woos his bride..."
John Holm, Douglas

The four cockpit sleep-outers had been very fortunate. The torrential rain that usually pounded down once or twice a night had spared them so far, but tonight, as they slumbered, trundled on top of two plastic cocoons, Mother Nature decided that she'd been nice for too long.

They'd all trooped back, exhausted and satiated from the eating and drinking and dancing. No one could stop talking about what a fabulous evening it was. Down in her cabin, Annie slid out of her creased and rumpled new yellow dress. She put on her shortie pajamas and was brushing her teeth when Suzie came into the cabin.

"Hi, Cousin." Annie spoke through a mouth full of foam. "Have a good time tonight?"

"It was fun," Suzie seemed to have forgotten her animosity. "And you?"

"Danced my feet off. I think we'll have a wonderful time at the wedding. Did you buy anything? I didn't see you in the shops." She rinsed her mouth, dried off her face and pulled the new pink dress out of its bag. "I got this at Flynn's dress shop for the wedding. Like it?"

Suzie gave the dress a cursory glance. "Nice. I did a lot of shopping, Elliott and me, that is. We...I bought a few dresses and a handbag and a hat." She motioned to a pile of boxes on her bunk, but didn't offer to show them to Annie. "Elliott got a lot of things too." She went into the bathroom and closed the door, turning to say goodnight before she shut it. Annie shrugged, folded her two dresses, and went up to the galley where Kat, Zandra and Paula were enjoying a few moments of talk before bed.

"I'd love a cup of tea, thanks," Annie accepted Kat's offer. "No. Nothing to eat." She fended off a plate of cake. "I ate like a proverbial pig tonight and probably can't fit into my new dress for tomorrow!" She patted her stomach. "I have done nothing but loll in the sun and eat since I got here. If I keep this up, I'll look like...well, like...well, fatter!" She giggled.

""Same with me," Zandra sympathized, "But look! Here I am with the cake!" They all chuckled, filled with happiness, a lot of good wine and good food. Zandra crossed her legs and giggled harder. "Please don't make me laugh. I am so full that I have to pee and if I laugh any more, I will wet over myself!" She laughed even harder and clutched at herself. "I'm too lazy to go down and use my toilet! Why can't we women be built in a better way, like a man, so that we can pee over the side of the boat?" This made the women laugh even harder and Zandra groaned with the effort of keeping dry.

"*Psst*!" Kat spoke in an excited whisper. "Are there any men around?" The women shook their heads for no. "OK, here I will show you Kat's Secret Method!"

"What?"

"Yes. From being on boats so much, you know. Sometimes it is not so much convenient to use the head or leave the wheel if I am on watch at night. The men, naturally, all they have to do is dangle their dingle over the rail." There was another gust of laughter. "We women are not so…what is the word? Anatomically fortunate. It is hard for us to urinate easily if we are not sitting down, no? And so…" She turned with an impish glow in her eyes, to open up a cabinet. She removed a plastic glass. "This is the way to urinate when you cannot get to a bathroom. Now, watch. I will show you Kat's Secret Method." She turned her back to them and stood for a moment or so, ostensibly looking out of the cabin window. She turned back, moving her hand and they saw that the plastic glass was filled with a yellow-colored liquid. "See?" She waved the glass. "You didn't even notice, really, that I peed, did you?" Paula, Annie and Zandra started at her, goggle-eyed. "And then, I can pour it away over the rail." Kat performed the action to her words.

"How? How did you do this maneuver?" Zandra gaped. Paula's mouth was opened and Annie started to giggle helplessly.

"What a marvelous trick! How'd you do that?" The women clustered around and Kat showed them. "So…helpful. So practical. We'll show those men!" Zandra grabbed a cup and turned away, clumsily adjusting her pajamas. She bent, laughing and turned, triumphantly holding her own yellow-liquid- filled trophy.

Paula began to laugh, feeling an unaccustomed warmth to these young women. What a wonderful group of ladies these three were! She wanted to gather them into her arms, hold them and keep them safe from all the horrors of life. She wished that the team of Paula and

Sharon were together again, just for a day or two, and both here on this boat, exchanging laughs and girlish secrets with Zandra, Kat and Annie. *We would have enjoyed ourselves so much! Oh, you would have loved it, my pet. Zandra is like a funny cousin, Kat is like the girl next door and Annie...Ah, Annie could have been the darling daughter that one of us might have had, if only we could have lived and loved like normal people. Ah, my best friend, we have had a lot, but we have missed a lot, too. Who would have thought that I'd be here, learning how to urinate in a crowd of women wearing my pajamas and hoping that no one can notice? Ah, I hope you are watching me from above, my dear friend. I hope you are laughing with us.* Unable to help herself, as her bladder was strained full with the product of too much liquid to drink and uncontrollable laughter, Paula took her own cup, turned her back, and crimson to the roots of her hair, peed.

The glass door slid open, letting in a blast of warm night air and Captain Jack, too. The women screeched and Zandra and Paula blushed furiously, each hiding their plastic glass behind themselves.

Captain Jack eyed the group. Annie snorted, trying to hold in her laughter. Zandra's face got redder and redder and Paula thought she would die from embarrassment. "Humpf," Jack said, his grin threatening to break loose, "peeing in a cup, ladies?"

***

As late as it was, Sampson Fullbright decided to call Carlton. "Carlton? Sorry to wake you, you dancing fool, you." Doctor Fullbright had stopped for an hour to watch the rehearsal dinner antics, then had gone to the hospital to finish up one more of the less-happy parts of his job description.

"Oh, Doc." Carlton made a groaning noise and turned away from Rebecca's side of the bed. "Only for you would I answer the phone at this time of night. Wassamatter? A pelican eat somebody? A giant squid leap out of the ocean and devour the bride? What?"

"No matter the hour, my man, you never lose your sharp sense of humor," Doctor Fullbright chuckled. "I just thought you'd sleep better knowing that the autopsy on Sing Fong confirmed accidental death." On the other end of the receiver, Carlton nodded, as if Fullbright could see him. As if he did indeed see him, Doctor Fullbright continued. "A fatal reaction to the toxin, most likely due to the previous bite, even though the sea creatures were dissimilar. We're putting it down as an accident, pure and simple."

"Not so pure and not so simple, but thanks, I'm glad that I don't have one more headache to investigate." Carlton scratched his head. "I'll see you tomorrow, Doc."

"Sleep tight," there was a wheezy chuckle and the phone was dead.

Wide awake now, Carlton padded into he bathroom and then came back to sit on the edge of the bed. He leaned over and kissed Rebecca's shoulder. She made an inarticulate noise and rolled over onto her back. Carlton looked at the clock. Three AM. He grinned into the darkness and finished waking Rebecca up.

***

The four members of the cockpit gang, sleeping soundly under light blankets in two heaps, felt the wind first. Duncan, more used to being in the outdoors, opened his eyes suddenly. The stars had disappeared and the sky was a muddy grey. On his arm, a drop of rain fell, alerting him. "Hey!" His whisper was sharp. "Rain!" Annie sat up, muzzy and confused.

"Rain!" On the other side of the trampoline, Hosea shook Zandra. "Here we go!" The rain began to intensify. Quickly, remembering Ducky's instructions, each couple scooted inside their plastic envelope, cuddling together and making sure that the Velcro straps were secure and tight. "You two prepared?" Hosea spoke out loud as the rain began to drum down. "We're snug and tight as bedbugs over here." He and Zandra were bundled into the plastic bedding. They covered their pillows, heads and faces with the flap, leaving a small sheltered opening for their eyes and mouths.

"I think we have it fixed," Duncan hollered back, as the rain began to drum down. "Hold on, my canny friends, hold on!"

Inside their cave, Duncan and Annie huddled like two spoons, curving their bodies together, giggling at the sensation which could only be described, as Annie said later, ... "Like being under a freaking waterfall!" The storm cloud centered overhead and the deluge dumped what seemed like tons of water on *The Southern Cross* and the harbor. Through the thundering sound of the rain, Duncan could faintly hear hatches being slammed shut and the sound of Captain Jack and Ducky yelling to one another. He grinned and pulled Annie closer, glorying in the unusual feeling of being dry and safe and warm and close under the effective plastic cover.

"What a pisser!" he exulted.

***

The bleating of six hungry nanny goats woke Zandra. She opened her eyes and was puzzled for a moment, enveloped as she was in a bright blue shroud, stuffy and crackling. "The rain!" she breathed, in voice filled with wonder. "Such rain! But, here I am - dry as an old lamb chop bone!" She poked Hosea and he groaned and snuggled into her shoulder. She sat up, peeling the plastic and Velcro, and ungluing her cocoon. The morning was sunny and bright, hot, almost, with a slight steam pouring off the quickly vanishing drops of last night's leftover moisture. On the right side of the tarpaulin, Annie and Duncan sat up simultaneously, goggle-eyed, blinking in the sun. "Are you as dry as I am?" Zandra laughed, a triumphant shout.

"I'll be dipped!" Annie pushed back the top of the tarp. "Did I imagine the rain or was it the Biblical Flood that we had here last night?" Duncan raised his arms to the blue, puffy-cloud sky.

"Glory be. That was the most remarkable...." The tarp's net jiggled as Ducky came toward them, bearing a tray. On the tray were four cups of coffee, four glasses of fresh-squeezed juice, and four croissants.

"For the victors, come the spoils. You are now fully-fledged members of the cockpit gang and you should be mighty proud of yourselves! You came through a deluge with nary a drop of water on you!" He gravely handed coffee to each of them. "I - J. Ducksworth Blyton, salute you!" He bowed, then laughed out loud. "What'ja think?"

"Fan-fuckin'tastic!" Annie's face was alight with glee. "That was the *best*!"

And twenty minutes later, Duncan was approached by Lannie. "Hey, Duncan, um, I know you and Annie...well, I know you might want to be alone, but ..."

"What is it, lad?"

"Would you mind if I came out tonight to sleep on the netting?" Lannie's face was wistful. "I think I was too hasty. I believe I am missing a marvelous opportunity to experience something brilliant."

Duncan bowed from the waist. "Lannie, my old man, on behalf of the cockpit gang, I invite you to take up residence in the blue bag on my left tonight." He rubbed his face with its early morning bristles. "And I hope it rains like a sonofabitch again tonight so you can see what I mean! What an experience, my lad. What a blooming thrill!"

Suzie was already in their cabin when Annie came down to change. "Did you get wet?" Suzie challenged.

"Nope. Dry as a desert rat and just as happy."

"Hmpf," Suzie muttered as she stalked out. "Elliott says you are a bunch of lunatics," and slammed the cabin door. Annie's smile beamed as she put on shorts and a halter top, and then bounded up to the galley to brag to everyone about their fantastic nighttime adventure. *I hope Elliott hears every delighted word,* she exulted.

***

"I'm not going to talk to you or see you all day," Arlis informed her betrothed. "That way, it will be as if I am a virgin bride." Her face told him that he had better not even comment. A smart man, Don just nodded, kissed her on her neck, winked and walked out the door.

Grinning, Arlis rounded up her mother, Carole, Don's daughter, Amy, and Esther, together with several of the other women guests who had been smart enough to book a facial, pedicure, manicure and hairdressing appointment with Gail and her expanded crew. "Here comes the bride…" she sang, as she marched over to the beauty parlor.

Don, freed of all responsibility for the morning, walked on the beach, allowing his fertile mind to think about the rest of his life.

Elliott and Suzie rented a small sailboat, gathered a picnic lunch, four bottles of wine and some other things that they felt were indispensable, and pointed the craft into the waves.

Ducky and Kat cleaned the galley and the heads, then, their duties done for the day, disappeared into the burgeoning crowd, Ducky towards Lisette's house, and Kat to a quiet restaurant in the Belonger quarters.

Captain Jack and Emma joined a large, raucous group of boat owners who commandeered a big table at Captain Fatty's and watched the parade of people who came and went.

Vinny, Sam, Claudia, and Martha re-prowled the shops, then went back to the boat to nap until the wedding. Paula, Michael Beck, Corliss and Elwyn went back to the art show, had lunch and then, little by little separated. Paula found herself alone, hot and exhausted. *I get so tired* *now. I hope I can finish all of what I have to do before...*She took the pins out of her hair, brushed it back up in a topknot, using her hands as combs, and stuck the bamboo clips back up to hold the hair out of her eyes and away from her sweaty neck. She needed to sit down and wandered into the air-conditioned lounge of The Green Flash. Cooled by the air-conditioning, she saw a table being vacated and slid into an empty chair before anyone else could grab it. She sighed. *I'm getting old. It will be over soon.* From her seat, she watched the ebb and flow of customers and vicariously shared snippets of conversation that circled around her. She ordered a glass of white wine.

"Excuse me," a voice spoke to her. She turned to see a tall man who also held a glass in his hand. "It's so crowded in here, may I share a space at your table?" Paula's first impulse was to refuse, but his smile was pleasant, and the lounge *was* mobbed with guests. She nodded without smiling and he sat down. "I'm Brian Carpentier," ...he pronounced his name with a French accent, *Brian Char-pen-tee-ay*.... "I'm down here on a charter boat, owned by some friends..." He waited to see if she would answer.

"Good morning, Mr. Char-pen-tee-ay," Paula smiled. "I'm here on Captain Jack's catamaran." She nodded and extended her hand across the little table. "I'm Paula Haskins."

He relaxed visibly. "Glad to meet you. I'm from New Hampshire...in America."

"I'm from New York City." She found herself unbending slightly.

"Ah, a fellow traveler....Howdy, I'm in sales...food sales," His smile was self-deprecating. "I sell English muffins."

Despite herself, Paula laughed. "I never thought much about how muffins might get sold."

"Unfortunately, my boss thinks about how they might get sold all the time!" Brain's laugh was nervous. "That's why I'm here for a whole week without my laptop. So I can get away from the everlasting thoughts of how many English muffins I have sold today and how many I must sell tomorrow." They both laughed and Brian finished his glass of wine. He beckoned to a waiter. "Can I buy you another glass of wine? The English muffin business has been generally good and I can afford two more glasses today." Her tiredness disappeared as she nodded again. Brian looked pleased. "My friends...they're from California...Gary and Mary Lou Kunkel...they just bought a new boat and are trying to get into the charter business." He gestured toward a cluster of boats at the water's edge. "Theirs is called the '*Folie a Deaux*'..."

"Ah?"

"It means a delusional fantasy shared by two people." He chuckled. "Poor Gary and Mary Lou have dreamed about having their own boat for years and years...and here they are with me, chartering with them - and I have known Gary since we were boys- and one other older and much-less-fun couple as their first guests." He waved his glass in the air. "I hope it all works out for them. This is a tough business, this boat chartering."

"Perhaps I can introduce them to Captain Jack," Paula was amazed to find herself offering. "He's been very successful down here and I think he knows everyone that a charter boat captain ought to know." The waiter came with their second glasses of wine, and they barely noticed him.

Sarah Lemonowski had a long talk with Lara and Jamie Vitiello, then went to the offices of David and Barbara Wessel, where she spent the better part of the morning. After their meeting, Sarah went back to shopping and David and Barbara took Teddy for a long walk along the sand to the place where Teddy had some unfinished business with an oleander bush.

Rebecca rehearsed one more time with her adult and children's group. Sweaty and satisfied, she sent everyone home to shower, rest and get ready for their performance.

Effalyn brought her mother to the harbor and they had tea and cakes with Aunt Fanny. "How're you doing with that lady who poisoned her husband?" Aunt Fanny asked.

"Mama, did you tell...?" Effalyn glared at her mother.

"Pshaw," Mrs. Penn waved a hand at her daughter's chagrin. "Everyone knows about it anyway." Effalyn rolled her eyes. Aunt Fanny swatted Effalyn's shoulder as she got up to wait on a customer who wanted six cream buns. As the door closed after the customer, Aunt Fanny sat back down, puffing.

"Blamed corns," she groused, rubbing her foot. "I was over in Charlotte Amalie yesterday, visiting my cousin, Doris."

"How's she managing with those three children?" Mrs. Penn was always interested in the doings of others.

Aunt Fanny chuckled. "She's a caution, that Doris. Has to be with those children." She leaned forward to tell a tale. "She came home to find the place in a mess. Someone had broken a window and there was greasy food all over the kitchen counter. The children swore, *swore* ...that none of them had anything to do with any of it."

"Humpf," Mrs. Penn knew better already.

"Well, naturally," Aunt Fanny agreed.

"So, how did she get them to confess?"

"She rounded them up, making sure that they all knew she was rounding them *all* up. Then, while each of them was watching the other, she brought them each into a separate room." Mrs. Penn nodded with satisfaction and Effalyn rolled her eyes at the triviality of the story. "Then, she went to the girl and told her that the older boy has said that he and the younger boy were innocent. The older boy said that the girl had done it all."

"I presume she went to the older boy and told him that the girl had squealed on him." Mrs Penn made an ummm-hmmm sound.

"Naturally. Then she went into the bedroom of the younger son...said a similar thing. And each time, each of the children saw her going from one to the other. Naturally, they were all guilty and pretty soon, they were all blaming each other and she got the whole story." Aunt Fanny dusted off her hands as the bell over the door tinkled and three customers came in.

"Works every time," Effalyn's mother finished her coffee and heaved herself to her feet. "I used to do the same thing to you and your sister."

Effalyn made a face. "You could always make me confess, Mama. You had the technique."

"Hmpf. Any mother could. Shoot, I could make bank robbers confess if only I had them all watching each other to see who blabbed first!"

"You are so right, girl." Aunt Fanny waved them goodbye. "Any good mother could."

***

And Annie and Duncan sat on the seawall, near the local fishing boat fleet. Outwardly, they talked, sharing more and more of their lives, hopes and dreams. Inwardly, they quaked with desire and hope.

CHAPTER FIFTEEN

"A bed, a bed" Clark Saunders said. "A bed for you and me."
"Fye, na, fye na," said Margaret May, "Till anes we marry be."
An anonymous ballad...

Jamie Vitiello, His Honor, the Mayor of Big Fish Cay, stood up and motioned to Pat Biase to play a loud chord on the piano. "Ladies and gentlemen! May I have your attention, please!" Dum-*dum*! The piano echoed. The noise of several hundred people dwindled as Mayor Vitiello beckoned them to come to their seats. "The wedding is about to begin."

The orchestra began to play as the guests took their seats. Outside the fence, the onlookers strained and jostled to get a good spot to watch. His Excellency, Jasper Ducksworth Blyton, Queen's Representative to the Crown, dressed in black satin robes, strode majestically to a spot just in front of the arbor. During the hour before the ceremony, the arbor had been bedecked in jasmine and fronds of fern and His Excellency admired the handiwork as he turned to face the audience of guests. He waited, like some noble dignitary of the Roman Court, still and solemn, until the whispers died down and a hush came over the crowd. He nodded and the orchestra brought their preliminary music to a halt. Joyce O'Sullivan stood up, a silver baton in her left hand, nodded to His Excellency and then, brought the baton down. The orchestra, careful and nervous, began to play the Triumphal March from Aida. The honored guests started down the aisle: Don's children, Arlis' friends, Don's family, Arlis' family, Don's friends, and then, with a measured tread, Arlis' mother, Alfrieda, lovely in pink and white.

Don, shaking like a man with Saint Vitus, took his place, his Best Man beside him. His Excellency, J. Ducksworth Blyton, turned and shook Don's limp hand. He winked at Don. "Lucky man. You'll be happy forever."

And, as Aida's music soared, Arlis' Matron of Honor, Carole, walked across the apron of patio and down to the arbor. She wore a sapphire blue dress and an amazing hat with matching flowers and feathers. The silence was absolute, except for one envious sigh from outside the fence.

At a nod from His Excellency, Joyce raised her baton again and the orchestra played their very first official rendition of Lohengrin's Wedding March. Everyone stood up and turned to see Arlis – dazzling in her virginal white gown – stand for one triumphal moment – alone, her arms filled with white blossoms - with just the shadow of Captain Jack Scambaugh at her side. Captain Jack bowed, crooked his arm and down they marched – Arlis to meet her love and be wed to him.

***

"Thank you all," Don stood up, his glass in hand. "Before we tuck into Leslie and Charlie's beautiful food, I want to thank you all once more for joining my bride, Arlis..." he began to laugh... "I guess by now you all know her name!" He was engaging and nervous. "I think many of you know that I am a struggling poet. Arlis is my muse. I want to share with you all my humble words to her on this happy occasion." He harrumphed and fingered the tightness of his tuxedo shirt collar:

"To, um, Arlis:
Norwegian woman with soft-smiled face,
How I treasure your warm embrace...
Kindness, caring, laughter, giving:
You make my life so worth the living!

Slow to anger, quick to smile,
Never trying to beguile:
Though smart enough to work each wile,
Doing that is not your style.
I'll say this and say it loud,
Shout it out in any crowd:
"To hold your hand just makes me proud!"

I'd walk with you on my last mile
For one more glimpse of loving smile.
Kindness, caring, loving, giving"
You've made my life well worth the living!"

He bent and kissed his wife and she began to cry.

From his table, Ducky made a face. "Geez," Ducky groaned, "Now Lisette is going to expect me to come up with something just like that!"

"And you'd better do a good job, laddie." Duncan's tone was lugubrious. "The leddies, they love that gooey treacle stuff."

Lisette, lovely in green chiffon, nodded with a kiss in the air toward Ducky's direction. "I will expect a sonnet on my pillow tomorrow."

"Who was the good-looking man you were with today, Paula," Annie leaned toward her. "Is he here?"

"A momentary fling. Long enough for a glass or two of wine," Paula's tone was joking, but behind her eyes, Annie could see some bottomless sadness. "For me, romance is not on the agenda. It is too late." Annie wondered what Paula meant, but didn't ask. "He was nice. A good companion, but his ship sailed early." Rueful, Paula chuckled. "Literally, I mean. They sailed to Road Town."

"Oh, noooo!" Annie squeaked, then dramatically smote her brow. "Never to be seen again?"

"Maybe...if our ships meet in the night," Her second glass of champagne had made Paula a bit tipsy. "He sells...are you prepared for this? English muffins." Annie collapsed with silly giggles and Paula joined her, eyes streaming with laughter.

"English muffins?" Duncan looked confused. "Wha's sae funny about English muffins?"

At the adjoining table, Zandra took Hosea's hand in hers. "So much romantic, that skinny beanpole. So tall, like some soldier. Who would think he has the soul of a poet?"

Hosea stroked her hand. "He can see...She is beautiful, inside and out. He saw her on the boat and fell in love..." Hosea stared straight ahead, his forehead wrinkled in thought. "He saw her perfection. Her sense of humor and the inner woman, too. Intelligent, romantic, soft, his dream."

"You sound as if you know her well, this Arlis."

"I am not speaking of this Arlis person." Hosea turned towards her. "I am speaking of you."

The purple and gold of the evening sky turned to velvet black. The stars came out and the moon was full and the Island Boys began to play. They started with easy, danceable tunes, getting old and young out on the dance floor; then, swung into a brighter beat with island music, some disco and a bit of rock 'n' roll. Arlis tucked the long train of her gown up, hitched it securely, and began to dance. As she twirled around, Ducky watched. "Look at the buttons on that back of her dress!" He marveled. "Gonna take ole Don an hour to get the dress off of her!" Lisette swatted him and made him get up to dance.

When the band couldn't play another note without wetting their throats, Brian Flynn announced that they'd be taking a break. "But..." He held up his hands at the groans of disappointment..."As we promised last night, we have a little entertainment for you. Rebecca Reese and her dancers, a few older and a few younger, are going to do a number for you!" There was raucous applause. "And *then*, we're all going to do the *limbo*!" Brian roared at the response. "And everyone – yeah, you too, Captain Scumbag – *everyone* is expected to get up and dance! Here they are: The Big Fish Cay Dancers!"

A CD blared. A few loud beats. The dancers moved into the center of the party, the adults first, and then the children. The audience cheered as the notes of *Hot, Hot, Hot* hit the air. The dancers began to gyrate and writhe, whirling to the hypnotic music. "*Feelin' hot, hot, hot...*" The younger dancers, Niccola, Emily-Anne, Cailyn, Allison, Meghan and Madeline and the not-so-young, Shirley Leach, Holly-from-the-Post-Office, and Marie Rudisol, The Fruitcake Lady, swooped and danced, spurred on by the cheers and clapping of the audience.

Mitchell and his buddy, Howard Doncaster, filled with self-importance, brought two poles and holders to the dance floor and then the carefully balanced a long, thin stick on the upper struts of the poles. Mitchell turned to the audience and bowed with great aplomb. "We invite all of you to dance the *limbo*!" And the music began. The children began to shimmy under the bar, the adult dancers each took the hand of one or two of the guests and pulled them into the line. Everyone was laughing and clapping and enjoying themselves. Arlis, in her magnificent gown, train flipped over her shoulders, bent backwards and shuffled under to thunderous applause. Don, with his height, had to cheat and bend forward. Boos greeted him and he gestured obscenely to the crowd.

Suzie and Elliott sat watching the party. Suzie's foot tapped. The music beckoned to her...called her...and she wanted to dance. She nudged him. "Come on. I want to dance."

His eyes bored into her. "Go right ahead, if that's what you want." His tone was ice.

"Come on, Elliott," Suzie wheedled. "Just one dance." She tried her best smile and put her hand on his thigh. "I've been so nice to you." Her face was flushed and hot. Her brain, over-stimulated by the drinks and drugs she had ingested, seemed to bulge and the blood in her veins was ginger-ale. She just *had* to dance! To move, to go crazy.

"Sit down, you slut!" Elliott's voice was louder than he had intended. His own brain was also pulsing. He felt his heart beating, almost as if it were outside of his body. Bam, bam, bam, bam, like some great tolling bell. "You'll do what I say, or else!"

"Hey!" Suzie was more than a little drunk. Stung by the injustice of Elliott's remarks, she retaliated, "I was nice about it last time. I did what you wanted. How about one dance? That's all. Come, on, Elliott. Do it for me."

"You're acting like a whore. Sit *down*!" He hissed; his tone acid.

Enough! She had enough! Her brain burned, unable to grasp it all. Angry and careless of the consequences, she stood up. "I *will* dance, you bastard," she hissed back, defiant.

His eyes were flat and dark and devoid of expression. He reached out and grabbed her arm, trying to pull her back. "No bimbo fucks with me!" His grip was iron. Like a crazed animal, she twisted, angry and suddenly out of control. He started to rise, to force her back and she slapped him and backed out of his grip. *Oh, shit! He'll kill me*!

Frightened, but unable to go back to him, she moved to the table where the four men from The Jumbie Jamboree sat. "Who wants to dance with me?" She twirled and sparkled, her hair loose and her cheeks over-bright. One of the men, the one that was tall and dark with the bushy moustache, got up, holding her lightly. They moved onto the dance floor. Suzie began to dance with abandon, glaring at the dark corner where Elliott sat. She saw the glowing tip of his cigarette. *Screw him*!

Elwyn asked Emma to dance and Captain Jack partnered Sarah Lemonowski. "Having fun?' he asked her as he heaved himself around the dance floor.

"I love it here!" She grinned at him, and he glimpsed the shy, lovely woman behind her quiet exterior. "This vacation has been the best time in my life!" His bushy eyebrows wiggled his pleasure at her pleasure. "As a matter of fact," she bent close to yell to him in the roaring noise, "I have a secret."

"A w*hat*?" He strained to hear her.

"A secret...I can't let you know yet, but you are going to be amazed at what I am going to do!" She whirled around him, laughing. He shrugged. He was the repository of so many of his passengers' secrets. He wondered just what she was up to, this quiet little mouse of a woman. His eyes asked her once again, but she only shrugged and clapped her hands in time to the music. "You'll see. You won't believe I have the courage to do what I am going to do." And with that, he had to be satisfied.

Carlton, Rebecca, Effalyn and Mrs. Penn sat at another table together with Lara and Jamie Vitiello, Trisha Flynn and Robin Blanchette. "Great party, Boss," Effalyn laughed. "Makes me feel as if I can forget all of our troubles."

"Ha," Carlton grunted. "How about a dance, Eff?"

Jamie bowed toward Mrs. Penn. "And I'd be honored if you would join me..." She nodded with delight and took his hand.

"I always did love to dance with a handsome man." They moved onto the dance floor.

As the music intensified, the dancers bumped into one another and laughing, moved back and away, only to bump into someone else. Suzie was gyrating wildly and her hand, bedecked with a huge jeweled ring, flew back, hitting out and connecting with Elwyn's cheek.

"Ow!" He stopped his dance and put his hand to his face. Suzie, in some psychedelic world of her own, never noticed and twirled past into the crowd.

"Oh! You're bleeding!" Emma cried. "She...her nails...her ring! You're cut!" She reached up with the sleeve of her dress, trying to staunch the drips.

"Here! Let me help, Mrs. Scambaugh." An arm holding a clean napkin reached up to Elwyn's cheek. "You remember me, don't you? I'm Effalyn Penn, the police detective?" She guided Elwyn to a chair. "Here. Sit down here and I'll get some...no, nevermind. Come with me and I'll get first aid inside the hotel." She gripped Elwyn's arm. "Oh! You *are* bleeding! Hold the bandage tight against the cut. She really got you with her nails and that ring." She turned to Emma. "Please just whisper to Detective-Inspector Reese about this and tell him we'll be in the hotel, getting this fixed up." She lowered her voice. "It is not too serious, I think. A few stitches perhaps. Tell him that there is no emergency."

"Silly girl, that Suzie." Elwyn said. "She has no sense at all." He walked with Effalyn, holding the napkin padded against his cheek. Effalyn agreed and then requested a first aid kit from the receptionist. Elwyn pulled the napkin away and looked at it. It was sodden with his blood. He swayed...a tall, strong man...and then crashed to the floor in a faint.

"Get some water!" Effalyn stooped and pressed the napkin back against the cut. "And hand me something...anything...to staunch this blood!" The receptionist ran to a table and grabbed a pitcher of water and a clean napkin. "Thanks." Effalyn cleaned the wound and reapplied the wet napkin. "Get me one more napkin and then get the first aid kit...thank you." She dampened Elwyn's forehead and loosened the collar of his shirt. He groaned and tried to rise. "Lie still. Just lie still and we'll get the bleeding to stop." She bathed his face again. "Don't be some big hero and think you have to get up and dance right now." Elwyn gave up his attempt to rise and lay back, allowing Effalyn to administer to his wound.

"Do we need an ambulance?" Carlton was there, holding the first aid kit and handing Effalyn the sterile bandages and tape.

"No. I think he needs some stitches, though," She gently, but firmly, taped the pad in place. "I think I should drive him to the hospital."

"Do I get any say in this?" Elwyn bleated.

"No," Effalyn and Carlton told him simultaneously. "You are the victim. You just lie there and do what we say." Elwyn waved his hand in submission.

"Let me get my car. You wait here with him." Effalyn whirled back to the party, grabbed her purse and keys, arranged for Lara and Jamie to bring her mother home, and drove to the street entrance of The Green Flash. Carlton had propped Elwyn up and then helped him to his feet.

"I feel better. I'm OK now." Embarrassed at his weakness, Elwyn tried to protest, but he swayed as he stood, holding tight onto Carlton's arm.

"No, Superman, you really must have the cut seen to. It's a wonder she didn't cut your head off with her talons," Carlton joked. "I'm Carlton Reece. I'm with the island police. Who are you, anyway?"

"Elwyn Langdon. I'm from Los Angeles, California. A passenger on Captain Jack's boat." Effalyn's car screeched to the door. Elwyn watched as Effalyn hurried in to fetch him. "She's lovely. Who is she?"

"My right hand man. Her name is Effalyn Penn." Carlton smiled gently. "She's going to bring you to the hospital and they'll patch you up and then she'll get you back to your boat." He scratched his head. "Actually, about twelve years ago, I met my wife suddenly at the scene of an accident, took her to the hospital and we fell in love right then and there."

"You don't say?" Elwyn leaned on Effalyn's arm and she helped him across the lobby, into her car, and to the hospital.

Carlton went back to the wedding reception, a huge grin splitting his face.

***

In the back of the festivities, at a darkened table, Elliott sat, nursing the remnants of his Scotch and nursing his anger at Suzie. A shape materialized and bent to speak with him. He listened and nodded, smiling faintly. The shape disappeared back into the darkness. No one noticed. Elliott checked his wristwatch and grinned wolfishly. Who needed that little slut? Not him. No sir.

The music was still pumping. The newlyweds were showing an admiring audience just how many Dark 'n' Stormys they could drink; Arlis had discarded the huge mass of flowers that had been her bouquet and the lady from the other side of the fence had appropriated a few blossoms from it to take home with her. Kat was dancing with the entire crew from Captain Dave's boat, with the captain himself in the middle of the stomping circle; Annie and Duncan were walking on the sand, hand in hand; Suzie, totally unaware of the drama she had begun, was draped closely in the embrace of Francesco, the tall, dark mustachioed man from the *Jumbie Jamboree*. Paula, having done all that she had hoped to accomplish had reached her limit on staying awake. She'd had enough of the music, the noise and the crowd, and looked around to find Ducky to see if he would ferry her back to the boat. She was exhausted and ready to go to sleep.

"This party looks like it will go on for hours. I am exhausted." Paula looked pale and nervous. "Would it be too much trouble if I went back to the boat? I just want to take a pill and go to sleep." Ducky grinned and assured her that he would zip her right back to the boat.

"Anyone else want to go back on this trip?" Ducky asked to find that Sarah, Michael, Corliss, Zandra and Hosea were also ready to call it a night. Ducky kissed Lisette lightly, "I'll be back in fifteen minutes. *I'm* not ready to call it a night yet!"

CHAPTER SIXTEEN

"...Other sins only speak, murder shrieks out!..."
John Webster, The Dutchess of Malfi

As he did every morning, Junie Winslow rose early...early enough to creep down to the harbor and snitch a loaf of bread from the bag delivered at Aunt Fanny's door. It wasn't that Junie was really a thief, no; it was that he was an oppor*tun*ist. Ready to take advantage of whatever might come his way. He munched on a still-warm end and gave each of his three rib-skinny island dogs a torn-off wedge. The sun was just peeking over the horizon and Junie's next stop would be to see if Old Peter's fishing trap held a small fish or two that wouldn't be missed. He whistled to the dogs and walked over the sand, still damp and cool from the night air.

Lots of garbage all over the place.... Junie, not being on the cutting edge of the island's social scene, hadn't been aware that a wedding had taken place here last night. He was observant enough, however, to notice that several half-empty beer bottles and one nearly full bottle of wine had been left on some of the tables. Skillfully, with a stealth born of years of laziness, he scooped up the warm beer glasses and drank deeply, belching at the combination of alcohol and bread. He took the bottle of wine with him for consumption a little later in the morning. A man had to have some distinctions, didn't he? And wine was a little too heavy for this early in the day.

"Hoy! Pal! Where are you, dawg?" He called. "Dusty! Hambone!" He tried a whistle, but his mouth was too dry. Maybe the wine *would* be a good idea after all. He sipped and then whistled again. A spate of barking in the coconut palm grove answered him. "Hey! You dawgs, come on!"

Hambone, the largest and mangiest of his animal collection appeared, trotting toward him, tail wagging in proud excitement. "Whatchu got?" The dog pranced clumsily and dropped a coconut at Junie's bare, splayed feet. He bent and looked at it as the other two dogs continued to whine and bark. "What th' hell...." Junie stopped, stuck the bottle of wine in the sand, and picked up the coconut. "*Yaaa*!"

He dropped it, jumping back as if stung by a viper. *Blood*! His hand was covered with sticky *blood*!

By the time Carlton, Effalyn and doctor Fullbright arrived, Junie's dogs had churned up the scene of the crime into a policeman's nightmare. "Christ! What the hell happened here!" Doc Fullbright stood staring. "Who the hell is *he*?"

"Don't know," Effalyn toed the sand. "I think he was at the wedding?" She turned to Carlton. "Do you recall him?" Carlton shrugged, trying to remove the grin on his face.

"He's sure dead." The doctor walked around the body. "Hey!" he yelled at Junie and the dogs. "Keep those mangy animals over there. Yes! You, too. You and the blamed dogs...don't move an inch!"

A crowd had begun to gather. Another police car screeched to a stop and Ganny Johnstone and Armand Hubert leaped out. "Keep those people back, boys," Carlton hollered. "Keep everyone away from here and then let's rope off the scene." He looked around in disgust. "Such as it is. What a mess!"

"Dogs destroyed any semblance of evidence." Effalyn stood, her hands on her hips, and surveyed the wreckage. "I think he was lying under the that big tree and a coconut hit him on the head," Effalyn herself didn't quite believe what she was saying. "A coconut," her echo was soft and wondering. "A coconut!" Her voice rose to a scream. "I just don't believe that *another* coconut killed somebody!"

"Hmmmm." Doctor Fullbright put on gloves and squatted by the body. Effalyn sighed and pulled out her own gloves and started her tape recorder. She held it near Doc's mouth. "Well-nourished man, perhaps in his mid-sixties. White. American or European...Dressed expensively. No...nope...nothing in his pockets, no wrist watch, no rings...no identification." He mulled for a moment. "But he had a watch on and he had a ring...looky here, see the tan lines?" He pointed. "On initial observation, I hate to say it, but...hit on the head with a coconut. Geez. One more blamed coconut." He sighed, deeply affronted at the fate that had shown him two deaths by coconut in a short amount of time. "Death probably occurred from a massive blow to the head." He motioned to Carlton to help him roll the body over. "I'm gonna make a guess that he was killed...let's see, it's seven now...maybe five or six hours ago. I'll stick my handsome neck out and say two in the morning." He stuck the probe into the body and Effalyn grimaced and looked away. Doc looked at the temperature and made a note on his pad. "Yeah, about two." He stood up, groaning with effort. "Poor sonofabitch! I wonder what made him take a nap under this particular tree". He looked up at the bunches of coconuts that hung down, then kicked at two of them that already had fallen on the sand below the tree.

"Here's the one that killed him?" Wordlessly, Effalyn handed him a plastic bag with the dirty, bloodied coconut in it. "Junie's dog was trotting around the beach with it in his mouth." She made another pattern in the sand with her foot. "I think the other dogs ate part of the victim." She pointed her toe at several small chunks of flesh that lay near the body. "See?" Again she pointed with her foot at corresponding bites on the corpse's arms and neck. "Nice, huh? Now let's all go and get some breakfast, how about?"

"Even I, with my reputation for food, don't feel like bacon and eggs just yet," Carlton bent and sniffed at the surrounding beach. "Footprints and paw prints all messed up…" He walked in a circle and then in a larger circle. "But here! Look at this! Someone lit a fire here…" He bent and poked at the few ashes that were left. "Not much left, whatever they burned." He took a plastic bag from Effalyn and carefully scooped in the sand, the burnt bits of wood and debris and then sealed the bag. "Find anything else?" Effalyn shook her head, defeated at the carnage.

"You two, get the morgue boys out here. Have them take Mr. X to the morgue. I'll do the autopsy right away. Don't believe that I'll find anything riveting, but maybe he swallowed poison or was also bitten by an anaconda!" The doctor shook his head with disgust. "Maybe an elephant sat on him and squeezed him to death! Never seen anything like this. Never. One dumb thing after the other."

"When the body's been removed," Carlton told Armand and Ganny, "see if you can find any footprints that can be casted." Armand and Ganny looked glum. "Cast them and then take a rake and go over this whole area. See if anything has been buried or …whatever." With a defeated shrug, he waved to his men. "Whatever."

"What now, Boss," Effalyn looked at him.

"Let's get some coffee, I need it by now."

"And maybe a roll and butter?" She queried.

"And maybe two. And a couple of eggs."

"You must be feeling much better. And the bacon?"

"I'm a growing boy, you know."

***

The passengers woke late. Most of them had drunk too much the night before and slowly sipped a reviving cup of coffee, getting their heads screwed back on correctly after their night of excess. Kat mixed up a huge pitcher of Bloody Mary's to get circulation going and then asked who wanted anything more than toast. No one did.

"We'll cast off in a half hour," Captain Jack announced.

'Um, I don't think Suzie or Elliott are here," Annie tentatively mentioned, biting her lip in embarrassment. "She...I haven't seen her and his cabin door is wide open and no one is there."

"Mmmmm," Captain Jack growled, his fingers fiercely combing his beard. "Where the hell are they? Did they decide to sleep out under the stars? Did they take a hotel room? Did anyone see them this morning?" He was met by puzzled shakes of heads.

"They didn't go ashore unless they swam," Ducky mused. "The Zodiacs are here and dry." He stood up, groaning, "I'm getting too old for all this partying." He stretched, his lithe, young body supple and beautiful. Annie, despite herself and her worry over Suzie, smiled in appreciation. She turned and saw Duncan watching her, his eyes speculative.

Ducky yawned, "Let me do a reconnaissance down below." Chuckling at the silly things that passengers did - not worried at all - he went down to the cabin area.

Jack shrugged and helped himself to another glass of juice. "They're probably drunk and lying somewhere on the beach." He made a sour face. "I'll go in and see if I can round them up."

"Aye, I'll come with you," Duncan offered. "Maybe they bunked down in the hotel lobby. Does anyone remember them coming back last night?" There was a chorus of negatives. Duncan and Captain Jack climbed into one of the Zodiacs and motored in to shore.

"Suzie doesn't swim well enough to go swimming." Annie's face was creased with worry. "I did see her last night, but she wasn't with Elliott. She was with some other man...dark and with a moustache."

"I think she and Elliott had some kind of a dust-up," Lannie offered. "I overheard them arguing and then she huffed off and began to dance. Elliott was sitting in the back, but I don't recall seeing him after that."

***

Carlton took a snapshot of Mr. X's face after Doctor Fullbright did a quick cosmetic fix-up so that a witness might not faint at the sight of the wounds, brain spillage and dog-bitten skin. Effalyn ran off several copies. Ganny and Armond hoofed off to the shopkeepers to see if anyone recognized the dead man, while Carlton went to The Green Flash and Effalyn took a motorboat to all the boats in the harbor.

Leslie and Charlie looked at the photo. "Ugh!" Leslie's face crinkled. "He looks awful!"

Carlton tipped his head judiciously. "You'd look pretty bad if someone bopped you on the head with a coconut."

"You think its murder?" Charlie's shrewd eyes were wide. Carlton shrugged.

"I think I remember him," Leslie squinted, her adorable tipped-up nose crinkled in thought. Charlie smiled fondly at her. Even when Leslie was looking at a photo of a corpse, she was his heart's delight. "I think he was in the bar yesterday." She thought back. "Maybe with a pretty blonde girl."

Charlie groaned, stretching his bad knee out. "Mebbe I do remember him. He was really handsome, right? Dressed expensively?"

"Not any more," Carlton's laugh was harsh.

"Poor man," Leslie's blue eyes were sad. "To think that such a joyous night should end like this."

"Was he a wedding guest?" Leslie shook her head and shrugged. She really didn't know.

"I wonder if he's the same man I'm thinking of," Charlie's tone was regretful. "There were so many people here…"

"Where is the wedding party now?" Carlton looked around.

"In the main dining room having brunch."

"Mind if I speak to them?"

Leslie shrugged. "Go ahead, it will either gross them out or make their day. How many couples can look back and talk about the corpse that was found in the aftermath of their wedding reception?"

Carlton walked into the dining room and Leslie followed him, curious to see what transpired. "Ladies and gentlemen, Mr. and Mrs. Gamble," he bowed to the head table. "I wonder if I may have a few moments of your time…."

***

Ganny and Armond showed the photo to all of the shopkeepers as well as any customers in the stores. Two women, one in Aunt Fanny's and one in Eva's Jewelry shop, thought they remembered seeing a handsome man, dressed expensively, walking with a pretty blonde girl. Another woman said she remembered him clearly, and he was limping and used a cane. No, she stated positively, he wasn't with anyone. She closed her eyes dramatically and offered that she recalled that he had a gold tooth, too. She was positive. Solemnly, Ganny took her name and address. The bartender at Captain Fatty's remembered Mr. X well. "He was drinking expensive Scotch and he was with two women, one a redhead and one a blonde."

The waitress shook her head. "Nah! He was only with one woman, the blonde. He drank single malt Scotches, maybe four of them, and she drank a Pina Colada. Several Pina Coladas." She jingled the change in her pocket. "He gave me a big tip – twenty bucks…" She grinned. "I clearly remember anyone who gives me twenty bucks. He was dressed snazzy. Had on an expensive watch and a gold chain or two. Money there." She nodded and the bartender shrugged.

"I thought he was with two women."

An older woman, sitting at the bar, came over. She pushed her way into the conversation and offered: "Yeah, he was in here yesterday. He was with a gorgeous blonde. He was nice, but you could tell that he could be a bastard if he wanted to be. She was sort of snotty." She made a motion with her head. "Asked me if I knew where a man might make a purchase…" Her voice was suggestive.

"What kind'a purchase?" Armond asked.

The lady rolled her eyes. "You know, a *pur*chase."

"Oh, a *pur*chase! And what did you tell him?"

"Me? Shoot, what would I know about such things!" The lady huffed and turned away. Armond gently took her arm and turned her back. The lady grinned, letting her gaze run up and down Armond's body, stopping at various salient points. "Well, I did see them, both of them, walkin' over toward the old Belonger quarter."

"Where they just might be able to buy drugs." Armond's face was disgusted.

"Well, I wouldn't know about those kind'a things." The lady grinned and shook her head. "Handsome man like you. Maybe you should go over that-a-way and see what you might see."

***

Effalyn visited boat after boat and at each, received nothing but heads that shook back and forth with negatives. No one recognized the photo. And then, she gently bumped her boat into the stern of *The Southern Cross.*

"*Oh, my God*! It's *Elliott*!" Kat screamed. "He looks...he...Is he *dead*? What happened?" In a moment, all of the passengers were crowded around. As the passengers gasped at the photo, Captain Jack and Duncan came back in the Zodiac. Duncan shook his head and announced: "We didn't see either of them and no one seems to remember them." He jumped off the Zodiac and saw the glassy-eyed passengers. "What's all this?"

The realization of what was happening hit Annie hard. "*Suzie*! What's happened to Suzie?" Annie's panicked voice nearly screamed.

"Who is Suzie?" Effalyn queried gently.

"My cousin! She was with Elliott!" Annie was becoming frantic.

Duncan put his arm around her. "Easy, Annie, love. Take a deep breath. That's better." He hugged her close. "Suzie's a survivor. She's going to be fine."

Kat patted Annie's arm. "I think she was with him earlier on, but I don't think she was with him at the end of the party."

"She left with some other guy," Sammy said. "Didn't you see her?" He turned to Vinny. "Some dark, bearded man."

"Yeah. She was dancing with him and Elliott was sitting at a table at the back. He was glowering and looked pissed off."

"Anyone want breakfast?" Kat came out of the galley with a basket filled with fresh-baked rolls. She was met with blank stares.

A small motor-powered dingy came toward the catamaran. Annie watched it approach. There, in the bow, was a wind-blown, blonde-haired woman in a crumpled dress. "*Suzie*!" screamed Annie. "Oh, Suzie! Thank God!"

"What's all the excitement?" The bulky man who was steering the boat threw the painter to Ducky and tied up to *The Southern Cross's* stern. Suzie, looking less than her usual perfectly coiffed self, was lifted up. "What's going on?" She patted her hair and tried to smooth her dress.

She looks so...tawdry, Annie thought.

"Elliott has had an accident," Captain Jack's face was somber. "A bad accident."

"Are you a relative of this man…Elliott…Elliott…what is his last name?" Effalyn queried.

Suzie's expression was bewildered. Effalyn judged her surprise was genuine. "His name? He's Elliott Barringer. Why do you want to know? What's happened? Did he have an accident?"

"Are you a relative?"

"No…no. I just…he…we are friends."

"Is there a relative on board?"

"No," Captain Jack's expression was somber. "No one."

"Then you, as Captain, will be our official contact until we can reach his attorney or a relative."

"What are you *saying*?" Suzie grabbed the photo out of Effalyn's hand. She looked at it in horror. "He…he looks…." She shook her head in confusion.

"I'm sorry to tell you this, Ma'am," Effalyn's voice was officiously stiff. "But he is dead."

"*Dead*!" Suzie's voice was a terrified whisper. "What happened?"

"We don't know, Ma'am. He was found on the beach."

"Was it a heart attack?" Duncan asked.

"No. Not a heart attack." Effalyn looked slowly around at the circle of faces. "Not a heart attack." There was silence. The passengers and crew looked at one another, their eyes worried.

Effalyn sighed. This part was always difficult. "I'm going to ask you to prepare to be here for at least today." She took out her mobile. "Captain Jack, I will need you, in the absence of a relative, to come and officially identify the body as your passenger." The Captain nodded, his usually jolly face somber. "I'm going back to get Detective Inspector Reese and we'll be back in about fifteen minutes to talk with all of you." She spoke rapidly into her mobile, nodded her head and prepared to get back into her boat. "Stay here, everyone. No one is to leave the boat."

"Elliott!" Suzie clutched at the dark man. "I've….please….I have…." She made a retching sound and bolted into the cabin. Effalyn made a move to stop her, but Suzie had fled, clutching her stomach. Effalyn shrugged and left *The Southern Cross*.

"And who are you, sir?" Captain Jack introduced himself.

"I'm Francesco Jeraldo." The man looked bewildered. "I'm a passenger on the *Jumbie Jamboree* with Captain Karen and Ed. What the hell is going on?"

***

Within fifteen minutes, Carlton had telephoned his superior, Superintendent Craig Buckley. "We'll keep the captain, crew and passengers until we get more information....Yes, sir. I know, sir....What do you want to do with all the wedding guests, the passengers on the other boats?"

"Get all their information. See if anyone witnessed the deceased at the wedding or afterwards. If you get anyone who saw him, interview them and find out what they know. Was there anyone there who knew him before?" Superintendent Buckley scratched his nearly bald head. "What else?"

"We'll get their contact information and, naturally, keep anyone who knows anything at all. The rest of the group...the wedding party...we'll let them continue home. Most of them are leaving today and...well..." Carlton let the thought of several hundred wedding guests, mad as hornets at being delayed, float in Buckley's imagination.

Buckley huffed with annoyance, but was a realist. "I reckon it is the best thing to do. We cannot keep all those people indefinitely." He longed for the old days, when he could hold up a passenger ship and all the passengers, damn the consequences. Ah, well. "And the cruising boats? How many of them and how many passengers?"

"Perhaps a dozen boats," Carlton hazarded. "Perhaps fifty passengers." He paused. "But the cruising boats aren't really going anywhere. They – the passengers – are all down here for a week or more at one island or another. Turnover day is at the end of the week, so they'll be available if we need them"

"Good man."

"I have patrolmen Johnstone and Hubert doing the preliminary interviews If they see any need for me to step in, I will. Otherwise, we'll let the boats go after we get their passenger information and itineraries. The only boat we are officially boarding right now is *The Southern Cross*."

"Hmpf. That's Scambaugh's catamaran, isn't it?"

"Yes, sir. He identified the deceased as one of his passengers."

"Good Old Scumbag." Buckley's laugh rumbled over the wires. "Give him my best and tell him I owe him a drink."

"Yes, sir. I'll tell him." Carlton hoped that the Super hadn't thought that perhaps Captain Scambaugh himself was also a suspect. Anyone on that boat might have killed the victim. He spoke once more, "Effalyn Penn and I are about to go to the catamaran. We'll search...what's his last name again?" Effalyn wrote furiously on a pad of paper and held it up. "Ah, Elliott, um, Barringer, that's his name. Don't know much more right now, but we'll be better informed within an hour....yes, sir. We'll search Barringer's cabin and interview the other passengers and crew." He listened for a moment more. "Yes, sir. I will." Carlton turned to Effalyn. "Let's go!"

CHAPTER SEVENTEEN

"...as idle as a painted ship upon a painted ocean..."
Samuel Taylor Coleridge, *The Rhyme of the Ancient Mariner*

"Boss? I got Thigpin Odette here." Ganny Johnstone's voice was excited. "Maybe he killed our coconut man."

Carlton held the mobile phone tight to his ear, trying to hear over the roar of the outboard engine. "You got what?"

"I was down in the Belonger Quarter. Heard a rumor while I was questioning the people in Fat Matt's Bar that Mr. X was trying to score some drugs and so I went to the Pink Iguana Bar....Yeah...Who do I see right away but ole Thigpin and he startles as soon as he sees me and tries to run out the back...Yeah...He's draped with a heavy gold chain around his neck and a faggot-y bracelet on his wrist and he's wearing a gold watch with enough diamonds on it buy half of the island....Yeah, no way Thigpin could ever afford a watch like this. Gold Rolex. Gen-yew-wine. He stole them from the corpse. He swears that the body was dead when he saw it in the early morning hours. Said he almost fell over it. He said he was just strollin' around the wedding celebration and went to take a piss in this clump of trees. Almost fell over the body...."

"Go on," Carlton's voice yelled through the telephone.

"Says the stiff was dead beyond all question when he found him on the beach. Says it was maybe three in the morning...two-thirty maybe. He's shaken and not too sure of the time. He's crying like a baby and swears on his mother's grave that he would never kill anyone. Says he saw a chance to steal his stuff ... 'Who could leave all that gold lying there?'...I quote him...so, anyway, he...Thigpin... took a necklace, a gold wrist chain and a watch, all of which he...Thigpin... was wearing, like I said, when I apprehended him."

"What do you think, Ganny? Your quick guess," Carlton bawled. "Did he kill him or just steal the jewelry?"

"Donno, boss. Thigpin Odette is scum, but I don't know that he'd murder someone he didn't know and then parade himself all over the island wearing the spoils. He's shrewd, but not stupid. I think Thigpin sold the stiff and a blonde lady some drugs, though. Don't know how that ties in with the murder. What do you think?"

"Keep him in custody. Let him know that we know he's been selling drugs. That ought to put the fear into him. Then, let him think *we* think he killed him." Ganny nodded into his phone. "Ought to be good for his character development." Carlton heard Ganny snigger in appreciation. "I'll be back in a few hours. Oh, and we think we know the identity of the body. A Mister Elliott Barringer. Passenger on *The Southern Cross*."

"Uh, huh," Ganny assented. "We'll keep Mr. Odette in a nice, comfortable cell. I'll put Mama Lucille back in his life again."

"Geez. He hates Mama Lucille!"

"What sleaze-bag doesn't?" Ganny chuckled. "She'll put the fear of God into him. He'll be in that jail for possession until he rots, nevermind what she'll do to him if she thinks he killed someone." He laughed, a high pitched cackle. "See you soon, Boss."

Carlton clicked his mobile shut. "Ganny found Thigpin the rat in a bar in the Belonger Quarter. Thigpin was wearing the dead man's wrist watch, bracelet and gold necklace." Above the pounding of her motor, Effalyn shook her head. "Ganny's got him in custody, swearing on his mother's hairnet that he only robbed him; that he stumbled on the corpse...already dead."

"Sounds like Thigpin. He's a nasty slug, but I don't think he'd murder someone, do you?" Effalyn slowed the engine as they approached *The Southern Cross*. All crew and passengers appeared to be on deck, waiting for them. Effalyn motioned her head towards the stern of the boat. "They all look apprehensive."

"Wonder which one killed him." Carlton made a motion with his hands. "Hold off docking for a moment. Let them all worry some more." Effalyn promptly took the engine out of gear and turned the tiller slightly so that the little boat drifted twenty feet behind *The Southern Cross'* stern.

"We'll obviously put off questioning Mrs. Marsden and Mr. Zuster until tomorrow. This mess takes precedence. I want to get those people who are probably clear off the island and keep only those to whom we really need to talk ." Effalyn nodded.

"Eff?" Carlton's voice was neutral.

"Uh, huh."

"That nice man from last night? What was his name?"

"You mean Elwyn Langdon?" Her face bloomed crimson.

"Him. He's on this boat, you know."

"I know. I presume he'll be one that you interview and not me." She bit her lip and looked out over the horizon.

"I think that would be the best."

"Of course."

"Boss," Effalyn bent to slip the engine into forward, but paused for a moment. "We were sure that Two-Tone's death was simply an accident. Why do we think this one is murder?"

"Damn good question, Eff. When you get an answer, please let me know."

In the end, they split it up, Effalyn doing the preliminary interviews of the women, and Carlton speaking with the men.

"What do you know about Elliott Barringer? Why would anyone want to kill him?"

Captain Jack eased himself down in to a cockpit chair. He had a folder in his hands. "Don't know much, really. Only met the man a few days ago. Here's his dossier, application, passport copy, sailing resume and all that stuff." He pushed the folder towards the middle of the table. "If you're looking for motive, let me be the first to tell you that almost everyone on the boat hated him…well, maybe hated him is too strong a word. Let's say all the passengers, me, Kat and Ducky disliked him intensely. The man was a weasel and a shit."

"That nice, eh?"

"Humpf. No one liked him at all. He was rude, arrogant, snide, nasty…"

"But, don't hold back. Tell me how you *really* felt about him?" The two friends laughed. "Shit, Jack, you might find yourself rotting away in prison if I can find out why you killed him."

"Man wasn't worth that much hate," Jack laughed, easy with himself. "But he *was* a bastard. Only person who saw any worth in him, and she was an idiot herself, was Suzie Ruutz-Reese, one of the other passengers."

"Suzie. The little blonde sex-pot. What was the story?"

"Well, you know this trip is advertised as a find-your-love cruise." Jack got up and pulled a cold soda out of the refrigerator. He waved it questioningly to Carlton, who nodded. Jack got another soda, popped both tops, and sat back down. He took a long swig, belched and then continued. "Surprisingly enough, we get a lot of people here who do fall in love. Shoot, that wedding yesterday - that was because of last year's trip." He paused again and drank. "We – Ducky and me – think that they were both using drugs. Anyway, this Suzie seemed to fall in a big way for Elliott. Except for last night."

"Oh?"

"Mmmm. Several of the other passengers said that they had some kind of an argument and Suzie smacked his face and went away with some guy named Francesco." Carlton rolled his eyes. "She...the little hussy..." he laughed half in disgust, half in appreciation, "spent the night with Francesco on board the *Jumbie Jamboree*. I talked with Francesco, and funny thing is, he comes from the same hometown that Suzie and Annie are from. Greenwich, Connecticut. He lived there until he was in his twenties and then moved back to Italy when his mother and father divorced. Suzie says she never met him before last night. Says what a shame that she didn't. Ha!" He spread his big hands out. "So she has a pretty good alibi."

Carlton looked glum. He opened the folder and scanned the sheets. "From Los Angeles. A lawyer." He looked up. "I hate lawyers." He ruffled the sheets and stacked them back neatly. "Do you have any more personal knowledge of this guy? Was he married? Kids?"

"I have the impression he was married and maybe more than once. No children, I believe. I think we can contact his law firm for further information of that kind."

"OK. Just for the record, where were you at two in the morning?"

"Sitting right there," Jack's chin pointed to the seats in the cockpit, where Effalyn was interviewing the women, one by one. "With Emma, Ducky, Lisette and Michael Beck, one of the passengers. We were shooting the shit and playing a few tunes. Went to bed about an hour later. All of us."

"Tough." Carlton stood up. "I was hoping to nail you for the murder right away."

"I'm sure, if you turn the thumbscrews on Emma, she'll squeal on me." Captain Jack lumbered up. "Who you wanna see next?"

"Send me Ducky. That way, I'll get to check your alibi."

***

"Any joy?" Carlton spoke quietly.

"Not much. Our hottest suspect, Suzie Ruutz-Reese, seems clear. She was the only one who really got to know him," Effalyn's face was deadpan, "Biblical sense and no common sense. But, as you know, last night seemed to be the end, figuratively and literally, of their romance. I can't see how she...Suzie...could have killed him. She was with this Francesco fellow for the entire night, unless they were both in it together?" She shook her head. "Nah. She's clear of the murder, but..."

"But, what?"

"She's scared of something. She's nervous and afraid and hiding something."

"The drugs? I think she was up to her pretty neck in drugs."

"Maybe. Let's see what we find when we take a look below." She rubbed the back of her own pretty neck. "And, um, Boss?"

"Hmmm?"

"About Elwyn. Is he clear?"

Carlton smiled, a genuine sweet smile. "Yes, my turtle dove. Your new friend seems innocent." He turned his head suddenly with a frown. "Unless, when you brought him back from the hospital, the two of you stopped at the beach and bopped Elliott over the head."

Effalyn raised her hands high. "You got us, Boss. You're too clever for me."

Carlton patted her hand. "He seems like a nice gentleman. Now," he turned and addressed the passengers in a loud voice. "I want you all to stay up here while Miss Penn and I do some checking down below in the cabins." There were a few gasps and some of the passengers seemed to move closer together as they realized that the police were seriously looking within the catamaran for a killer. "Maybe Kat can get you all some brunch and we'll be as quick as we can." He raked the faces of the passengers. Suzie Ruutz-Reese looked sly and triumphant; Claudia's face was upset; Lannie was visibly worried and Paula looked pale and sickly.

***

"Boss!" Come here, please." Effalyn's urgent whisper found him, his hands covered by the ubiquitous latex gloves, rummaging through piles of clothing in Sammy and Vinny's cabin.

"What did you find?" He looked glum. "I hope it's more interesting than the seven bottles of rum I found in Vinny James' suitcase."

"Come to Annie and Suzie's cabin."

She pointed to a carefully folded-back edge of the lining of Annie Sabatino's suitcase. "See the baggie? Drugs?"

"Annie's luggage? That nice little girl?" He bent closer. Then closer. He gingerly opened the plastic bag and sniffed, then dipped his little finger into the white powder and tasted it. "Bleah!"

Effalyn's face drooped. "She would be the last one I suspected of this." She looked around the cabin. "Unless...unless...someone *else* put them in her suitcase instead of her own suitcase."

"Someone else? Hmmm? Who else lives in this little cabin? Who else? Perhaps her dear cousin, Suzie?" Carlton's face was angry. "You don't think one cousin would do that to her own cousin, do you?"

"Ah! I remember now! Suzie said she was about to be ill just before I left the boat to come and get you. She either *was* sick, or *pretended* to be sick and ran down to her cabin..." Effalyn made a tsk-tsking sound. "She had a large pocketbook with her. Hmmm, she may have stashed the drugs then, knowing that we were coming back." She shook her head. "I never should have left them alone. Never should have let her come down here."

"We all learn by making dumb mistakes," Carlton's voice was gentle. "You were alone and did the best you could under the circumstances. Don't worry too much. Come on, my turtle dove, let's get Ganny and Armond out here pronto with the kits and, if Suzie did plant the stuff, with some luck, she was careless and we'll have her fingerprints all over this." He carefully folded the slit bottom back and closed the suitcase. "Unless she was smart enough to wear gloves when she stashed this. Or, maybe we're seeing this all wrong and Annie really is the druggie."

"Somehow, it just doesn't seem that way to me." Effalyn rubbed her chin.

"Me, too. I see the long-fingernailed hands of Suzie Ruutz-Reese all over this."

He made several mobile phone calls and then joined the group to have lunch. The passengers, unable to go to their cabins, were restless and jumpy. They ate their food up on the trampoline, speaking in hushed voices to one another. Captain Jack, Carlton and Effalyn sat at the Nav Station, keeping an eye on the passengers and the passage-way to the cabins. The air was tense.

Carefully, Effalyn paged through the passports, the medical records and the resumes of the passengers. "This is interesting, Boss. You know, the man who died, Elliott…? He was also born in the same town as Annie and Suzie. Greenwich, Connecticut. It's here on his passport and also on his sailing resume." She read, 'Sailing Experience: Sailed as a young boy at the Greenwich Yacht Club…Graduated from Greenwich High School…' Coincidence, huh? There's an awful lot of 'Greenwich, Connecticut' in this mess…"

"Hmmm." Carlton mused. "Maybe I'll give a call to the police up there. See if any of them has a record. For all we know, even that sweet little Annie could have been a drug offender for years. She could be a thief…or arrested for drunken driving…who knows. Let's check."

"Whatever you say, Boss."

"We'll have to check all of them…not just Annie and Suzie. Any of the passengers could be violent or have a pattern of hurting a spouse or a child or picking bar fights." Carlton bit off a huge wedge of sandwich, chewed thoughtfully and swallowed. "This is a toughie, with all of these total strangers, all out of their familiar elements."

"Sarah Lemonowski, the woman from England…" Captain Jack dusted off this crumb-strewn shirt, "She has some kind of secret. She hinted that we would be astonished when we found out, but I don't have any idea if it has anything to with any of this."

"We'll talk to her and try to see what's her story." Carlton made a note on his napkin and stuffed it into his pocket. Effalyn watched him and smiled to herself. He'd forget the note and when Rebecca washed his pants, the note would be destroyed. She surreptitiously made her own notations and circled it and put a star at the top.

"Maybe Thigpin did it after all," Effalyn's voice was hushed as she doodled on her notepad. "Or maybe the coconut just fell on Mr. Barringer." Their musings were startled at the sound of a motor launch approaching.

Ganny and Armond and two officers from Spanish Town, a man and a woman, hopped onto the boat. They were laden with crime scene equipment. "OK, everyone, please line up. Patrolmen Johnstone and Hubert will be taking your fingerprints."

"Why our fingerprints?" Zandra's voice was fearful. 'We have done no harm."

"Is this all necessary?" Hosea demanded. "Do we have our rights here?"

"It's for elimination purposes," Carlton tried his most sincere smile. "No one is accusing anyone of anything. And the faster we can eliminate you from our concerns, the faster Captain Jack can get you on your way."

"I think I ken," Duncan MacKinnon nodded. "As I am completely innocent, a naked babe in a cloud, naturally, you can take my fingerprints." He held his hands out.

"Me, too," Annie came forward. "Let's make this as easy as it can be," she smiled at Carlton. "I have no fear. You can do my fingers."

Effalyn's eyes met Carlton's for a moment. The tension relaxed. *We have nothing to fear. Why not let them take my fingerprints? After all, I have done nothing. Why should I protest? If I do, they might think I have something to hide.* The passengers' thoughts were clearly etched in the air. *Thank you, Duncan and Annie,* Carlton sighed to himself. These two were making it easy for them. *Obviously, Annie had no idea that the little bag is sitting in her suitcase, or she wouldn't have been so eager to comply. Or did she think that she'd hidden it well enough so that it wouldn't be found? Who knows?*

Elwyn, his face bandaged, presented himself to Effalyn. "Here are my hands for you to inspect," the rest of his face was bland. "As I was with you most of the early morning at the hospital, I hope that you don't think that I am a suspect." He tried a smile, but it slid off his face. Elwyn was intelligent enough to know the danger they were all in.

"I'll reserve judgment," Effalyn put her hand to his face and patted it. "How's the injury?"

"Hurts like a sonofabitch, but, as opposed to being dead, I guess it is nothing." He put his hand on top of hers. "Makes you think, doesn't it? This is so unusual, so weird for all of us, but you, my sleuth woman, you get to see this kind of thing all the time, don't you?" Effalyn nodded, her mouth wry. "I, um, really enjoyed having you take care of me last night. I was going to call on you this morning to see if we might be able to have dinner one night soon, but I'm not sure if that's a good thing to do now that this has happened."

"I...I think we could...but, before I say anything, I'll have to clear it with my boss." She bit her lip. "This is so peculiar. I never had a...date or a social engagement..." Her lovely complexion darkened at the word engagement. *Was she being too blatant? Would he think she was angling for something more?...* "A further meeting, I mean, with anyone who might have been a suspect." She giggled and he smiled, wanting to know this intelligent, complex woman better.

"I'd hate a little murder to get in the way of our getting to know each other under more, um, normal situations. I want to show you my better side, not just the manly one that faints at the sight of my own blood." His own grin was rueful. "How can I get in touch so I can take you to dinner? We'll be here in the islands, but not around Big Fish Cay, for a week or so and I can leave the group anytime and come back here."

Effalyn gave him her mobile telephone number and then added her personal number. "I'd like to have dinner with you." She ducked her head, embarrassed but delighted at his attention.

"As soon as my name gets wiped off the suspect list, I will call you." He pressed her hand. "I promise."

The other police were introduced as Josephine Jean and Norman Sweetman. They went below to continue a more thorough search and to package up everything in Elliott Barringer's cabin.

Carlton, armed with both Suzie's and Annie's fingerprints, went back down to their cabin with the special camera and a box of dusting powder and captured the outlines of the prints on the suitcase, the area that had been slit open, and the outside of the baggie. "I need a microscope," he groaned to Effalyn. "I just can't eliminate her from this with my naked eye." He rubbed his chin. "I think I have to take her in."

"Annie?"

"Yes." He backed away from Effalyn's fierce glare. "I know, I know," His hands went up defensively. "I know I'm wrong, but I can't just ignore the drug situation because I like that little Annie and think her cousin is a snake. I've got to act on it." His face was lugubrious. "You stay here and keep everything going. Make sure your handsome pilot doesn't try to fly away." His grin softened his words. "I'll bring Annie in with Ganny and the evidence and have the lab take a look at it all."

"On your head be it." Effalyn wasn't happy. "You're the boss, so naturally I go along with whatever you do, even though I don't like it." The look Carlton gave back to her was sour. *Sometimes this job just sucks.*

Ganny bagged the entire suitcase and carried it to the smaller motorboat. As he carried it, the passengers muttered and Annie gasped, her face a furious red. "What are you doing with my things?" Her voice was a tiny scream.

"I'm afraid you'll have to come with me to the station, Miss Sabatino." He took her arm gently. "I have some further tests and questions to ask of you."

"Duncan!" She turned to him in terror. "What shall I do?"

"You can'na just take the girl! You have no right! What the devil has she done?" Duncan thundered, his face tight and furious. "Stay here, Annie!"

"Mr. MacKinnon." Carlton's face was calm. "Please, try to be reasonable. This is routine and we need her to do some tests that we cannot do here on the boat. Please don't make this more difficult than it already is."

"Duncan!" Annie almost shrieked.

"Let's go, Miss Sabatino." Carlton ushered her to the stern. Frightened, but afraid to make a scene, Annie stumbled into the small rowboat, helped by Ducky's strong arm and his confident wink that all would be well. Just wait.

Elwyn restrained Duncan. "Keep a stiff upper lip, my man. This will all work out in time." Duncan twisted away, but didn't follow. Effalyn watched the rest of the passengers. Most were horrified and Zandra was openly weeping. Suzie, Effalyn noted, had a strange look on her face and kept away from the others. *Hmpf,* she said to herself. *That one is awful big trouble.*

As the motorboat pulled away from *The Southern Cross*, Duncan suddenly leapt overboard, fully dressed, and began to swim to shore, his arms and legs straining in the water. Even with his strength, he trailed woefully behind, his arms churning manaically, as the motorboat picked up speed.

"Hey!" Effalyn tried to stop him, but as she sprung to the rail, he was already swimming strongly in the direction of the dock. She looked around, as if to find Armond, but then shrugged her shoulders. *Ah, what was the worse that could happen if he swam ashore? He'd swim to the dock and then what? Walk to the police station soaking wet? Get a taxicab?* Her face was resolute, but inwardly, she was grinning. Let the Boss handle this one! See what he'd do when the Scottish-Ox-in-Love turned up dripping at the station. "All right, everyone. Let's line up. I want to go over your papers and information again. Let's start with you, Miss Hoovenmeyer." Zandra blew her nose and sullenly sat down. "Is this your passport?" Zandra nodded....

***

Carlton and Ganny didn't speak on the way to the station. Annie sat, huddled and terrified in the back seat. Carlton almost turned around to tell her not to worry so much, but, at the last moment, decided to play by the rule book. He said nothing at all.

Doctor Fullbright was waiting for him when he got to the station. "Ganny, take Miss Sabatino to Room Three," he ordered. Nodding and in silence, Ganny guided Annie to a smallish room, painted in light blue. The room had one small, grated window, a table and three chairs.

"Can I get you a cup of tea?" Ganny asked. Annie shook her head. *Anything to eat or drink would make me vomit*, she thought.

Then, fearful of all of the visions of TV cop shows she had watched, she changed her mind. "A cup of tea, please." She relented. "Two sugars, no milk." After all, they might try to starve her to make her talk. *Talk*? Talk about *what*? Why was she here and why did they bundle up her suitcase? The piece of art that she bought? Was it a counterfeit? *What*? She shuddered and looked around the bleakness of the room. *Suppose they did bring her tea and then she had to use the toilet? And they might not let her until she confessed. Confessed to what? What would she do if she had to pee and they tried to keep her in the room? Aha! She could pee into the teacup*! She snorted with nervous laughter. *Would they just stand by and watch her? Would they pretend to not notice that she had turned around to have some privacy? Oh, Lord! What was she going to do? Damn Suzie anyhow!*

"I think it was murder, all right," Doc Fullbright told Carlton. "Preliminary autopsy shows some kind of barbiturate in him. Maybe chloral hydrate or some kind of quick-acting sleeping pill." He sat down heavily, puffing air out. "Who is that girl you're holding?"

Carlton quickly outlined what they knew. Ganny came back out and took the suitcase, together with Suzie's and Annie's prints, and the print card from the deceased's fingers upstairs to the lab. "They have to check those prints *immediately*!" Carlton growled. "Before I really make a fool of myself."

"What the heck can you do?" The old doctor rubbed his finger alongside his nose. "You can't just ignore the drugs. You gotta do what you gotta do."

"I'm going to talk with her now." Carlton turned, his stomach churning, a sour taste in his mouth. "Jeez, I hope this is all a big mistake."

"You want moral company? You want me or Mama Lucille?" The doctor's old eyes twinkled. "I'll prop you up, my friend."

"I wouldn't mind you being there. I always appreciate your point of view." He sighed. "And we might as well get Mama in here too."

In three minutes, a huge black woman, dressed in a blue dress that fit her like a circus tent came into the room. "What's happenin'?" She asked, her grin showing three gold teeth. She sniffed the air. "Hmmm...I detect a kanits around here." She giggled, an attractive sound from such a large lady.

"I give up already." Carlton raised his hands in surrender. "What the hell is a 'kanits'."

"Ha!" Mama Lucille exulted. "Gotcha again. My dear man, a kanits is a bad odor. A bad smell. Something smells around here, no?" She appealed to Carlton. He nodded. "And being that something smells, you called for Mama." Her eyes danced. "And so? You want me?"

Carlton grinned lasciviously at her. "I always want you, Mama. Fat lot of good it does me. You never agree to mess around with me." She slapped him on his arm and rolled her eyes.

Mama Lucille was a Virgin Gorda legend. She was born in the poorest of the poor sections of the island. Her life as a girl was hard, as her father drank and her mother couldn't cope with life. Or perhaps her mother couldn't cope with life and that was why her father drank. Whichever, little Lucille was left to bring herself up, cook her own meals, keep her mother and the house clean. Any money that came into the household was quickly tipped down her father's throat. When Lucille was thirteen, she left school for good and got a job cleaning houses for other island women who had it better than she did. At fifteen, her father came home one night roaring drunk. He picked up a knife and killed Lucille's mother and then slit his own wrists to bleed to death. Lucille, hiding in the bedroom, watched and listened to the escalating argument, her mother's cries and her father's anguish. Afterwards, she calmly called the police and watched as they tried to deal with the bloody carnage that remained of her life.

It took Lucille a few weeks to get used to her new situation. Their violent deaths saddened her as she loved them both, but, in a peculiar way, she was relieved that she only had to care for herself from now on. She worked harder than ever. At sixteen, Lucille, a skinny slip of a girl, married Big Joe Carrington and the tenor of her life changed.

She and Joe were very happy together. So happy that they had eight children right in a row. As Joe's name started with a 'J' and her own name started with an 'L', they named their children names that started with the letter that was in-between. Kyle, Kendrick, the twins; Kitty and Kara, Kimmie, Kalen, Keesa and Klayman. When Kyle was ten, Big Joe was killed in a traffic accident caused by a truck filled with cement blocks, driven by a no-good islander who was high on drugs. The accident left Lucille alone with the children and not much in the way of income, as the driver of the truck had no insurance and no assets. Lucille went back to work, this time snaring a good job as a prison guard on the night shift; a job with good pay and good benefits, including schooling for herself. She worked on the night shift so that she could be home to care for the babies during the day. She had no time for schooling during those years, but only grinding work and taking care of her darling children, and she earned the respect of everyone who knew her. As soon as her children were partly grown up, she went back to school and then, with her precious diploma in hand, went on to study Criminal Justice. In time, her evenhandedness and success with even the most violent prisoners earned her one promotion after another. During the prison break and riots of 1993, Lucille single-handedly talked seven violent men into putting down their arms and surrendering, saving the life of two prison guards who were being held hostage.

Her life was easier now, but Lucille missed Big Joe every moment of the day and twice as much at night. To console herself, she began to eat more and more, until her figure became legendary and, in the island way, her name changed from Poor Lucille With All Those Little Children, to Mama Lucille, The Caretaker Of The Jail.

Her children were a testament to her stern, but loving upbringing, each of them graduating from high school and then studying at the tuition-free University of the Virgin Islands. Kyle was now an attorney in St. Thomas; Kendrick a dentist in Puerto Rico. The twins became aeronautical engineers and worked at the Kennedy Space Center in Florida. Kimmie married her high school sweetheart and was the mother of four young children, helping her husband with his accounting business in Road Town. Kaylen was training to be a dermatologist, and Keesa and Klayman were studying for their Doctorates in Computer Sciences. Mama Lucille was very proud of each and every one of them, and they were proud of her.

"The only thing is, Mama," Kyle teased her. "You still love to talk like an island child. You know better, Mama."

And Mama Lucille would swat at him, big lawyer or no big lawyer. "I had no time to learn what you children learned. I talk like I always talked. Jus' regular talk."

"Hmpf," Kendrick hugged her. "You know more words than anyone I know."

"I really didn't have no proper schoolin' as a chile," Mama demurred in an exaggerated accent. "I *am* jus' an island girl."

"Ha! You can speak better than the Queen when you want to. You only put on the poor island girl accent when you want some sympathy." Kyle laughed. "You, of all people, have the best vocabulary I know. After all, you learned all those words from The Reader's Digest every month."

"Yes," Mama nodded, a grin splitting her broad face. "That little magazine didn't even cost me a penny. I jus' waited until someone threw it away and then I brought it home to study the words." She nodded her head. "An' I learned them all...words like calmodulin...barghest...genipap."

"Stop swearing, Mama!"

"You might say I was a logolept, mightn't you?"

"What the heck does that mean, Mama?"

She looked demurely up at her son. "A person who is obsessed with words. A logolept. That's me, right?"

"Like I said, Mama, don't swear!"

"Ha!"

Mama Lucille now ran the entire prison system for the island and was on the Board of Directors for Prison Reform for the entire British Virgin Islands chain. She was known to be scrupulously fair. Kind and understanding, when the situation warranted, but stern and judgmental if a prisoner was difficult. She had a distinct bias about men and women who abused liquor and drugs, having seen the consequences in her own personal life. She was aware of her prejudices and strove to be more than fair with substance users.

"But it rankles me when they let themselves be eaten up by those poisons," she would say. "And it *really* rankles me when they hurt others. And," she mumbled time and time again, "given the magnitude of their problems, they always do."

A penitent prisoner, genuinely trying to get himself on the straight and narrow, would find Mama his best pal, encouraging him to study and better himself, often taking the prisoner into her home when they were released. To make the transition to life outside of prison, Lucille could be found browbeating her friends to help them to find a job. For years after their release, she would keep tabs on their lives to be sure that they didn't slip back. These people loved Mama Lucille. On the other hand, a prisoner who used his time in jail to learn tricks on how to lie more successfully, cheat or to be a slicker criminal once they got out, would find her a wrathful tiger just waiting to bite them where it really hurt.

***

As they trudged to Room Three, Carlton quickly explained the outline of the situation to Mama Lucille, who, in a lifetime of police work, had seen and heard everything under the sun. She nodded somberly.

"Lessee what's what," she murmured and she rubbed her ham-fisted hands together. "Mama will see."

***

Pat Biase and Joyce O'Sullivan were working hard, taking down the art exhibit, folding chairs and unpinning the banner that had waved over the art show. "Hey! Look at that!" Pat stopped, a chair in his hand, and watched as a man climbed out of the water, fully dressed and dripping. The man was breathing heavily. Joyce stopped folding the banner and watched as the man approached them, his face white with effort and strain.

"I say, pardon…" The man wheezed, obviously at the end of his strength. "I need…I must find…the police station." He bent from the waist as a spasm of cramp hit him. "Oh, my! Oh!"

"Are you ill?" Joyce asked, concerned that the man was going to lie down and die in front of them.

"No…no…oh, oh!" The man clutched both arms around his stomach. "There…" he breathed a little better. A slight bit of color was coming back to his face. "I…need…the police station."

"Is this an emergency?" Pat was sympathetic. Whatever had happened, this man was in some kind of trouble. "Can we help you?"

"I…need…I have to get…the police station." He frantically slapped at his trouser pockets. "A taxi…no money…on the boat…" He flailed his arms toward the water.

"You need some money for a taxi?" Joyce peered closely into the man's face. Although he was wet and disheveled, he didn't look crazy.

"Please, oh, please…" His eyes were frantic as he begged her. "I…I need…"

Pat whistled at a taxi that was parked at the front of Captain Fatty's. He dug into the pocket of his shorts and pulled out a few crumpled bills. "Here. Take it and pay me back when you get yourself together."

"God bless you, laddie." The man eased himself up into a standing position. "How can I find you…to pay back…?"

"Don't worry too much about it, but, if you must, I'm Pat, the artist. Everyone around here knows me." The taxi pulled closer.

"I…must go…my blessings to you both…" The man staggered into the taxi, shut the door and collapsed back against the cushions as the taxi drove off.

Joyce stood with her hands on her hips, watching the taxi disappear towards the police station. "I could never live anywhere else," she said. Pat nodded and together, they finished folding the banner.

***

"I won't tell you," Annie's bottom lip stuck out. "I'm just not going to talk about it!" How could she tell about Suzie and the cocaine? Never!

"Honey," Mama Lucille patted her hand. "You jus' gotta tell me. You can't hold this in any longer. I know I look fierce, but, believe me, I can be your friend." Her dark eyes showed a depth of compassion, but Annie was too frightened to tell them her suspicions about Suzie. She couldn't …she just couldn't…. Mama Lucille bent forward again, "Now, how did them drugs get in to your suitcase? Did you use them or put them there?" Annie shrugged, terrified to tell the truth, thereby getting her cousin into very hot water and maybe a British Virgin Island prison, and terrified that if she didn't speak up, she herself would spend the rest of her life in the selfsame prison.

Mama Lucille looked up at Carlton. "OK, honey. We gonna talk about other things now. Tell me how you came to be on this trip to our little eyot and how you know this man who got killed."

"What's that mean, Mama? Eyot?" Carlton sighed. He never, even if he studied The Readers Digest from now until eternity, would know words like Mama Lucille knew words.

"Why, Carlton. I thought you knew! Eyot means little island!"

Relived that the subject had turned from drugs to vocabulary, Annie began to relax. She readily told them all about Suzie wanting a roommate, how they applied for and got a cabin, and how they had met Elliott. "He was just another passenger to me. I barely spoke to him."

"Did you like him?" Carlton probed gently.

"No, I didn't" Annie answered, worrying herself with her honesty. *Should she say this truth? Would they think she killed him because she didn't like him? No, that was silly. Or should she pretend that she liked him a little bit? No, that was silly too.* "He was a nasty, sarcastic person, with a barb in every sentence he spoke. I think he liked to hurt people and make fun of them." *Well, that was true enough.*

"Did your cousin, Suzie like him?" Effalyn asked. Annie shook her head and shrugged. She wasn't going to answer any sort of questions that involved Suzie.

"Did you know Elliott in Greenwich?" Annie's eyes goggled. *In Greenwich?*

"In *Greenwich*? How would I know him in Greenwich? He's from the West Coast."

"He lives there now, but he was born and brought up in your home town." Carlton informed her. "He was older than you. Did you know that?"

"I had no idea. I...I wouldn't ...I never saw him or heard of him before I met him on the boat. Was it only a few days ago?" She shook her head again. "It seems like fifty years."

"You mentioned that you came from a big family. Might someone in your family have known him?"

"Perhaps. I have no idea." She shrugged, now genuinely intrigued.

"Do you think Suzie knew him from Greenwich?"

Although they were back on the subject of Suzie, Annie felt she was on firm ground and answered the question. "I'm positive that she had never heard his name before. We got a list of passengers...you know...before the trip and Suzie and I discussed every name, wondering what they were going to be like. She...she talked about him...his name...because he had a single cabin and she thought...you know, that he had to be rich if he had a private cabin. But know him? No." Annie's hair flew out of its ribbon and fanned the air as she shook her head from side to side. She reached back and tried to smooth it into some sort of neatness. "No. I would have known if his name was familiar to her. No. Not at all."

"Funny, isn't it? That you all came from the same town?" Carlton shuffled some papers on the table. "I mean, isn't that quite a coincidence?" He thought about the man...Francesco...that Suzie had been with the night before. He, too, had a connection with Greenwich, Connecticut. Was there anyone else with a past in that town?

"Did you or Suzie know Francesco, um, Jeraldo in Greenwich?"

"Never heard of him and I'm sure that Suzie didn't know him before she met him down here." She spread her hands out in supplication. "But, you know...Greenwich is a big place. A lot of people come and go through Greenwich. It's a well-known town and a lot of corporations have offices there." Annie sipped at the dregs of her tea, feeling comfortable with the path of the questioning. "As a matter of fact, Paula's good friend...I can't remember her name...Shannon or something like that, ah, Sharon...Sharon Nye...Paula asked me if I knew her family, but I never knew anyone named Nye....anyway, as far as your coincidences go, Paula had a best friend who came from Greenwich, too." Carlton's eyes slid to Effalyn's and she wrote again on her notepad.

There was a knock on the door and Ganny Johnstone stuck his head in. He was grinning broadly as he motioned to Carlton. Carlton got up and went to the door. The two men stepped outside, shutting the door behind them. Inside, Mama Lucille shifted her bulk on the chair. "You gotta tell me about them drugs, darling. This is serious. You can trust me, I promise." She put her work-hardened hand on Annie's arm. "You don' have any idea of how serious this is." Her dark eyes were somber.

Doctor Fullbright nodded. "Annie. We want to help you, but you must help us. How did those drugs get into your suitcase? Are they yours? Or, do you think someone put them there to make a fool out of you. Get you arrested instead of...whoever put them there?" Annie shut her eyes, hung her head and refused to speak.

The door opened again. Carlton came back in. He sat down heavily. "The tests are back on the fingerprints." He turned to Annie, leaning forward towards her, his face impassive. She backed away, frightened now. "You know what we found, don't you, Annie?" She blinked back her tears and saw a gleam of humor behind his blank face. Timidly hopeful, she nodded. "You're clean on the prints." Annie's eyes began to tear up again. *Oh joy! Oh joy!* She knuckled her eyes and grabbed a tissue to blow her nose. *Thank God! They knew that she hadn't....*

Carlton continued: "You know that you're innocent and that there are none of your prints anywhere near the drugs." She bit her lip hard and nodded again, a tiny nod. "That there are none of your prints on the baggie, none on the edges of the suitcase near the baggie, nor anywhere near the area that was ripped open, don't you?" Again, she gave a nod of her head, her eyes now huge and sad.

"And now...officially...we know it, too. So just who might have planted the cocaine in your suitcase? Who might have gone into your room? She screwed you badly, didn't she? Your own cousin." His voice was hard. "Nice family feelings there, huh?"

There was a distraction outside the door. A banging and yells and a scuffle. Carlton jumped up and opened the door. Ganny was struggling with a wet and disheveled maniac.

"Duncan!" Annie screamed with delight. "Oh, Duncan!"

"Oh, Geez!" Carlton groaned. "Just what we need. The hero from the Black Lagoon. All right, Ganny, let Mr. Lochinvar loose. He's been riding hard to save his lady." He hid a grin. "Come on in, Mr. MacKinnon, you swimming fool...you cave man, you." He motioned for Duncan to join them.

"Annie! Did they hurt you, lass? I'll...I'll..." He looked wildly around the room, his hands clenched in fists, wanting to punch someone...anyone.

Annie stood up, knocking over her chair, and ran to him. He clasped her in his arms and held her tight. "My wee darling! My love! Are you all right?" Annie's face beamed. Now that he was here, what did it matter if she was being interrogated in a police station? "Did they hurt you?" Wet and disheveled, he glared at Carlton.

"I'm fine, Duncan, my dear. Fine. No one beat me with a rubber hose or anything." She turned and smiled tremulously at her captors. "This is Mama Lucille and this is Doctor Fullbright. They have been very kind to me, although I have been very obstinate with them."

Carlton stood up, trying not to laugh at the romantic comedy being played out before him. "Ahem...sit down, Annie...you here and Duncan...take my chair. Nevermind your wet clothes. I'll, um, ah, stand for a while." He rubbed his face and tapped at the table. "This, um, has been a remarkable time. Ah, yes. Well, um, Duncan, we were just informing Miss Annie that the drugs found in her suitcase...ah, hidden in her suitcase...well, we are sure that she had no idea they were there."

Duncan looked incredulous that *anyone,* anywhere should think such a thing about Annie. He opened his mouth to remonstrate, but closed it again as Carlton began to speak.

"And now we want Annie to help us figure out just who might have *put* the drugs into her suitcase."

"It's yon wee skunk Suzie, her cousin!" Duncan was thunderous. And his voice slipped further and further into a broad brogue. "Did she do that to you, my wee hen?" He shook Annie gently. "The scunner! The bitch! I'll kill her meself."

"Ahem," Carlton interrupted. "This is really not for publication just yet, but...what the hell...you all know what the story is here. We do know it was Suzie as her fingerprints are all over the salient places." He looked down at the table. "The dead man's fingerprints are all over the baggie, too, but not on the suitcase. I think he and she shared some of the, um, cocaine, and then she held the baggie and the envelope in her purse. When we boarded the boat and she discovered that Elliott was dead, she scuttled down into your cabin and planted the evidence on you, Annie." His expression was grim. "We are going to have to arrest her, Annie." Annie's face blanched. "You know the penalties here for drug use and possession. I know you want to shelter her, but she's a big girl, and she was perfectly happy to see you jailed for her crime."

"The rotten woman," Duncan spat out, holding Annie tighter.

Mama Lucille sighed, and then grinned at Duncan. "You're obviously from Scotland, you glaikit man." Duncan's head snapped back.

"Glaikit? You know the word 'glaikit'? What kind of an island woman are you?"

"One who knows some Scottish fol-de-rol." She threw back her head and roared at his confusion." When she stopped laughing, she got up. Stooping over, she hugged Annie. "You poor thing. You do have a rat for a cousin. I haven't met this Suzie yet, but I don't like her already. I presume, when we get her in jail, I'll be seein' a lot of her for a long time." She stood up, towering over Carlton, her hands on her massive hips. "I can almost forgive someone for the drugs, but I can't forgive her letting you – family, no less - take the troubles she caused. For that, she'll be sorry, believe me." She patted Annie's arm again. "Good luck to you. You're a sweet and loyal girl. But don't put that loyalty where it doesn't belong." She lumbered out of the room.

"Let's get you back to the boat, Annie. And yes," he held up his hand to stave off her question, "We *will* be arresting Suzie."

He ushered them out of the room. "Come on, you wild man, you. We'll drive you out in the boat this time and you won't have to swim the English Channel again."

"Such love! Such bravado! Such courage!" Doctor Fullbright tipped his head to Duncan. "*Homeric*! You are a remarkable man, sir!"

***

"As I see it, several of the passengers have pretty solid alibis," Effalyn mused. "Some of them returned to the boat about midnight. Sarah Lemonowski, Paula Haskins, Michael, um, Beck, Corliss Curtis, Zandra Hoovenmeyer...what kind of name is that? ...and Hosea Balleau...they went back early. There wasn't a boat available to any of them. Unless one of them swam to shore and killed Barringer, they couldn't have done it."

"Any one of them might have swum back to shore and killed him. Look how easy it was for that Duncan guy to jump in and swim to the dock."

"It would have been difficult. Unless the timing was just right, there were Zodiacs coming and going and then, after three in the morning, Captain Jack and others were sitting right smack dab in the middle of the cockpit. No way that they would have missed someone who was swimming to the boat and climbed aboard, wet and dripping."

"That lets Paula out completely. She can't swim a stroke."

"Who says so?"

"Everybody."

"Humpf. And your poor, wounded Mr. Langdon. He was with you at the hospital most of the night and went back with the last group around three in the morning. He's in the clear, too."

"Captain Scambaugh, not that I would dream that he was guilty, was with his wife, Ducky Blyton, his girlfriend, Lisette and – who else – ah, Michael Beck. They're all out of the loop."

"Who does that leave?"

"Kat, the cook, but as to why she'd kill him, I can't figure out."

"He criticized her cooking?" Carlton winked.

Effalyn paid him no attention and continued, "Suzie is in the clear for the murder, at least. She was with that Italian man, Francesco all night. So – left without an alibi are the two young men, friends from New Jersey." Effalyn checked her list. "Samuel Gallofrito. Vincent James. Then, Sarah Lemonowski, Duncan MacKinnon, our Scottish long-distance swimmer, Annie herself, Martha Temple-Wright, Claudia Van Voorhees, and Laddie Olmstead. A nice round group of suspects."

"Can you tell who is who yet? I know Suzie and Annie and Duncan...the rest of them meld into a big amorphous group to me."

"Some of them stand out. Michael Beck, perhaps because of his Irish lilt. Paula Haskins because she is so pale, elegant and frail. Those two boys from New Jersey? I can't tell one from the other. They look alike and talk alike and I can't remember which is which."

"The same with me and those two cousins from South Africa...Claudia and who?"

"Martha."

"Martha. They are like twins. Which is which, even when I know, I forget, they look so much alike. Claudia could pass for Martha and Martha could be Claudia. I would never know the difference." He shrugged. "I think I remember a case from when I was at the Police University. There were two brothers and they looked almost alike. One did the murder and the other confessed. The witness identified the second brother and they put him on trial and convicted him. Then, the first brother, the real murderer, confessed and the second one retracted his confession. No one knew which was which and I think they got away with murder."

"God forbid we get anything that complex. These cases lately have been screwy enough! Sting rays and snakes and coconuts! Nevermind the plants that killed poor Mister Marsden!" She re-checked her notes. "Anyway, the people who stayed late. They all came back later on the boats at about three. Any one of them could have killed him and then strolled back to the party."

"When did Kat come back?"

"Even later," Effalyn flipped a page over. "She says she was with Captain Dave's girls, but everyone was dancing, up and down and around. Any one of them could have sneaked out, bashed him, and come back in, jiving and dancing and no one would have even noticed that they were gone."

"But why?"

"We'll find out."

"OK. Get Ganny to go over to the hotel and release everyone from the wedding party and so forth. He's already got the passenger information and itinerary of all the other boats." Carlton got up and dusted off the seat of his pants. "I'm going to call the police chief in Greenwich - that town keeps popping up with too much frequency for my liking - and Barringer's law firm. I want you to check and re-check the dossiers and folders on all of the other passengers. See if you can find any other connection with Greenwich, Connecticut. Find out if anyone had Barringer as an attorney. Anyone have him represent a relative? Anyone know his name from anywhere?" He rubbed his neck. "And then, when we have a spare moment, I want to get over to Mrs. Marsden's house and go over her statement again."

"Shouldn't take me but ten minutes to do all that," Effalyn smiled gently.

"You, go, girl."

"You are watching too much American television. Your slang is getting to be too much!"

***

Carlton called Elliott's law office and asked to speak with the managing director. A gentleman named Shane Zarhor finally came onto the telephone and introduced himself as Senior Partner. Carlton explained the reason for his call and was rewarded with a swiftly indrawn breath from Mr. Zarhor.

"Sonofabitch! He's dead, then? This isn't some sort of a joke, is it?" Carlton assured him of the seriousness of Elliott's demise. "Shit! Who killed him?"

"What makes you think it was murder, Mr. Zarhor?"

"Because anyone who knew him, even remotely, wanted to slit his throat."

Zarhor told him. "He's got to be the biggest asshole in the legal world. Everyone loathed him. How did he die?"

"Got hit on the head with a coconut. Bashed his brains in."

"A coconut! Ha! Best news we've had in years!"

"Well, we like to keep it civil down here, even if he wasn't a popular person."

"Ha!"

Carlton scratched his head. He'd do his best to catch Elliott's killer. That was his job. A detective. No matter how horrible a human being was, no one deserved to die with his head caved in and then his flesh eaten by a couple of mangy dogs. Not even this son of a bitch. "How long has he worked for your firm, and if he was such a jerk, why was he still employed there?" Carlton was curious. What kind of man was this Elliott Barringer to enjoy so much derision and hatred?

"He's been here for more than twenty years now. His father bought him a lifetime position here with the previous partners. We're stuck with him." Zarhor's voice boomed through the receiver as he acknowledged just what this news meant. "By God, we aren't stuck with him anymore! This is a red-letter-day for us!"

"Tell me more. Was he married?"

"Yeah, lots of times. I think all of his ex-wives, and I believe there were four of them, would happily confess to killing him."

"Any children?"

"No...and there's a sad story, Detective Reese. My wife's cousin was his second wife. He abused her mentally and physically, kicking her down a flight of stairs when he heard that she was carrying their child." Carlton made a soft, swearing sound of disbelief. "Yes, it's true. She's in a mental home now and has been since he ruined her life and her health. She's a zombie now." He laughed, a nasty sound. "And you wonder that we are going to throw a party right after I hang up with you?"

"We have no real suspect here. Is there anything you can tell me about his life that would throw any light on who might have come down to the British Virgin Islands to kill him?"

"I don't know anyone who is down there," Carlton could hear the man thinking. "I'll ask around and see if I hear anything."

"I'll FAX you a list of the people involved. See if you recognize any of the names. I'll also want from you a list of his cases for the past ten years or so. Who he defended, perhaps unsuccessfully. Who he prosecuted, perhaps successfully. Who...although there seems to be a parade... really had reason to want him dead."

"I'll gather up his files and make a list. I can't tell you everything due to confidentiality, but I'll make sure that you get the gist of everything. I think I'm intelligent enough to perceive if there is anything, anywhere, in our files that could help you."

"Thank you. If needed, I can come out to California to check your files out."

"Well, you send me your names...let me go through things and I promise I'll give it my undivided attention for the rest of the day. I'll ask around the office and call you when I have a dossier prepared. I'll be sure that I get it done by tomorrow."

Thank goodness Zarhor was a reasonable man, even if he was an attorney. So many of them were pencil pushing geeks, mired in procedural minutia and officious in hampering the police. "I appreciate all that you are going to do, Mr. Zarhor. With no issue, and all of his wives divorced, who is his next of kin? Who...he was a wealthy man, wasn't he?"

"Tons of money. Most of it inherited from his father. He inherited a lot from his father other than money. His selfishness, his temper, his brutality to anyone who got in his way..." He laughed, a ripe guffaw.... "He was his daddy's son, all right!"

"And who gets it now that he's dead?"

"I think the bulk of it goes to his college, with some money to three cousins. I'll pull out his will..." He yelled to someone in the office, "Marisa! Elliott's dead!" Carlton heard a screech on the other end. "Yes! Amazing. Somebody bonked him on the head with a ... are you ready? ...a coconut!" Carlton heard the incredulous screams through the line.

"I shouldn't spread this around, but, maybe you deserve to know that he was partially eaten by some beach dogs before we found his body." *Ooops*, Carlton thought, *I probably shouldn't have said that, but what the hell, this man has already told me a dozen things about Barringer that he shouldn't have told.*

"You have certainly made my day, sir!"

"And I want to know if anyone knew him when he lived in Connecticut." Carlton's big toe was tingling over the Greenwich coincidences.

"Before my time here, but again, I certainly will ask everyone. Maybe old Simonson, who worked with Barringer's father, might know. He's known Elliott since he was born."

"You are a prince, Mr. Zarhor, I look forward to receiving the files and dossiers you promised. Anything further that you may glean from your inquiries, no matter how trivial, will be most appreciated." Carlton thanked him again. "I know I can rely on your discretions on this matter."

"What will you do with, um, his, um...remains, when you are through with the investigation?"

"I will await instructions from you, Barringer's cousins or his executor." The two men hung up, mutually delighted with the exchange.

***

"Yes. The Chief of Police. And his name is? Horowitz. George Horowitz. Thank you. This is Detective Inspector Carlton Reese from the island of Virgin Gorda in the British Virgin Islands. I have to speak with him personally....Yes, thank you. I'll hold." Carlton opened the Barringer folder while he waited. Then, he pulled Suzie's folder and Annie's folder in front of him, and, after thinking for a second, also pulled Paula's folder and opened the piece of paper that mentioned Francesco Jeraldo's connections with Greenwich.

***

"Ready for a drink?" Carlton stuck his head into Effalyn's office.

"A drink? A *drink* drink?" her eyes were wide with surprise as he nodded, unable to keep the grin from filling the bottom half of his face.

"A *biiiig*, drink drink."

"Are you smoking something?" Carlton never drank during the day. "You'd better watch out that Mama Lucille doesn't catch you!"

"I think I've got it." He motioned to her, pumping his fist into the air. "I just finished talking with an old man who worked for Elliott's law firm. Worked there when Elliott was just a pup. A nasty pup. Long time ago. He gave me some ideas." He grinned like a Cheshire cat. "And then I had a very long talk with my counterpart in Greenwich, Connecticut. Many things that go back many years. It's gonna' take me some thinking to put it all in order, but I think this calls for an early tentative celebration of sorts, maybe a little glass of champagne."

Effalyn rarely uttered a swear word. "No shit?" She leaped up. "You've figured out who killed Barringer?"

"Tut, Tut, Mizz Penn, such language from an officer of the law," His bright eyes were dancing. "As I said, I have a lot of new pieces to my jigsaw puzzle. I haven't quite put it all together, and there are still a lot of pieces missing. But I think, given some sneaky police work and some luck, I may have the right stuff to somehow make some sense of all of it." He slapped the doorway. "Let's go!"

***

Suzie was allowed to take a small carryall with her. The carryall contained two changes of clothing, underwear and a pair of flip flops. She also was permitted to take her toothbrush, toothpaste and a comb and brush. "What about my make-up?" In her fear, she was nasty. "Are you fuckers going to deprive me of my things?"

"For now, just what you have in the bag is all you are allowed." Ganny wasn't cowed by her. "You don't seem to understand the gravity of what is happening to you, Miss. You are being arrested for drug possession and hiding and planting evidence." He motioned to her to precede him. "Come along nicely and I won't put cuffs on you."

Suzie began to sob. This was a nightmare. "Can any of you help me?" She begged to Captain Jack. "I need a good lawyer. I have plenty of money. Money is no object. Just find me someone who can get me out of this mess."

"I'll go over immediately and get you an attorney," Jack felt sorry for her, even though, at the same time, he despised her. Suzie was a wealthy and pampered American, not used to laws that were not like the ones in her homeland. He had tried mightily to warn her about drug usage in the islands. He sighed. She was in for a huge shock. Drugs were treated with great seriousness and Mama Lucille, the Wardress at the jail, was known for her harsh and unyielding stance on substance use. As Mama Lucille's niece had been raped and killed three years ago by a drug dealer, and Big John, Mama's husband, had been killed by a drug-crazed truck driver many years ago, Captain Jack understood Mama's position, which, of course, also properly followed the laws of the British Virgin Islands. "I'll try to send Harry Glass over to the jail immediately to see you. I hope he can help get you through this."

Suzie glared at Annie. "You bitch! You got me into this!" She hissed at her cousin. Annie drew back into the shelter of Duncan's arms. "You and your old-man lover!" Her venom was palpable. "You snitched on me to get me into trouble!"

"Suzie," Annie leaned forward and held out her hand. "I've never said anything to anyone about you. I'll try to help as best I can."

"Get away from me, you traitor!" Suzie's face was ugly with hate. Ganny motioned her towards the stern of the boat and she stumbled, hampered by her fear. She got into the boat, handed in by Ducky. This time, Ducky didn't wink or give the thumbs-up sign. His expression was shut and somber. His face frightened Suzie. *Maybe I'm stuck*, she thought. *Maybe I won't be able to get myself out of this*! "Don't let them take me to jail, Ducky! *Don't*!" Suzie's wail drifted back.

"Shit," Ducky stepped back. "She's going to have a bloody awful time."

"She deserves it," Hosea muttered. "She played with danger and laughed. Now, she will be suffering." Zandra touched his arm and they went up to the bow together.

"What shall I do?" Annie grabbed Captain Jack. "I have to help her."

"Why don't you come with me to the attorney's office? Let's see what he says."

"Can I come with you, Annie?" Duncan's face was somber. "I hate her for what she tried to do to you, but, nonetheless, puir lassie, I feel very sorry for wha' is going to come."

"Will they really keep her in prison?" Annie's mouth trembled. Captain Jack nodded. "Oh, she'll just die!"

"She will not die, but certainly she might wish she did," Kat watched the boat get smaller and smaller. "Some do not listen. They think they are bigger than the laws here. We try to tell everyone about drugs. We put it in writing. We warn everyone…but some just cannot believe that the law means *them*. They think the law is only for other…how do you say it?… suckers, the poor or the ugly. They feel it is fine to do what they want, to break the law." She sucked in her breath. "And then, when they are caught, they want all the people to jump and excuse them."

"Ready?" Captain Jack asked Duncan and Annie. "Let's go."

"Can I come on shore?" Lannie asked. "Are we able to leave the boat now?"

"How long are we going to be here in Big Fish Cay?" Martha wanted to know.

"Until the police let us leave." Jack's strong shoulders slumped. "Don't forget, they suspect that one of us killed Elliott, nevermind the drug situation. We are all still murder suspects."

CHAPTER EIGHTEEN

"If you have tears, prepare to shed them now…"
Shakespeare, Julius Caesar

"You think it will work?" Effalyn's face was doubtful. "It seems very contrived to me."

"I can't see how we can get evidence any other way. I think we can rely on the psychological make-up of our murderer. That's the way I see it. I'll check the suitcases and see if there's a hidden area where papers might be, but otherwise, I can't let murder go unpunished just because I wasn't smart enough to connect the dots and the victim was a shit."

"I don't know. I can't quite see how you are going to do it. And then, I don't quite see what it will get you. You have to manipulate so many people and you'll have to be incredibly lucky with the timing."

"It will expose a huge lie. If I get that, I think I can break our killer down."

"OK, let's make a detailed plan…" Effalyn took out her notebook. "When is he coming?"

"Tomorrow early afternoon plane."

"That'll be very interesting. He seems to agree with you?"

"He thinks it is worth the trip. After all, he's got a personal stake in all of this and he has all the old information, the autopsy report and all that."

She wig-wagged her head, trying to think of what she'd be doing in this unusual situation. "OK. Our plan…I hope it works. Let's try. What's first?"

"First, talk with Captain Jack and Kat and then Captain Dave.

"And then?"

"Second, get Rebecca to let me do this."

"Ha!" Effalyn crowed. "If you can do *that,* you can do anything! And third?"

"Rehearse Niccola in her part."

***

The bland, smooth attorney, Harry Glass, had come to the British Virgin Islands from England twenty years ago. There was a rumor that he had been involved with the wife of one of his richest clients, but no one knew the details. All anyone knew was that Harry Glass charged a lot of money and got good results. If you were in a bad situation, Glass was the best to get…if you could afford him. Mama Lucille called him a porbeagle…and then explained to everyone that 'porbeagle' was a word for a particularly nasty species of shark.

Harry's first move, after his introduction to Suzie, was to have her sign a huge retainer over to him. "You get what you pay for," His sonorous voice made her feel better. *Maybe, with enough money*, she thought, *I can buy myself out of this mess. Goddamn that Elliott and his hypnotic promises and the attraction to the forbidden cocaine and marijuana.* "That will be our line of defense, Suzie…you don't mind if I call you Suzie, do you? Good. We'll try to convince them that you were a poor and helpless innocent girl. That this monster…this Svengali… started you down the path to drugs. He used you, didn't he?" Suzie, venal and grasping, but not stupid, nodded vehemently. Of course he used her, the blackguard!

"Good, good. He had you in his clutches, didn't he?" Again, Suzie nodded, hoping against hope that no one had seen her obvious enjoyment and desire for better and stronger drugs.

"Annie!" She lifted her head in anguish. "Annie knows that I….she….my cousin." Suzie paused and marshaled her thoughts. *Annie, I'll blame it all on Annie.* "She hates me. She's always hated me. She's jealous of me. I'm popular and pretty and she's…well, she's not. She'll try to get me in more trouble." Suzie could see it all now. The trial. She, Suzie, dressed in pale grey, her hair in a vulnerable, but yet crisp chignon. Her make up would be subdued, with shadows under her eyes and wan cheeks, so that the jury would know that she was the victim….And Elliott, he was dead and gone. He couldn't tell the truth about her and her urging him to get even stronger stuff. Her red mouth curved upwards like that of a satiated kitten. Annie would be the one who they blamed. Annie, who was jealous and always had been jealous because she, Suzie was prettier and more popular. Suzie licked her lips and began to lie and lie to Harry.

Harry sighed inwardly. In the twenty plus years that he had been defending criminals, he had heard it all. And here it came, heavy and acrimonious from the innocent-looking, beautiful, treacherous face before him. To save her own pretty ass, she'd gladly throw her cousin into prison. Ah, well. It wasn't his business to question his clients too closely. If he probed, he might learn the truth and that was the last thing he wanted her to tell him. All right. The whole thing was Elliott's fault. And if it wasn't Elliott's fault, it was the cousin's fault for exaggerating poor little Suzie's, um, ah, problems. He wrote and wrote on the large yellow pad.

"I need to get bail. I need to get out of here," Suzie pulled urgently at his sleeve. "I can't be in this pigpen. They don't know who I am. These people, this slutty black matron, Mrs. Lulu or whatever her name is, she hates me already."

"Mama Lucille? What happened?" He hoped that Suzie was smart enough not to rile Mama Lucille.

"She wanted me to do stupid things." Suzie tossed her head. "And she laughed when I asked to have a hairdresser come in and fix my hair." Suzie's face was fierce with hatred. "The dumb woman. The bitch! She doesn't realize who I am! I'm not going to take orders from her. I'm an American. A rich American. Far above any of these native types...I don't have to listen to them... I'm just not in their class..." she laughed and Harry began to chew at his fingernails. "And their class is all low!" Suzie laughed again and looked to him to appreciate her wit. He wondered if he should warn her about Mama Lucille and the people of the island's judicial systems dislike of Americans who tried to throw their weight and money around, assuming that anyone who lived in Virgin Gorda and who was black was also stupid. He opened his mouth, but Suzie's voice ran on. "I have to get out of here and be free. I don't care what I have to pay. I want to get out!"

Harry shrugged. This little bimbo was going to be her own worst enemy. "I'm going to try. If we go for bail, it will cost you." He tapped his pen against the table. "But, Suzie, for your own good, you ought to be at least polite to Mama Lucille. She's the key to you getting decent treatment here."

"I don't give a damn about her and her fat ass. I don't have to bend down and kiss it – ever! She'll be sorry if she messes with me." She grabbed Harry's hand. "Fix it, Harry!" she ordered. "Get me out of this hell hole."

"I'll do what I can. It will be very expensive."

"I don't care what it costs me! I can afford it, whatever it is! Offer that big, fat lady a bribe. Get to the judge. You ought to know who to grease!" Suzie's face didn't look so pretty any more.

"That's not the way it goes here. I'm sorry. This island is run very honestly as far as the law goes. No one involved with the police here would *ever* take money to dispense the law." Harry looked shocked. "They would come down on you even harder if you tried to subvert justice. Don't even think about trying to bribe someone, Suzie. It will only cause you more grief than you already have." Suzie threw her head back and glared at him. He got up and patted her hand. She was his favorite kind of client, rich and devious. He'd see what he could do. He smiled again at her, holding her hand lightly and only releasing it when Suzie took her checkbook out again. She was a pretty little thing, and obviously sex-starved and had little in the way of decency or morals. Just his kind of woman.

***

"Did I embarrass you? Did you think I was some kind of bull, trying to get to you?" Duncan held Annie in his arms.

"No. Actually, I was sort of thrilled at what you did. I was terrified, but underneath, I felt like some kind of old-fashioned maiden and you were a knight on a white horse. You came riding…well…swimming…to rescue me and I was tickled pink. Thank you, Duncan. I was frightened, but as long as I knew you were coming along after me, I felt that everything would come out all right." Her eyes shone as she looked up at him. "And I was impressed. For an old geezer, you were pretty athletic, swimming and running and getting right to the police station for me."

"Well, lassie, I almost wheezed to death." He patted his stomach, still washboard stiff, "I had a fright there along the line, as I was manfully trying to catch my breath and not keel over, that I was going to have to lay me doon and dee." He held her tight. "All I could think of was you, ma' wee Annie-Laurie, being beaten with a rubber hose by the big, bad policemen. I wanted to gather you up and keep you safe forever." He nuzzled her hair and smelled its sweet, fresh fragrance. "And I do mean forever." He bent backwards and looked at her. Shyly, she raised her eyes to him. "We must have a lang crack, ma' wee hen. A lang crack about marriage."

"A...what?"

"You'll have to start learning Scots brogue. A lang crack is a long talk. I can see many, many hours of close and personal tutelage." His bright blue eyes bored into her astonished brown ones. "Will ye marry this auld man, my wee Annie? Will you come to Scotland as ma' bride?"

Annie's mouth opened. *Scot*land? So far away? And his children? What would they think of her as a stepmother? Did she love him enough to change her life completely? Was it true love or only the proximity of the stars and the turquoise waters?

She'd have to think about it all. This was a decision that she just couldn't make in a moment... and....oh, for goodness sake, she barely *knew* this man...and he *was* older...and...and... her mouth opened to tell him of her doubts and hesitation... "Yes," she blurted out. "Yes, Duncan, my Lochinvar. I *will* be your bride and you will be my darling husband."

We will leave them for the moment as they whispered and kissed and planned their lives together, sometimes being in Scotland and sometimes being in America. It looked like they were able to work it all out fine...just fine.

***

"I'm sorry, Suzie. There's to be no bail." Harry was almost frightened to tell her. Her wrath was fierce.

"What the hell do you *mean,* no bail?" She screamed. "Do you think I'm going to rot in this fucking place?"

"You have no choice, Suzie. Bail was denied. There isn't anything else I can do about it." He spread his hands in frustration. "Drug usage here is not tolerated at all. Your arraignment is in five days. I was able to get them to move it up."

"What the fuck am I paying you for?" The words were spat at him. "I'm a rich American! Get me out of this fucking prison!"

"I'm doing my best, believe me." Harry sat down and handed Suzie a box. In the box were two cartons of Marlboro Lights, three bags of candy, a package of gum and two paperback books. "Here, these are for you."

Suzie threw the box on the floor. "Shit!" She cried. "I don't want this crap! What am I going to do?" The last word was a long, drawn-out wail.

"Your cousin is here. She wants to see you." Harry's tone was neutral.

"Fuck her too!" Suzie kicked at the pile on the floor. "Damned if I'm going to let her see me like this! Look at my *hair*!" She reached up and pulled at the bird's nest that her usually expensively coiffed hair had become. "And look that my *nails*!" she screamed. "I look...horrible and old!"

***

Carlton and Captain Jack had a long and detailed conversation. Then, Jack called Captain Dave and made arrangements for the next morning. Luckily, Captain Dave had an open schedule and was able to be accommodating. Kat was coached in her part of the drama. There was nothing more for Carlton to do but pray that it all would fall into place.

"Hey, everyone," Captain Jack announced. "Some good news at last. We are going to change our schedule slightly so that we can enjoy ourselves tomorrow, but still be available to the police, if needed." The passengers crowded around. "I have arranged that our deep-sea fishing expedition, which was to have taken place on Friday, to be moved to tomorrow." There was a murmur of excitement. "We'll be picked up at six...early...tomorrow for a full day of fishing with Captain Dave and his famous crew." There were appreciative cat-calls and whistles from a few of the male passengers. "We'll be catching...well, hopefully catching...large trophy fish and Captain Dave will arrange to have the fish shipped back to your homes, if that's what you wish. He'll explain everything to you when you get on board."

"I'm going to stay here," Kat interjected. "I hate fishing and the day is so long. The waves are horrid and I don't enjoy the rocking of the boat. I'm going to just relax on our boat, maybe read or sun-bathe...just take it easy..." She looked around. "If anyone is too tired or doesn't want to face a whole day out in the briny deep, feel free to stay with me." She looked at the group and her glance stopped at Paula. "Paula? Want to keep me company in this lovely calm harbor instead of the rough seas outside in the ocean area?"

"I...I think that is a good idea for me." Paula's face was pale and lined. "I think that I will skip the fishing. I'm sort of ....afraid of ...the water, you know. Too deep and I..."

"Great!" Kat's smile beamed. "We'll just relax here together." She winked at Captain Jack and he gave her a thumbs-up.

"You may be better off here, Paula. It's a very long and arduous day," he concurred.

"Maybe I will stay here, too." Sarah chimed in.

"No, Sarah!" Michael Beck pulled at her arm. "You said you wanted to catch a wahoo. Come on! When will you get another chance to go fishing like this?"

"Oh, all right. I'll go." Michael grinned at her and Captain Jack's weathered face looked relieved.

"I've never caught a fish," Lannie confessed. "How do you hook it? Will they bait the line for me for me, or do I have to touch that slimy stuff? How do you get it in the boat?"

"Have no fear," Ducky assured him. "Those expert fisherwomen will teach you everything they know."

"Everything?" Lannie shuddered deliciously.

"Everything...if you're lucky!"

CHAPTER NINETEEN

"...He was a murderer from the beginning...."
The Bible according to Saint John

The morning dawned bright and warm. The *GKB* picked up the passengers early and departed, leaving Paula and Kat on board *The Southern Cross*. They waved and then, taking coffee with them, went back to bed. "I rarely have this kind of opportunity," Kat yawned and stretched. "I'll see you in an hour or so."

Except for *The Southern Cross*, which was still being kept in Big Fish Cay by the police, the rest of the charter boats upped anchor and sailed or motored to their next destination. Paula sat on the deck; her back supported by a cushion, and watched the boats, the water and the distant harbor. She had a book with her, but was too exhausted to read. With no one on the boat except Kat, Paula permitted herself to cautiously take off her long-sleeved top and bare her arms and shoulders to the sun. There was no one to see the purple bruises and contusions that marred her skin. She sipped at a glass of iced tea and wondered what her future might hold. And whether or not she really cared. She was so tired. So tired. She watched other boats coming into the harbor to replace the ones that just left and noted a fishing boat that anchored nearby. An old man and an old woman, both with conical hats pulled over their heads, dropped lines over the gunnels. They sat, patiently waiting for a fish to bite at their bait. *They looked peaceful*, Paula thought. *If only I had nothing to worry about except catching a fish or two*. Sighing, her eyes slowly closed and she was startled by Kat's voice calling to her. In a panic, she pushed her thin arms into the sleeves of her shirt and managed to get it on before Kat clambered up next to her.

"Hey, Paula, ready for a nice trip to the harbor shops?" Kat's face was expectant. "Without the rest of the crowd, we can shop 'til we drop."

"You go by yourself, Kat." Paula drooped back against her cushion. "I just fell asleep and I think I'm just going to stay here and rest."

"You sure? I hate to leave you alone."

"I'm sure." Paula smiled. "I've bought everything in the shops anyway." She waved her hand. "Go and enjoy yourself."

"Want me to bring you back some lunch? Or can I prepare a salad or something for you before I go?"

"Nope. I ate a big breakfast and might just have a piece of fruit later." Paula waved her glass. "But, maybe, before you go, can you refill this with iced tea? I'm too lazy to even get up."

Kat filled her glass with tea and added a scoop of ice. She brought the glass to Paula and added a banana and three oatmeal cookies on a plate. "Just in case you get peckish. I would not want for to you fade away." She bent down and patted Paula on her shoulder. "Oh, by the way, Captain Jack received a telephone call this morning. He was informed that they have found Elliott's murderer."

"They did?" Paula sat up, startled. "Who? ...I mean, who...killed him?"

"A person who is a beach bum ...A funny name...I do not remember the name...a funny name." Kat pulled her hair back into a pony tail and looped a band around it. "He was...this man... always in difficulty with the police. He is the one who said that he saw the body lying there in the darkness and he took Elliott's watch and things. He had all of Elliott's jewelry on him. The authorities presume he killed Elliott to get the gold necklace and the wristwatch. A man who is not too intelligent, no?"

"Did...did he confess?" Paula's face felt hot.

"No. He is screaming that he is innocent." Kat made a face of derision. "Of *course* he is proclaiming that he is innocent. Stupid man, wearing all of that gold in the daylight hours where all could see. Flashing the wrist watch! Stupid bugger! Bad enough that he is up to his neck in suspicious drug stuff...they think he was selling Elliott and Suzie some bad thing like cocaine..."

"Oh, no!"

"Oh, yes! The police have had their eye on him for ages. He is...how do you say it?... A shiftless bum." Kat shrugged her shoulders as if to flick the thoughts of a beach- bum-turned-murderer away. "He *claims*..." the word dragged sarcastically out of her mouth... "that he only sold him the drugs. He fell down on the ground to protest that he never would kill anyone! Ha! As if anyone would believe him with his neck and wrists dripping with Elliott's gold!"

Paula gulped. "But...maybe he...didn't do it after all. Just because he was wearing the jewelry...that doesn't mean..."

"Ha!" Kat made a sound of disbelief. "He...Thigpin! That is his name, is that not an incredible name? Thigpin!" She shook her head slowly from side to side. "Why would anyone believe him? He swears that Elliott was cold and dead when he found him. He swears that he never touched him except to rob him, but who the heck is going to think that he is telling the truth? He is only trying to save his neck...literally!" She laughed.

"Will they hang him?" Paula's voice was barely audible. "Do they hang people here who...?"

"Unfortunately no. They just keep them jailed for the rest of their lives. I disliked Elliott intensely, but for Thigpin to kill him...well!" She turned. "It is getting hot now. I think I will go onto the shore. I will see you in two hours, Paula."

"Bye, Kat." Paula's voice was subdued. If Kat had turned around, she would have seen a strange expression on Paula's face.

Kat started the Zodiac and circled the boat, waving at Paula. Paula waved back and watched Kat's silver carrier get smaller and smaller as it zoomed into the harbor. Paula sighed and slipped down further on her pillow. She closed her eyes, but, somehow, couldn't get back to sleep.

At the dock, Kat jumped out, tied up the Zodiac, took out her mobile phone and called Carlton's private number.

***

As their plane rose into the sky, the new Mrs. Don Gamble looked out over the receding green mountaintops. "This was the best, Don. I'll remember every moment forever." She took her husband's hand. "I'm the happiest and luckiest woman alive."

"I'll agree," Don reached over and kissed her cheek as the flight attendant came to their seats.

"Champagne? Wine?"

"Champagne, darling?" Don winked.

"I guess they don't have Dark 'n' Stormy's on the plane?" Arlis asked the flight attendant, who shook her head regretfully. "Then champagne it is."

"We just got married on Virgin Gorda," Don proudly informed everyone within hearing distance.

"Champagne is just what you need!" The drink foamed into their glasses. "Happy life together!" Several of their fellow passengers winked and nudged, smiling at their obvious delight. Everyone certainly loved a newlywed.

"Happy life, Don." Arlis clinked her glass to his.

"Happy life, Arlis." He mouthed a kiss before sipping.

"We had a murder at the wedding!" Arlis informed the startled but fascinated flight attendant.

"No kidding? What happened?"

"Well..." Arlis leaned toward her. "Don and I met last year on this cruise on a catamaran called *The Southern Cross*..."

***

A small motorboat bumped into the stern of The Southern Cross. "Ahoy! Anyone home?"

Paula awoke with a start, confused and groggy. She'd been sleeping soundly and the shout roused her. "Who...?"

"Hello! Anyone here?" It was that policeman, the nice one, even though he had taken Annie away...Inspector Reese. Paula rolled over and knelt to get up, pulling herself erect with the help of the railing.

"Hello?"

"Oh, it's you, Miss...Mrs...?" The policeman scratched his head. Paula was surprised to see that he was wearing a cast and his right arm was in a sling. *I wonder what happened to him*? A young girl, barefooted and wearing a sundress, tied up the motorboat and hopped onto the catamaran. She hunched her shoulders in awkward silence and smiled shyly at Paula.

"No one here but you?" Carlton looked around, as if hoping that Captain Jack would materialize. He waved his arm awkwardly. "I have my chauffeur with me today." He laughed with embarrassment. "I slipped and fell and shattered my elbow. Can't do diddley-squat, so I've borrowed my daughter to help me today." He ruffled the girl's hair with his left hand. "Niccola, this is, uh, Mrs....um..."

"I'm Paula Haskins. Miss Haskins." Paula smiled at the child. "How are you, Niccola?"

"Fine, thank you, Miss Haskins." The little girl grinned and ducked her head. "I'm helping Daddy today."

"Sure is hot, isn't it?" Carlton brushed at his forehead. "I guess they gave me a little bit too much painkiller." He laughed in a rueful boom. "I feel a bit dizzy."

"Can I get you some water, Inspector?" Paula made a motion towards the galley.

"No...please, Miss Haskins. Niccola will help me." He motioned with his chin, "Some water, honey?" Niccola nodded, her smile changing to a look of worry, and slipped into the cool recess of the galley.

"Please sit down," Paula pulled at a chair and motioned Carlton to sit. He sat, gratefully, sighing and rubbing at his head. She sat next to him, leaning forward.

"I have a few questions for you, now that you're here and I'm here." He looked around. "Where is everyone else today?"

"Gone fishing with Captain Dave." Niccola brought back two glasses filled with ice and water and put them on the table. She grinned again. *She'll be a charmer when she grows up*, Paula thought. Niccola hunched her shoulders again in the coltish way that so many young girls moved. She drifted towards the back of the boat. "What kind of questions?" Paula brought her wavering attention back to Carlton.

"Oh, just a few things to wrap up our investigation. You seem like a sensitive and intelligent woman. You may just be the one to assist me."

"Whatever I can do..." Paula gnawed at her knuckle.

"Well, as I told Jack Scambaugh, we have found Elliott's murderer..." Carlton paused. "The man who drugged him, lured him into the copse of coconut trees and then bashed him over the head." Carlton rose half-way out of his chair, brought his good arm up and swung it down sharply. "*Bam*!" That's what it must have sounded like." Paula jumped. "That coconut hitting Elliott on his head and smashing through his skull...must have been a mess, all his brains spilling out." Paula's body moved backwards and she motioned her hands forward as if to push herself away. "*Smack*!" Can you imagine the sound it made?" Carlton's voice dropped an octave. "His whole head was mashed in...and if that wasn't bad enough..." He peered at her intently... "The dogs that found him started to eat his brains and the flesh on his head." Paula shuddered and looked sick. "I wouldn't have thought that Thigpin Odette could have killed a man like that...but he did." Carlton sat back, as if drained. Paula was hypnotized by his voice. "I knew he was a bum, Thigpin was. I knew he sold drugs, but never had enough evidence to jail him. I knew he was a lowlife and good for very little except fathering children and drinking rotgut whisky, but I never thought he was mean enough to kill somebody." Carlton's head wagged from right to left in a slow, sad way. "He'll never see the light of day again. He'll *rot* away in prison," Carlton relished the word. "Rot…rot away."

The silence stretched out. "Maybe…" Paula's voice was tentative. "Maybe he didn't murder anyone…"

"No?" Carlton was incredulous. "He had the gold chain. He had the wrist watch. He admits that he stole them. He tells us that Elliott and his girlfriend of the moment…what was her name? Suzie? Suzie…they bought drugs from him. It logically follows that Thigpin killed him, right? If not him, who then?" He stood up awkwardly, balancing himself with his one good hand and chuckled, "Couldn't have been you, Miss Haskins." He loomed over her and she shrank in her chair. "You could not have committed the murder." Carlton's head moved from right to left. "Not you. You were on the boat and you can't swim. Isn't that right, Miss Haskins?" His voice thundered in her head. "Isn't that *right*?" She opened her mouth and a gasp escaped. She put up her hands once again as if to ward off evil. He stood to his full height and then…his head snapped backwards as if some phantom assailant had punched him. His face crumpled and grimaced…he grabbed his chest…he staggered and overturned his chair, grasping at anything that would keep him upright. Paula screamed and tried to hold him up, but he fell hard against her and slumped to the deck. His eyes rolled back and he twitched and shuddered, holding his good hand on his chest. Bare feet thumping on the teak deck, Niccola came running. Carlton clawed at his throat, making horrible gasping and mewling sounds and then….he lay still.

"He's having a heart attack!" Niccola screamed. "Daddy! *Daddy!*" She tried to shake him, to make him speak. Frantic, she stood up, her hands twisted in her hair, her face ashen. "Oh, God! What shall I *do*?"

"I'll….can he take some water?" *How stupid I sound*! Paula's heart hammered in her breast and she stammered with helplessness. *My God! He's dying and I don't know what to do*! She tried splashing water on Carlton's face, but he lay immobile, his mouth open slightly, his breathing labored.

"Can we call…? Do you know how…? The radio…? No? I don't know either!" Her voice shrieked. "I'll go…it will be the fastest way… and get the doctor!" Niccola whirled and jumped into the little motor boat. She pulled at the cord…nothing happened. "Oh, oh! My Daddy!" She stood up in the wildly rocking boat and pulled again. This time, the force of her pull jerked her off her feet. As Paula watched, Niccola tried to grab at the side of the boat, floundered for a moment, and then fell overboard with a huge splash.

Paula ran to the stern. There was no sign of the child. "*Niccola!*" Paula's voice screamed. "*Niccola!*" There was a thrashing in the water and Niccola's head appeared. She was coughing and sputtering and flailing her arms.

"*Help*! *Help*!" The child caught sight of Paula's anguished face. "Help me! I can't *swim*!" She beat her arms and sank again with her mouth open, screaming.

Paula bent over the deck, trying to reach her. She cried and screamed, calling out, but the child had disappeared. Paula stood, frantic and undecided. She gave Carlton's body a hunted glance, saw that the fishing boat that had been nearby all morning had noticed their plight and was heading their way. Saw that it was too far away to make a recovery. Closed her eyes and moaned and then dove into the water with a clean jackknife as close as to where the child had sunk as possible.

On the deck, Carlton sat up and watched, his hand to his chin. Thank goodness for miracles.

Paula's head appeared, her hair plastered to her head, her long-sleeved shirt clinging to her body. In her hand, she grasped the top of Niccola's tee shirt, holding the child's head carefully out of the water. With a practiced side stroke, she kicked and swam, pulling Niccola with her, to the swimming ladder. There, she handed her bundle to Carlton, who had discarded his sling and false cast. He pulled Niccola up, then put his hand out to Paula.

"You tricked me. All of you. You knew all the time," she said dully, as he helped haul her on board. "You did all of this...." She lay on the deck, coughing and spitting. "You knew I could swim."

"Yes, I knew." Carlton turned for a moment. "Are you OK, Nicky?"

"Fine, Dad." Niccola looked down at her bare feet. "I'm fine."

"And she swims like a fish, doesn't she?" Paula's voice was sad.

"As well as you do." Carlton sighed and got to his feet. "Come on, Paula. Let's sit down and talk."

The small fishing boat reached *The Southern Cross*. Paula laughed with bitterness. "Why didn't they get here a few minutes sooner? *They* could have saved her and you'd never have known that I can swim."

"I knew, Paula. Ever since I spoke with George Horowitz, the police chief from Greenwich, I knew."

"George!" Paula gasped. "*George*? *My* George? He's the...po*lice* chief?" Carlton nodded. "And Effalyn Penn, my associate, is the fisherwoman on the boat." Paula shrank into herself as Effalyn took off the conical hat and sat down next to her.

"Don't worry, Miss Haskins. We understand what you did." Effalyn took Paula's cold and stiff hand into hers. "You're shivering. You just tell us all about it and we'll help you as best we can. I promise." Carlton nodded in somber agreement. Effalyn went below to get towels and some dry clothing for Paula.

"I think it all goes back to Debbie Nye's suicide, doesn't it?" His voice was gentle. "You were avenging your dear friend's sister's death."

Paula began to laugh, a high giggling sound that went on and on. Carlton's eyes signaled Effalyn's. She dropped the dry clothes and rushed into the galley for a glass of brandy. Paula's laugh never stopped until Effalyn returned with the brandy. Paula grabbed the glass, took a huge gulp, coughed and then suddenly ceased laughing and drew a huge breath. She hiccupped and laughter turned to sobs.

"You only think you know it all." She cried, her hands clawing the air. "You *don't* know it at all! And what does it matter now, anyway! I'm *not* Paula Haskins...Paula is dead. *I'm* Sharon Nye and that bastard Elliott," she spat his name out, "as good as killed my sister, my mother and my father and ruined our lives! I'd kill him again, if I could!"

CHAPTER TWENTY

*"Revenge triumphs over death; love slights it;
honor aspireth to it; grief flieth to it…"*
Sir Francis Bacon, on Death

At the police station, they took her into the small room. Her suitcase, as she requested, lay on the table. Effalyn sat next to her, looking like a fierce lion mother defending her cub. Mama Lucille and Carlton sat at the other side of the table. And Captain Jack sat quietly in a corner, out of the way. Dressed now in warm, dry clothing, Paula took a packet from the suitcase, where it was hidden under the lining. It was wrapped in silk. In it was an envelope and a letter. The letter nearly fell to pieces. It had obviously been read a thousand or more times. "This came to me when I turned twenty-one. Up to that time, I never knew why Debbie hung herself. I never dreamed…"

More tears stained the paper as she read:

"To my darling sister, Sharon:
    By this time, you are grown up and perhaps can understand why I did what I did. I always loved you and pray that you can find it in your heart to forgive me for the grief that I know I will be causing you and Mommy and Daddy.
    You are too young to have known the horrors of Elliott Barringer.
    He was in the class ahead of mine and always was a terrible boy, mean and nasty – really nasty - to everyone, teasing me and taunting me and everyone who wasn't in his little clique. Everyone who wasn't rich and snobbish and cruel. His father was on the Board of Directors at Daddy's bank. I think Elliott was attracted to me in some perverted way, and that's why all of this began.
    He seemed to pick on me a lot, always making smart remarks and touching me in terrible ways. You are old enough now to understand that kind of thing, but I could never have explained it to you then. He would put his hand on my bosom

and then whisper that he'd have his father make Daddy lose his job if I wasn't nice to him. I tried hard to keep out of his way, but I could tell that he was getting bolder and bolder. Who could I tell? No one. Daddy…never! Mommy…even more never! There was no one who could help me. Maybe if George had been older…but he tormented George too. I could tell. George's face would get white with anger sometimes and I would ask him what was wrong. George, like me, was the perfect victim to a sadist like Elliott. His evil was his strength.

One evening, three months ago, when I had stayed late at school for practice and was walking home alone, a car pulled up. Elliott and three of his friends stopped me. They dragged me into the bushes and did terrible things to me. Elliott raped me while the others held me down and then he made the other boys rape me too. He said I was such a slut that I'd do it with four boys at a time. He held my head still and spit into my face. He said that if I ever told anyone who had done this, he'd see to it that my father would get fired and arrested for taking money from the bank. He said that no one would believe me and that the other boys would swear that I slept with them and anyone else who wanted sex. He said that he'd tell everyone that I pursued him.

I tried to reason with him and he pinched my breast, hard enough to bruise me, and told me that no one would believe my father if his father brought charges against Daddy. They threw me on the ground, and then, laughing, they drove away.

I won't try to tell you the torment I went through, trying to hide every time he was near, fearing that a telephone call would come or that the police would come to the bank and arrest Daddy. But he never did anything, except look at me intensely. It frightened me completely.

And then, like some radio soap opera, my body changed and I knew that I was going to have a baby. Whose baby was it? Who knows? I only knew that I would break Mommy and Daddy's heart and bring shame on our whole family. They were so proud of me and you, my darling. I don't think I could have borne being the cause of their despair. And thus, after anguish that I hope you never have to know, I thought that this was the best way for all. The baby would have been all wrong.

I don't know what else I can do.

I pray that you will forgive me and have some love left in your heart to understand me. I will look down upon your life, my darling sister, and plead with God to understand and keep you safe. Even if it means losing my own soul unto eternity.

My love is always with you,

> Your weak and loving sister, Debbie"

Carlton blew his nose and harrumphed. Effalyn was weeping openly. Mama Lucille threw her ample arms around Paula...for they could only call her Paula...and promised, "I'll treat you like a sweet baby, you poor lamb." She made a sign known only to the island people. "And that devil...well, even though I am a woman of the Law...I'm glad that he is dead!" She glared at everyone in the room, defying them to contradict her.

"Paula?" Carlton asked gently, "I will always think of you as Paula...tell me just how this all came about."

Paula dried her own tears and carefully folded her sister's letter. She told them about her life as a child; how wonderful Debbie was, about George, their family and how happy they all were... "We were so normal. Our life was the best." And then, she explained how it became after Debbie's death. About her parents, her anguish, George, and how she met the real Paula Haskins. "We were sisters. Immediately...soul sisters. She had been through a terrible childhood. I know it sounds peculiar, but we saw into each other's heart. We helped one another to cope with our wounds and, although the wounds never really ever healed, we managed to limp along in our lives together."

She touched the letter again with her fingertips. "Paula always had precarious health. Then she'd see a doctor and would seem to get better, but it was only a matter of time before her illness grew stronger and stronger. When we were both thirty, Paula became really ill...desperately ill, with no chance of recovery. It was a rare disease and there was no cure, although we tried doctor after doctor all over the world. When it became evident that she only had a few months to live, Paula made me promise that I would do exactly as she wanted me to. I didn't know what she had in mind, but at that moment, I would have laid down my own life to make her better, and I agreed. She told me that we were moving to London and that we would be switching names and identities.

"'What?' I said to her. 'What for?'"

" 'Now, hush, Sharon,' she ordered me. 'I've known that I was sick ever since we were in school and I've been planning for this for years.' She was laughing. 'Remember our college class pictures?' "

"And then I remembered. When we were graduating, she made me promise to do a thing...she wouldn't tell me what and she made me promise. I didn't know what she had in mind, and so I promised. At the time, I thought it was just a silly whim, but now I understood. What she wanted me to do was to change places with her when we took our college yearbook pictures."

"Why?" Effalyn wondered.

"Why? So that, if anyone looked back and was suspicious, they would see that Paula's name was under *my* picture and *my* name was under her's. That way, she set the stage for her deception."

"I don't understand," Mama Lucille's eyes were squinched up. "For what?"

"So that I would be her, when the time came. And she would be me. And I would have her fortune to help me find Elliott and kill him."

"She knew?"

"She was with me when the letter came. She and I had no secrets from one another. She knew everything." Paula took another small sip of the brandy and gasped as the fiery liquid ran down her throat. "She not only knew, she helped me to find him and keep track of him until we could figure out a way to kill him that would go undetected," Paula smiled with rue. "I guess we just weren't smart enough...or that I just wasn't smart enough..."

"Why didn't she just leave you her money?" Effalyn's brow was furrowed with perplexity.

"She couldn't under the terms of her legacy. If she died, all the money went to a carefully selected group of charities." Paula grinned, an urchin's grin and shrugged. "And when I die, which will be soon, the money will still go to the charities." She sipped again at the brandy and this time, the brandy slid down with a warm glow. "I have been sending monies to the charities all along, so I don't feel that they have been cheated." She shrugged, her thin shoulders moving helplessly. "Oh, certainly, we committed fraud, we did. But what the hell...we were going to commit *murder*! So what was a little fraud?"

"And so you moved to London and you switched identities?" Carlton was following the story with fascination. "And then what happened?"

"I became Paula and she became me. No one knew or cared. We looked very similar, and when you meet two women that look alike, sometimes you can't quite remember who is who."

Effalyn nodded. "I guess it was easy. I still can't tell you which of those cousins from South Africa is Martha and which one is Claudia. I just think of them as the cousins from South Africa."

"Yes. Our passports had to be renewed and we just switched identities. I posed for her passport and she was on mine. No one ever suspected that her picture was on my passport and that I had become her. We looked very much alike and...who would care?"

"You wouldn't get away with that nowadays," Carlton said sternly.

"You might." Effalyn's voice was thoughtful. "I think those two boys from New Jersey...they could have switched identities...who would know? Their physical characteristics...height...their faces and hair...they are so similar...who could tell if both of them were in on it?"

Paula rubbed her hands together, as if they were cold. "No one suspected anything. As I said, who would? And, eventually, the woman named Sharon Nye died in London. There was no one but me...Paula...to mourn her. Her ashes were scattered over the ocean when I returned to New York as Paula three months later. As she always corresponded with her attorneys by mail, there was never any suspicion. I never aroused any suspicion whatsoever. I was circumspect. I never spent much money. Only what I needed to live modestly and to pay for the three private detectives who kept me informed of Elliott's life and whereabouts." She took a deep breath and looked at each of them. "I'm not sorry that I did what I did. And I am fully prepared to pay the price."

"But you won't pay it for long?" Effalyn's voice was soft. "I helped you out of your wet things and saw those bruises and marks on you. I think you are very sick. You have...? What?"

"Raving, angry, advanced breast cancer. It came upon me last year and there really was no beating it. I refused all chemotherapy and treatment, as it wouldn't have made much difference at all. Wouldn't have prolonged my life. I have about three months to live. But I really don't care to live any longer. I suppose I will escape the trial and the punishment here. I know I am going straight to prison." She held her hands out to Mama Lucille. "You can whip me all you want for three months or so."

"Oh, my sweet pea!" Mama Lucille took Paula's hands in hers. "I'll feed you up and make you better." Paula shook her head no. There was no salvation or miracle coming to her.

"You knew...? How did you know?" Paula sought Carlton's face.

"I spoke with Elliott's law firm. I spoke with an old man who worked with him a long time ago and I spoke with George. All the co-incidences of Greenwich. And George has never forgotten Debbie's death. Never." Carlton smiled. "He'll be here this afternoon and he's going to be in for a huge surprise. He thinks, as I thought, that you are really Paula."

"*George*!" Paula's mood changed and her face became pink and excited. "He was a wonderful boy. He loved my sister and she loved him." Her face darkened. "They...they probably would have married...maybe...if...if Elliott...and all this..." She began to weep again, soft sobs. "He was such a destroyer. He destroyed all of our lives. All of our happiness."

Mama Lucille gathered her into her capacious arms and rocked her. Paula sniffed and dried her tears.

"How did you figure to murder Elliott?" Effalyn leaned forward, enthralled by the melodrama of Paula and Sharon.

"I found out that he was coming on this cruise. One of his clients gave him the trip, telling him that he thought he needed some relaxation. Naturally, I had paid the client to do so. I thought that if I could get him away somewhere, I could find a way to kill him, even if I had to do it myself." She drew herself up. "As a matter of fact, I wanted to do it myself." She turned to Captain Jack, who had sat quietly in the back of the room, listening to Paula's tale. "It was the newspaper you sent me that gave me the idea."

"Me?" Jack's face was perplexed. "Me?"

"Yes, there was a story in the newspaper about a man who was killed by a falling coconut."

"Oh, Two-Tone's death! That's what it was! You read about Two-Tone!" Effalyn breathed heavily. "Imagine that!"

"Two-Tone?" Paula blinked. "His name was Two-Tone?" Effalyn was quick to assure her that it was only a nickname and Paula smiled, nodding. "Thank goodness for Two-Tone. Was he murdered too?"

"No, as far as we know, it was an accident." Carlton stated. And then, "Unless you came down and tried a dress rehearsal?" Paula laughed, no, and then couldn't stop laughing until she began to cry.

"All right, everyone get outta here and let this poor woman rest." Mama Lucille shooed at them.

"But wait!" Carlton stopped them before they rose. "I want to know how you killed him. I mean, we'll never get you to trial, but I'm curious as to how you managed it all." There were nods and murmurs all around....*How the heck did you do it? How'd you get him to go under the tree? How'd you hit him? Were you sure he was dead? How did you get back to the boat?* "You owe it to us to explain."

"Nothing matters now," Paula shrugged. "I have no more secrets. I wasn't sure that I was going to be able to kill him that night. I watched and waited for the right time and took advantage of timing and luck. When I saw that Suzie had gone off with that other man – and by the way, I never knew him - Francesco Jeraldo? - in Greenwich either... It was really just a coincidence that he, too, had lived there. Anyway, I saw Elliott alone and I knew he had been trying to purchase some drugs. I, um...well, you don't know it – and I'm not going to tell you who he is – but one of my operatives...my private detectives... is down here and helping me." She put her hands out, palms up and made a stop motion. "No, I'm not going to tell you who he is. And no, he doesn't know that I was going to kill anyone. So, don't even *try* to figure out who it is!" She glared at Carlton, who was looking baffled and upset.

"Anyway, I went over to his table when he was alone. I told him that I had medical morphine for my pain and that I would go back to the boat and get it, if he paid me two thousand dollars. He just laughed and told me that I didn't look like a broad who needed money. I told him that looks were deceiving. And indeed my looks *were* deceiving to him. There was no way that he could know who I was, the bastard." She sniffed back a tear. "I made plans to meet him at two o'clock in the grove of coconut trees. He'd bring the money and I'd bring him a month's worth of morphine. Then, I told Ducky that I was tired and wanted to go back to the boat, thereby giving myself a cast-iron alibi, or so I thought. I went back, and slipped into a black bathing suit and flippers. I carried a bottle of brandy that I had doctored, a long black dress and a headscarf in a plastic bag and swam into the beach. I changed in the clump of coconut trees and waited for him. When he came, I offered him a drink and he, as I thought he would do, chugged almost the entire bottle of brandy. There was a huge amount of sleeping medicine in the brandy and he – almost immediately – sat down dizzy and disoriented. I leaned him back against the tree, picked up a large coconut, thought about my sister, my mother and my father...and smashed it against his head." There was a swift, indrawn breath somewhere in the room, but Paula's voice was steady and even. "I whispered that this was for Debbie...and for my mother...and for my father...and for all the grief and misery he had caused people...I made sure he was dead and he was. Otherwise, I would have hit him again and again and again." Her eyes were burning bright. "Oh, I wore rubber gloves from Kat's kitchen when I hit him with the coconut. I brought a pack of matches, too. I made a little fire and burned the gloves and then smothered the ashes with sand. I thought it would make even more confusion to the police if there was a fire to discover." Her face crumpled. "I put all my clothing and things back into the plastic bag, got back into my swim suit and flippers and swam back to the boat."

"Why didn't anyone see or hear you get back on the boat?"

"Not because I was so clever...no. Just good timing and some luck." Paula grinned, her mood lifting. "Everyone who came with me on the Zodiac was already asleep. Ducky had gone back to the wedding party and I put the flippers away and dried off my bathing suit with a towel. I was actually sound asleep when the rest of the group came back from the wedding. I awoke for a moment and could hear you..." she smiled at Captain Jack..."You were singing and playing a lovely song. Something about Wynkin, Blynkin and Nod. A child's lullaby. I just rolled over and went back to sleep."

"Why did you confess so readily?" Carlton had his own ideas, but wanted them confirmed.

"Oh, nothing matters anymore. But there were two things. One, I couldn't let that poor man, Thigpen Odette, be incarcerated for what I had done," Carlton nodded with an inner glow of satisfaction. He was right again. "And two, I accomplished my revenge. That was all I wanted to do I was consumed by revenge. I know I committed murder...I killed Elliott. I thought about it and planned it for years, so, I am sure that it will be considered as premeditated." Her voice jerked upward. "Premeditated! It was all we talked about and planned! It was the most premeditated killing in history!" She sighed. "And I know I will be judged by God...and very soon, too. But I think I can talk him out of being too hard on me." Carlton's face was thoughtful. He hadn't considered that part.

"And you'll have your good friend Paula to help Him make His decision," Effalyn nodded firmly. "God's going to understand." Carlton looked at his right-hand-woman. She certainly had put herself squarely on Paula's side. And why not?

"I hope so, Effalyn. I hope so." Paula bowed her head. She was exhausted.

"Come on, child," Mama Lucille's hand was supportive. "Let's get you in to a nice and comfortable cell. The nice one that get's the morning sunshine. And then, I'll make you some soup. You'll feel much better after you've had some of my soup." She helped Paula to her feet and walked out of the room, holding her around the waist, protecting her as best she could.

Carlton, Effalyn and Captain Jack sat for a few moments, each with his own thoughts. "My, my," Effalyn said. Jack and Carlton nodded in fervent agreement.

CHAPTER TWENTY-ONE

"Shall this, our lofty scene be acted o'er..."
William Shakespeare, Julius Caesar

"Still, she's a murderer," Effalyn's mother crossed her arms, her face stern and implacable. "She can't just get away with it."

"Of course, she's guilty," Effalyn opened the door to Aunt Fanny's Tearoom and ushered her mother inside. "But she's dying and very frail and sick. She'll never live long enough to be tried for her crime."

"God will judge her." Effalyn's mother sat down, her spine rigid. "He sees everything."

"If He sees everything, then she'll be just fine. She's suffered, Mama. She's tired of this life. She's ready to face Him." Her mother sniffed, showing clearly what she thought of people who tinker with the Lord's Commandments.

Aunt Fanny shuffled over with a pot of tea and a plate of shortbread biscuits iced with pink frosting. "Here. Let me sit down." She plopped herself into a chair. "Ohhh, I'm tired." She waggled her feet in the air. "My poor dogs are crying." She poured each of them a cup of tea. "So, I hear that the American lady confessed."

"How did you hear so fast?" Effalyn wondered out loud. "It's only been a few hours since we arrested her."

"It's all over the island." Aunt Fanny licked the icing off a cookie and then proceeded to eat it, bite by bite. "Consensus is that he deserved it."

"Consensus is correct," Effalyn drained her cup and poured herself another.

"Hmpf," Effalyn's mother sniffed. "That man was bad to the bone. I blame his mother and father for not showing him right from wrong." Aunt Fanny tsked her agreement. "You have to teach your children."

"Guess he never wanted to be taught," Aunt Fanny mused.

"Children are easy to bend to the right. Even if you have to fool them sometimes for their own good." Effalyn's mother thought of the years gone by. "Even you, Effalyn, and you were always...well, almost always...a good girl. I had to bend you now and then. I had to show you right from wrong." Effalyn smiled tenderly and put her hands out. One touched Aunt Fanny's work-worn hand, and one touched her mother's.

"You bent me well, Mama."

***

"If you managed to pull off that farce on the boat, we can pull off a scam with Mrs. Marsden and her pal, Neil."

"You think it will work?"

"It's worth a try. My mother and Aunt Fanny were talking this morning about bending children the right way. It reminded me about another conversation they had...a few days ago...you know...your mother is probably the same way. They always love to talk about how they fooled their children. They were talking about how to make children snitch on one another. I think we can use their lesson."

"What do you plan to do?"

"First, we need the cooperation of Professor Stambaugh. She needs to bring a camera and maybe even those two experts that she had here the other day. Make it all look very, very professional and thorough. Scare the hell out of them. I think Mrs. Marsden will be the one to crack first."

Carlton nodded. "And then what?"

"Then, I think Neil Zuster will crack the loudest. I think he's an even bigger rat than Mrs. Marsden."

"How do you want to set it up?" Carlton grinned, thinking that Effalyn, if this worked, would emerge as a superstar detective.

"I've given it some thought and want your opinion on what else we need. Here is my plan: We need two patrol cars with lights and sirens and Ganny and Armond and you and I in full uniform...We want to look very overwhelming and official." Effalyn made some notes on a pad of paper. "And we must make sure that they are both at home. It would be even better if their neighbors were at home and might be outside to watch the whole show....I'm going to call Mrs. Leuzarder, Marsha and Len,...those two will brighten up the spectacle... and the other people on the other side..." She looked at her notes... "Mr. and Mrs Kochanek. The more, the merrier. I want to make it into as big a circus as possible. A huge and very public drama. I want old Neil and Mrs. Marsden to feel as if they are in a public boxing ring...each of them fighting to prove that the other was the really bad one. I want them to squirm...and worry...and tattle-tale on one another."

"You're a tough detective. I hope it works."

"It has to!" Effalyn slapped the desk. "My ego is on the line here! I can't let *your* plan be successful and *my* plan fail!"

***

In the end, they decided to bring along Doctor Fullbright, too. "He can take Mrs. Zuster to the hospital for tests. And be sure that he announces what he's going to do in a very loud voice. I want to be sure that everyone hears him loud and clear."

They agreed that they would pick up Mrs. Marsden first. "I'm going to call her and tell her that we're all coming. Give her more time to stew." Effalyn called Mrs Marsden and in a very official voice informed her that the police and a group of poison plant specialists were to visit her in fifteen minutes. Before Mrs. Marsden could ask any questions, Effalyn hung up the telephone, presuming that Ellen Marsden would call Neil Zuster immediately.

In a stately procession, four police cars and a large ambulance drove to Fifty One Overlook Drive. The siren was off, but all of the police cars had their lights blinking and the red lights on the roof revolving in scarlet splendor. As if on cue, several neighbors popped out of their homes to wonder what was happening.

Professor Stambaugh and the Corkes got out of one of the police cars. They collected a number of cameras, tripods and photo paraphernalia and made a lot of commotion. Ganny and Armond got out of one of the police cars, Effalyn and Carlton each stepped out of a car, and Doctor Fullbright, wearing a purple suit, rose majestically from the front seat of the ambulance. Ellen Marsden came to the door. She was dressed in a flowered housedress and her hair had just been washed and was set into large, pink curlers. She half-opened the door and peered nervously at the crowd on her doorstep. No one said a word.

"What...? What do you want?" Her voice was loud and raw and she patted the curlers on her hair, seemingly embarrassed to be caught in such dishabille. "Who are all of these people?" Her neighbors and a few passers-by moved closer. Ellen Marsden stopped touching her hair and clutched at her throat. "Wha...what is all of this?" She tried to speak in an imperious way, but her voice came out as a bleat.

A Fat Virgin Death

Carlton took out his badge. "Ellen Marsden?" He asked, his voice stiff and officious.

"Yes….yes…what…?" Carlton held his badge up to her face and she backed away, afraid to touch it.

"Under Statute Sixty-Three of the Law of Virgin Gorda…" Effalyn flicked a questioning glance at him. *Statute Sixty-Three? What was Statute Sixty-Three?* "I am informing you officially that Plant Poison Specialists from The University of The Virgin Islands and The University of Massachusetts in the United States are taking photographs and collecting specimens for evidence in the matter of your husband's death." He motioned – a sweeping gesture with his arm - for Carol, Randy and Mary to proceed. They looked severely at her and marched, equipment in tow, to the back of the house. Mrs. Marsden and the crowd of neighbors watched them, openmouthed.

"What? Poison? You…you can't…"

"*Madam!*" Carlton thundered. "You have no say in this! I represent the law!" The crowd gasped and drew even closer. The neighbors from next door, Len and Marsha, came rushing over with their dog, a huge mastiff named Boober, straining at his leash, barking. But other than Boober's howls, the group was again silent.

Mrs Marsden's mouth opened and closed and she made a tentative motion to dash inside her house, but Doctor Fullbright moved his imposing body between her and the door. "Not inside, madam," he informed her.

Randy and Mary and Carol came around the corner of the house. Randy hefted the camera and the two women had their arms filled with leaves and branches. Mrs. Marsden gasped again when she saw them. "We have all the evidence," Randy informed Carlton in a loud voice. "I have all the photographs I need."

"Good. As soon as we get the plants from Neil Zuster's garden, we will have everything we need for a conviction." There was a gasp and a tiny wail from Mrs. Marsden. "Get all of the evidence to the laboratory so it can be matched to the poison found in Mr. Marsden's body." Mrs. Marsden seemed to sag. There was a collective sigh from the crowd on the street and even Boober stopped barking and stood at attention, his long tail up in the air, sensing the tension. Carlton turned to Mrs. Marsden and held her elbow. "Will you please come with us to the police station for questioning, Mrs. Marsden. This is an official request." Mrs. Marsden's eyes rolled, showing the whites. "We will be picking up Mr.

Neil Zuster on the way." Ellen Marsden's face blanched and she seemed unsteady on her feet.

Carlton coughed with officious seriousness. He guided her to one of the police cars. Ganny slid into the driver's seat and Effalyn got into the back seat with Mrs. Marsden. Everyone else got into their cars and the ambulance and the entourage drove away with the sirens howling and the lights flashing.

"I think she's in big trouble," Ann Leuzarder remarked to the crowd at large.

"What happened?" A tall woman with a straw hat perched on her head asked.

"Didn't you hear? She poisoned her husband. Fed him plants until he died!"

"Really?" The woman took a closer look at the Marsden's house. She wanted to be able to describe it in detail to her husband when he came home from work.

***

"Are you all right, Mrs. Marsden?" Effalyn bent towards her.

"Am I...? Am I being arrested?"

"No. We're just questioning you officially." Effalyn patted her hand. "I shouldn't be telling you this, but...well, I think you are being set-up by Neil Zuster." Effalyn made a face. "Men! You know how they are! Promise a woman anything, but when the chips are down, why, they leave you with all the blame!"

"Blame? What did he tell you?"

Effalyn lowered her voice and turned her head closer. "I shouldn't be saying anything." She tipped her chin toward the back of Ganny's helmeted head. "I don't want Officer Johnstone to hear me. But we women have to stick together."

"What? What did Neil say about me?" Her voice rose in panic.

"That everything was your idea. That you were the brains of the whole situation. That he had no idea that you wanted Mr. Marsden dead." Effalyn's face was the picture of sorrow and betrayal. "I think he's planning to get you jailed. He plans to turn in all the evidence and that way he'll be a hero. He'll walk away with no penalty at all or, at worst, a slap on the wrist. Hmpf. I even heard that he and his wife have come into some big money and plan to move back to Europe."

"The *bas*tard!"

"That's what I heard. I thought you should know so that you can be ready to tell us what really happened." Effalyn patted Mrs. Marsden's hand once more. "Again, I want you to make him sorry he was born. Men!" *Oh, Mama, you ought to see your lying daughter now*! Effalyn hoped that all of these lies would produce a gushing confession.

"What should I do? How…? It wasn't my idea at all! It was *his*! He's the one who planned it all. Looked up the poisons. He made me…he…he wanted to kill his wife, the snivelling bitch! It was all his idea!"

"Look, Mrs. Marsden, it isn't me that you should tell, not unless you want to make an official confession." Mrs. Marsden looked frightened and started to cry. "I mean, whoever confesses first…If there are two people and they try to blame each other – the one that tells us just what happened and tells the truth, well, that's the one who will get the mercy of the judge."

"If I make a confession…what…? *Oh, God*! Why did I ever let that man…Oh! Oh!"

"I do have a tape recorder here." Effalyn reached into her purse. "I can tape you telling me your side of the story…" Her eyes asked and Mrs Marsden nodded, hesitant and unsure. "Let's see…" Effalyn fiddled with the knob of the recorder as the procession of cars pulled up in front of Neil and Damson Zuster's house. Mrs. Marsden watched, like a trapped rabbit, as the police, Dr. Fullbright and the botanists all got out of the cars. Randy, Carol and Mary lugged their cameras out and stood, while Carlton knocked on the door.

Ellen Marsden turned to Effalyn, tugging at her sleeve. "I'm afraid. I want to tell you my side before he starts to tell lies."

"Are you sure?" Effalyn held the tape recorder out. "I don't want you to be retracting your story later."

"I swear. I swear." Her voice rose an octave. Effalyn searched her face and then nodded, as if confirming something.

She pushed the button and the tape began to whir softly. "This is Detective Effalyn Penn of the Virgin Gorda Police. The date today is….." Mrs. Marsden watched Effalyn's lips moving. Here eyes looked dazed and confused. *If she hadn't stuffed all those plants into her husband's gizzard, I might find it in my heart to feel sorry for her,* Effalyn thought. She continued dictating into the recorder…. "I am in the back seat of one of our patrol cars with Mrs. Ellen Marsden, widow of Antony Marsden, recently deceased. Mrs. Marsden, will you state your full name…"

"Ellen Marsden."

"And are you giving this interview and taping this conversation of your own free will?"

"Yes…yes, I am." Ellen gasped as she watched Neil Zuster being brought out of his house. He was struggling and angry, and when he saw her sitting in the back of the police car, began to swear and shake his fist at her. "Oh, he'll be so angry at me…so angry…perhaps…I…maybe, I shouldn't."

Rats, thought Effalyn. "That's your prerogative, Mrs. Marsden. I'm sure that Neil Zuster won't have any such scruples." They watched as Neil was stuffed into the back of the other police car. He glared out of the window, his hands moving in angry gesticulations.

Doctor Fullbright came out of the Zuster's house with Mrs. Zuster. She appeared pale and ill and he helped her solicitously into the front seat of the ambulance.

"What's she doing? Where are they taking her?"

"I think they are taking her to the hospital to have tests done on her stomach contents and blood."

Mrs. Marsden's face blanched again. "Why are they doing that?

"To see if there is any trace of the poisons. Mrs Zuster has been complaining of fatigue and illness…and the botany experts tell us those symptoms are consistent with early signs of plant toxins."

"You can tell that? If they are still alive…you can tell…?"

"Oh, certainly. I'm sure that her husband will be singing his song about how the whole thing came from you." Effalyn shook her head in pretended disgust. "He's going to try to save his own skin."

"You mean that he's going to tell them that this was all my idea?"

"That's what I think. Of course, I have no idea of what he's really going to say." The tape rolled and Effalyn sat, silent.

The botanist group came back towards the cars, the camera and branches again filling their hands. Randy, who enjoyed amateur theatrics back home, was in his element and would dine out on this story for years to come, waved the branch enthusiastically. Mrs Marsden bit her bottom lip. "Maybe I should tell you just how it all happened…" her voice was tentative.

"I must warn you that anything you say…" Effalyn droned the necessary warnings and then held the microphone up.

"He came to me about two years ago. He said that he loved me and there was a good way that we could be together and get the money that... He told me that he was tired of the whining of his wife and confessed that he wanted to kill her and marry me." She took in a deep, shaky breath. "He suggested that he and I should work together....first to poison Antony and then, a few months later, to more slowly poison his wife. He...he told me about a book he had read about plants that were poisonous. That I should let Antony...have...he was beginning to be ill, anyway....and that there were plants here in our gardens that would make him act ...like Alzheimer's. He...I didn't really want to kill Antony, but Neil...he...he seduced me and made me swear that I would do what he wanted me to." Her eyes flickered from left to right... "He brought some books over to my house and showed me about the effects of the plants." She rubbed her forehead, pushing hard, as if she had a headache and continued. "I...swear that I wanted no part of the scheme, but he begged me and made love to me and finally forced me to...." Her voice droned on, insisting that she was innocent, really...that all of the plans had been made by Neil, and that she was under his spell. Effalyn listened, and prayed that a good judge would put them both behind bars for a very long time.

In the other police car, Neil was told that Ellen was most likely giving her version of their murder, probably blaming him and trying to exonerate herself.

"Bitch!" Neil spat. "This whole thing was her idea. I was crazy about her. She wanted her old man dead and so she suggested that I help her. She had these books...all about poisons found on the island..." He began to babble, faster and faster. "It was all her. I was really innocent. She gave him the poisons...."

In the driver's seat, Patrolman Armond Hubert coughed to conceal his laughter. The boss was milking the man like a goat. Ha! He and his murdering girl-friend would try to scratch each other's eyes out before the day was over. Nothing like honor among thieves and murderers, huh!

The entourage stopped first at the hospital. The ambulance went to the front door. The police cars were behind, each of them with a good view of the entrance-way. Ellen Marsden and Neil Zuster's faces were pressed again the glass in their respective autos, watching as Damson Zuster was helped into the hospital, held up by Doctor Fullbright's sturdy arm. As the doctor and his new patient approached the hospital doors, they were burst open by a team of nurses and doctors, pushing a fully equipped stretcher. With a great show of medical legerdemain, they solicitously assisted Mrs. Zuster onto the stretcher, attached cathodes and intravenous lines, fussed around the stretcher and finally retreated into the bowels of the hospital.

Neil Zuster's eyes were glazed over. There was a touch of spittle at the corner of his mouth as his mind churned furiously. *Damn! They were going to stick a tube down Damson's belly and the evidence against me will come spilling out!*

At the police station, as the cars were emptying, Neil lunged toward Ellen, shaking his fist and screaming at her. "You bitch! I'll kill you! This was all your idea! I'm innocent! You'll spend the rest of your life in prison! You...you...."

Ellen shrank back against Effalyn, nearly collapsing into her arms. "He...he..." She began to sob. "We're done for, aren't we? Both of us?"

Effalyn nodded her head slowly. "Yes, we'll be arresting you both."

A phalanx of newspaper reporters appeared, as if from nowhere. Their cameras snapped. One reported tried to stick a microphone in Ellen's face. "Lady! Mrs. Marsden! Did you poison your husband?" Ellen cowered and Effalyn spoke sternly to the reporter, as she hustled Mrs. Marsden inside.

Ellen Marsden howled. "My hair! They've taken a picture of me with curlers in my hair!"

***

At noontime, Annie and Duncan arrived at the jail. Again, Suzie refused to see them. Mama Lucille came bustling downstairs to see them.

"She's heading for a fall. Not even to see you! She still thinks that her money will magically open the door of the cell and she'll be able to waltz right out." She made a sound of disgust. "She isn't learning yet."

"How can we help her," Duncan stood with his hands clasped. Annie was upset that Suzie was in prison, and he would do anything – anything – to make his Annie smile. "What do you suggest?"

"If she refuses to entertain you, she refuses. We can't make her see you." Mama Lucille scratched her head. "Maybe you can speak with the Officer of the Court. He's a wise old coot and has been here longer than Methuselah."

On her suggestion, Annie and Duncan asked for a short meeting with the Officer of the Court. He was an elderly black man, with a wreath of white, tufty hair that sat like a halo on his otherwise bald head. His teeth were white and square and his eyes were a deep, dark color. "I am Officer Daniel. How can I help you?"

Duncan explained their dilemma. "We are on a chartered catamaran. I believe that we are going to leave this side of Virgin Gorda tomorrow morning to sail to The Baths and then spend a day in Spanish Town. We want to help her and perhaps testify on her behalf."

Annie wrung her hands. "You can't keep her down here in prison for the rest of her life! She'll wither away and die."

Officer Daniel's eyes were sad. Annie's stomach fell to the bottom of her shoes. This man had seen evil and murder and remorse. There was nothing that hadn't passed him by. How could she convince him that there was some worth in Suzie? Suzie certainly refused to help herself. The police had told her that Suzie had spit at Mama Lucille, thrown her food on the floor and cursed at anyone and everyone who had come her way. Pissed that her lawyer hadn't been able to get her out of jail, she had screamed at him and told him that he was fired. Shrugging, he left the jail, telling her to call him when she changed her mind. After all, he had already cashed her retainer checks.

"How do you suggest that this Court can help her?"

"Can we find a way, perhaps to have her do some humbling community service?"

"And what do you suggest?"

"Is there a home here for your drug abusers? Or perhaps a home for people who are trying hard to get back on their feet? Maybe Suzie can work there in some capacity...clean bathrooms...cook...do her work during the day and go back to jail at night? Sort of a probation?" Annie bit her lip. "So that she can have some freedom until they hear her case?"

"I'll be happy to put up bail money to assure that she doesn't run away," Duncan really didn't trust Suzie, but was willing to make an attempt to help her.

The old man looked at the papers in Suzie's file. "I am sure that she will be found guilty and that she will be incarcerated for many years, no matter how much it upsets you and your family." Annie began to weep, realizing how futile her efforts were.

"I can't bear for her to be shut up in prison! She'll...she'll..."

Officer Daniel patted Annie's hand. "We all write our own story in the book of life." He stood up. "In the end, no one is responsible but you. I am touched by your concern. I will think about your suggestions. I will talk them over with Mama Lucille. No one can make your cousin see that the road to her freedom lies within herself and herself only. You and I," he turned from Duncan to Annie, "can only help her if she wants help." He rubbed his hands together. "Give me two days and come back on the day before you leave Spanish Town."

With that faint hope, they had to be satisfied.

***

Carlton met the ferry boat from St. Thomas at Spanish Town and hopped on, brushing past the Customs men to greet a tall man with graying gingery hair. "George Horowitz? Chief Horowitz?"

"Detective-Inspector Reese? I'm pleased and proud to meet you. What an amazing story all of this is! How is it all going with you?" The two men shook hands and then stood, a foot apart, looking at one another.

Carlton grunted. "This is the most remarkable case. Wait until you hear about what has happened since I spoke with you. You have a big shock coming." A Customs Agent stepped toward Chief Horowitz. Carlton waved him away.

"Nevermind him. He's with me on official business." Carlton led George around the Customs Area and out to his car. "Welcome to Virgin Gorda."

***

Revised Itinerary of *The Southern Cross*...

Wednesday, December 22 – We hope and pray that all of you will join with us in coping with the extraordinary events of the last few days. All of you are aware of the magnitude of these events and the aftermath, which will be leaving us with three passengers less for the remainder of our cruise. I am pleased that none of you saw fit to take *The Southern Cross* up on our offer to refund your money and get you home sooner. Kat, Ducky, Emma and I are delighted that you all have decided to continue with us and enjoy, or try to enjoy, the rest of the voyage.

This morning, we will continue most of our original itinerary, with a few changes. After breakfast here in Big Fish Cay, the police have given us permission to continue our voyage. We will be weighing anchor at 9AM and traveling to The Baths, one of the most remarkable natural stone formations in the world. Snorkeling here is excellent as you swim through huge granite boulders with magical pools of water, sunlight and shadows. We hope you take advantage of the remarkable walking trail through the boulders. Lunch will be served as a picnic on the fine, white sand of Devil's Bay. In mid-afternoon, we will sail the short distance to Spanish Town and The Virgin Gorda Yacht basin. Once again, we will be tied at the dock, making for easy egress. Our afternoon will be at leisure. You can shop in the many stores and boutiques that line the harbor. Night will find us traveling by jitney to the Olde Yard Inn, known for excellent cuisines and a magnificent garden.

Thursday, December 23 - Breakfast in the tiny, exquisite garden in the middle of Spanish Town. The restaurant is noted for its rum and banana pancakes and for its island rum punch. Today we can ride on horseback up to the top of the mountains where the old copper mines once supplied copper to the world. We will lunch at the Copper Mine Restaurant and then come back down the mountain to enjoy speedboat rides and water skiing. Dinner is at the Parrott Club, a private golf and tennis club tucked into the hillsides. It is a formal place, and jackets are suggested for the men. The women can show off one of the lovely outfits that have been purchased in one of the shops.

Friday, December 24 – Breakfast on board and then an early departure as we cruise to the North sound of Virgin Gorda. *The Southern Cross* will be traveling in ocean water and you will hang onto your hats as we skim the waves at more than 18 knots. The truly brave can ride on the trampoline, holding on tightly, for the ride and drenching of their lives. We will turn the boat before we reach Portugal (ha) and head into North Sound and The Bitter End Yacht Club.

As you all have suffered some deprivation, we have arranged a two night stay, including Christmas Eve and Christmas Day at the Bitter End. Those who wish to get off the boat are being offered private cabanas at no cost to any of you. The Bitter End has wonderful dining rooms, a chance to water ski, sail smaller boats, para-kite, SCUBA dive, take a snorkeling boat to the outer reefs of Necker Island (the fantastically expensive playground island of such luminaries as Princess Diana, Barbra Streisand, Mick Jagger and Elton John. – The cost of

renting Necker Island for a week is in the $200,000 range, but you can take a good look at the island from the snorkeling boat for free). The Bitter End also has an Olympic sized fresh water swimming pool so you can cool down and wash the salt away. And may I mention again that all food, beverages, costs of boat and equipment rental…everything…including the luxurious world-renowned spa…with no cost to any of you. The Bitter End Yacht Club will be hosting a Christmas Eve Disco Party, a Christmas Day Brunch, with special gifts for each of you, and a Christmas Evening Old English Dinner. We hope you will stuff yourselves and be ready to cast off on Sunday morning, December 26th.
………more later ………

***

At Mama Lucille's suggestion, Paula was moved to a private wing at the island hospital. "She's not gonna' run away. She's probably never even gonna' leave the hospital alive," Mama told the authorities gruffly. "She's got plenty of money. You can charge her double for the room."

No one questioned Mama's suggestion.

CHAPTER TWENTY-TWO

*"What is longer than the waves? What is deeper than the sea?
Love is longer than the waves. Hell is deeper than the sea..."*
old riddle

"George? Oh, George, is this you?" Paula put out her arms. "It's really me...yes, little Sharon. Oh, George...Debbie...Can you forgive me? Oh, *George*!"

And after a period of tears and touching, gentle hugs and incoherent cries, Paula...for, again, we will know her forever as Paula...showed George her sister's letter.

***

Harry Glass finally convinced Suzie to see her cousin. "She's working hard to help you. She and her boyfriend...that Scotch guy...have finally convinced Mama Lucille to give you a bit of a chance to redeem yourself instead of spending your life here inside a prison cell. And it won't be a nice private prison cell like this..." Harry spread his arms wide. "No...this cell is a deluxe hotel room compared to the one you'd be in if they arraign you for drug possession and attempting to fake the evidence against your cousin."

Suzie's eyes narrowed. She wanted to spit in Harry's face, but the few days of imprisonment with the slowly dawning realization that her money, her charms, her beauty and her temper were not going to set her free, had made her cautious. Maybe she'd have to pretend to be nice to Annie. Maybe that was the only way. "All right, I'll see her." Her voice was grudging.

"And my advice to you is to be nice to her. Be helpful. Try to convince her, and Mama Lucille, that you may have seen the light of day and redemption."

"You're asking a lot from me."

"You're paying me a fortune, Suzie. Try to listen to what I say to you in return for all that money. You're not a stupid woman, although, God Almighty, you're a stubborn one. You have no status here. You have no rights. You are scum to these people. They think badly of you for the drug situation, but that's nothing to how they feel about you trying to implicate your cousin." He stood over her. "Annie's your only chance and if you don't understand that, you're going to die right here on the island, in a room with three other vicious women with strange sexual practices – each of them stronger and meaner than you, one toilet and no chance to ever get out. Does that make *any* impression on you?"

Cowed by the thought of the room with three other convicts, Suzie nodded again. "I said I'd see her, didn't I?" *What does he mean, Strange sexual practices? Not...? No way!*

Annie and Duncan entered Suzie's cell. Suzie half-lay, half-sat on the cot. Annie was astonished at how terrible Suzie looked. Suzie, who was always perfectly groomed, Suzie who always was dressed expensively in the height of fashion. Suzie, whose make-up and hair was always perfect. "Gee whiz, Suzie," Annie gasped. "You look awful!"

"Thanks a bunch. You'd look awful too, if you had to look at these four walls and that fat Mama Pajama all day."

"I...I didn't mean....well, of course...you are...you haven't..." Annie didn't know what to say.

"What do you want, Miss Goody?"

Annie squared her shoulders. She was trying to help, but Suzie, as always, was making it hard. Annie gulped and tried to not tell Suzie that she'd like to kick her – hard – in the rear end. "Look, Suzie. I'm trying to help you. Duncan and I have been talking and pleading and promising that you'll try to cooperate. If you do, or if you can try, maybe we can get you on a probation program instead of having you put into prison for the rest of your life."

"You love this, don't you," Suzie lit a cigarette. "You always were jealous of me and now you think you have me where you want me..." Annie bit her lip, trying not to cry.

"*Enough!*" Duncan roared. "You, Annie...Out. I'm going to talk with your cousin for exactly three minutes. If I can't make her empty, gormless head understand what is facing her if she doesn't wise up, I'll be leaving this cell and you and your cousin will most likely never see one another again." He gently pushed Annie out the door.

Duncan turned towards Suzie. Suzie had sat up and her eyes were wary. 'What are you going to do? Beat me up?"

"No, Suzie. There would be no point to that," Duncan smiled with tired eyes. "You'd probably enjoy that." Suzie gasped, surprised that he understood her so well. "I'm going to spend two minutes telling you what you are going to do, and then, you will either spend thirty seconds telling me that you will do it, or I will say good bye forever." He paced the cell. "This is the point of no return for you."

"Go ahead," she chewed at her lower lip. "I'm listening…"

"Well, listen hard…"

***

"Neil R. Zuster and Ellen J. Marsden, you are both being arrested for the murder of Antony Marsden and the attempted murder of Damson Zuster. What say you?"

"I plead 'Not Guilty'," Neil said in a strong, loud voice. He stared straight ahead and did not look at Ellen.

"And you, Mrs. Marsden? How say you?"

"I plead 'Guilty with Extenuating Circumstances'." At Ellen's side, with her check in his pocket, stood Harry Glass.

"Bail is denied on both cases. You will be imprisoned until arraignment can be scheduled."

The Judge pounded on the podium and motioned for the officers of the court to take the prisoners away.

"Wait! *Wait!*" Neil struggled to turn around. "I want to speak out!"

"Oh, Mr. Zuster, you will have plenty of time to speak out. Make no mistake about it. Plenty of time." The Judge pounded once more and turned to the next prisoner.

***

"Coffee, Eff?" Carlton ushered her out to the car. Standing in front of the car was Elwyn Langdon, fresh from Doctor Fullbright's ministrations of removing the three stitches on this chin.

Effalyn stopped suddenly and a tide of crimson stained her cheeks. *Was it possible that he could know that she had thought of him every moment that she wasn't thinking of how to get Ellen Marsden and Neil Zuster to confess?* Elwyn stepped forward wondering if Carlton could tell that he had spent almost every waking moment thinking of Effalyn. "Can I speak with her for a moment? Carlton smiled, a broad smile, and waved the two of them toward the front of the car.

"*The Southern Cross* is leaving tomorrow morning. Is there a chance that we can have dinner tonight? I know it's very short notice and I'm usually a more thoughtful dinner date, but this is the first chance I've had..." He toed the sand with his foot. "I, um, ah...really would like to see you."

"I'd really like to see you, too." Effalyn touched the tiny bandage on his chin. "Where shall we meet?"

"Meet? I will meet you at your home, if that's all right. I want to meet your mother."

"Oh, she's very anxious to meet you, too. She's a tough one where me and men are concerned." Effalyn laughed out loud. "Can you take her questions?"

"With delight. Where shall...? What's your address?"

Carlton got into the patrol car and turned on the air conditioning full blast. He whistled softly as Effalyn, smiling, slid into the front seat.

"Everything is coming up roses today, yes?"

"Roses and orchids, thanks, Boss. By the way, what was all that stuff about Statute Sixty-Three? What Statute Sixty-Three?"

Carlton laughed, a rollicking sound. "I made it all up!"

"You scoundrel, you!" Her tone was filled with admiration.

"You really did well with your plan to get Marsden and Zuster to sing. Together, they'll be an opera." He turned to her. "You did well. I probably didn't need to throw in my line about Statute Sixty-Three, but...I was swept away by the drama of it all!" Effalyn ducked her head and thought about what she was going to wear tonight.

***

"I can't stand it anymore, Em," Captain Jack griped to his wife. "I'm tired of solving other people's problems, tired of putting up with jerks and selfish, over-sexed women. I'm sick of the capriciousness of the idle rich, up to here..." he put his hand up to his eyebrows ... "with settling quarrels and trying to sniff out passengers who try to break the law. I need a rest." He sighed and put his bearded head on her shoulder. "I need some tender, loving care."

"And you deserve it, darling." She kissed him tenderly. "I'm leaving all the mess at the office and coming with you for the rest of the trip. After all, it's almost Christmas."

"Oh, gee whiz..." Jack looked stricken. "I haven't even gotten you a present yet."

"You will, you big lug. You will." And with that, Captain Jack was happy again. He wondered if he should tell Emma about selling *The Southern Cross*. Maybe he could have the plans for *Music* drawn up neatly, printed on some stiff parchment paper, rolled into a scroll and tied with a pink ribbon. He could give the scroll to her on Christmas morning. Good idea.

***

Effalyn and Carlton stopped into the hospital to see Paula. George was there with a box filled with Aunt Fanny's famous cream buns. Effalyn went to ask the nurses if they might bring coffee and tea into the room.

"Of course," the thin nurse with the spiked hair, the delightful German accent and the name tag that said "Call me Christa!" jumped up. "She's our heroine! I told my husband that if he ever stepped out of line, I was going to do a 'Paula' on him!" She laughed and promised to bring refreshments into the room in a jiffy.

Carlton regaled all of them with the success of Effalyn's drama. "I feel badly, sometimes, fooling perpetrators," Carlton looked at Paula with a sheepish grin. "But, I think sometimes that most people, in the end, are glad to confess."

"I didn't realize how it would weigh on me," Paula agreed. "I'm not sorry I killed Elliott, but...when you told me that you might be imprisoning that other man, Thigpin, for what I had done...I...I'm glad that you tricked me. I think I would have confessed without your little charade, but, now that I have had a chance to mull everything over, I think you did the right thing." She turned toward George. "Seeing George again was worth it all."

George took Paula's dry hand. "We're going to fatten her up and make her well."

Paula shrugged. They all knew that she would never leave the hospital alive, but these people were her friends. Strange to think that the police who tricked her and arrested her would be thought of as friends, but the world was strange sometime.

"I told... Paula...Sharon...Oh, whatever. I'm just going to continue to say 'Paula'"...he laughed. "It's easier that way...Anyway, I said that Elliott had tormented me, too, when I was younger. He made crude remarks about me not being a big football hero, called me names and jeered at me and my family because we were Jewish." George sniffed and his eyes began to fill as he thought of those horrible taunts so long ago. "Elliott's father owned the building where my father's store was located and his bank held the mortgage on our house. He told me that if I protested or squealed on him that he'd see to it that we were thrown out on the street. When you're a teen-ager and sensitive about a pimple on your face, for God's sake, that kind of threat was terrifying to me." His eyes misted. "I can just imagine how broken-up and helpless Debbie was." He wiped a tear away. "If we had only talked with one another…shared our fears…maybe…maybe…"

"I wonder how many other lives he destroyed." Effalyn poured out the coffee and handed the buns around. "The bastard. Even Suzie, as nasty as she is, was too weak to fight him. He really put the icing on her cake with his smarmy charm and snake-oil persuasion."

"Maybe," Carlton was fair. "We all hated him and it's easy to put all the blame on him, but Suzie was a willing participant, from what Duncan told me. Annie didn't want to snitch on her cousin, but she told Duncan that she…Suzie…was just as guilty as Elliott when it came to wanting more and more thrills from drugs. She egged him on to go from marijuana to cocaine."

"What will they do to her?" George, as a law man, was always interested in other people's cases.

"She finally saw some sense, showed some remorse, sincere or feigned…who will know?... and the Court agreed to a five-year probation plan."

"Five years!" Paula gasped. "Such a harsh punishment!"

"Not really. The usual punishment for that kind of drug possession, plus her planting evidence on an innocent person…which is thought of as being a worse crime here…is twenty years in jail with some hard labor attached."

"Wow." Paula was thoughtful. "What would happen in these instances in the US?" she asked George.

"Similar punishment. Maybe ten to fifteen years," He bit into his cream bun. "Again, as much for the trying to implicate an innocent person as the drug charges. We're getting stiffer and stiffer sentences from judges in America and it's about time. When you think of the needless deaths and the ruined lives of innocent people that follow drug usage…." He shook his head. "It's tragic."

"Paula?" Effalyn's voice wheedled. "One last end to the string of questions...Who was your private detective? The one who helped you to follow Elliott?"

"Never you mind, Eff. It will be a little puzzle for you to try to solve."

"Oh, come on, Paula. Who was it? One of those boys from New Jersey?"

Paula shook her head.

"Is it...could it be...Elwyn?"

"You'll never know, will you?" Paula chuckled and changed the subject. "What will happen to those other people...the ones who murdered that poor old man with plant poisons?" Paula asked, her face a mask of innocence.

"Most likely life in prison for both of them. Premeditated murder."

"No matter which one insists that he or she is innocent?"

"Neither one of them is innocent."

***

"Where is he taking her?" Aunt Fanny dusted off the counter and leaned over to talk to Mrs. Penn.

"Some fancy restaurant, I suppose."

"Is he nice?"

"We'll see. Effalyn is in a tizzy over him. I hope he's a good man."

"He's divorced, isn't he?"

"Divorced!" Mrs. Penn looked scandalized. "No! He's a widower. A respectable widower."

"I'll say a prayer that she gets him if she wants him."

"Amen to that. Good thing we told Effalyn how to handle those two murdering plant people."

"Good thing she had the sense to listen to our advice! Want another bun?"[4]

---

[4] Aunt Fanny's cream bun recipe can be found at the end of this book. Yum.

CHAPTER TWENTY-THREE

"...and he has left a lot of little things behind him..."
Rudyard Kipling in The Absent-Minded Beggar

In the middle of July in the summer of the year following the aforementioned cruise of *The Southern Cross,* a group of people boarded planes and flew to the British Virgin Islands once again.

They had all been invited as special guests of Jack and Emma Scambaugh to spend a week on the final voyage of *The Southern Cross* as owned by Captain Jack.

The catamaran had been sold. Its new owners were Karen and Ed Cosgrove. They, in turn, had sold the *Jumbie Jamboree* to Mary Lou and Gary Kunkel, who, in turn, had sold the *Folie a Deux* to David and Barbara Wessel. David and Barbara outfitted the boat for the two of them and added an innovative "poop pit" for Teddy's comfort. Sarah Lemonowski ran their office so efficiently that the Wessels felt that they could retire.

Jack's gift to Emma, the sailing vessel *Music,* danced in her slip at the marina, awaiting her maiden voyage to Bermuda with only Jack and Emma aboard.

The special guests on *The Southern Cross* included Arlis Fuglie (for she, as independent as she was, had kept her maiden name) and Don Gamble (for he, as intuitive and as in love as he was, let her), had flown down a day early, leaving their cats, Tinker and Chance, in the good care of Arlis' mother.

Annie and Duncan MacKinnon traveled from Scotland, glad that the trip was in July. Had it been much later, Annie, in her fifth month of pregnancy, might not have been able to fly.

In the month preceding, Duncan had mailed a large and heavy package to Big Fish Cay. It was a hamper from one of the most exclusive department stores in the British Isles – Fortnum & Mason – and it was filled with hundreds of boxes of delicacies...kippers and meat pies...clotted cream...shortbread fingers, jams, crystallized fruits, toffee, ginger cakes...all the best that Scotland and England had to offer. The package was addressed simply to: Pat the Artist, c/o Big Fish Cay

Art Society, Big Fish Cay, Virgin Gorda. The card that was tucked into the hamper said: "To my benefactor from a wet Scottish swimmer". Pat shared some of the goodies with his fellow artists, but the best things he kept for himself.

From Greenwich, Connecticut, Police Chief George Horowitz and his wife Cheryl came to the islands. Cheryl was a bit worried about being sea-sick, but her doctor at home had assured her that the little prescription patch behind her ear would do the trick.

Zandra Hoovenmeyer and Hosea Balleau flew from Israel, where they both lived now. Captain Jack was going to lead Zandra down the aisle on the third day of the cruise. The wedding wasn't going to be a big extravaganza, but a tiny, quiet ceremony for the passengers and crew and a few select island guests: Carlton and Rebecca Reese, Mama Lucille, Effalyn, her mother and Elwyn. The ceremony and dinner afterward would be held at The Green Flash and Leslie and Charlie were in charge of making it exquisite and memorable.

Hoping that they would sell as many paintings as before, The Big Fish Cay Art Society, under Lara Vitiello's direction, planned to stage another art show and Pat Biase and Joyce O'Sullivan collected paintings from Lara, Lou Seraso, Tony Ginise and Bob Cherico to display. In addition, the Island Boys Band had been hired to play peppy dance music after the ceremony. Madeline, the Flynn girls, Niccola and Mitchell were extremely disappointed that they weren't asked to do the limbo again. "Hmpf, grown-ups," Mitchell griped, "They don't understand that we kids really like to show off!"

Madeline had to be satisfied that Jamie and Lara had asked to her baby sit for Mikayla. "At least I'll make some money," she told her brother with lofty condescension.

A week after the cruise was over, Ducky and Lisette would be departing to England to continue their studies. Kat and her friend Belinda would depart the islands, headed for Ireland, to Eigan Bally, the little town where Michael Beck operated his funeral parlors. Kat and Belinda planned to open a pub, attempting to brighten up the taste buds of the Irish with Jamaican jerk and island cooking. "Will they like roti, Michael?" Kat had written.

"The food here is so bad that you could serve cat scraps and they'd come every night," he had written back. "I have a wonderful cottage ready for you two. An old lady lived in it for her entire life. It's filled with lovely antiques and she just put in a new bathroom and central heat. I got first dibs on it because I was so nice to her family two weeks ago when she died."

"Have you heard from any of the others?" Kat wrote back. "I got a nice letter from Claudia. She's marrying one of the doctors at the hospital, and Martha is marrying the man who owns the farm north of their property. Lannie also sent me a wonderful invitation to the opening party for the new magazine he's going to publish in Dublin. It's called Wild Mountain Thyme, and I understand all of the advertisement has been sold out for the upcoming year! Good for Lannie! We're all invited …me and you, Belinda and your new girlfriend Maeve. We'll all be going to Dublin for two days to party hearty! We'll be in Ireland in three weeks. What news do you have?"

"I heard from those New Jersey boys. Vinny is marrying his high school sweetheart, Laura, and Sammy is marrying someone much older than he is. She's been divorced twice, but he feels that she's going to be the love of his life. I wish I could be with all of you in Big Fish Cay. Such memories! Tell everyone 'hello' from me and if anyone else is coming to Ireland, they can have a nice, comfortable coffin to sleep in! Ha, that ought to bring them. See you and Belinda at the airport! Love, Michael."

Elwyn, who owned a part-share in a Lear Jet, flew the plane down to Virgin Gorda. Effalyn and her mother met him at the tiny island airport. "My!" Mrs. Penn gushed. "I can't believe that you flew all this way in that little bitty airplane!"

"I'm going to take you and Effalyn up day after tomorrow. We'll buzz the islands and maybe meet *The Southern Cross* at Banjo's on Jost Van Dyke."

"You're drunk if you think you'll get me up in that contraption!"

"We'll see, Mama Penn. I'll bet you a cream bun that you'll even enjoy it!"

Mrs. Penn gave him one of her special looks. "We'll see."

***

Suzie was permitted to meet with Annie and Duncan. "Suzie! I almost didn't recognize you!" But this time, Annie's astonishment was complimentary. Suzie, deprived of beauty services, had cut her hair short. The blonde color that had been bleached and processed into her hair for so many years had all grown out. Now, Suzie's hair was cut into an Eton crop, almost like a young boy, and its natural color, a dark blond streaked with a few gray highlights, made her look softer, less harsh.

"Like my hair-do?" Suzie's sarcastic drawl hadn't changed. "I cut it myself, once a month when Mama Pajama lets me use a pair of scissors on myself. She stands over me like King Kong to be sure I won't stick the point into my eye..." Suzie chuckled, seeming more like her old self... "Or even worse, into *her* eye!"

"You look fabulous!" Annie's astonishment was sincere. "You look ten years younger than before!"

"Really?" Suzie ruffled up her hair. "Thanks."

"How is it all going?" Annie was afraid that Suzie might jump at her, but she answered the question thoughtfully.

"It's going well. Its not the way I planned my life, but, considering what it might be like," she shrugged. "It's OK."

"What do you do?"

"I'm incarcerated here. I have a cell to myself, for which I pay the Government of The Virgin Islands a small fortune, but it's worth it to me." Suzie shuddered. "I think it was the thought of those roommates coupled with your wrath, Duncan, that made me see a glimmer of sense. I, um, go to work, as they call it, after breakfast every day. I run a program for young women who are pregnant and are trying to get off drugs quickly enough so that their babies are born non-dependant. It's not a pretty life."

"Yours or theirs?" Duncan's face was a study.

"Theirs." Suzie looked clearly at him. "My life, well, maybe for the first time, I'm taking responsibility for the mess I made. That's my own problem and I have to find my own solutions for coping. I do get a lot of help from Officer Daniel and Mama Lucille. She's not such a bad old roly-poly, when you get to know her. But these poor girls, they never saw what hit them. They got hooked when they were twelve or thirteen, turned to prostitution to feed their habits and then turned to theft and worse to keep their pimps happy. I'd like to think that maybe I've made a difference in some of their lives." She bit her lip. "This is my life for a long time and I'm trying to make it useful."

"We understand you are doing a rather good job." Duncan patted her on her shoulder. "Mama Lucille said that you slip back now and then, but it keeps her on her own toes to cope with you." Suzie gave him a rueful look and shook her head.

"I can only face each day and hope that I cope with it." She stood up and went to the table at the side of the room. "Here," she picked up a long green box. "Here are some flowers for you to take out on the water this morning." She handed the box to Annie. "Say a prayer for Paula from me and tell her that I understand what she did. I'm sorry that I never got to know her and learn from her."

"I'm sure that she understands. Goodbye, Cousin. Maybe one day…after your problems are over…maybe you can come to visit…" Annie's words tumbled over one another. She bent and kissed Suzie's cheek. "We leave our love."

"Maybe," Suzie made a wry face. Then she smiled, a genuine smile. "Be sure to send me a picture of your baby!" Suzie waved them goodbye, her smile slipping as they left the cell. Annie turned around to see Suzie sit down suddenly on her cot, and hold her head in her hands. Her shoulders were shaking with sobs.

***

On the morning of the wedding, five hours before the ceremony, *The Southern Cross*, with all of its passengers, crew and many honored guests, sailed out into the sparking blue ocean. There, under the hot sun, Reverend Emanuel Emanuel intoned a moving epitaph and prayed for the souls of Paula Haskins, Debbie Nye and Sharon Nye. The guests joined hands as Captain Jack scattered Paula's ashes into the ocean, then each of them spoke a few words and tossed a flower into the waves. "Goodbye, Paula. We commend your soul to God."

Finis

HEARD AT BANJO'S:

ANOTHER TRIBUTE TO CAPTAIN JACK SCUMBAG AND A FAREWELL TO HIS SOUTHERN CROSS

Oh Jack and Emma sailed Da Cross, way out into da sea, And joined ole Bomba and de Sarge wid Jumbie Jamboree..
Jack sells da boat to his ole frens, and dey sell Jumbie too…An' all of dem, and all of you, come here for calaloo!
Now Jack an' Emma, dey will sail da Music far away…But dey'll be back to play wid me, on some great future day.
We'll miss dem bof, we love dem so, and hope dat dey'll be back…For who can I make fun of like I do wid Captain Jack?

Oh, Captain Jack, you Scumbag Man, you sail into da sea
Oh, Emma too, da bof of of you, please come and play wid me…

Da Jumbies showed up everyplace and drove da po-leece mad, snakes and fishes go amuck…oh dear, it was so sad!
Carlton Reece and Effalyn, dey chase da Jumbies out, Turn dem upside down and den, dey make da Jumbies shout!
Captain Jack and Emma too, dey see da fishies float. Catchem all and den dey go to live on dere new boat.
Captain Eddie and de Sarge dey now run Southern Cross. Karen really runs it, she is his new boss! Ha!

Oh, Captain Jack, you Scumbag Man, you sail into da sea
We'll miss you two, we'll wait until , you're back to play wid me….

Mama Lucille, she keeps da peace and fun out in de jail. Takes da bad men from da dock and shows 'em how to sail
She take da tiger outta men and shows 'em how to purr…Even me, da Banjo Man…I'm sure afraid of her! Ha!

RECIPE #1 – THE FAMOUS MANGO WANGO

1 large scoop of vanilla ice cream
1 cup mango puree
½ cup coco-loco
½ cup dark rum

Add to a blender full of ice…whirr around until the ice is pulverized

Pour into a tall glass, garnish with a slice of mango, a wedge of lime and a dusting of nutmeg

Add a straw and enjoy.

RECIPE #2 – MRS. PENN'S FAMOUS ISLAND RUM AND COCONUT CAKE

THE CAKE
2 ¼ cups cake flour
1 egg plus 5 egg whites
¾ cups Cream of Coconut
¼ cup Dark Rum
1 tsp. EACH vanilla and coconut extracts
1 cup sugar
1 tsp Baking Powder
1 ½ sticks Butter
2 cups lightly toasted coconut

2 round 9" pans, greased and dusted with flour
325 degree oven – bake for 30 minutes

THE FROSTING
4 Egg Whites
1 cup Sugar – pinch of salt
1 pound Butter
¼ cup Cream of Coconut
1 tsp EACH Rum and Coconut Extract
2 cups lightly toasted coconut

1. Cream butter, add sugar and whole egg. Add Cream of Coconut, Rum and extracts
2. Mix flour, baking powder, and add dry ingredients to butter and sugar mixture
3. Whip egg whites until glossy. Carefully fold into mixture and add toasted coconut. Do not overmix. Cake batter will be streaky.
4. Divide batter into pans. Bake until slightly dry with cake pulling away from sides of pan. Cool cakes and remove carefully from pans.

FROSTING:
1. In a double boiler, over simmering water, mix egg whites, sugar and a pinch of salt.
2. When sugar has melted and mixture is very hot to touch (230 degrees), put mixture into mixer. Beat until cool, glossy and doubled in volume.

3. Beat in butter, bit by bit. Add Cream of Coconut and extracts. Cool.
4. Frost cake, lavishing the icing in swirls, especially on top of cake
5. Pat toasted coconut on the sides of the cake.

RECIPE #3 – KAT'S INTERNATIONAL FALLS HOT CHEESE BALL SALAD

CHEESE BALLS
1 cup blue cheese crumbled (can use gorgonzola)
1 cup Panko bread crumbs (can be found in Oriental aisle in grocery store)
1 egg white
½ cup vegetable oil or canola oil for browning balls

SALAD
4 cups assorted baby greens – (can use a bag of mixed baby greens)
2 ripe pears, cored and sliced (can also use 2 apples, or 2 Asian pears)
½ cup pecans (or walnuts)
Optional: Thinly sliced onions, tiny ripe tomatoes
Enough Italian dressing (or whatever kind you wish to use) to cover the salad lightly

1. In a large bowl, mix the salad, but do not put the dressing on yet.
2. Make the cheese balls: With your hands, press the crumbled cheese into small balls.
3. With a fork, beat the egg white slightly – dip each cheese ball into the egg white and then roll each in the Panko bread crumbs. Let the balls dry for 10 minutes.
4. Put ½ cup of oil into a large frying pan. Heat to smoking. Add the balls and roll them in the hot oil until they are brown and crispy on the outside.
5. Toss the balls into the salad bowl, add dressing and serve **IMMEDIATELY**, while the balls are hot.

RECIPE #4 – AUNT FANNY's CREAM BUNS

ISLAND BUTTER DOUGH
1 cup warm milk
2 packages dry yeast
4 ½ cups all purpose flour
1/3 cup sugar
4 sticks of butter at room temp.
2 large eggs plus one egg yolk

CREAM FILLING
2 cups milk or half and half
½ cup sugar 4 egg yolks
¼ cup cornstarch
2 tablespoons butter
1 tsp pure vanilla extract

Make the dough:
1. Put the milk (about 110 degrees) into a small, ceramic bowl. Sprinkle the yeast over the milk and stir until dissolved. Let sit about 7-10 minutes until foamy.
2. In the bowl of your Kitchen-Aid mixer, put the flour and sugar and whirl until mixed. Add ½ stick of butter and mix until incorporated. Mixture will be mealy.
3. Add yeast and milk and mix for a moment or two, then add eggs and yolk and mix until just combined. You do not want to over-mix this dough.
4. Turn dough onto lightly floured board and pat into a rectangular shape (about 18 x 10)…like a piece of paper…with short side facing you, evenly distribute the remaining butter over the central 2/3 of the dough. Fold the dough up 1/3 of the way, as if you were folding a business letter. Fold the top 1/3 down to seal in the butter. Pat the dough gently, but firmly into a neat rectangle.
5. Roll the dough again into a 18 x 10 rectangle. Then, fold into thirds as described above. Refrigerate for 3 hours.
6. Repeat #5 two times more, refrigerating at least 1 hour between turns.
7. Wrap dough tightly in cling wrap and refrigerate overnight. The dough can be frozen at this point and used at a later

date. If freezing the dough, be sure to thaw overnight in the refrigerator before using.

THE PASTRY CREAM:
1. Combine milk and half of the sugar in a small, heavy saucepan. Cook over medium heat until mixture is simmering.
2. In another medium sized bowl, whisk the egg yolks and the remaining sugar.
3. Whisking as you work, pour half of the hot-milk mixture into the bowl. Slowly add the rest of the hot-milk mixture, whisking as you pour.
4. Pour mixture back into same saucepan as used for the hot-milk mixture. Cook over medium heat, whisking constantly so that the pastry cream does not burn. Cook until mixture thickens and coats the spoon you are stirring with.
5. Put hot mixture into your Kitchen Aid mixer. Add the butter, bit by bit, and beat on medium speed until the mixture cools. When it is cool, add the vanilla extract.
6. Cover with cling wrap, pressing the wrap directly on the surface so that no "skin" forms on the custard. Refrigerate until very cold.

PUT THE BUNS TOGETHER:
1. Roll out the chilled dough on a lightly floured board to a rectangle 15 x 12. With a sharp knife, cut the rectangle into twenty 3-inch squares.
2. With a small teaspoon, put a small scoop of chilled pastry cream into the center of each square
3. With a small brush, wet edges of each square with water and gather the edges together around the pastry cream, pinching the seams together to form a smooth ball.
4. Gently roll the balls to be sure that the cream is completely enclosed. Place each ball on a lightly greased cookie sheet about 3 inches apart. Cover with plastic wrap and let sit at room temperature until each ball has doubled in size.
5. Meanwhile, preheat oven to 375 degrees. Bake, rotating pans so the buns turn golden brown but do not burn, 25 to 30 minutes.

6. Brush hot buns with melted butter and roll gently in granulated sugar to coat.
7. Serve at room temperature.

ALSO WRITTEN BY J. Tracksler :

The Tears of San'Antonio
The Botticelli Journey
Murder at Malafortuna
The Ice Floe
Deceit
Cherubini
Worse Than A Thief

And coming soon:
The Metropolitan Opera Murders
Panis Angelicus (The Bread of Angels)

Printed in the United States
98423LV00003B/168/A